If it's only
L♥VE

If it's only LOVE

New York Times Bestselling Author

LEXI RYAN

Cover and cover image © 2019 by Sara Eirew
Print ISBN: 9781089361886
Interior designed and formatted by

E.M. TIPPETTS
BOOK DESIGNS

emtippettsbookdesigns.com

Other Books by
LEXI RYAN

The Boys of Jackson Harbor
The Wrong Kind of Love (Ethan's story)
Straight Up Love (Jake's story)
Dirty, Reckless Love (Levi's story)
Wrapped in Love (Brayden's story)
Crazy for Your Love (Carter's story)
If It's Only Love (Shay's story)

The Blackhawk Boys
Spinning Out (Arrow's story)
Rushing In (Chris's story)
Going Under (Sebastian's story)
Falling Hard (Keegan's story)
In Too Deep (Mason's story)

LOVE UNBOUND: Four series, one small town, lots of happy endings

Splintered Hearts (A Love Unbound Series)
Unbreak Me (Maggie's story)
Stolen Wishes: A Wish I May Prequel Novella (Will and Cally's prequel)
Wish I May (Will and Cally's novel)
Or read them together in the omnibus edition, *Splintered Hearts: The New Hope Trilogy*

Here and Now (A Love Unbound Series)
Lost in Me (Hanna's story begins)
Fall to You (Hanna's story continues)
All for This (Hanna's story concludes)
Or read them together in the omnibus edition, *Here and Now: The Complete Series*

Reckless and Real (A Love Unbound Series)
Something Wild (Liz and Sam's story begins)
Something Reckless (Liz and Sam's story continues)
Something Real (Liz and Sam's story concludes)
Or read them together in the omnibus edition, *Reckless and Real: The Complete Series*

Mended Hearts (A Love Unbound Series)
Playing with Fire (Nix's story)
Holding Her Close (Janelle and Cade's story)

OTHER TITLES

Hot Contemporary Romance
Text Appeal
Accidental Sex Goddess

Decadence Creek (Story and Sexy Romance)
Just One Night
Just the Way You Are

For all my readers who want to visit Jackson Harbor.
I'll meet you at Jackson Brews.

ABOUT
If it's only Love LOVE

From *New York Times* bestseller Lexi Ryan comes a sexy new standalone romance in the bestselling Boys of Jackson Harbor series. Meet single dad Easton Connor as he leaves the NFL and returns to Jackson Harbor to fight for another chance with the love of his life.

I don't regret much.

Not my decision to enter the NFL draft before finishing college.

Not fighting for custody of my daughter—even if, biologically speaking, it turns out she's not mine.

And certainly not seducing my buddy's little sister ten years ago.

But when it comes to Shayleigh Jackson, my no-regrets attitude stops there. I screwed up royally where she's concerned. Then I made another mistake when I let her shut me out of her life.

Now after more than a decade living in different time zones, I'm coming home to Jackson Harbor. My first priority is keeping my daughter away from the media circus in Los Angeles, but the moment I see Shay, I know something else brought me back here. Now I'll stop at nothing to win her back.

So what if she won't speak to me? So what if she's changed? So what if she's fallen for some douchebag professor? I've never gotten over her, and I know she feels the same about me.

I've let her go twice. I won't make that mistake again.

SHAY

I was seven when I fell in love with Easton Connor. He was four years older than me and best friends with my brother Carter, but that didn't matter to me. I never thought of him as too old back then. Never thought of him as off-limits.

When I fell off my bike while racing down the street after my brothers, it was Easton who circled back to help me. Easton who took me inside, helped me clean the bits of gravel out of my knee, and then dabbed it with hydrogen peroxide. Easton who turned my tears into laughter by telling me about Carter's inability to speak every time he saw his crush in class.

I decided right then that I was going to marry Easton. Because I was seven and didn't understand the realities of romantic love. Because Easton hadn't yet become *the* Easton Connor. Because I hadn't hit puberty and become *chubby Shay*. Because I still believed in fairytales, I believed I would marry this boy with the light brown hair and blue-green eyes.

It was my secret. One I vowed to keep to myself until the time was right. Easton didn't know my plans.

And I had no idea he'd break my heart.

Part I.

Before

April 27th, draft night, thirteen years ago

"Shay!" Easton hoists a shot glass in the air and wriggles it in offering. "Tequila? What do you say?"

Carter spins on him and frowns. "What the fuck, man? Don't give my little sister alcohol."

"Shit, sorry," Easton says, but his mischievous eyes are on me as he says, "I always forget she's so young."

The tequila must be going to his head, because there's no other explanation for the way he's looking at me. His eyes drop to my mouth, and warmth spreads through me. If I didn't know better, I might think that . . . No. That doesn't make sense. This is *Easton.* My friend now, sure, but East is everything. Girls everywhere are crazy about him—a football star on the brink of NFL fame, he could have any woman he wanted.

Carter grabs a beer and leaves the kitchen and pushes out the back door to join the party. And then it's just me and Easton. Alone with a bottle of tequila and the full shot glass that's still in his hand.

He flashes a glance over his shoulder toward the back door. "Does Carter have any idea that you're not a little girl anymore?" he asks, closing the distance between us.

I bite my bottom lip. My skin flushes hot when he's this close, and I swear he's looking at my lips again. Do I have something on my face? Spaghetti sauce from dinner or something? I discreetly wipe my mouth with the cuff of my sweatshirt—or as discreetly as I can when he's so close.

Easton grins, as if he knows he's making me uncomfortable and likes it. "Have you ever done this before?"

A thousand possibilities fly through my mind at that question—most of them involving the hands and mouth of the man asking. "Done what?"

He lifts the shot glass and sniffs the tequila. "A snakebite. Salt, tequila, lime."

I shrug. I've had alcohol before. My family isn't exactly puritanical when it comes to alcohol. But I've never done a shot, and certainly never a *snakebite*. Whatever that is. "How do you do it?"

Grinning, he hands me the shot glass then grabs the salt shaker from the counter. He lifts my free hand to his mouth and licks the inside of my wrist. My breath whooshes out of me at the sensation of his hot tongue on my skin. I want to close my eyes, but he's watching me, and I'm afraid he'll laugh if he has any idea what affect he has on me.

Grinning, he sprinkles salt on the wet patch of skin before putting the shaker down and grabbing a wedge of lime from the counter behind me. "Lick the salt. Take the shot. Suck on the lime."

"Lick, shoot, suck." I nod. "I can do that."

His nostrils flare and his pupils dilate, turning those blue-green eyes dark. "I think I'd like to see you try."

I swallow hard. Is Easton Connor coming on to me? I don't want to be the idiot who believes that could be true. I don't want to be the dumb fat girl who fell for the practical joke because she believed a guy like Easton could be attracted to her.

I don't know how long I stand there trying to decide, but my skin tingles where he licked, and my mouth has gone dry.

"Want me to go first?" he asks, his voice a little husky.

I nod.

He takes my wrist and brings it to his mouth, licking off the salt. Shocks of pleasure roll down my spine and settle into a riot of butterflies in my stomach. He doesn't even take the shot glass from me, just wraps his hand around mine and leads the glass to his mouth so he can shoot it back. Then he pops the lime in his mouth and makes a goofy face at me as he sucks the juice.

"Got it?" he asks, still squinting from the sourness.

"I think I can do that."

He refills the tequila then looks over his shoulder again.

"Why are you so worried about Carter seeing?" I ask. "He knows I've had alcohol before. He's just being a prude about the shot."

"I don't want him pissed at me," he says, shrugging. "God knows he did worse than take a couple of shots when he was sixteen, but—"

"I'm seventeen. Eighteen in a few months."

He slowly turns his attention away from the back door and back to me. "My timing is shit."

"Timing for what?"

His eyes are so intense on mine, but it's a good kind of intensity. Like he *sees* me. Has anyone ever looked at me before? Really *looked*? "Nothing." He lets out a puff of air and shakes his head. "Then Carter really would kill me."

I laugh. "You're ridiculous."

"What? Why do you say that?"

"You just got drafted into the NFL, and you're acting like you're attracted to me."

His gaze skims over me, from my hair all the way down to my bare feet and the bright pink polish on my toes. "What does one have to do with the other?"

I don't understand what's happening here. Am I dreaming? Has he had more to drink than I realized? I throw the shot back before I can lose my nerve, totally forgetting the salt.

I shudder. "That's *awful!*"

He laughs. "You did it wrong. Are you always this terrible with directions?"

Only when you're here. Only when you're looking at me like this and making me think I can have things I can't. But as awful as the taste was, warmth blooms in my chest. It's more intense than the effects of the glass of wine I drank with Easter dinner, and I do like that.

"Now I risk getting you drunk if I make you do it the right way."

"I'm not drunk." I shake my head. "I don't feel anything."

He grunts. "Give it a minute." He steps around me and stands at the counter, pouring himself another shot. I guess he's not going to drink it from my glass this time. It's dumb to be disappointed.

He doesn't bother with the salt or lime, just throws it back. Doesn't even grimace. Then he braces his arms on the counter and hangs his head.

I'd have to be emotionally stunted not to feel the change in his mood. He just went from playful flirt to morose jock in the span of a blink. "What's wrong?"

He shrugs. "Nothing."

"Liar."

He drags a hand through his hair and finally turns to me. He leans back against the counter. "Can you keep a secret?"

"Of course."

He hesitates a beat, and I see the emotions playing across his face—he's trying to decide if he can trust me with this, or if he even wants to own up to whatever it is.

"I never told anyone when I caught you with that dirty magazine when you were thirteen."

His eyes widen and he grins. "Oh, fuck. I'd completely forgotten about that. Jesus." He scrubs a hand over his face. "Okay, fair enough. That kind of discretion so young is definitely meaningful."

"Meaningful? Are you kidding me? That's preteen blackmail gold, and I never used it. Not even when you wouldn't dump that girl you took to senior prom."

His forehead wrinkles, and I can tell he's trying to remember his date.

"Hilary," I remind him.

"I didn't know you wanted me to dump her."

"I didn't realize I needed to spell it out for you. I told you she was a bitch and you deserved better."

"Honestly, I was eighteen, and she was hot and willing. I probably didn't care that she was a bitch."

"She called me a *fat tagalong*."

"What?" The tops of his ears turn pink—a tell I learned long ago means he's angry. "You never told me that."

I shrug. When Easton was with Hilary, I was fourteen. I'd foolishly believed that he wouldn't notice I was fat if no one ever told him. Not the dumbest thing I've let myself believe in the name of loving him, but not a delusion I'm particularly proud of either.

"You're not fat," he says.

I fold my arms and arch a brow. "Come on, Easton. I might be naive and shamefully inexperienced for a girl my age, but my eyes work just fine."

He holds up a finger. "One, so do mine, and you're *not* fat. You're not skinny. You have a nice body."

A *nice body*. The words are both the balm and the blade. On the one hand, I'm intelligent and rational enough to know I should be glad he thinks of my body in better terms than I do. Intellectually, I know *nice* is as good as it's going to get for a girl like me. On the other hand, part of me wanted to believe I saw heat in his eyes earlier. As irrational as it is, I want to believe he might think I'm beautiful, even while I know I'd never believe it if he used those words.

Emotions are dumb.

He holds up another finger. "And *two*, I'm going to need you to tell me what you mean by *shamefully inexperienced*."

"Absolutely not."

"Please?"

My face is on fire. Why did I say that? I would be fine if no one ever knew the extent of my innocence, but Easton is the last person I want to admit it to. "Forget I said anything."

He steps closer. "I'll tell you my secret if you tell me yours."

"You go first," I blurt. Because who am I kidding? Anyone who had to guess would know I've never kissed anyone. It's not like I've ever had a boyfriend.

His eyes soften and something like pain flashes over his features for a beat. "I wish the Demons hadn't drafted me."

I don't know what I expected him to say, but that came out of left field. Easton's dreamed of the NFL his whole life, and tonight we're celebrating him being selected in the first freaking round of the draft. Now he's telling me that achieving this lifelong dream is what has him down. "Why'd you enter the draft if you didn't want to be picked up? Carter said you could've waited until next year and finished school."

"I wanted to be drafted. I suck at school and I . . ." He chews on the inside of his cheek. "I wanted to be drafted, but I was hoping Chicago or Detroit would draft me. I'm scared to move so far from home. Which I realize is dumb, but . . ."

"It's not dumb." Easton had his pick of colleges, and he went to Starling College in Grand Rapids. They have a good football team, but he could have gone to Florida or LSU—teams whose football programs are practically NFL breeding grounds. I figured it was because he wanted to stay close to home, but it never occurred to me that those preferences would hold true three years later. Only, this time the choice is out of his hands. "You can visit, though, right? A contract that big means you can fly home as often as you want."

His gaze locks on his feet. "Right. Of course. It's stupid, I know."

"It's really not."

"Don't tell anyone. I don't want to come across like the ungrateful rookie or like I'm too immature to handle the move."

"I promise." I squeeze his wrist, but I'm suddenly all too aware of the fact that I'm *touching* him. His skin is warm under my fingertips. I can feel his strength and the power of his big hands. How many times have I imagined those hands on me?

I jerk away, but he grabs my hand before I can get far.

"It's your turn," he says, threading his fingers through mine. *What is he doing?* "Why do you think you're shamefully inexperienced, Shayleigh? Your friends aren't pressuring you to have sex, are they?"

Sex. Oh my God. He thought I meant *sex*. Now my dumb secret feels even more mortifying, but he's still holding my hand, and even as embarrassment warms my cheeks, I don't want him to let go. "No one's pressuring me."

The back door clangs closed as Carter pushes into the kitchen. Easton jumps back and drops my hand.

"What are you two talking about in here?" my brother asks. He crosses the kitchen between us and opens the fridge. "Don't you know the party's outside?"

Easton's throat bobs and he tucks his hands in his pockets.

"We're just catching up."

Carter pulls out another beer and uses the opener on the wall to pull off the cap. "Well, I hope you're finished, because people are starting to wonder if you already moved to L.A. or something."

"Relax, Carter," I tell him. "The night is young."

He frowns as he looks back and forth between me and Easton. "I don't like you two being alone in here together."

I snort and for the millionth time in my life wonder what it would be like to *not* have five overly protective brothers. "Why not?"

Carter stares at Easton for a long beat. Easton gives a subtle shake of his head and Carter sighs. "Because you're my little sister, and this punk breaks hearts in his sleep."

"My heart is fine." *Liar, liar.* Does Carter know how I feel about Easton? I've never told anyone. "We're just talking."

Carter taps Easton's arm with the neck of his beer. "You. Outside. We're celebrating your news, after all. And anyway, that redhead Tri-Delt showed up and is looking for you."

Easton heads toward the back with my brother. "Why didn't you say so sooner?" He opens the door and turns back to wink at me before heading toward the lakeside bonfire with my brother.

I guess Easton doesn't want to know my secret after all. I dodged a bullet.

So why do I feel so disappointed?

Easton

"**Y**ou have to fucking stop." Carter stomps away from the house and toward the bonfire blazing on the beach.

"Stop what?"

"I already told you she's off-limits."

The Jackson brothers have been telling me for *years* that their sister is off-limits. It just didn't matter until last summer. I'd been busy with school and hadn't seen Shayleigh in months when I came out to the Jackson family cabin with Carter. Shay was here and suddenly she was . . . *more*. It's not like I didn't know she was pretty before. She's always been *pretty*. She's also always been really fucking special to me. Something about Shay brings me peace when I need it the most. She's the only person I've ever met who can chill my anxiety just by sitting next to me.

But sometime between when I'd seen her at Christmas and

when I came out here last summer, she went from the pretty-but-quiet little sister of my best friend to the kind of beautiful it's hard to look away from. Or maybe it happened long before last summer, and the swimsuit brought it to my attention. Because Shayleigh Jackson in a swimsuit, with her long legs, soft thighs, and full breasts—*no idea* when that happened. She wasn't simply the Jackson sister anymore. She was a fucking siren, and I was going to drown trying to resist her. With her dark hair falling around her shoulders and that wide smile and easy laugh, how could I *not* notice?

And I noticed a few too many times, because Carter caught me staring and tore into me.

Carter looks to the house then to me, and I can practically see him calculating the pros and cons of locking his sister away to protect her virtue.

"I told you I wouldn't hurt her," I say.

Carter grunts. "Somehow, that's not comforting." He sighs. "She's seventeen."

"I know."

"And you're moving to California next month."

"I know."

"She's so smart, East. She's only a junior, and she's already got colleges chasing her. Did you know she's fluent in French?"

Did you know she's incredibly fucking insecure and has no idea what her value is? I don't ask.

I know I shouldn't be the man to show her just how beautiful she is, but I want to be anyway. "Does she . . . does she have a boyfriend?" I ask. Carter's glare would melt a lesser man, but I turn up my palms. "I'm not asking your permission to take

15

her virginity. I'm asking if she has a boyfriend. This is normal conversation."

"I can't believe you just said that," he growls.

"What?"

"I don't even want you *thinking* about my sister's virginity."

"Again, I'm asking about a boyfriend."

"No. She doesn't. She's too focused on school to date, I think."

Or she's too convinced that she's . . . What did Hilary call her? A *fat tagalong*? Jesus. If I'd known, I never would have let that fly.

Carter studies me. "Why?" One word, hundreds of warnings.

I shrug. "Just curious how much she tells you."

Carter frowns. "Wait. What's that supposed to mean? Do you know something? Does she have a boyfriend?"

"You really are the protective big brother cliché." I press my palm between his shoulder blades and give him a good shove toward the beach. "The party is waiting."

As I suspected, it's less than fifteen minutes until Carter is completely distracted and I can head back to the house without him noticing. I used the time to circulate and listen to everyone's congrats. Carter's right. I should be out there. This is my celebration. Lifelong dream accomplished. But there's only one person I want to celebrate with. One person with killer soft curves and a beautiful smile who owes me a secret.

Shay's not in the kitchen where we left her. Did she go down to the bonfire and I missed her? I check the basement. Nothing. I head back to the kitchen and grab a beer from the fridge, ready to give up. Then I hear the screech of old pipes and realize a shower is shutting off.

Grinning, I stride toward the stairs and climb to the second floor. By the time Shay pushes out of the bathroom in a puff of steam, I'm leaning against the opposite wall, arms folded.

She jumps. "Jesus, Easton. Are you trying to give me a heart attack?"

I don't answer. My own heart is having some issues. Mainly, it's racing like it's trying to force me forward with its momentum—toward her.

I did not think this through.

She's in a fluffy light blue robe. It's tied at the waist but gapes open at her chest, giving me a view of the swell of her cleavage. Her wet hair is combed out of her face and falls in light waves down her back.

It would be so easy to tug on the waistband of her robe, to pull her to me and slide my hands inside, to cup her breasts and lower my mouth to hers. Easy, but a fucking death sentence.

"Easton!" She tugs the top of her robe tighter. "Ohmygod. Were you just looking at my breasts?"

I take a deep breath and drag my gaze back up to meet hers. "I love that you call them *breasts*."

"What else am I supposed to call them?"

I shrug. "Most girls your age would dodge calling them anything at all. Or maybe vaguely refer to their *chest*."

"I think you're wrong. I'm *not* twelve anymore."

I hope my arched brow conveys the *obviously* I'm not allowed to say.

She swallows. "And, well . . . I guess I'm not afraid of words."

What are you afraid of?

It's a question I won't ask. Not when it would invite her to turn it back on me. I don't want to talk about my fears any further than I did in the kitchen. Not tonight. Not when she's so close and soon she'll be so damn far away. I didn't anticipate it would bother me so much, but the realization eats away at my gut. "That's good," I say. "Because you owe me a few."

She blinks. "What do I owe you?"

"Words."

"Must you speak in riddles?"

"Your secret. I told you mine, so now it's your turn."

Her face pales, and I wonder just how innocent she is that she doesn't want to talk about it. "You already guessed it. I'm gonna go get dressed."

She turns toward her room, and I grab her wrist to stop her. "We can do this one of two ways," I say, and she slowly turns back to face me. "You can just tell me, which would be fair, since that was our deal. Or"—I lift the beer I grabbed from the fridge—"we can play a game."

She studies the bottle. "What kind of game?"

"Never Have I Ever."

She snorts and folds her arms. "Seriously? As I mentioned a minute ago, I'm not twelve anymore."

I turn up the palm of my free hand, moving it up and down opposite the beer in the other hand, as if I'm weighing them against each other. "Your choice."

"Fine, the game, but I'm getting dressed first."

"If you must," I say. I can't stop grinning. Damn it. She does that to me.

I wait in the hall while she disappears into her bedroom, my eyes fixed on the door the whole time. Carter would definitely kick my ass if he knew I was about to play a drinking game with his little sister. But it's not like we're playing with tequila. One beer split between the two of us can't get me in too much trouble. That said, if she's as innocent as she claims, I'll be the one doing most of the drinking.

A minute later, and the door swings open. Shay's gotten dressed, but she's not in her normal clothes. She's wearing pajamas. These aren't the kind of pajamas that are meant to seduce—they're gray cotton. A long-sleeved T-shirt with a lace cutout down each arm, and matching shorts that show just enough leg to remind me there's more that I want to see.

She catches me looking and scowls. "My clothes smelled like smoke from the bonfire, and the only other outfit I have with me is my work uniform for tomorrow."

"I wasn't complaining."

"I know." She frowns. "You're weird tonight."

"Nah, I'm weird every night. You've just forgotten because you barely ever see me anymore."

"True." She motions me to follow her, and when I freeze, she says, "I'm not going to jump you if you come into my room, weirdo."

Damn shame.

I swallow hard and step inside "her" bedroom. This isn't the Jacksons' full-time home, but their vacation place. They rent out this cabin to tourists—a ten-year plan to get it paid off sooner, Carter told me—so it's definitely not as personal as her room at home, but it is hers. As the only girl, she's the one Jackson sibling to get a room of her own, and there are little decorative touches in here that show this room is truly Shay's. The bookshelf overflowing with well-loved paperbacks, the map of Paris that hangs over the queen-sized bed, and the glasses that sit on the bedside table—no doubt for reading after she takes her contacts out.

I remember when she got glasses for the first time. She was so excited. But then some jerk at school teased her about them, and she came home with them tucked into her backpack and told her mom she wouldn't wear them anymore. She lost that fight, of course, and wore glasses until her mom relented and let her get contacts when she started middle school.

"I can't keep much here," she says as I look around. "We still rent it out sometimes. Less now, though."

"Carter used to be jealous that you got your own room."

She shrugs. "Well, I used to be jealous that my brothers had each other and I didn't have a single sister."

"And now?"

She sweeps her hair over one shoulder and starts braiding the wet locks. "Now I'm grateful to be the only girl. I get along better with boys than I do with girls anyway." Her fingers work efficiently, and she ties off the braid at the end.

"Maybe that would be different if you had sisters."

"Maybe, but I think my family is perfect just the way it is." She makes a face and seems to rethink her words. "No, not perfect at all. Just perfect for me, I guess."

A pang slices through my chest. *Jealousy.* Their family is incredible, and somehow they all know it. I don't have any siblings—none that I know of, at least, though there's no telling how many kids my father has brought into this world and walked away from. I don't even have a dad who gives a shit. Just Mom, and I'm grateful for her every day. Mom and I are partners; the

Jacksons are a team. When life feels like a constant blitz from the defense, it's hard not to be jealous of the people who are making plays with a solid O-line—even when your partner is the best in the game.

"What are you thinking about?" Shay asks.

I shake my head. "Just how lucky you all are." I let out a breath. "And how much I hate my father."

Shay's expression turns sad. "Have you talked to him?"

"Oh, yeah. He was watching the draft and called right away."

Anger flashes in her eyes. "Of course he did."

"'Congratulations, son,'" I say in my mocking impression of my father's voice. "'I knew you could do it. Aren't you glad you got my athleticism and not your mother's? Now let me talk out my ass about NFL contracts like I know anything at all.'"

"Fucker." Shay's uncharacteristic curse makes me smile.

"Exactly."

"Did he ask for money?"

"Not yet. I'm sure he will. But I've trained my whole life to tell him no, just like he told Mom no when she asked for help."

Her fingers brush mine, and I look down to see her taking the beer from my hand. She takes a long drink from it, her throat bobbing as she swallows, then hands the bottle to me. "To knowing when to say no."

I take a sip and nod before holding up the bottle. It's nearly half drained. "We don't have much to work with here."

She shrugs. "You'd better make good use of your turns, then."

"So we're playing that we take turns saying something and drink if we've done it?"

She nods. "Which is why I had to drink so much to start.

That beer is pretty much all yours."

"We'll see about that." I smile and lift it to my lips. I imagined us sitting on the floor, face to face as we took turns, but this is better. Standing, I can be closer to her. "Never have I ever celebrated Father's Day with my dad."

She snags the beer from my hand. "That's cheap." She takes a sip then studies me for a long beat before saying, "Never have I ever had sex."

Cutting right to the chase. "There's no rush, Shay. Seriously. Don't let anyone make you feel like—"

She clears her throat and presses the cold bottle into my hand. "Drink."

"Right." I take a sip, mindful of keeping it small so we can keep this going. "Never have I ever had a crush on a brother's friend."

"You don't have any brothers!"

I shrug. "I don't make the rules."

She takes a drink.

She has five brothers, four of them older than her. The possibilities are endless, but there's only one possibility I'm interested in hearing her confess to. "Who?"

She laughs. "That is not how this game is played, cheater." She taps a finger to her lips. "Never have I ever gone skinny-dipping."

"Seriously? Your family owns a house on a lake, and you haven't even *once*?"

She makes a face. "With my *brothers*? Hard pass." She hands the beer back to me.

"Fine." I watch her over the bottle as I tilt it to my lips and swallow. "Never have I ever gotten Shay off with my hand."

22

She folds her arms, all smugness, until the logic of my statement sinks in and red blossoms in her cheeks. "Are you seriously asking me if I have masturbated?"

My cock has been half hard since she stepped out of the shower, but at that, it goes the rest of the way. "Again with the precise word choice." I shrug. "And in all fairness, you could turn around and do the same to me."

She rolls her eyes and takes the beer. "I'm not wasting a turn like that." She drinks.

I thought I knew what I was doing when I said it, but the image of her in bed flashes through my mind as clear as a photo—her hand between her legs, pleasure on her face, all that dark hair splayed across the pillow as she arches into her own touch.

So fucking hot.

My cock strains against the fly of my jeans. I'm playing with fire right now, but I can't muster any motivation to back down. "Not all girls do, you know," I say. "Some are afraid to touch themselves."

"Yeah, well, I was raised around five boys who talk about masturbation as if it's a sport half the time and as if it's as essential as water the other half. I didn't exactly have to go up against some massive stigma the first time I tried it."

"And how was it?" I swallow. "When you . . ."

She snorts. "You are twenty-one years old, and you can't say the word *masturbated*?"

"Why would I when it sounds so much hotter when you say it?" I grin at her immediate and vivid blush, then nod to the bottle. "It's your turn."

She lifts her chin and holds my gaze as she says, "Never have

I ever had someone other than myself get me off."

"Why not?"

She shoves the bottle into my hand. "Quit cheating with your unsanctioned questions and drink."

Just how innocent is she? I look at the bottle. There's hardly a full drink left. Mindful of this, I take a sip and then push all my chips in. "Never have I ever kissed anyone."

"You filthy liar."

Grinning, I tilt the beer to my lips, taking the drink I owe for speaking a *never* that I *have* done. I arch a brow. Waiting. Because surely this beautiful, smart, funny girl has been kissed before. Surely, some guy saw her for what she was and won her over so he could taste those pink lips.

But when I offer her the beer, she shakes her head.

"Never," she whispers. "Pretty lame, huh?"

"It's not lame. Just . . . surprising."

She scoffs. "What's so surprising about it?"

I open my mouth, but before I can find the words, I'm interrupted by the sound of doors closing, footsteps, and laughter booming from downstairs.

The party's moved inside. That means Shay's five brothers are downstairs while I'm standing here so close to her, thinking about what it would be like to be the first man to kiss those lips. "Do you . . ." I swallow. Her lips part, and I swear there's some invisible cord between us that goes taut, draws me forward. "Do you want to?"

Her brow wrinkles as she cranes her neck to look into my eyes. "Want to what?"

I dip my head, lean my forehead against hers. "Be kissed."

She presses her hand to my chest, and my breath catches as I wait for her to close the distance—those final inches between our lips.

Instead, she shoves me hard. "Out!"

I stumble before catching my balance. "What the hell?"

"I don't want your pity kiss, East." She's avoiding my eyes, but I don't miss the hurt that flashes across her face.

"It wouldn't be—"

She squeezes her eyes shut. "Just go."

"Easton? You up here?" Jake's voice. *Fuuuuuck. Not now.*

Shay steps around me and opens the door.

"What's he doing up there?" Carter calls from the stairs. "Shay? That rich asshole with you?"

Jake pokes his head around the doorframe. "You two decent?"

Shay rolls her eyes. "Come in, Jake."

Jake's all smiles with a side of drunken stumble as he comes into the room. "*There's* the guest of honor. What are you two doing up here?"

"Telling secrets and braiding each other's hair." Shay's smile is tight. "What else?"

Jake chuckles. Unlike Carter, he's completely clueless about my attraction to Shay. He grabs the empty beer from my hand. "You need more!"

Carter rushes into the room. "What's going on in here?"

"I found him," Jake says, slinging his arm around my shoulders and leading me out of the room.

I look back at Shay, but she's busy scanning the books on her bookshelf. Could she truly not feel this thing between us? *Pity kiss?* The fuck? How could she even think that was what I was offering?

"You okay?" Carter asks her. "What were you two doing?"

Jake and I are already at the stairs when I hear her say, "We were fucking, Carter. Doing the dirty with the door open and my brothers downstairs. Can't you tell? I'm going to turn up pregnant with Easton's love child any day now."

"You're not funny," Carter says, but I can hear the tension leave his voice. The typical Shay smartass response was possibly the only one that would put his mind at ease.

When I turn back to them, she's pushed Carter out of her room and is closing the door after him.

Never been kissed. I can hardly wrap my brain around it.

I can't focus on my book, but I can't sleep either. Who could with the party roaring downstairs?

I roll over and bury my face in a pillow, muffling my frustrated scream. I can't believe I told Easton I've never been kissed. I could've lied. He never would've known. But the worst part is that I also admitted to having a crush on one of my brothers' friends. I won't make the same mistake if he asks about that again. Sometimes we have to lie to protect ourselves, and I know better than to leave my heart unguarded against Easton Connor.

I clutch a second pillow to my chest, my skin all tingly with memories of him in my room—standing so close and passing the beer to me while we traded secrets. His body so close as he touched his forehead to mine and asked if I wanted him to kiss me.

Could it hurt to close my eyes and let myself imagine what it would've been like? I'm totally unworthy, and he's a fucking football star—now a first-round NFL draft pick—but it would hardly be the first time I've indulged such a fantasy. In an alternate reality, I could have accepted that kiss. I imagine myself as the tall, thin beauty my mom was at my age, and I imagine him as *just Easton*—the boy who patched up my knee when I fell off my bike and who told me jokes when I was sad. In that alternate reality, it wouldn't have been a pity kiss at all but something he wanted as much as I did.

He wouldn't have asked with words. He would've asked with the slow descent of his mouth to mine, and I wouldn't have pulled away. He would've tasted like beer and been gentle, and I would've been a naturally good kisser. So good, he would've groaned into my mouth like the heroes in romance novels do.

I flip over in bed again, whimpering in frustration.

My bedroom door clicks, and I stare at it in the darkness. Is Carter checking on me? I don't know why he's suddenly so worried about me and Easton being alone together. Probably because I got boobs. *Finally.*

"Shay? You awake?" The husky whisper is a tripwire in my stomach, causing all my internal organs to detonate before clumsily righting themselves.

I roll to my side, watching the door as I hold the pillow to my chest. "Yeah. Everything okay?"

The sliver of hallway light grows as East steps into the room. "Could I sit in here with you?"

Oh, shit. I know that tone in his voice—the subtle tremor of anxiety that sometimes hits East so hard he can't function. I would do anything to make it better, but luckily, it doesn't take much. I scoot to the opposite side of the mattress and pat the bed beside me.

Easton releases a long breath, and the light shrinks again to nothing as he shuts the door behind him. He lies down on his back on top of the covers. "Sorry," he whispers.

I put my hand on his chest, right on top of his racing heart. "I'm here. It's fine."

He places a hand on top of mine. "Thank you."

Gone are the days of self-deprecation for these spells of anxiety. The first time I witnessed one of his attacks, he was a junior in high school and it was the night before he was supposed to take the SATs. I found him in the corner of our basement, shivering and sweating. It freaked me out to see him so panicked. He couldn't catch his breath and his skin was so hot that I thought he had a fever. I had no idea what to do, so I just sat down beside him and held his hand. Eventually, he calmed enough to tell me it was an anxiety attack, and not his first. School was always a trigger for him—especially anything that made him feel like he might lose a chance to play football.

After that night, it wasn't uncommon for him to seek me out during the tough moments. For whatever reason, I've always been able to calm him. He told me he was comforted to have me beside him whenever he had to suffer through a full-blown attack.

"Just breathe." I scoot closer, keeping my hand on his chest under his.

I hear him fighting to control his breathing, and his heartbeat slows incrementally. "Thank you."

"Try to sleep, East. Everything seems worse in the middle of the night." I stay close, willing my calm to seep into him until the steady, even beat under my hand lulls me to sleep.

I fade in and out of consciousness, dreaming of our drinking game, of our conversation from earlier, my brain replaying and rewriting the words as his grip on my hand loosens.

And when the words I needed earlier tonight register in my brain, I don't know if they're from this Easton or from my dream.

"It wouldn't have been a pity kiss."

Easton: Thank you for last night. You are the literal chill to my crazy.

I clutch my phone in my hand as I read and reread the text. I fell asleep next to Easton, but when I woke, the morning sun slanting through the curtains, he was gone. I thought I'd find him downstairs with the rest of the hungover crew, but apparently he had to drive back to Jackson Harbor before anyone was up.

I didn't expect to hear anything from him until the next time he came home but . . . he texted. I try not to let it mean more than it does.

Me: You're not crazy. You have a lot on your shoulders. It's understandable that your anxiety would flare up.

Easton: It's easier to manage it when you're there.

I squeeze my eyes shut. Does he have any idea what words like this do to me? The hope they give?

> *Easton: Do you think your parents would let you finish high school in L.A.? I'd give you room and board in exchange for your chilling effect in my life.*

> *Me: Oh, absolutely. Let me just go tell Dad. He'll be totally cool with his only daughter moving to L.A. to live with and serve a pro football player.*

> *Easton: Serve? Please don't say it that way to your dad. I like my face as it is.*

> *Me: Say it like what?*

> *Easton: Like I'm buying sexual favors.*

> *Me: I think we've established I'm not the girl for THAT job.*

> *Easton: I'm saying I wouldn't want to pay you.*

> *Me: If you did, you'd demand a refund. Because, if you recall our conversation, I'm CLUELESS.*

> *Easton: No. I don't want to pay for your sexual favors for the same reason you don't want a pity kiss.*

My cheeks are on fire. Luckily, I'm alone in my bedroom and no one can see my awkward nerves at having this conversation with Easton. Is this a conversation, or is it . . . *flirting*? I stare at the screen while trying to decide how to reply. His next text comes through before I can.

> *Easton: Will you come see my new place when I get settled?*

Yes! Yes! Yes! I don't trust myself to reply. I'm trying to be cool, but my insides have zero chill when Easton is pouring on the attention like this.

> *Easton: I'm not sure how I'm supposed to start this new life without my rock to ground me when my crazy comes out.*

> *Me: Talking to your doctor about a prescription might be a start. And you know I'm not joking.*

> *Easton: I know. I just don't want to need it.*

> *Me: There's no shame in it.*

> *Easton: Thank you. For that. For everything.*

I reread those words over and over, my heart swelling so big there's no room for me to draw breath into my lungs. Maybe I'll never have Easton the way I wish I could, but at least I have this.

Whatever it is.

My brothers are lounging in the family room, barely awake and worshipping their coffee mugs, and the kitchen is clean, the counters sparkling. There's no sign of the dirty cups and beer bottles I expected to find littering the main floor. Instead, the only evidence of last night's celebration is the three black trash bags piled by the garage door.

"You all got to work early," I say to the boys.

Jake rubs his eyes. "Not us. East felt bad about leaving us with the mess, so he cleaned before he left."

"Nice."

"Is it just me, or has he been acting weird since the draft?" Jake asks.

Carter squeezes his eyes shut. "He's acting like he doesn't want to go. Which is ridiculous."

"It's just a lot. I think he's still processing," I say.

Carter frowns at me. "Since when are you two besties?"

"We're not besties. I'm just a good listener."

Carter grunts and mumbles something about how I'd better be "listening and nothing more," and my cheeks heat.

I don't want to pay for your sexual favors for the same reason you don't want a pity kiss.

Maybe that just means he doesn't want to pay for sex. Maybe I'm being a naive girl with a crush to think it means he wants *me*.

December 31st, eight months later

*E*aston's home.

    I've never felt shy around him, but tonight I watch him play cards at the kitchen table with my brothers and feel weird about saying a simple *hello*. The sound of laughter and clinking of beer bottles fills my family's vacation cabin. A fire roars in the living room. As far as New Year's Eve parties go, this one is pretty tame. My brothers and a handful of their friends from school, Easton, and as of ten minutes ago . . . me. I'm standing just outside the kitchen, fidgeting with my purse, and wondering if I should have come at all. I don't think anyone's noticed I'm here. I'm sure Easton hasn't, not when there's a girl with big boobs, blond hair, and a tiny waist standing behind him and giggle-whispering in his ear.

    I don't know why the idea of being in the same room as him

is making my heart race. I haven't seen him since draft night, when he gave me my first shot of tequila and fell asleep next to me, but we text sometimes. Well, my brothers text him all the time, and I'm in that loop, but sometimes he checks in with me. A message on my eighteenth birthday, a check-in at midterms, a goofy story about a guy on his team. Nothing profound or incredibly meaningful, but every time I get a message from him that isn't also sent to my brothers, hope swells so big in my chest that I can hardly breathe.

Everything and nothing has changed since he left. His whole life is different. He's living in L.A. and wrapping up his first season in the NFL. He even dated an underwear model for a few weeks last fall. But I'm still the same girl he fell asleep next to. The one who's never been kissed and can't get over her childhood crush, even though she knows he's entirely out of her league.

It's twenty minutes until midnight, but I'm suddenly too tired and too self-conscious to announce my arrival. I slip up the stairs and head to my bedroom, changing into flannel pajamas before sliding into bed and cracking open *Harry Potter and the Chamber of Secrets*. I've already read it three times, but there's something about returning to a favorite that is as comforting as a well-worn blanket.

It's not long before I hear the sounds of everyone downstairs counting down to the new year. I wonder if Easton's kissing that pretty blond girl. I wish I didn't care.

I close my book, roll to my back, and stare at the ceiling. I could have gone to a party with kids from my high school tonight. There's a cute boy in my honors English class that asked if I'd be there. His name is Steve, and the way he smiled when he said he hoped to see me made me blush. But I came here instead, and I don't even bother lying to myself about why. I wanted to see Easton.

There's a knock on my door, and I roll my eyes. I bet one of my brothers is checking to see if this room is empty so he can hook up with someone. "I'm in here," I say, not bothering to hide my annoyance.

The door cracks. "That's what I was hoping."

Easton. My heart sprints, stumbles, falls flat on its face.

He steps into my room, grinning, and shuts the door behind him. "Why weren't you downstairs?"

Because I realized I'll never be pretty enough, and I hated myself for thinking that way. Even if it's true. I sit up in bed and lean against the headboard. "I didn't want to be around so many people."

This is a ridiculous explanation when I could have stayed home tonight, but he nods as if it makes perfect sense. "I kind of feel the same. Do you mind if I hide in here with you?"

"Won't your date be disappointed?"

He arches a brow. "My *date*?"

I'm making a fool of myself. "The blond girl who was rubbing herself all over you?"

He lifts his chin. "Ah. I think her name's Sasha, but I'm not interested. I'd rather hang out with you . . . if you don't care?" The question is laced with enough doubt that the shield around my clumsy heart falls.

I swallow and will my pulse to slow. I don't want to be so desperate for his attention, but here I am. "Sure. I'm just reading."

Grinning, he crosses the room and studies the books on my

shelf before grabbing my copy of *The Stand.*

"King," I say, nodding. "Good choice."

Easton toes off his tennis shoes and stretches out in bed beside me—him on top of the covers, me beneath, just like on draft night when he was having an anxiety attack. He opens his book and I open mine.

"Happy New Year, Short Stack," he says softly.

The old nickname makes me smile. "Happy New Year."

I wake up to the feel of a calloused hand on my stomach, fingertips sweeping underneath my shorts. My body is awake—every nerve ending at full attention—but my mind is foggy and I have to blink into the darkness a few times before I remember where I am and who I'm with.

Easton.

Easton is touching me.

His fingers sweep across the waistband of my panties, and I gasp, arching instinctively. I must've fallen asleep while reading. The lights are off and he's spooning me, his front flush to my back, and when I shift, the hard length of him presses along my ass. "Easton?" My thighs clench, and it's all I can do not to tuck my hips and lead that hand to where I want it—where I've imagined it a thousand times before. "Are you awake?"

He moans into my neck and grips my hip, holding me against him.

The instinct to arch into his touch is so strong, but I have to know if this is real. "Easton?" My mind is foggy from sleep, but my body is more alert than ever. Every inch of my skin is aware of every movement he makes.

Suddenly he releases my hip and pulls away. My body goes cold everywhere he was touching me. "Shay?"

I drag in a ragged breath. *Shit, shit, shit.* "Yeah?"

"Fuck. I'm sorry. I was dreaming and . . ." I hear his swallow in the darkness.

I roll to face him, but I can barely make out his silhouette in the inky blackness. "What were you dreaming about?"

He releases a raspy chuckle. "Isn't that obvious?"

I bite my bottom lip. "So *who* were you dreaming about, then?"

He lifts his hand to my face, tracing the line of my jaw. I wish I could see his eyes, his expression, anything that might hint at his thoughts. "I thought that might be obvious too," he murmurs. "I'm sorry. You fell asleep, and I didn't want to leave, but I never meant to—"

"It's fine," I blurt. *Please don't stop. Please don't tell me you don't want this.*

His hand stills on my jaw. "It's not. Touching you while you're sleeping. That's . . . It's not cool."

"I . . . liked it."

He's silent for a long beat. Is he sorry I stole his easy out, or is he reconsidering his decision to throw the brakes on what we started in our sleep? "Yeah?"

"Do you want to . . ." I swallow hard. I want his hands on me again. I would trade all my pride for the relief of his touch. "Do you want to keep going?" As soon as the question is out, I wish I could snatch it back. Too needy, too desperate.

His fingers slip from my jaw and run down my neck—so slowly that the speed of the touch itself is a seduction. Rough fingertips graze my collarbone, and I bite back a moan. I never would've imagined my collarbone could be an erogenous zone. "More than I've ever wanted anything."

My breath catches. Maybe I can have this. Here in the dark. Just once, before he returns to his new life and forgets about me. "I'm not asleep now."

"Neither am I." His voice is as rough as the fingers slipping over my sleep shirt and between my breasts. "I'm going to kiss you now."

Please. I'm shaking. I barely trust myself to speak, so I nod and hope he can make out my consent in the darkness.

His mouth finds mine, and my whole body clenches at the electricity in the contact. It starts with a brush of lips, then a hand in my hair and his tongue touching mine. I swallow a moan and inch closer, parting my lips farther.

His kiss is nothing like I imagined it. It's better. Every stroke of his tongue stokes the fire inside me, tightens that sweet ache between my thighs.

When he breaks the kiss, we're both breathing hard and my lips feel swollen. "I wanted to do that last spring. I wanted to be your first kiss."

"You were," I admit. "That was, I mean."

His breath leaves him in a rush. "I'm not sure I trust myself with you."

I wish I'd lied—that I told him I was more experienced than I am just so he wouldn't be scared away. But this is Easton, and between us, honesty has always been the only choice. "I trust you. Completely."

He groans, and the sound is temptation and agony and pleasure all wrapped in one. "That's why I should keep my hands to myself." He cups my breast, his thumb grazing across my nipple. I swear his breath catches in tandem with mine. "Tell me what you want. I'm not trusting my judgment here. I need you to tell me this is okay." Even as he says it, he rolls me to my back and crawls over me, bracing himself on one elbow and using his free hand to toy with my breast. He lowers his mouth to my collarbone, explores with his tongue and nipping teeth before kissing his way up my neck and whispering into my ear. "You're in the driver's seat."

"I want everything."

"Shay." My name is the most erotic sound when he's breathless. "I should stop."

I whimper. "Please don't." Maybe I should be embarrassed by the desperate plea. Maybe I will be later. But right now, all I care about is getting more of him. "Easton, I need you."

He shifts over me, pressing the heat and weight of his powerful thigh between my legs. "Can I make you come?"

I arch into that pressure, and my cheeks heat when I realize how easy it would be to rub against him—how much I want to. "*Please.*"

"You might be the death of me."

I rub myself against his thigh again, and he hisses.

"Tell me you want me to touch you, Shay. Tell me I can put my hand between your legs and you'll still talk to me tomorrow." He shifts his thigh, putting pressure just where I need it. "Christ,

I can feel how wet you are through your shorts."

"Sorry." But God, I'm not really. Any embarrassment I feel about my reaction to him is overridden by my need for friction. My only chance of keeping my hips still is if I glue them to the bed.

He chokes out a low laugh. "Don't ever apologize for that. It's so hot." He sucks my earlobe between his teeth. "Feeling you grind against me is hot as fuck too. Don't fight it."

"Easton . . ." I slide my fingers into his hair and tug. "I want this."

A shudder rocks through him. "Me too." He lowers his mouth to mine and kisses me slowly—a long, lingering kiss that scatters all thoughts from my brain. When he pulls back, I swear he's looking at me. Maybe my body is better in the dark. Maybe he won't notice the extra weight I carry in my waist or how chubby my thighs are. He traces my lips with his finger. I catch it between my teeth, and he groans before withdrawing. He traces a wet path down between my breasts, over my stomach, and tucks his finger beneath the waistband of my panties. "I want to touch you here," he says, kissing my neck. "I want to feel you."

I lift my hips off the bed and toward his hand. "Easton, please."

He nips at the tender skin beneath my ear. He slips his hand under the cotton and grazes a knuckle over my clit.

"Shit!" I gasp.

I almost expect him to laugh at my outburst. Instead, he groans. "You're already so damn wet. Did you wake up like this?"

"Yes." *Because it's you*, I want to say. *Because I've wanted you for so long.*

He slides his fingers over me. "I fucking love the feel of you on my fingers."

My body winds tighter, tighter, *tighter* with every word he speaks. He's barely touched me, and I already feel close. "East."

He pinches my clit between two fingers, and I gasp. "Shh," he whispers, his mouth over mine. "I want to hear you moan, but I need you to be quiet." He sweeps his lips along my jaw again then slides a finger into me.

My body locks up, clenching tight around him. A single finger, but he's stretching me so much.

"Relax," he whispers. "Fuck, you're wet. Are you okay?"

"I've never . . ." I draw in a breath, because my body has already adjusted to the stretch of his thick finger, and pleasure has chased away the discomfort. "Not this."

"Not even with your own fingers?"

"No. Just . . ." I can't speak. Can't think. His hand has found a delicious rhythm, pumping in and out of me, stretching me. Every time he plunges in, I want more—*deeper*—and every time he pulls out, I feel like part of me is missing.

"Good," he growls against my neck. "I have no right, Shay, but I wanted it to be me. I want everything to be me."

I barely register his words as pleasure knots in my gut and ratchets up my spine. He presses his thumb against my clit, and my body jerks. That thumb strokes, and my whole body shakes as I climb, climb, climb.

"Don't fight it. Just let yourself feel good."

I tug his hair. I'm clinging to him, to this moment, to the edge of a mountain I'm sure I've never seen before. His finger pumps faster and he presses his mouth to mine, swallowing my moans as I give in to the pleasure and let my orgasm pull me apart. I cling to him, shaking and boneless.

Even when I'm nothing but trembling aftershocks, he's still kissing me, his hand moving in soothing, gentle strokes between my legs as I come down.

"I think I lied," I say when he finally frees my mouth.

"About what?"

"I thought I'd given myself orgasms, but they were never like *that*."

He groans, a long, low, tortured sound. "It's different with a partner. Better. More intense."

"I guess I should return the favor." I roll to my side and reach for him, pressing the flat of my palm to his hard length. He stops me with a hand on my wrist. "What's wrong?"

He brings my hand to his mouth and kisses my knuckles. "Nothing's wrong. Everything's great."

"You don't want me to touch you?"

He blows out a breath. "I want so much. But not tonight, Shayleigh. Not when I have to leave tomorrow." He pulls me into his arms and presses a kiss to the side of my neck. "I don't deserve you."

*E*aston woke me up this morning with a whispered apology. He promised his mom he'd have lunch with her before he leaves, and he flies back to California tonight. I desperately wanted him to stay—to kiss me more and touch me again, to convince me last night wasn't just a dream—but I didn't want to seem desperate or clingy. I smiled and told him to tell his mom I said hi, and he kissed me on the forehead and made me promise I'd text when I woke up.

> *Me: Texting, as promised.*

> *Easton: Good morning, sleepyhead. How are you this morning?*

> *Me: I'm good.*

> *Easton: Are you? I hated leaving after what happened last night.*

I hated for you to leave too. I wanted more. But I can't tell him that. Even if my fingers itch to type the words. I'm a coward, so I stick with something safe.

> *Me: I'm really fine. How's your mom?*

> *Easton: Good. We're making plans for her to move out to Cali this spring.*

> *Me: Oh, wow. It will be nice to have her closer.*

> *Easton: I wish I could move you all out. It's nice to want things, right?*

I bite back a smile, remembering our conversation last April, when he said he wished I could move out there.

Me: Maybe I'll look into UCLA's French literature program.

As soon as I send it, I wish I worded it differently—or that I hadn't shared it at all. Easton knows I've been planning to stay close to home for college. University of Chicago has been my top choice for years, and I just admitted I might apply to a college across the country to be closer to him.

Two minutes later, he still hasn't replied, and that does nothing to ease my anxiety.

I look at my phone every thirty seconds while I get dressed. Why did I say anything? By the time I head downstairs to join the hungover masses and clean up, I'm ready to invent the technology to delete texts after sending them.

It's not until we're all piled into Jake's car and on the interstate headed back to Jackson Harbor that Easton replies. The text is so far from what I was hoping that tears sting my eyes.

Easton: Don't change your plans, Shay. University of Chicago is your dream. I'm just joking around.

Part II.
Now

Shay

Twelve-and-a-half years later

Jackson family brunch has never been a relaxing affair. Every single one of my five brothers has managed to fall into a committed relationship in the last three years. Add in my two nieces and soon-to-be nephew, and our numbers have more than doubled. There are too many of us for even the simplest meal to be anything short of chaotic. And I *love it*.

But today, I'm grasping for my typical contented family-time happiness and coming up short.

Easton Connor is back in town and going to be in my personal space any second now. Well, not my *personal space* personal space—not like touching me. But in this kitchen. Sharing a meal with me—with *us*—for the first time since my father's funeral. Not only will I have to face him, I'll have to *talk* to him. I'll have to play nice, because no one knows what happened between us.

If I have my way, they never will. I won't let Easton ruin my day.

When the doorbell rings, my body locks up and the crowd clears out of the kitchen, leaving me blessedly alone for a moment before what feels like an impending apocalypse.

"About time you made it home for a family brunch," Carter says at the front door.

Easton's deep chuckle is warm and familiar, like fingertips running up my spine, like hot breath in my ear . . . like stolen kisses and my first shot of tequila.

I reach for the coffee carafe, only to find it empty. Everyone assumes that the Jacksons—craft beer connoisseurs that we are—love nothing more than we love beer. They assume wrong. In my family, coffee ranks high above even our favorite brews.

I grind some beans and dump them into the coffee filter. It's a three-cup-minimum day. I've been working nonstop between finishing my dissertation, keeping up with the four classes I teach at Starling University, and job hunting. The stress is finally catching up to me, and there's never enough sleep or enough coffee.

"East!" Brayden calls. I hear him jog down the last few steps and consider that perhaps Easton is the miracle worker he was deemed his second year in the NFL, because I didn't think anybody but Molly and Noah could pull Brayden away from work that quickly. "Congrats on the retirement! How's it going?"

I squeeze my eyes shut and listen to my family *ooh* and *aww* over him. Easton and Carter may have been the closest growing up, but Easton was friends with all my brothers, and he's Jackson Harbor's only claim to fame. Everyone's buzzing about him moving back home.

Tuning out the conversation coming from the front of the house, I focus on the coffee dripping all too slowly into the pot when every instinct screams at me to run to the bathroom and check my appearance. I changed three times this morning before making myself put on my favorite stretchy jeans and a Jackson Brews T-shirt. Because nothing says "I don't care that you broke my heart" like wearing the exact same outfit I do behind the bar at our family's brewpub.

"Hey, pretty," Teagan says, wandering in from the living room.

"Morning, beautiful." I turn away from the coffee pot to smile at my best friend. Teagan looks stunning today, as usual. Her dark hair is pulled off her face, and she's rocking a sweater dress that shows off her curves. I'll be shocked if Carter is able to keep his hands off her—not that he typically bothers trying. He's a fool in love.

"You okay?" she asks.

I nod, then cut my eyes toward the front of the house. "They're acting like a bunch of puppies running to greet their master."

She laughs. "But are you okay?"

My history with Easton is a secret, but when I found out he was coming to town, Teagan saw the panic in my eyes. I admitted I used to have a thing for Easton. She prodded for more information, but when it comes to Easton, I'm a vault. "I'm fine." I smile, but judging by the snort of laughter that slips from her lips in response, it's not convincing.

She opens the fridge and pulls out a bottle of champagne.

"Seems like a good day for mimosas. Want one?"

Carter's laughing at something Easton said. Why didn't I just come up with an excuse to miss this morning? I'm staring down the barrel of my dissertation defense and have a pile of revisions I need to work through in the next two months, never mind the midterm essays I haven't graded yet. No one would've held my absence against me.

I wave her off. "I'm good with coffee."

She hums and grabs some champagne glasses from the cabinet.

I'm urging the coffee to brew faster and doing a pretty decent job ignoring the conversation at the front of the house when I hear Easton ask, "Is Shay here?"

The words are like a pair of jumper cables to my heart. Does he really care, or is he just being polite?

"She's in the kitchen making coffee," Carter says.

"Of course she is." Easton chuckles. God, that *laugh*. It transports me to another time. If I close my eyes, I'm in his bed in Paris, the Eiffel Tower twinkling in the dusk beyond the window, his smell all over me.

I draw in a breath, and when I open my eyes, he's standing in front of me—the man I once loved so desperately, the only guy to ever break my heart.

Easton's eyes go wide, and his jaw slackens as he takes me in. His eyes skim over me, from my dark ponytail down to my beaten-up black Chuck Taylors then back up. "Shayleigh Jackson, what a sight for sore eyes."

"Hey, East."

Teagan nudges my arm, then shoves a glass of champagne

into my hand. Because, obviously, she's the best friend ever and knows me better than I know myself. "We're out of OJ," she says brightly.

I take a sip of the champagne and give Easton a small smile.

"You look . . ." he starts.

I arch a brow, waiting for him to finish that sentence. There are many directions he could go with this. A polite "great" would work. Or maybe the healthy muscle tone I've gained since I last saw him calls for "incredible." I really hope he doesn't say "all grown up" or any shit like that. I can't be held responsible for what my fists will do if he treats me like a little girl.

Carter's found the champagne, and he offers Easton a glass.

East nods his thanks before turning back to me. "You look well," he says softly. *Well.* How . . . clinical. And somewhere in my chest, the remaining kernel of the girl I was winces. That girl wished every day that she could be thin, that she could walk into a room and drop jaws, that she could be more than "the smart girl." The idea that she still wouldn't be that even if she did lose the weight was a fear she didn't even admit to herself.

But that girl didn't know who she was. And this girl—this *woman*—does. So I look him over brazenly, taking in the breadth of his shoulders, the corded muscles of his arms, the way his L.A. Demons shirt stretches across his chest, and, finally, the subtle wrinkles at the corners of his eyes. "So do you." I tap my glass to his, but I don't take another drink. Despite Teagan's good intentions, I need to keep my wits about me today.

And for the last two months, I've anticipated his return with a mix of dread and curiosity. I feel more than a little guilty about the number of times his impending return has intruded in my thoughts during my scarce alone time with secret kind-of-boyfriend, George. I wonder if I would've even gone home with George that first time if I hadn't learned Easton was coming.

And I can't help but be grateful that I did. It's better that I'm not single.

I place my champagne flute on the counter and trade it for a mug full of coffee.

When it comes to Easton Connor, I cannot be trusted.

Easton

Seeing Shayleigh Jackson for the first time in almost seven years is like an iron fist to the solar plexus. I'd be a liar if I said I hadn't thought about her in our time apart, and an even bigger liar if I denied doing a little Internet stalking to prepare for this meeting today. Her Facebook account's locked down tighter than Fort Knox, so I couldn't get much there aside from her profile picture and a handful of pics both she and Carter are tagged in. Instagram and Twitter were no more fruitful.

This profile is private.

I'm sure I'm being defensive, but it felt like those words were directed at me. Like she's kept everything private just to shut me out. I'm not entirely paranoid. She's done worse to keep me away.

Luckily for me, there's still Google. The Starling University website didn't disappoint. She's a lecturer there, teaching classes in postmodern fiction and contemporary women's lit. According to her bio, she's working on a dissertation on the intersection of pop music and contemporary American women's poetry, which sounds so much like Shay that I had to smile. Life is full of shitty surprises, but I'm glad some things stay the same.

No amount of research could've prepared me for what it would feel like to stand here. To be close enough to touch her. And I swear I can smell the lemon and lavender soap she fell in love with in Paris. I want to know if she still uses it. I want to know if she's found an American substitute, or if down-to-earth, practical Shay pays to have fancy Parisian soaps shipped to her in Jackson Harbor.

I sent her a box of it for her twenty-fifth birthday, and the store contacted me a month later letting me know it had been returned. Would I like to send it to another address?

I didn't bother. *Message received.*

"How's the dissertation coming?" I ask her now. It's hard to free myself from the tangle of memories when she smells like my favorites.

"Whoa!" Levi says, making a face.

Carter shakes his head and stage-whispers, "We aren't allowed to ask that question until after she defends."

Shay rolls her eyes at her brothers. "It's fine. I just don't like to be *harassed* about it, and for a while there, these guys thought I'd finish faster if they just asked more." She gives a pointed look to each of her brothers, as if daring them to deny it. "It doesn't work like that."

"You're planning to defend this spring?" I ask. I want her attention so badly that I feel like a fiend, but her curt nod tells me the desire to catch up doesn't go both ways. If I were wise, I'd let it go, but I can't.

"Easton, it's so good to see you! I always knew fate would lead you back home," Mrs. Jackson says, forcing me to turn away from my study of the woman I've missed so damn much.

I open my arms and wrap my surrogate mother in a hug. Her hair is shorter than she used to wear it. Carter tells me that's because she lost it fighting cancer, and when it grew back, she decided she liked it short. "It's good to see you, Mrs. Jackson."

"Please, you can call me Kathleen now."

"That's sweet of you, Mrs. Jackson."

She chuckles and pulls back, rubbing my arm. "I was so sorry to hear about your mother passing."

I nod. "Me too. Thank you."

She looks around. "Where's Abigail this morning?"

"She's back in L.A. with her nanny. I have a lot of business to take care of on this trip, and I didn't want to overwhelm her with everything else going on."

Kathleen nods, as if she knows "everything else" means the fact that my daughter found out in the worst way possible that she's not really my daughter. *Fucking Scarlett.* When I discovered her lie six years ago, it was hard to swallow, but I realized if she hadn't lied, Abi would've never been in my life. Since Abi's easily the best thing that's ever happened to me, I couldn't stay angry about it. But then Scarlett had to go and reveal the truth in a drunken reality TV rant that the whole world would see.

The kids at school were relentless in their teasing, and the cameras I've kept away from Abi her entire life swarmed closer and closer.

"Breakfast?" asks a bright-faced woman with honey-brown hair.

Levi grabs a plate. "Finally. I'm starved."

"Pardon my children," Kathleen says, frowning. "They forget their manners when they're hungry." She points to the honey-haired woman. "This is Nic, Ethan's wife. I think you met Lilly at Frank's funeral," she says, pointing to a little girl who's at the breakfast bar filling her plate. She has dark hair like her dad and is around the same age as my Abigail.

I grin at her. "You were barely talking then. Just two years old. I bet you don't remember me."

Lilly shakes her head. "I thought you were bringing me a friend."

Gratitude washes over me. *We won't be alone here, Abi. We have family.* "Next time. I promise."

Kathleen points to a woman with a dark bob who has a baby on her hip. "You remember Ava, I'm sure. She's Jake's wife now, and this is their daughter, Lauren." She turns to the brunette hanging close to Levi. "That's Ellie, Levi's fiancée."

"I know Ellie," I say, waving at my Realtor. "She's been house-hunting for me."

"Are we still on for this afternoon?" she asks.

I nod. I'm here to see the latest house she's found for me, and if all goes well, I'll be putting in an offer first thing tomorrow and closing before leaving Jackson Harbor. "Looking forward to it."

"Good. Then, of course, there's Teagan," Kathleen says, pointing to an olive-skinned woman who's been inspecting me like I'm an interesting artifact since I walked into the room. Teagan's been keeping close to Shay, and I wonder how much she knows about our past. "Teagan is Carter's girlfriend."

Brayden clears his throat. "My fiancée, Molly, isn't here this morning. She and her son Noah are wedding dress shopping with her mom in Chicago this weekend, but I'm sure you'll meet her this week."

I sweep my gaze across the kitchen and try to take in all the faces. "Wives, fiancées, girlfriends, babies. You all have been busy," I say, and everyone laughs.

"Now we can eat," Mrs. Jackson says.

I fall back and watch with a pang of nostalgia as the familiar Jackson brunch ritual plays out. Everyone fills their plates and mugs, the brothers poking fun at each other, Mrs. Jackson smiling proudly at her children.

Shay catches me watching. "We've squeezed around that table for years, but it just got to be too much." She shoves a plate in my hand. "So now we split up between the kitchen and the dining room."

"It's different," I say softly. On the one hand, it's just like they did it when I was a kid. I have fond memories of sleeping over on Saturdays and waking up Sundays to a massive meal with this family that became so precious to me. On the other hand, the differences are impossible to ignore. There are so many more people, and it's crowded, but most notably, Frank Jackson isn't here to keep his arm around his wife and steal kisses like they're teenagers.

"The only thing guaranteed in life is change." Pain flashes over Shay's face, and I'm thrown back to her father's funeral and the feel of her in my arms as she cried. The way her sobs were so powerful, they shook me. The way I took her grief in my hands and made it so much worse.

I open my mouth to apologize—for that night, for the years I let her shut me out—but I snap it shut again. There are too many eyes on me right now, and I don't think Shay wants them to know why I owe her an apology.

Shay

After brunch is cleaned up, everyone scatters. Levi and Ellie leave to run some errands, Ethan, Nic, and Lilly head out to a movie, and everyone else heads to the basement to play games. I use my revisions as an excuse to stay upstairs with my laptop, but I can't face my dissertation while I'm this distracted, so I sit at the kitchen table and respond to student emails instead.

Lucky me, I have an email from a student about his two-week-late paper as an outlet for my frustrations. I'm a lengthy paragraph into a careful recap of my course policies when I hear the basement door open and close again. I know without looking that Easton just came back upstairs. Why is that? Why do I *feel* him when he's around, even after all these years?

I lean closer to my computer, pretending I'm not aware of every step he takes, pretending I don't notice when he pulls out the chair beside me and sinks into it.

When I look over at him, he's turned toward me, elbows on his knees, deeply engrossed in a study of the tiled floor. Fine. If he's not going to tell me what he needs, then I'm not going to ask. I go back to my email, realize my last sentence is nearly incoherent, and delete it.

"You're giving me the silent treatment?"

Sighing, I pull my gaze off my screen and turn to him. "What gives you that idea?"

He lifts his head, and those sea-green eyes search my face. Whoever gave Easton Connor those eyes wanted to torture me. No one should have eyes that make you feel lost and precious all at once. It's not fair. "You barely talked to me at all at brunch."

"That doesn't mean I'm giving you the silent treatment."

Leaning back in his chair, he folds his arms. He's not buying my shit, and I don't care. "You blocked me on social media—I sent requests."

I snort. "Really, Easton? Do you care if some girl from back home keeps her accounts private?"

"You're more than that to me, and you know it."

"Am I?" My heart is doing some really crazy racing-and-stuttering thing in my chest. Like someone's trying to test its accelerator and its brakes at the same time. "I don't go years without talking to the people who matter to me, so I guess I don't know anything."

"Would you have talked to me if I'd tried?" He swallows, his eyes scanning my face over and over. What's he looking for? A sign that he didn't screw things up with me? Proof that maybe we can still be *friends* after everything? He can keep looking, but he's not going to find it.

"It doesn't matter." I close my laptop. "That was all a long time ago, and I'm not some moon-eyed girl anymore."

"Have dinner with me," he blurts.

Clearly, guilt over the past has made this man lose his mind. It's bad enough that he's moving back, but he can't seriously expect me to want to spend time alone with him. "Why?"

He blinks. "Because I missed you? Because I want a chance to apologize properly?" He looks out the window over my shoulder and frowns. "I'm not wrong, am I? You've never told your family . . . about us?"

I shake my head and slide my laptop into my bag. "I don't hate you, I don't need to go to dinner to hear you apologize, and my family doesn't need to know about our mistakes."

His throat bobs as he swallows. "Was that all I was to you? A mistake?"

I'm too tired to deal with this today. Merely sitting beside him is more emotionally taxing than I was prepared for. "What else would you call it?"

"Bad timing?" He shakes his head. "I'm back here now. For real. We're going to have to talk at some point. You can't keep pushing me away."

"Just because I'm not available to you doesn't mean I'm giving you the silent treatment. And just because you're moving home doesn't mean I'm obligated to have dinner with you. You and I have said all we need to say." I sling my bag over my shoulder and do my best to ignore the hurt in his eyes. Even after everything, I can't stand the idea of causing him pain, so I attempt to soften my words. "Welcome back to Jackson Harbor. I'm sure your daughter will love it here."

Easton

"The master looks right out to Lake Michigan." At the top of the stairs, Ellie turns left and opens a set of double doors that lead into the master bedroom of what I hope will be my future home. She strides in, her heels clicking on the hardwood floor.

I turn to follow, and the view stops me in my tracks. The lake stretches for miles, and the rippling water glitters like diamonds in the sunset.

I would've thought I'd become accustomed to views like this. After thirteen years in the NFL, the best has become my new normal. Hell, I've owned my penthouse in Laguna Beach for ten years, and its view of the Pacific is hands-down more impressive than this. But I'm speechless nonetheless. Something about being back in Jackson Harbor makes the last thirteen years go away. Once again, I'm just the son of a single mom, scraping by on next to nothing. Once again, I'm a kid who's grateful he has football and a best friend with the coolest family in the world.

Once, a house like this was only a dream, and now I'm a couple of signatures from grabbing it for myself—free and clear.

"Is it okay?" Ellie asks, misinterpreting my silence for disapproval.

Nodding, I cross the room to stand by the windows. I've been waiting for something like this to come on the market, and came to town just to see it before finalizing my offer. "No, it's great." I flash her a smile over my shoulder. "Thanks for catching it for me."

She beams. "That's my job."

"There are other bedrooms on this floor?"

"Yes. It's a split floor plan up here. The master's on this side, and then there's an office between you and the other bedrooms." She nods toward the door. "Let me show you the one I think your daughter would love."

I follow her down the hall, stopping along the way to admire the massive office with its wall of walnut built-ins. I love all the wood tones in this house, from the trim to the timber beams in the family room downstairs. Right before Scarlett finally moved out, she remodeled my Laguna home into a monochromatic wash of white and gray. It felt like a high-end hotel. *This* feels like home.

"Big closets," Ellie says when I follow her into the room at the end of the hall. "And she might not care about that now, but there's a good chance she will when she gets older."

I grunt. Abigail might only be nine, but she already cares about clothes more than I ever have. The room is a good size, and

I can already picture where I'll put her bed, a desk, and a small TV area with her fuzzy pink beanbag chairs. It might not have the massive windows that the master has, but it does overlook the water.

"She'll love it." I swallow, hoping I'm right. I need to get her out of L.A. The media circus that's rained down on us since her mom's follow-up tell-all interview has been intense and worse than anything we've had to deal with before. Abi wants it to end, but like any nine-year-old would be, she's nervous about leaving all her friends.

"I'm sure it's scary," Ellie says softly, "picking up your whole life and moving here. But there's nowhere I'd rather raise a family."

Grinning, I look pointedly at the ring on her finger and grab the opportunity to change the subject with both hands. "Are you and Levi planning a family?"

Her cheeks bloom red. "Eventually. We're not in any hurry."

"It's hard for me to imagine that little punk settling down. He was always up to something." I smile, memories filling my head.

"He's changed a lot since you moved away." She studies me for a long beat before adding, "Everyone has."

Hell, don't I know it. "You're friends with Shay?"

She nods. "I'm not as close to her as Teagan is, but we're friends. We all try to get together for girls' night at least once a month—though now it's more like quarterly. Everyone's so busy. But Shay's been finishing up her dissertation. We have to drag her out of the house every so often so she doesn't work herself into the ground." She cocks her head to the side and says, "But I thought it was Carter you were so close to."

Busted. "I was close to the whole family. They treated me like one of their own."

"Of course they did."

"There's room for everyone," we say in unison, reciting what seems to be the Jackson family creed.

"They were there for me through some tough times too." She scans the empty room, but I get the impression she's really just stuck in her memories.

"Carter was my best friend growing up." I shove my hands in my pockets and make a show of checking the closet. I've already had a private inspector go through the house, and I knew I'd buy it before I flew here to see it. I just wanted to make sure it felt right before I committed. Maybe I also wanted to see Shay before I'm busy settling Abigail into Jackson Harbor.

And didn't that go great?

"And you and Shay . . .?" Ellie asks.

I arch a brow, waiting for her to finish that sentence and wondering how close she really is with the Jackson sister.

She shakes her head. "Sorry. I'm being unprofessional. Your history with her is none of my business."

Did Shay say something? I bite back the question. It won't do anything but make me sound like an insecure teenager. But damn, where Shay's concerned, that's how I feel.

I glance around the room again. "So let's do some paperwork and make this official."

Shay

"**A**re you okay?"

Jerking out of my thoughts, I realize my date is staring at me, his deep brown eyes crinkled in the corners. "I'm fine. Why?"

"You've been poking at that pasta for ten minutes." George Alby flashes me his panty-melting bearded smile. His signature charm only compounds my guilt. "You just seem distracted. Is it your defense? Because you have nothing to worry about. Hammer out those revisions, and you'll have a dissertation worth publishing."

"It's not that." After I failed spectacularly at quieting my brain enough to nap, George and I decided to meet for dinner at our favorite diner. The place is just off the interstate in a tiny town halfway between Grand Rapids and Jackson Harbor. These are usually my favorite nights with him—when we can be in public without hiding our relationship. Tonight, I've barely touched my food, and his plate is clear. I'm proving to be a crappy date.

George nudges his empty plate to the side and folds his arms on the table. "So tell me what it is." He looks around the restaurant in amusement. "Is this a breakup dinner?"

I gape. "No, of course not! Why would you even think that?"

"It's just a matter of time, isn't it?" An insecure smile flashes across his ruggedly handsome features, and my heart tugs. "Until one of these universities on the other side of the country drags you away from me?"

I don't want to move across the country. But is that because I don't want to leave George, or because I don't want to leave my family? He and I have never set out to have something long-term. I'm not even sure what this thing *is* between us. He's more than my fuck buddy—and I'm pretty sure that label would offend him down to his bones—but he's not quite my boyfriend either. And the fact that we agreed from the beginning to keep this relationship a secret hasn't given us any reason to iron out what we are to each other.

I blow out a breath. "I'm sorry I'm distracted. It's not about you."

"Shay . . ." He takes my hand and toys with my fingers. "You can trust me with whatever's going on in your head. I don't scare off easily."

But everything in my head is awful. My head is full of a laundry list of Easton's qualities and all the ways George. . . *isn't him.* "Did you know Easton Connor is moving back to Jackson Harbor?" I can tell by George's baffled expression that he has no idea who Easton is. That makes me laugh. "Easton Connor, the quarterback? Two-time Super Bowl MVP?"

George wrinkles his nose and shrugs. He's adorable, and normally a show of NFL ignorance would be a point in his favor, because it means never having to answer all the crazy fan questions about what it was like to grow up with Easton. Tonight it irritates me. And the fact that I'm irritated is irritating. I blame Easton for it all. He's like a drug. He messes with my brain on a chemical level.

"Easton Connor is an NFL player who grew up in Jackson Harbor," I explain patiently. "He was best friends with my brother Carter growing up, and he was at brunch today."

George tilts his head to the side. "Okay . . ."

I look away. I don't want to admit my complicated past with Easton to anyone, but sharing it with an academic who sneers at professional athletes is really high on my list of *do not want*. "We haven't seen each other in years, and it's messed with me a little."

"You're struggling because you've reconnected with your brother's childhood best friend?" he asks. "Or you're struggling because he used to be something to you?"

"He was never anything to me," I blurt. *Way too defensive.* "Not officially, at least."

"He hurt you?"

I feel like that description is simultaneously too harsh and too weak. "Yes, but he never intended to. He was hard to get over."

"Your first love?"

My eyes fill with hot tears. Totally unexpected and even more unacceptable. *Stupid emotions.* "I don't know if I'd use that word." Though with Easton, there's no other word that comes close to what I felt. "My family never knew."

He cocks his head to the side. George really is a grade-A listener. "Why was it a secret?"

Because it wasn't real? Because Carter would've killed him? Because I wasn't enough to make it worth telling the truth? "It was never really a thing, but a . . ." I shrug.

"He slept with you and you fell for him, but nothing came of it."

Wincing at that painfully accurate summary, I shrug again. *Excellent communicating, Shayleigh.*

"And then he left for the NFL and forgot about you?"

I bite my bottom lip. "Not exactly. We . . . reconnected a couple of times over the years."

"Let me guess—when you were convenient."

It's not a question so much as an assumption, and I don't fully understand why it cuts so deep. Because it feels too accurate, or because George can't imagine me being something more than a convenient diversion to someone like Easton?

George nods slowly, taking my lack of response as confirmation. "Does he know how you felt about him?"

"I think so." I thought he felt the same, and then he was just a young guy desperately trying to do the right thing. I had to let him go. "It's not a big deal, but it's something I need to process."

"Are you sure that's all?" He reaches across the table and runs a fingertip over my knuckles. The touch should be comforting, but I want to shake him off. I'm such a mess.

"What do you mean?"

"I mean, should I be worried that you're going to throw away a bright future for this guy?"

"No. Of course not. That's not why I . . ." I shake my head. I'm not even sure what *future* he's referring to. My career, or my relationship with him? Surely the former, right? "I've just been thinking about the past. I'm fine. I'm *not* looking to reunite with Easton, I promise."

He squeezes my hand. "Good." He nods to my plate. "Are you done?"

The smell of my favorite pasta carbonara turns my stomach tonight, but George had ordered my usual for me by the time I arrived, and I didn't want to be rude. "I don't have much of an appetite."

Standing, he pulls out his wallet and throws cash on the table to cover our meal. He leads me from my seat and cups my jaw in both hands, kissing me long and full and . . . *Damn.* This is why I fell into bed with him that first time. He can listen, and he can *kiss.* I never thought I'd find myself in a relationship like this, and yet here I am, sneaking around. It's not that what we're doing is against the rules, but it's certainly frowned upon. At the very least, it will make people think twice about my accomplishment when I finally get my doctorate.

"You're way too good for some guy who gets paid to knock other guys around on a field," he whispers against my mouth. "Just remember that."

I grimace, wishing he didn't have to bring his anti-athlete snobbery into this. And seriously, who doesn't know that quarterbacks do the ball throwing and not the knocking around?

"Ready to go home?" he asks.

Home. The place we stay when we sleep together is hardly home to either of us.

George has a daughter in Chicago and lives there Thursday night through Tuesday morning to be with her. He teaches a Tuesday/Wednesday/Thursday schedule at Starling and lives in a studio apartment near campus those days. This weekend was one of the rare exceptions when he stuck around Starling for department obligations.

His phone buzzes on the table, and he cuts his eyes to it before looking back to me. "Do you mind? I'm waiting for a call from my secretary about arrangements for next month's speaker series."

"On a Sunday?"

"No rest for the wicked." Winking, he grabs the phone and swipes to answer it. "George Alby speaking."

I point to the bathroom, and he nods toward the street and mouths, *Meet me outside?*

"Sure."

In the bathroom, I wash my hands and breathe. Until I started talking about Easton, I didn't realize how much I was dreading tonight's conversation. If someone accused me of intentionally omitting my history with Easton from what I've shared with George, I would've denied it like crazy. But now? Now I realize I didn't want to talk about it because I knew George would make me face a past I'm not ready to face.

It's not like Easton and I are going to try to have something real now that he's back home. I wouldn't want that even if I was single. I have too many feelings of rejection and heartache where he's concerned to ever want that.

I close my eyes and remember the buzz that went across my skin when Easton found me alone in the kitchen. The way I could

73

feel him enter the room. Intellectually, I'm totally on board with letting Easton go forever, but my pheromones haven't gotten the message yet.

With a deep breath, I push out of the bathroom and back into the restaurant toward the front.

"Ma'am?" Our waiter from earlier nods to our table. "Your date left his jacket."

"Oh, no! Thanks." I grab George's jacket off the back of the chair. When I sling it over my arm, something falls from the pocket and bounces off my shoe before rolling under the table. "Shit." I drop to my knees and reach under the table.

When my hand closes over the soft velvet box, my heart seems to stop in my chest. *No. We're not there yet. Surely this isn't . . .*

I stare at the box, terrified to open it and find out what's inside.

"Ma'am? Are you okay?" the waiter asks.

I quickly hide the box under George's jacket and stand. "I'm just clumsy. Thanks again."

Through the windows at the front of the restaurant, I can see George pacing the sidewalk as he talks with his secretary. That's one of the things I love about him—he's passionate about his job. While I enjoy my time in the classroom, George thrives on all of it—the advising, the committee work, the publishing. The man even gets a freakish pleasure from grading papers.

And he really is a good listener, and fun to be around. There's a lot to love about him, but I don't even know if I could say that I love *him*. We've never even met each other's families.

I didn't think he wanted to change that.

I clutch the box in my hand. Maybe it's not what I think. Maybe he bought me a necklace or earrings. Maybe it's not even for me.

Holding my breath, I open the lid and shut it just as quickly. My eyes burn, and I'm not sure why. I am definitely overreacting. There has to be a reasonable explanation for George bringing a giant solitaire diamond ring to dinner with me.

I shove the box into the pocket of his jacket and head out front.

George's eyes go wide when he sees the jacket over my arm. "I can't believe I forgot that."

"The . . ." I clear my throat and force a smile. *There's no way that ring is for you, Shayleigh. Chill the fuck out.* "The waiter made sure I didn't forget it."

He drags a hand through his hair, making a mess of the dark blond curls before tying them back into his signature manbun. When he takes the jacket from me, he pats the pockets before his shoulders relax and he smiles at me. "Sorry. I'm just a little frazzled tonight. Come on. Let's go."

I take a deep breath. "Actually, I think I want to head home." I squeeze his arm, an effort at reassurance for myself as much as him. I'm totally not running away from a romantic evening with George that may or may not include a ring. That would be unreasonable when there's no reason to think that ring is for me. Maybe he's . . . holding it for a friend. "I'm going to hole up in my apartment and work on my revisions all day tomorrow."

"I understand." He pinches my chin and smiles down at me. "You can make it up to me next time."

At some point, we're going to have to talk about the future, and about what happens to us when I leave Starling for a job with another university—no matter what fell out of his pocket. But I'm a coward and can't do it tonight. Not with Easton's smell in my nose and my body still buzzing from our reunion.

Easton

The last time I was in the Jackson Brews bar, it was a hole in the wall, bordering on a dive bar. At the time, Jake was trying to turn it into something more. I can't say I totally understood his vision at the time, but the transformation he's created here is phenomenal.

Despite the snow outside, every booth in the bar is full. Patrons crowd around the tables, mingle at high-tops set around the pool tables, and lean against any free space at the bar. Waitstaff bustle about in jeans and red Jackson Brews T-shirts, and I nearly do a spit take when I see the back of one.

Jackson Brews
The bar, the beer, and oh Lord . . . the BROTHERS!

I spot Jake behind the bar, his messy skater hair hanging over one eye. I grab a stool just as its occupant leaves. "Nice place, Jake."

He grins at me. "I forgot how long it's been for you. You probably haven't been here since . . ." The amusement fades from his face. "Probably Dad's funeral, huh?"

"I didn't make it over here during that trip," I say, still taking it all in. Even the ritzy bars in Laguna smell a little like stale beer, but this place is sparkling. The pride in his ownership is evident. "I should've made the time. Seriously. I'm sorry I didn't."

Jake waves away my apology. "Don't give it another thought. What can I get you? Beer? Food?"

I glance at the chalkboard menus over his head. "How's the Jackson Haze?"

"Well, it's one of mine, so it's excellent, of course. You like hazy IPAs?"

"I do. Let me try that one."

"Got it." He pours my beer and listens to a waitress from the floor rattle off an order for her table. This place isn't all that's evolved. Jake has too. The whole family has.

"I can't believe you and Ava ended up together. I think she spent more time at your house when we were growing up than I did." I shake my head. "I thought you two would never see what was right in front of you."

"I'm the luckiest ass you'll ever meet," he says, and I can see in his eyes that he means it.

I see another waitress wearing a BROTHERS T-shirt. She slides into a booth with a group of women—no, she can't be a waitress. Unless she's on a break or something? "What's up with the T-shirts?"

Jake plops a coaster on the counter in front of me and sets my beer on it. "The girls thought those up one night after they'd had too many drinks. The customers love them. Brayden hates them."

Brayden was always the uber-responsible Jackson brother. "Who are 'the girls'?"

"You know, all our . . ." He waves a hand.

"Your women?"

"More or less, but Shay is among their ranks and would punch me if she heard me describe them that way, so I was trying to come up with a better descriptor."

I grin. "Of course she would." And since I came here hoping to run into her, it's all I can do not to scan the bar again at the mention of her name. I accused her of giving me the silent treatment, and she proved she wasn't. What I should've said was she was shutting me out. Because she is. She has for years. I fucking let her because it was easier than facing the fact that my decisions hurt her.

I sip my beer, not tasting it when I'm so busy thinking about Shay. How did I forget the way her eyes seem to pull me under? How did I forget the way she can use that smart mouth of hers to take control of any situation?

"What do you think?" Jake asks.

I snap my head up. "What?"

Jake folds his arms. "The beer?"

I have no idea. "It's great. Really smooth, Jake. Well done."

He smiles. "Thanks. I'm pretty happy with this one."

I take a breath and a chance. "Jake . . ."

He arches a brow, waiting. "Easton?"

Fuck it. What do I have to lose? "Is Shay seeing anyone?"

He shakes his head. "Not that I know of. Why? . . . Oh, fuck." His lips twitch. "You still have the hots for my little sister?"

Jake knew about it too? I must've done an even worse job hiding it than I thought. "To say the least," I mutter.

"I would've thought thirteen years in L.A. and all those actresses and models in your bed would've cured you of that."

"*One* actress and *one* model," I say. But it wouldn't matter if there were a hundred of each. I'm pretty sure this thing I feel for Shay is incurable. "Did Carter tell you or Shay?"

"Carter told me that you— Wait. Shay knows?"

"Shay knows what?"

Speak of the devil. My skin tingles at the sound of that voice, and I slowly turn to see Shay striding toward the bar. The sight of her steals the breath from my lungs. She looked beautiful this morning in a T-shirt and jeans, but tonight, her legs are on display. Her little black dress clings to the luscious curves of her ass, and her pink sweater brings out the color in her cheeks. She's fucking irresistible—even when her eyes flash with annoyance at the sight of me and she braces her hands on her hips like she's preparing for battle.

Jake looks between me and his sister, then shakes his head. "Nah, I'm not touching this."

She arches a brow. "Shay knows *what*?"

"You know that I think you're beautiful," I say, leaning back in my chair. "At least, I *think* you know."

Something like hurt flashes across her face, but she shakes it away and turns to her brother. "I need the biggest fucking martini you've ever served, and I need it now."

"Okay then," Jake says.

"Bad day?" I can't help smiling, because *she's here.* I can tell the feeling isn't mutual, but my day just got a hell of a lot better.

"Weird night," she mutters. Shaking her head, she steps behind the bar. "Never mind, Jake. I think this calls for more than vodka."

Jake steps back, clearly smart enough to know when Shay's on a mission and he needs to get out of her way. "Do you want to talk about it or—"

"No." In a series of jerky motions, she grabs vodka, Baileys, Godiva, and Kahlua from the shelf.

Jake grimaces as she pours shots of each into a martini shaker. "What the hell are you making?"

"A martini."

"Yeah, I guessed as much," he mutters. "But what the hell kind of martini is that?"

"It's called And the Kitchen Sink. Star made them at her annual fundraiser for the women's shelter. It's a dessert martini. I only had a sip of Nic's because I was afraid of the calories, but I've decided *fuck it.*" She ducks down and pulls open the fridge under the bar. "Do we have any heavy cream?"

Jake's brows have totally disappeared under his messy hair. "Who are you, and what did you do with my calorie-conscious sister?"

Shay sighs dramatically and grabs her martini shaker, disappearing into the kitchen.

We both watch the door, waiting for her to return. When she does, she's capped off the martini shaker and is shaking it so hard her tits bounce—not that I'm looking.

Jake cautiously grabs a martini glass off the shelf and hands it to her.

"Don't judge until you try it," she says, pouring.

"But I don't *want* diabetes," he says with a grimace.

"Whatever. Suit yourself." The glass is filled to the rim when she pulls the shaker away, and she sighs, satisfied. But then she just stands there and stares at it.

"Are you going to try it?" Jake asks.

"Of course I am."

"Okay, because it looks like you were just going to admire it all night."

She bites her bottom lip, pulling off some of her pink gloss. Her hand shakes as she brings the glass to her lips. I wonder if Jake sees it too. I wonder if he, like me, knows this is what happens before she melts down. But maybe not anymore. She said she's changed, and after seven years without seeing her face, I can't claim to know shit.

Jake ducks his head and whispers something in her ear, and I know he sees it too—is probably offering to go somewhere and talk with her, if I had to guess. I've missed this family and their closeness, the way they can fight like rabid dogs one minute and have each other's backs the next.

Shay shakes her head. "I'm a little stressed. It's fine. I just need to self-medicate for a minute."

Jake gives her one last long look and nods before disappearing into the kitchen.

God must be smiling down on me today, because sometime during Shay's martini-making production, the guy who was sitting next to me cleared out, leaving cash for Jake.

I nod to the vacant barstool. "Sit here, Shayleigh. We'll self-medicate together. Unless you *are* giving me the silent treatment, that is."

I wait for it—that smile of hers that makes me believe that somehow everything will be okay, the comforting stillness of sitting next to her, the warmth of her laughter. Hell, it's been too long since I've heard that sound, since I've watched joy blossom on her face and felt like maybe I was born to put it there. *I've missed her.*

Except Shay doesn't flash me her smile or sit by me. She certainly doesn't laugh. She slides her sweet concoction in front of me and says, "On the house. I have to get out of here."

"I thought you needed a drink."

When she meets my eyes, I'm taken back to Paris, to my hotel room in Chicago, to her bedroom out at the lake and the hundred other times she met my eyes and I felt like Superman. "I was wrong." She turns around, but instead of leaving through the front, she ducks out from behind the bar and stomps off to the bathroom.

I get it. I fucked up with her. Fucked up phenomenally. But how am I supposed to apologize when she won't even talk to me?

I slide off my stool and follow her. She's standing at the sink, arms braced on the counter, head bowed. "Shay?"

She rolls her neck and sighs. "Easton, this is the women's room."

I nudge the door shut behind me and flip the lock. "I noticed." I fold my arms. "I saw my chance and took it."

She draws in a long breath. "Your chance for what? Creepy

bathroom stalking?"

"My chance to talk to you alone. You're avoiding me."

Her eyes flash. "We have nothing to talk about."

"Are you sure about that?" I stalk toward her. The pull to her is magnetic, and it's a miracle I've kept my distance this long. Hell, it's a miracle I ever let her go to begin with. "I can think of a lot of things we could talk about. Should we start with Paris or Chicago? Or maybe we should start with New Year's Eve out at the lake?"

"None of the above." She turns to me, her expression resigned as she leans a hip against the counter.

"Do you have any idea how much I've missed you?"

"You *missed* me? Is this some alternate-facts shit? Because last I checked, you had my number. You could've called or sent me a fucking text message. You weren't missing me. You were living your life."

"I hated myself for missing you. I thought I needed to make it work with Scarlett." I swallow and step closer. The truth burns my throat, searing off a piece of my pride. "I thought I could do it if you weren't a choice. I thought I could get over you. I was wrong about all of it. No amount of time can change the way I feel about you."

Her breath catches. "Easton—"

I slide my hand into her hair and skim my thumb across her bottom lip. "There wasn't a single day that went by that I didn't think about you."

I lower my mouth to hers before she can reply. The first touch of my lips to hers, and everything snaps into place for me. This is what I want—where I want to be, where I belong. Her lips part on a gasp. I touch my tongue to hers, and she presses her palm to my chest.

"Fuck you." She shoves me back—*hard*—and I stumble. "I didn't say you could do that."

Shaking my head, I force myself to back away another step. I didn't come in here intending to touch her, and with my recklessness, she's even less likely to talk to me.

She lifts her chin, her eyes blazing with anger I totally deserve. "Did it ever occur to you that maybe *I'm* not single? Did it ever occur to you that I might have a boyfriend? That maybe I haven't spent the last seven years waiting around for you?" She folds her arms, disgust clear in the curl of her lip. "You are so self-centered."

I shove my hands into my pockets so they don't get me in trouble. My pride is bruised as fuck, but this conversation isn't over. "It *did* occur to me. That's why I asked Jake. He said you weren't seeing anyone."

"So Jake is an expert in my love life now? You think he knows about every guy I've dated? Every man I've taken to bed?" She huffs out a breath. "Even if I were single—which, sorry to disappoint you when you're stuck in Jackson Harbor with no one else to fuck, *I'm not*—how egotistical do you have to be to assume I'd want to climb back into bed with you?"

There's so much happening in that sentence that I'm not even sure where to start. Maybe I am self-centered, because I start with the part that hurts the most. "You *are* seeing someone."

She folds her arms protectively across her middle. "Yeah."

"It can't be that serious if you haven't introduced him to your family."

"Don't make assumptions about my life."

"Do you love him?"

There's something else in her expression—pain? Awkwardness? I can't tell. "It's complicated."

I step forward and lift a hand, but I stop myself, turning around gripping the doorknob before I make the mistake of touching her again. I feel her eyes on my back. "I never expected you to wait for me. You deserved better than that." When I look at her over my shoulder, her expression is tight, her chest heaving like it would have if I'd had the chance to finish that kiss. "I stayed away because you deserved better than *me*."

Part III.

Before

Shay

February 24th, twelve years ago

Easton: Carter said you're staying home when everyone visits next month.

Me: Sorry. I can't believe you're bringing all the Jacksons to LA. Big shot.

Easton: I miss everyone. I swear I'm not trying to show off.

Me: I'm just teasing you. I'm sure it'll be awesome. Mom is buzzing about it. I hope you have fun.

Easton: Is everything okay?

Me: I have tests for school and I have to get my final papers done early before graduation.

Easton: Because you'll be in New York while everyone else takes finals.

Me: Spying on me?

Easton: Carter and Jake crow about you like they're responsible for your brain or something.

Me: That's kind of sweet.

Easton: I wish you were coming.

I put my phone down and force myself to back away. It's been less than two months since Easton spun my world on its head and made me believe that someone like him could be attracted to me. No, not just someone like him. He made me believe that *he* could be attracted to me. That he *was* attracted to me. And that's the kicker, because I don't want someone *like* Easton. I never have. I want *Easton*. But I'm no longer the twelve-year-old girl who'd follow him around when he stayed over on the weekend and quietly dream of our future wedding. I've grown up, and I'm smart enough to know that's not in the cards for a girl like me. Easton very gently reminded me of that when he told me not to apply at UCLA.

I still want to hide every time I remember I said that. What did I think? That Easton was going to want a college kid hanging around just because we fooled around in the middle of the night? Did I think he'd miss out on all the women who throw themselves at him on a daily basis for *me*?

So I checked myself. Remembered the limits of our relationship: *friendship*. When I went back to school after the holiday, I said yes to a date with Steve and decided it was time to force myself to get over Easton Connor. I've been doing great at not obsessing over him too, and then he has to throw out an *I wish you were coming*?

It's such a painful tease that I almost hate him for it. But I know that's not fair. He's just being my friend. Like he always has.

My phone buzzes again, and I immediately snatch it off the counter to see if it's another text from him. *I'm weak.*

> *Easton: I hope you have the time of your life in New York. I expect you to tell me about it.*

> *Me: Sure. I'll post pics.*

April 18th

> *Easton: Family reunion isn't the same without you, Short Stack.*

I read Easton's text three times before I make myself flip my phone over and pretend I didn't see it. I have the house to myself, and my boyfriend and I are using the time to study. Because Steve and I are just cool like that.

My family is in California at Easton's, and I've spent the last two days since they left vacillating between regret over my decision to stay home and relief that I was smart enough to make that choice. Despite what I told my parents, I could've gone. I could've worked on my papers on the plane. My finals will be a cakewalk. I don't need to study much. But I'm here, and the riot of fluttery insects making a mess of my stomach after just one text is enough to remind me I made the right choice. If I'd gone to L.A., I would've left my heart there with Easton. And I can't do that. I need my heart.

The cutie math nerd across the kitchen table from me might object to me giving it to someone else.

My phone buzzes again. I watch Steve scribble in his notebook before I look.

> *Easton: Hold up. Carter said you're going to New York with your BOYFRIEND.*

> *Me: Not exactly with him. My boyfriend is also in my honors English class and is going on the same trip.*

> *Easton: You didn't tell me you had a boyfriend.*

> *Me: I didn't know you required updates on my love life.*

> *Easton: Now you know. I require updates.*

Me: His name is Steve. He's smart and fun and sweet.

I stare at the screen too long. Aside from when he was asking me about the trip last month, we haven't gone back and forth texting like this since before New Year's. He sends me goofy memes from time to time, and we're on a couple of group text loops together in which my brothers break down his games play by play and he pretends to appreciate their advice when he has a whole team full of well-paid professionals who know way more about football than they do.

He doesn't reply. I bite back a sigh and put the phone down. I want to believe I've moved on, but a few text messages from him still get me tied up in knots. *Pathetic.*

Steve looks up from his notebook and grins at me. His eyes cut to the clock meaningfully. When he arrived tonight, he was all over me. I told him we had to study for one hour before we could make out. Now time's a-ticking.

I return his smile, my cheeks heating and my thoughts blessedly turning away from Easton and back to Steve and an evening in the house alone. Right where they should be.

Then my phone buzzes again.

Easton: Is he good to you?

Me: I wouldn't be with him if he weren't.

Easton: So I guess this means . . .

I swallow hard. How do I tell him that I need him not to do

this? How do I explain that his flirting messes with me without revealing that I've had a crush on him my whole life? Because despite my stumble with the UCLA thing, I think I've managed to hide the truth of my lifelong crush from everyone.

Me: It means I have a boyfriend, and I owe you no more secrets.

Easton: Ah. Message delivered. Have fun in New York. Behave.

Frowning, Steve pushes his notebook away and leans back in his chair. "Who's blowing up your phone?"

"Easton." I bow my head and pretend to study the irregular verb conjugations for my French exam.

Steve clears his throat. "Easton *Connor*? You're texting Easton *Connor*?"

I lift my head and smile. Steve's eyes are wide, and he looks like a starstruck little boy. "You know he's a family friend." I wave a hand, indicating the empty house. "And that he's the reason we're here alone right now?"

"Yeah, but I didn't know you *texted* with him."

I shrug. "Not that often. He's just thinking about me, since my family is there and I'm not."

Steve pushes his chair back and walks around the table. Taking my hand, he pulls me out of my chair and steps close. He's tall—taller than Easton, even—and I have to crane my neck to look up at him. Unlike Easton, with his effortless athletic grace, Steve is gangly and a little awkward. More than once he's reminded me of the Great Dane pup the neighbors adopted last year. The dog grew so fast that he could hardly walk straight. Now, like every time the comparison comes to mind, I feel guilty for it. Steve might not be an athlete, but he's absolutely adorable. Anyway, it's not like I'm some prize in the physical beauty department.

He presses a chaste kiss to my lips. "I'm glad you decided to stay home."

I loop my arms around his waist. "Are you?"

He dips his head and nuzzles my neck. "Yeah," he says against my ear. "We have the whole house to ourselves." He skims his hand up my side and under my shirt, and I laugh. He stills and pulls back. "Seriously?"

At the petulance in his tone, I train my expression to neutral. "Sorry. I'm ticklish."

He blows out a breath and shakes his head. "I thought you were laughing at the idea of enjoying an empty house with me." He nods toward the clock. "Time for our study break."

"I guess it is." I skim my fingers over the sparse stubble on his cheek. He has no business trying to grow a full beard, but he's been working on this since Christmas break, and I'm not going to be the one to tell him it needs to go. "What do you want to do?"

He arches a brow, as if this is the dumbest question in the world. "I mean, we could . . . You know . . ."

I frown. Steve's pretty articulate. He doesn't stumble over words, so his vague reply takes me a minute to understand. "Sex?"

The word is a giant record scratch in the empty house.

"Wow. Not the reaction I was expecting." He steps back, and my hands fall to my sides.

"Sorry, I just . . . I didn't realize we were *there*."

"Isn't everyone?" His smile is a little goofy when he adds, "And when's the next time we're going to have a house to ourselves like this? I want to take my time with you, not have some sloppy first time in the back of my car."

My jaw works. I appreciate the sentiment, but should we really be making the choice because it's *convenient*? "I don't know."

"We're seniors. It's not like we're kids anymore." He shrugs. "But maybe you don't want to do that with me. Whatever."

I gape at him. He's never acted like this, and I don't like it. "Are you seriously *pouting* right now?"

"I'm not pouting."

"Yes, you are. You're pouting because I don't want to have sex."

"Maybe I'm just hurt. Did you think of that?" His chest rises and falls with his deep breath. "Shit. This isn't how I wanted this conversation to go. I sound like an ass."

"Yeah." I hug myself. "You really do."

He turns to the table and messes with the stack of flashcards I have there. "Please forget I said anything?"

Steve is a nice guy, and I meant it when I told Easton he was good to me. Jerks have no appeal. But sex? I'm not even sure I love him.

I push away the thought quickly. Who said I have to be in love? I like him. I respect him. We have fun together. Isn't that enough?

I close the space between us, but he still feels miles away. I run a hand down his arm. "Hey. I'm sorry I freaked out, but I need you to understand that my freak-out isn't about you."

When he turns his eyes to me, I see the hurt there, and it twists in my chest. "Let me guess—it's about Easton Connor."

I blink at him. Because that came out of nowhere. Because he's being irrationally jealous.

Because he's right.

Easton

The Jackson crew wanders along the sand in front of me, soaking up the evening sun and laughing. I'm so glad to have them here, but I can't believe Shay didn't come.

I get it. She has other responsibilities, other things in her life to focus on than her brother's old friend. I tried to tell myself it didn't matter. Lied to myself about how much I wanted her to see my new life. Now her family's here and it's great, but it's also . . . lonely in a way I can't explain to anyone.

Doesn't she know that she's half the reason I arranged this trip? But I guess she wouldn't. When she suggested she'd change her college plans to be with me, it scared the shit out of me, and I've done everything I could to hide my feelings since. She's so smart—and not just compared to me. Compared to *anyone*. She's brilliant, and I won't be the reason she doesn't chase her dreams. When I was starting at Starling College, my course load was intense. I'd never been pushed academically like that, and my anxiety was off the charts. Lucky for me, Shay was taking a couple of courses there—a high school freshman taking French at a four-year college, because she's *that* kind of smart. I got to see her a couple of times a week. She's the only one who could help me relax enough to make it through those major projects. My grades weren't great, but I don't think I'd have passed if it hadn't been for her. If I'd been put on academic probation and kicked off the team, I never would've been drafted by the Demons. She's the reason I got to pursue my dream, and I won't stand in the way of hers.

But she didn't tell me she has a boyfriend.

It was only a matter of time, but it was still a punch in the gut when Carter's little brother, Levi, made a joke about Shay being alone at the house with him. I didn't want her to wait for me, but I guess I thought she might. But now she has a boyfriend, and they're going to New York together. Because he's smart enough to be in the special group that takes the trip. Smart like Shay. I bet she likes that.

I wonder if she calms him when he's stressed. I wonder if he's ever wondered if there's something wrong with the way he was made, only to have her put a hand on his arm and make him feel like he's whole, like he's *enough.*

I pull my phone from my pocket. *I owe you no more secrets.*

She's right. She doesn't owe me anything. But I want it all anyway.

Shay

I can't sleep.

I roll over and stare at the clock. Three a.m.

Steve left five hours ago, reluctantly still a virgin. I assured him that my reasons for waiting had nothing to do with Easton, that I just wasn't ready. *I'm an evil liar.*

Guilt had me inviting him for a soak in the hot tub, and after a heavy make-out session that ended with us back in the house, his swim trunks were on the floor, and my hand . . . well, my hand was right where he wanted it. After that, I think we were both a little more convinced that I'm not hung up on Easton.

But I have another five days full of prime virginity-losing opportunities, and I wonder if Steve's right. Maybe now's the time. We might not have another chance to be alone like this until we're in college, and even then there will be roommates to work around and neighbors on the other side of thin walls. I can't deny that our circumstances are ideal, but I always imagined I'd be in love when I lost my virginity. Will Steve wait that long?

I grab my phone off the nightstand and scroll through the pictures Mom sent me earlier. My stomach twists with longing. This is the first time I've missed a family trip, and seeing my brothers lined up and walking barefoot down the beach makes me feel . . . homesick.

I laugh at myself. How silly. *I'm* the one at home.

I click over to my text thread with Easton. It's midnight there. I bet he's still awake. And because I know he'll tell me the truth, I send him a message before I can talk myself out of it.

> Me: Would you have dated someone in high school who didn't put out?

> Easton: I did a few times. Not every relationship got that far.

> Me: But did you end things because you weren't sleeping together?

I stare at my phone for a long time. The bouncing dots that indicate he's typing appear and then disappear. Shit. I probably sound like an immature child.

> Me: You can be honest with me. I won't judge you.

> Easton: If my answer was yes, you fucking SHOULD judge me.

I can practically hear his voice just reading the words. I can see his nostrils flare in disbelief. *I miss him.*

> *Me: So . . . why didn't you answer?*

> *Easton: Because this conversation makes me want to come back to Jackson Harbor and beat the shit out of this boyfriend of yours.*

Crap. I clearly didn't think this through. I'm an asshole who's going to get my sweet, awkward math nerd boyfriend pounded by an NFL quarterback. Cause of death: irresponsible texting.

> *Me: I never said I was talking about my boyfriend.*

> *Easton: But weren't you?*

> *Me: Not exactly.*

> *Easton: What does that even mean?*

> *Me: It means I was asking in general terms, but I'm not saying he's going to break up with me if we don't have sex.*

> *Easton: You wouldn't be asking if you didn't think it was a possibility.*

I throw myself back on my pillows and whimper. I'm making

a mess of this. I don't want to throw Steve under the bus, but I truly do want advice. I could talk to my brothers, but they're irrational when it comes to me. They'd freak out if they knew I'd let a boy up my shirt, let alone if they knew I was thinking about having sex. I could talk to my girlfriends, but I want a guy's perspective on it.

> *Me: I'm afraid he's going to get sick of waiting.*
>
> *Easton: Nah. If he loves you, he'll wait forever.*
>
> *Me: And if he doesn't love me?*
>
> *Easton: Then you shouldn't have sex with him anyway.*
>
> *Me: Hypocrite.*
>
> *Easton: How do you figure?*
>
> *Me: You've NEVER had sex with someone you didn't love?*
>
> *Easton: Let me get back to you.*
>
> *Me: Need time to get the list together?*
>
> *Easton: Need time to put together my defense.*

I'm still laughing when his next text comes through.

Easton: This isn't about me. It's about you, and YOU deserve the love, the roses, the fucking fairytale. Don't settle for less.

I turn off my screen and close my eyes. I clutch the phone to my chest, and I'm smiling as I fall asleep.

Part IV.

Now

Shay

Teagan pulls her door open before I have a chance to knock. "I thought you might come over. Do you want to talk?"

"No. I want to go to the bar and drink until I forget that Easton Connor just walked back into my life and set off a bomb in the middle of it."

"Okay." Because she's the best fucking friend ever, she grabs her purse. "Let's go."

I shake my head. "Tried that already, but he was there."

"So you *don't* want to go to the bar?"

"I want to go and him not be there." I growl. I sound mental. "He had the nerve to kiss me."

Teagan's eyes go wide and she does that fish-mouthed trying-to-speak thing for a few beats before shaking off her shock. "Easton Connor kissed you?"

"Yes." I stomp into her house and toss my purse onto the couch with more force than necessary. Teagan and Carter live together in the little two-story craftsman Carter's been fixing up for a couple of years. Isaiah, a high school senior and the son of Carter's late friend, lives with them in the refinished attic. Carter has pretty much gutted the whole house and put it back together one piece at a time. It's adorable, and when he's around, I love talking to him about what comes next in this massive makeover. But tonight, I'm glad he's not here, because the last thing I want is for him to hear me rant about Easton. Easton and his presumptuous bathroom kissing. "Self-centered, egotistical *motherfucker*," I mutter.

"Wow. Okay." Teagan closes the door and joins me in the living room. "So you didn't want him to kiss you, but he did. What did you do?"

"I went off on him, and then I left because I just . . ." I try to drag a hand through my hair and end up making a mess of my ponytail.

Teagan shakes her head and straightens the blanket on the back of the couch. "You know what? I think I'll go get us a couple of beers."

"Do you have anything stronger?"

Biting her lip, she looks at the ceiling, thinking. "I might have some tequila left over from a chicken recipe I made last weekend?"

Tequila. The word washes an Easton-scented memory over my senses. Thirteen years later, and I can still recall the feel of Easton's hot tongue on my wrist where he licked off the salt. The man is imprinted in my mind permanently. But I don't want him to be, and the last thing I need is a drink that will bring those memories even closer to the surface. "Beer is fine."

I follow as she heads to the fridge.

Her dark hair frames her face as she leans in to inspect their beer selection. "I have a porter, a growler of that new hazy IPA Jake won't shut up about—oh, or we could share this bomber of blueberry sour if you want."

"I think my boyfriend is going to propose," I blurt.

Teagan straightens, eyes wide.

"It doesn't make any sense, but I saw the ring."

Teagan lets out a long breath. To her credit, she doesn't screech, *What boyfriend?*

"It's too soon. We're not there yet, but maybe he wants to propose before I accept a job somewhere else. But I don't know for sure, because I was a distracted mess tonight. I wanted to tell him about Easton being in town and how it means something to me." I mess with my hair again and decide to give it up and take out the hair tie. "I was trying to do the right thing, but I didn't know. . . I didn't realize . . ."

She shuts the fridge. "You're sure you don't want that tequila?"

"Can't. Easton memories."

"Shit." Teagan grabs a stool. She climbs onto it and digs through the cabinets over the refrigerator before coming out with a bottle of amber liquid. "Found this." Of course Carter would have bourbon in the house. I'm pretty sure all my brothers keep it around. "Any objectionable memories with this?"

I shake my head. "Thanks, Tea."

"Not a problem." She grabs two glasses from the cabinet, pours us each a couple of fingers, and hands mine over. "Drink, and then start at the beginning."

I take a sip, closing my eyes as the warmth from the liquor coats my throat and blooms in my chest. I'm not a big bourbon drinker, but it feels appropriate tonight. "I'm not ready to start at the beginning."

"Okay. Then start with tonight. You're . . . seeing someone? And it's serious? Who is he?" I can tell she's trying to hide it, but there's undeniable hurt in her voice, and I feel like an ass for keeping secrets from my friend.

"I've been seeing someone from work."

"For how long?"

I shrug. Do I count the first time I felt like he was flirting with me? The first time I accepted an invitation to dinner? The first time I slept with him? "I don't even know if 'seeing' is the right label." I swallow hard, shame dogging me. "We've been sleeping together, but we haven't had a chance to figure out if we want it to be more than that." It's not exactly officially against the rules to sleep with members of your dissertation committee, but it's certainly frowned upon. George and I seemed to have an unspoken agreement from the first morning I snuck out of his Grand Rapids apartment that we wouldn't let what we'd done get out. Even without official repercussions, information like that could damage *both* of our reputations. He doesn't need people thinking he's a sleazy professor, and I don't need people thinking I only made it through my doctorate because I was sleeping with the man in charge of deeming whether my work is worthy. "You've actually met him before. His name is George Alby."

"But isn't George . . . ?"

"He's the chairman of my dissertation committee."

"Oh," Teagan says. She takes a long swallow of her bourbon, coughing as it goes down.

"I never set out to sleep with him, and when it happened, I blamed it on the wine, too little sleep, and maybe general loneliness." I roll my glass between my hands. "I didn't think it would happen again, but it did. Then after the third time, it just became something we did. I'd go to his apartment for dinner after meetings, and we'd talk and end up in bed. When we went to the conference in Florida in February, I had my own room but barely spent any time in it."

"Wow. And now you think he's going to propose?"

I can see it in her face, the *Already?* The *Are you really that serious?* Or maybe those are my thoughts and I'm projecting. "George is great." I swallow. "And I care about him, but because of our weird situation, we've never had a chance to be a normal couple. I'm afraid that if he finds out how much that ring freaked me out, I'm really going to hurt him."

"Oh, honey." She puts her glass down and squeezes my free hand. "If you're not ready, you have to tell him."

"Can I tell you something terrible?"

"What?"

"I don't think I would've ever slept with George if I hadn't known Easton was moving to town."

It was almost four months ago that I found out Easton was looking for a house in Jackson Harbor. At the time, I didn't understand why he suddenly wanted to move back here. He hasn't lived here since high school. Why now?

But that's what I get for swearing off celebrity gossip. Apparently, his ex, the diva popstar Scarlett Lashenta, got drunk on her reality TV show and confessed on camera that her daughter isn't biologically Easton's. The news blew up because the real daddy is some now-famous rapper Scarlett thought was going nowhere when she found out she was pregnant.

Easton has always managed to stay out of the celebrity drama and keep his daughter out of it too, despite Scarlett's penchant for staying in the middle of it, but the cameras were all over him after the news hit. And then they realized he'd known that Abigail wasn't his for years and he'd stuck around anyway. *Cue the mass swoon.*

Which is ridiculous. Why do we swoon over guys who are actual *fathers* to their children? If he's raised her since birth, why would it be anything but expected that he'd stay by her side, despite a lack of blood ties? But I guess that just shows that the press doesn't know Easton as well as I do, because none of his decisions regarding Abi have surprised me. Even his impending move back to Jackson Harbor fits now that I know more of the story.

Before, the news threw me. I vacillated between panic and dread and . . . excitement. It was the last that may have been responsible for my rash decision to accept George's invitation back to his apartment for a glass of wine.

Teagan grimaces. "That makes sense."

"What do you mean by that?"

"It just helps explain it a little, I guess. Sleeping with a professor isn't like you, but sleeping with your *dissertation chair*? Shay, that's almost reckless."

I lift the bourbon to my lips again, but the smell turns my stomach, so I put it back on the counter with a clunk and busy my hands by pushing it around. "I know, I know. But now here we are. George told me after we . . ." I want to say *started dating*, but that would be inaccurate. George and I didn't start dating as much as we started sleeping together. "After we started seeing each other, he admitted that he's been interested in me for years and I never seemed to pick up the hint. I had to be faced with this not-even-an-ex coming back into my life before I noticed the really incredible guy right under my nose."

"It's not like you were planning to use him to get Easton to notice you." She hesitates a beat, squeezing my hand a little tighter. "Were you?"

"No. Of course not." My feelings are messy right now, but I am sure of that. I wasn't after jealousy. I was after protection— someone to be a barrier between me and East. *I'm a total ass.* "It was more like I was trying to put some distance between Easton and my heart."

"That's one hell of a crush, girl."

I let out a dry laugh. I never told anyone in my family about what happened with Easton and me. The truth would change the way they look at him. I can't do that to him or my family, though it's Carter who'd be the most pissed. Teagan, on the other hand, won't likely put a fist in Easton's face if I tell her. "I didn't tell you the whole truth about me and Easton."

"You don't say." She arches a brow, unsurprised. "I won't tell Carter, if that's what has you worried."

I swallow. "I appreciate that."

"It was more than a crush," she says, and it's not a question as much as a statement of the now-obvious.

I nod. "We fooled around a couple of times." That's the

extremely watered-down version of the truth, but I'm not up for sharing the whole story. I'm not sure I ever will be.

Her eyes widen. "You *fooled around* with Easton fucking Connor and kept it a *secret*?"

"Oh, yeah. My brothers would've killed him." My eyes burn. I'm so damn tired. "What if I push George away because of what I think I still feel for Easton and everything's different? What if what I feel is all past tense? I can't change how I felt back then. Our history is going to be there as I move forward, no matter what."

"Have you considered talking to Easton about all this?"

I huff out a dry laugh. "He keeps trying to talk, and I keep running away. I think he only kissed me tonight to get my attention." I bite the inside of my cheek as if it's some magical pressure point that can keep me from crying, but when I look up at my friend, I see her through a film of my tears. "I'm a coward."

"You're not." I can tell from her expression that she has questions—so many questions that she's too good of a friend to ask right now. "You have a lot on your plate. The defense, job applications, and now a possible proposal? Just give yourself room to breathe. Give your feelings some space to be before you judge them. If Easton really wants a chance to talk the past out with you, he'll wait."

"I don't want to make a choice I'll regret." I swirl my bourbon in my glass, wishing my stomach would cooperate so I could chug it. The oblivion of a good drunk would be welcome about now. "Tell me about your day. How are things going with the new girl at work?"

"Work is fine and my day was boring. Don't change the subject."

I cut my eyes away and sigh.

Teagan squeezes my wrist gently. "When I worked surgery, we had to tell patients that they weren't to make any major decisions post-op. I'm your nurse and I'm telling you to treat yourself as a post-op patient until further notice. No decisions." She gives me a sad smile. "If I had to guess, I'd say you've been so secretive about this whole Easton thing that you don't even know how you feel. Figure that out first and don't make any decisions in the meantime."

I smirk. "Does that also mean I can't operate heavy machinery?"

She gives a pointed look to my barely touched glass. "Not for the reasons I anticipated when you walked in the door, but maybe this calls for a sleepover. I miss Carter while he's at the fire station. You can keep me company."

"Deal," I whisper. "But I'm emotionally exhausted, so don't take it personally if I fall asleep before ten."

"I'll make your bed."

Easton

"**D**id you know your sister is seeing someone?" I ask Carter as he finishes his last set of squats Monday morning.

He grunts. "I think there's a guy from school she goes out with sometimes. Nothing serious, though."

"Does he make her happy?"

"Never met the guy. She doesn't really talk about him, but I assume he's decent enough."

Decent enough. Nah, I'm not gonna step aside for *decent enough.* "He can't be that good if she hasn't brought him around."

Carter freezes then slowly reracks the barbell before turning to me. "Why?"

His glare could knock a lesser man over, but I just shrug. "Because if he's not the most wonderful thing that's ever happened to her, if he doesn't treat her like an absolute goddess, I'm going to do everything in my power to convince her she should be with me and not him."

The ire in his eyes morphs into shock. "Excuse me?"

"Come on, Carter. You know I've had a thing for Shay since she was sixteen."

"Since you were a fucking college student drooling over my baby sister. Yeah, I remember."

I nod to the barbell in the rack. He has one hand wrapped around the knurling, squeezing like I imagine he'd like to do to my neck. "You gonna let me squat that or just grope it all day?" He scowls, but I grin slowly. "She's not a baby anymore, and you don't fucking scare me."

"She's not like the girls you're used to, East." He steps away from the rack and helps me add another bumper plate to each side. "If you're hoping to fuck her and walk away, save yourself the beating, because I won't let that happen."

I duck under the barbell, position it on my shoulders, and walk it off the rack. "Who said I want to walk away?"

"Are you serious right now?"

"I have feelings for her, Carter. Deal with it." I rep out a set of five and rerack the weight.

When I turn back to him, he's studying me. His eyes flash but he sighs. He scans the gym around us before stepping closer to me. "If you hurt her—if you make my sister cry one fucking tear—I'll punch you in the nuts so hard you'll feel them when you gargle. You get me?"

If I hurt her? *Too late for that.* But I smile and smack Carter on the shoulder. "She's grown, C. Thirty, last I checked. I don't think she needs her brothers to play guard dog anymore." *And the last thing I'm going to do is hurt her again.*

Shay

"We'll fly you in on that Thursday morning, and the interview will take place that afternoon. I'll make sure they give you early check-in at your hotel. That way you don't have to walk into the interview straight from such a long flight," Sally says. She's the administrative assistant for the English department at Emmitson University, and she's been the point person for every portion of my application process, including the virtual class visit the hiring committee did with my American lit class last week. Apparently they liked what they saw, because now they want to fly me out for an in-person interview—the final step in the hiring process.

"That sounds good," I say.

"Would you be okay with one of our graduate students picking you up at the airport?"

"Absolutely." This isn't the first time I've scheduled a flight to

L.A., but it'll be the first time I actually go. Easton lived there for thirteen years, but only next month, when he's officially moved back to Jackson Harbor, will I actually make the trip. I swallow a bubble of hysteria.

"Everyone's looking forward to meeting you, Shayleigh, myself included. You've been such a pleasure to work with through this process."

"Thank you so much, Sally."

"Don't hesitate to call if you have any questions or need to make any adjustments to your travel plans."

We say our goodbyes, and I put down my cell phone and take a deep breath. Then another. If I were home, I'd probably go take a nap, which is exactly why I'm working in Jake's old apartment above Jackson Brews. There's a bed here, but since I know how often my brothers sneak up here with their respective girlfriends/ fiancées/wives, I find any comfort it might offer pretty easy to resist.

I'm two months away from defending my dissertation and finishing up a twelve-year stint in higher education. But every time I get a call for an interview for a tenure-track position, I wince. I've worked my ass off for this—for the alphabet soup behind my name and the chance to get tenure and teach something more mentally stimulating than freshman comp. All the dissertation research killed something inside me, so I applied almost exclusively at small colleges with heavier teaching loads and smaller publishing expectations. I don't want the pressure of publishing articles every semester—of finding something new to say in a field already crowded with voices. But after teaching for the last few years and confronting the reality of students caring more about grades than knowledge, even the classroom has begun to lose its appeal. And the hard truth is that I'll probably need to move across the country if I want a good job in my field. The most promising jobs are in California, Maine, and Oklahoma.

Ugh.

My stomach hurts.

I'm growing more and more obsessed with the possibility that this degree was a giant waste of time. I'm either going to have to admit that I don't actually want the prize that's at the end of this finish line or strap myself to a job that might just be okay in a place that might make me miserable.

The sound of the rattling doorknob draws my attention away from my computer, and I look up to see Easton pushing into the apartment. "Hey, beautiful."

"I should've locked the door," I mutter.

He places two glasses on the table and a pitcher of beer, then flips around the chair opposite me and straddles it. "How's your day been?"

I roll my eyes. "What do you want?"

"Jake said you need to take a break." He lifts the pitcher and carefully pours. "Sent me to remind you."

His long-sleeved T-shirt stretches tight across his chest, making it difficult to keep my eyes on my laptop, where they belong. "I'm fine, but thanks anyway."

"What's got you so tied up in knots?"

I frown. "Who says I'm tied in knots?"

He points to the space between his eyebrows. "Right here. It gives you away every time. You get this little indentation there when you're trying to figure out a particularly vexing problem."

I snort. "Maybe I'm just not as young as I used to be and need some Botox."

"You don't need shit." He nods to my computer. "Is it your book? Do you need to brainstorm a plot problem?"

My eyes go wide, and I look over his shoulder to make sure no one has followed him up here. "Would you shut up?"

He folds his arms on the back of the chair, frowning. "Why?"

"I haven't told *anyone* about the books."

"Books. *Plural.*" He grins like I just told him I can secretly fly. "You've been busy."

I roll my eyes, sighing. "Well, it's been a lot of years, so yeah . . ."

"And you did tell *someone*. You told me."

I did. Somehow, I admitted my deepest secret—my secret hope—to Easton years ago. In my defense, it was a post-coital confession, and he'd just given me a series of mind-blowing orgasms that loosened my tongue and made me feel brave and invincible. He made me feel like I could have things I never believed possible. Things like *him*. "It's not a thing, so please don't go yapping about it."

"Not a thing, and yet somehow while finishing a PhD, teaching a full course load at Starling, and being the perfect daughter, sister, aunt, and friend, you've managed to go from a few chapters on *a* book to *books*—plural."

"It's not anything. Just . . ." I shrug. *Just a thing I want too much to pursue. Just a dream that's so much part of my soul that I don't know if I could handle the blow of inevitable rejection.*

"Just what?" he asks, propping his chin on his hands. "Just a lifelong passion?" He smiles, all angelic and shit, but I know better.

"Just a hobby," I say, even though the words feel like a betrayal to some growing seed buried deep inside me.

He tilts his head to one side, then the other, as if he's trying to use the light to better see through my bullshit. "For such a confident woman, you sure are scared."

I shut my laptop. "What do you need, Easton?"

"A tour."

"What?"

"The Starling football program offered me the position as their quarterback coach. The campus has changed a lot since I went there, so I want to get a feel for it before I make a decision."

Easton. Living in Jackson Harbor, coming to Jackson family brunch, hanging at Jackson Brews, and working at *Starling*, where I spend my weekdays. Is he trying to force me into an emotional meltdown? Hell, maybe it's good that my career trajectory is about to corner me into a move. That might be the only way to avoid him. "I'm sure the football people would be happy to take you on a tour. I don't know anything about that side of campus."

"And they don't know anything about *your* side of campus, but I want to get a feel for the whole thing."

I grunt. "You're telling me the layout of the English department will be integral in your decision to coach a bunch of football players?"

He sips his beer, watching me.

Sighing, I try again. "The people in admissions get paid to give tours. The lovely folks in fundraising and alumni engagement would probably carry you through campus on a golden sedan chair. The administration would probably make the college president himself take you on the damn tour if they thought you'd take the position."

He nods. "You're probably right."

Thank you. I turn my attention back to my laptop, still ignoring the beer he poured me. It doesn't even appeal to me right now, which is good, since I'm so tired that I'd probably pass out after drinking half of it. I shouldn't have worked through my spring break. I can't afford to burn out right before the finish line. "So . . . good luck with that. I'll see you around."

I can feel his gaze on me. Hungry and intense. By the way he's devouring me with his eyes, you'd think I was in a slinky formal gown and not the clothes I wore on my afternoon run. "You're right," he says, "but I still want you to do the tour."

I refuse to look away from my screen and reread an email about a department meeting. "It's nice to want things."

"Which is why I mentioned it in my meeting this morning. I said Shayleigh Jackson is an old family friend and I'd love for her to show me around the liberal arts side of campus." When I finally lift my eyes, he's grinning like a kid caught with his hand in the cookie jar and not like a grown man cornering me into spending time with him. "I guess you'll get a call about it soon."

"I guess I will," I say tightly.

Easton

Glasses. Sloppy bun. Pencil skirt. Oversized cardigan. No makeup, but a little gloss on her lips.

Shay agreed to meet me at the coffee kiosk in the lobby of the campus library Wednesday morning, and I'm sure she had no idea that her choice in attire would inspire some serious sexy librarian fantasies.

She grabs her coat off the back of a chair and shrugs into it. "Good. You're on time. Where do you want to start? I want to be back in my office by ten."

I grin at her. I'm not about to let her abrasive attitude scare me off. I brought a new fledgling NFL team through its growing pains and to three Super Bowl wins. I *am* persistence. "Coffee?" I ask, ignoring her scowl.

She opens her mouth, and I know she wants to refuse like

123

she refused the beer I brought up last night, but this is Shay and *coffee*. I know her weaknesses. "I guess we can drink and walk."

I'm going to win her back one little victory at a time, and we'll call this victory number one. "Americano, splash of half and half?"

Something in her expression softens, but she lifts her chin, fighting it. "That would be perfect, thanks."

I head to the counter to grab our drinks, and she stays at her table and pulls out her phone, an action surely meant to put me in my place. Sure, she might have to show me around campus, but she's not going to pretend to be happy about it.

"What can I get you?" the barista asks me. His tone sounds as disgusted as his facial expression looks.

"Two grande Americanos. One black, one with cream."

The dude rolls his eyes. "They come black. Cream's behind you."

"Right. Perfect, then."

The library seems like an odd place for a coffee stand, but apparently the kiosk is part of the college's efforts to turn the library into a comfortable "hangout" space students will want to use rather than a dusty grave for research they can find online.

I turn and see a tall, bearded hipster dude smiling at Shay. He's older—not so old that he's given up on the gym, I notice, but definitely old enough that someone should tell him to cut off the manbun. He plops his briefcase on a table and steps close to her. It's not exactly inappropriate, but it's definitely inside her bubble. When he adjusts her scarf, she flashes him a grin that I haven't seen in way too many years. It's a grin of adoration and pure feminine satisfaction.

What in the actual fuck is happening here?

Shay says something and then nods. The hipster dude's eyes go to me, and I hear him ask her something that sounds like "That's him?" and Shay nods again.

"Sir?" The cranky barista nudges the drinks toward me on the counter. "Your drinks?"

"Thanks." Giving him a smile he doesn't deserve, I grab the drinks, add a splash of cream to Shay's, and head over to meet the guy who seems to think he can look at Shay like . . . like she's *his*. "Your coffee," I say, handing it to her.

She gives a tight smile and takes it. "Thanks. Easton, this is Dr. George Alby. Dr. Alby is a professor in the English department and the chair of my dissertation committee. His collection of essays on Bradbury's influence on contemporary literature just won the Reichart Prize of Excellence—one of the highest honors in our field."

"I'm impressed," I say with a smile that probably says I'm not. But at least I have something to smile about now. *Dissertation chair, not boyfriend.*

"Dr. Alby, this is Easton. He's the old family friend I was telling you about."

I have a large-ass list of career credentials, and she's going to tell me about his prize while only giving me "family friend." Fine, then. I offer George my hand. "Nice to meet you, George." I'll be damned if I'm going to call him *Dr. Alby.*

George's attempt at a firm handshake is laughable. Dude might still know his way around the gym and have eight to ten years on me, but his hands are as soft as a five-year-old boy's. And yeah, I'm judging. "You're getting a campus tour today?" he asks.

"Yeah. Shay's nice enough to show me around."

She shoots me a death glare that says she's *not* doing it out of the goodness of her heart.

"Well, you're in for a treat," George says, beaming at her. "Shay's the best company you could ask for."

"I know she is. That's why I wanted her to do it."

He loops his arm around her shoulders—again, not exactly inappropriate, but definitely more intimate than colleague or mentor. Body language is everything, and his says, *She's mine.* I wonder if he knows about her secret boyfriend. "You played football?"

I almost laugh at his blasé tone. As if he's asking if I played on the intermural team at some accounting firm, but I manage to keep a straight face. "A little."

Shay rolls her eyes. "Easton was MVP this year. He's just retired and wrapped up an impressive career with more than four hundred passing touchdowns and over fifty thousand yards."

I smirk at her. *Someone was paying attention.*

"I don't really follow sports," George says. "Seeing grown men give each other concussions isn't my idea of fun."

Football isn't for everyone, and hell, I've had enough concussions that I'm legitimately concerned about the future of my brain. Nobody wants to end up in a nursing home, drooling into their Jell-O before the age of fifty. And yet I bet George's idea of "fun" is about as stimulating as watching paint dry.

George can't keep his eyes off Shay, and it makes me want to punch him. Something about the way he looks at her is so *possessive*. Do most dissertation chairmen look at their students like they plan to strip them bare and fuck them silly? "Let's meet after my three o'clock so we can talk about the chapter I want you to rewrite."

I don't miss the way she tenses a fraction at those words. "I can't tonight. I promised Lilly I'd take her to gymnastics and watch her new bar routine."

"Come by my office after you're done giving your tour, then." He winks at her then turns to go, not bothering to say goodbye to either of us.

Dude is so slimy I want a shower. "So that's the chair of your dissertation committee," I say when he's pushing out of the library.

"Yep." She takes a sip of her coffee.

"Did you have any say in who you got to work with?"

She frowns. "Of course."

"And you chose *him*?"

She rolls her eyes. "I'm lucky to have the opportunity to work with Dr. Alby. He's a fantastic mentor."

"He doesn't give you a creeper vibe?"

Her eyes flare. "George is a good guy. Don't be a dick." She looks at her watch pointedly and gives me a plastic smile. "I don't have much time, and my boss would kill me if I didn't give you that tour you want so badly, so we'd better get moving." She turns and walks toward the exit with the long strides of a woman on a mission. The view from back here isn't bad at all, but I'm disturbed enough by the bad vibes from Professor Douche that I'm almost too distracted to appreciate it.

I'm quiet while I follow her out of the library. The sidewalks that were crowded with students ten minutes ago have cleared out, and with two long strides, I've caught up to her and am walking by her side. "You two are . . . interesting."

She meets my eyes. "What's interesting?"

I shrug. "I wouldn't expect someone in his position to be so territorial around you." The answer I'm looking for is right there in the way she drops her gaze to her shoes. *Shit.* "You're dating *him*? The hipster academic with the manbun?"

She flinches and looks around as if she's checking to make sure no one's overheard "Would you be quiet?"

I lower my voice and try again. "Tell me you're not dating Professor Douche."

"I'm not sure dating is the right word."

I stiffen. "You're *fucking* him." My words come out a low rumble instead of the matter-of-fact statement I was aiming for. She doesn't look at me, and I know it's true. "You're fucking the chair of your dissertation committee. Isn't that . . .?"

She shoves her hands in the pockets of her coat and increases her pace. "Isn't it what?" she asks, jaw tight, gaze straight ahead. "It's not against any official rules, if that's what you mean."

Riiiiight. "Then why the secrecy?"

Her shoulders hunch around her ears. "Because it is frowned upon. I'd appreciate it if you kept this between us. People would . . . they'd make assumptions about both of us."

"Assumptions like he's taking advantage of you through his position."

Stopping suddenly, she spins on me, her eyes wide. "No one coerced me into anything. I know what I'm doing."

"Do you?" My hands curl at my sides, but fuck it. I can't stand this close to her and keep my hands to myself. I tuck a loose lock of hair behind her ear, skimming my fingers over the soft shell.

She closes her eyes but doesn't pull away. "You don't look like you're sure of anything, Shayleigh."

When she lifts her eyes to mine, her expression is one of resigned sadness. "Whether I am or not isn't your concern anymore."

I'm going to change that. "You don't love him." Maybe I'm reassuring myself. Maybe I'm reminding her.

"I care about him. We care about each other." She narrows her eyes. "Stop looking at me like I'm some challenge. You only want me because you can't have me."

"That's not even a little true." I hum. "Wait, before I forget . . ." I pat my pockets before finding what I'm looking for. "I'm supposed to give you this." I hand her the business card. "One of my teammates on the Demons has a sister who's a literary agent. She specializes in young adult lit and romance, so assuming you're still writing that, you should send her an email. Make sure you include his name in the subject line."

She stares at the business card. "I know this agent. Callie Weiman reps some big names in YA. Last I checked, she wasn't open to queries."

"But she's willing to consider *yours*."

She blinks up at me. "Why do you do this?"

"Do what?"

"Just enough to keep me on the hook. Just enough so I can't ever really let you go."

The words are a knife to the gut and a balm all at once. I wonder if she realizes she admitted she still has feelings for me. I don't want to hurt her. I hate knowing that I have. But if there's any chance for us, I have to try. "What if I don't want you to let me go? What if I want you to forget your professor and give me a fucking *chance*?"

She holds my gaze for so long that I almost expect her to agree, but then she takes a step back, emphasizing that distance between us, and releases a breath. "Come on, Easton. Let me show you around campus."

*O*peration Freeze Him Out died before we even started the tour. Easton is connecting me to a top YA agent. It might not amount to anything—nothing matters if the book isn't good enough—but just the fact that he did it makes those old gooey feelings come back. I was doing a hell of a job trying to turn cool again when, ten minutes into the tour, his daughter called and I watched his face transform as he talked to her. I've never doubted that Easton was a good dad, but seeing the love on his face when he spoke with Abi made it impossible to stay irritated with him.

The tour was pretty uneventful from there. Easton didn't make a pass at me, and I didn't break down and beg him to stay away so I can ignore the most painful piece of my past. All in all, I'm gonna call it a win.

We were stopped half a dozen times by students who

recognized him and wanted an autograph, and Easton handled each one with his signature charm and ease, signing ball caps, scraps of paper, even the shoulder of one girl who confessed before turning away that she was going straight to her tattoo artist to get it inked on her forever.

When I wrapped up the tour back at the library where we started, I thought he'd ask me out again or give me more shit about my relationship with George, but instead, he stared at me for a long time. "Thank you for today, Shayleigh. I wouldn't have wanted to see this place through anyone else's eyes."

And I melted all over again. Because this is Easton, and I've always been putty in his hands. The years apart have changed a lot, but apparently not that.

I knock on George's office door before cracking it enough to stick my head in. "Hey, you."

George looks up from a stack of papers and grins. "Hello, Shay. Come in. Shut the door behind you."

I step inside and lean against the door as it clicks closed. It's the first time we've been alone since dinner Sunday night, and I don't feel any more prepared for the conversation we need to have now than I did then.

"What's that look about?" George asks. He comes out from behind his desk and takes my purse, tossing it onto a chair before turning back to me.

"What look?" I smile as he slides his hands behind my back, pulling me against him. I blink when I realize . . . George is *hard*. It's nothing I haven't felt before, but George usually refrains from touching me at all on campus. Even this morning's affection in the library was out of character. He isn't a public-displaysof-affection kind of guy. He's certainly not a rub-my-erection-against-you-in-my-office kind of guy.

He tucks my hair behind my ear and drags his fingertips down my neck. "Like you're worried about something. Did your tour with the football player go okay?"

Swallowing, I nod. "It was fine. I wasn't thinking about that, actually."

"Then what?" He lowers his mouth to my neck and flattens me against the door.

He's definitely hard. And definitely looking to do something about that now. *In here.*

Earlier in our relationship, I would've been turned on by the thought of him touching me in his office, but today, with my mind so tangled up in my future—and, let's be fair, with Easton—sex in George's office is the last thing on my mind.

"Tell me what's bothering you," he murmurs against my neck, his hands busily unbuttoning my coat.

I bite my lip. I should ask about the ring. I should tell him that Easton kissed me Sunday night. "Did I ever tell you that sometimes I write fiction?"

He pulls back and looks down at me with wide eyes. "I don't think you've mentioned it. That's great. Have you thought about sending it to literary journals to diversify your CV?"

Of course he'd reduce this confession to its value on my curriculum vitae. It's the resumé for academics, which we try to make as long as possible by including every accomplishment we've ever come by just to prove our worth. "It's not the kind of thing literary journals would publish."

"You're being modest." His gaze sweeps over my face, lower,

settling on the bit of décolletage exposed by my shirt, and I want to smack him for not focusing on the conversation at hand. Doesn't he understand this is important? "You're more talented than you think."

"I'm not being modest. I'm saying it's not right for a literary journal because it's not literary. It's genre fiction. I've been writing for years and have a few novels completed."

"There's nothing wrong with writing stuff like that for fun." He lowers his face, kissing the swell of cleavage as he tugs ineffectually at the hem of my pencil skirt.

I brace my palms on his shoulders and gently push him away. "George, I'm trying to have a serious conversation."

His eyes are hazy with lust, but he takes a deep breath and backs up to his desk, leaning against it and folding his arms. "Sorry." His lips twitch. "Tell me about your genre fiction."

But I don't want to. Not when he has that smug look on his face. Not when I know the only words he'll speak with more derision than "genre fiction" are "romance novels." I'm not sure if categorizing my books as young adult romance would make them better or worse in his mind. "Never mind." I grab my purse and slide it onto my shoulder. "I need to get going so I'm not late for Lilly's practice."

George's expression shifts—the smugness gone and replaced by . . . panic? "Shay, I'm sorry. I want to know about your writing."

I nod. Maybe he does. Maybe he'll respect what I've done since he knows me and my other work. Or maybe he'll think I'm wasting my time. Either way, I don't want to be around him right now. "Another day," I say, avoiding his eyes. "It's not important."

But it is. More important than I've wanted to admit to myself.

So important that I only trusted the secret with Easton, who's kept it for me all this time. I cringe. I may not know what to call what I have with George and I might be too much of a coward to ask about the ring, but I owe him honesty. "I need to tell you something."

George tilts his head. "What is it?"

"Sunday night after we had dinner, I went to the bar. Easton was there."

His face goes slack. Even pales a little. "Okay . . ."

"He kissed me." I told myself it wasn't a big deal, but seeing George's face as I say the words makes me feel like shit. "I didn't kiss him back. I pushed him away and told him I was seeing someone." I swallow hard and step toward him, touch his chest. "It won't happen again, but I wanted to tell you."

He presses my palm to his chest, then dips his head to kiss me. It's slow and lingering, and I wait for it to fill me with warmth. It doesn't. When he pulls away, his eyes are dark. "Did his kiss feel like that?"

"No," I whisper. Because it didn't. Easton's kiss felt like a promise. Like praise and worship. In the two seconds his lips touched mine, I was destroyed and rebuilt. No, George's kiss feels nothing like Easton's.

"Good," he whispers, and I don't correct him. I can't bring myself to explain that it's not good. It's a mess. Everything's a mess. "Can you drive back after Lilly's class tonight? I want you in my bed."

I wait for the tingle that should shoot through me, for the temptation of George's bed to make me change my plans. It doesn't come. *Fuck you, Easton.* "I really need to work on my revisions. I might be able to get them done early if I put my head down."

He blows out a breath and straightens. I can practically see him mentally readjusting his expectations. "Early would be great. You could take a break."

I look around, surveying George's office. I've been teaching at Starling in a temporary position for the last two years, so it's not like I don't know what my life will be like if I find a tenure-track job. Teaching, grading, faculty meetings, advising undergrads, and so fucking much committee work. Of that list, the only thing I find rewarding is the actual time in the classroom. I love watching students connect with literature—sometimes for the very first time in their lives. I love taking them by the hand and showing them that even though writing terrifies them, they have the tools they need to write a compelling paper. But the rest? *Insert cringe.* "I think I need the extra time to explore my options for next year. I've been so busy finishing this degree and getting qualified for tenure-track positions that I'm not sure I've given enough thought to whether or not that's what I really want."

"Shay . . ." He studies me, disappointment creasing his brow. "Don't let this guy ruin your plans. I know he's all flash and money, and I'm sure that's appealing to you after working so hard and earning so little, but don't let him ruin everything you've worked for." He wraps his hand around my wrist and rubs his thumb against the pulse point. "Don't let him ruin the few months we have left together."

"I can't deny that seeing Easton again is messing with my head." I wave a hand between our bodies. "Messing with this."

He nods. "I noticed."

"And I am sorry about that. But the need to re-examine my career isn't about Easton. It's about me." But maybe I needed Easton to remind me that I'm more than the alphabet soup behind my name, and that I've never cared about my career as much as I care about my family.

Part V.

Before

May 16th, ten years ago

The beach is a balm to my lonely soul. Always has been. I grew up on the coast of Lake Michigan and spent weekends running barefoot in the surf and high school nights kissing girls on blankets in the sand. Lake Michigan is no Pacific Ocean, but it's so vast you can't see anything but water along the horizon. The waves are nothing compared to the monster currents of the Pacific, but they're there, even if they're only a few feet high.

As hard as it was for me to leave home when I was drafted by the Demons, I'm grateful I landed by the sea. I walk along the beach every time I need to think. It helps me chill. Helps me organize my thoughts. And tonight, my thoughts are on my other family, the one I left behind when I left Jackson Harbor.

It's been two years since I've seen any of them. I thought I'd visit, but then Mom moved out here to be closer to me, and . . .

well, my good intentions weren't enough to get me back home.

Carter and I haven't exchanged so much as a text in months. I'll get a random message from Shay from time to time, but nothing like those damn "Should I sleep with him?" texts she sent me in the middle of the night two years ago. She's still with Steve, so I guess she's probably answered that question by now.

If I'm honest with myself, that's a big part of what keeps me from flying back to Michigan. Every time I think about booking a ticket, I imagine seeing her with him. I know how unfair and unreasonable my jealousy is. She isn't mine. Never has been. I tell myself it's easier to stay away, but I think staying away from Shayleigh might be the hardest thing I've ever done.

And this month she's in Paris for the first time. With her boyfriend, through some program with their college.

I glance at the time on my phone.

She's nine hours ahead of me, so it's dinnertime there. Is her boyfriend romancing her in front of the Eiffel Tower? Is he telling her how gorgeous she is as they walk the halls of the Louvre? Does she believe him, or does she still doubt her beauty?

Fuck it.

I unlock my phone and pull up my text app.

Me: How's Paris?

Shay: Paris is great. Boys are stupid.

If there was any doubt in my mind that I'm a selfish asshole, the big-ass smile those words bring to my face would have confirmed it.

Me: All boys, or one in particular?

Shay: Who breaks up with a girl IN PARIS?

My breath rushes out of me. Fucking Steve. I thought he was supposed to be the smart kid. I should've trusted my instincts.

Me: A very, very stupid boy. Are you okay?

Shay: I'm fine. I guess I should've seen it coming. We get a free day tomorrow and I had it all worked out. We were going to spend it together, but now he tells me we're through and he's going to spend it with Heather. Heather, my roommate. Heather, who was supposedly my FRIEND.

Boys are the worst. And that's where she went wrong—dating a *boy*.

Shay: Why couldn't he have done this before we left? Now I'm on this trip and trying to act like I'm fine. I'll never forgive him if he ruins Paris for me.

Me: What did you plan for tomorrow?

Shay: Eiffel Tower, of course. BECAUSE ROMANTIC.

Me: Do it anyway.

Shay: I know. I know.

Shay: It's dumb, but I've imagined my first top-of-the-Eiffel-Tower kiss since I was ten.

I grin, and I can't help but be glad he's an idiot. This Steve guy has gotten so many of her firsts. He doesn't deserve that one too.

Apparently I don't reply fast enough, because her next text comes through before I can.

Shay: Okay. It IS dumb, but I can't help it.

Me: He's doesn't deserve you or that kiss.

Shay: Or maybe I'm a bore who "studies too much and isn't fun anymore."

I sincerely hope Heather has crabs and shares them with Steve. It's the least he deserves.

Me: Nah. I'm right on this one.

Shay: It's time for our nighttime bus tour, so I have to put my phone away. Please don't tell my family what happened. I don't want them to worry about me.

Me: You can always trust me with your secrets.

Shay

I scowl at my phone. Did I think Easton was going to text me all weekend just because I'm heartsick?

He could've at least responded to my last message. I sent it this morning because I needed to complain to *someone* that Heather and Steve sucked face the whole bus tour and then she snuck him into our room after she thought I was asleep. *Assholes.*

Easton didn't reply. There's a time difference to account for, but still. It's almost six p.m. here, so that means it's almost nine in the morning in LA.

Easton is right about one thing, though. I should spend my evening doing everything I planned, and while our whole group will go to the Eiffel Tower together next week, I really wanted to go alone first, when I wouldn't have professors droning on about the architectural wonder of it. I want to enjoy it on a visceral level the first time I go, and I shouldn't miss out just because Steve decided he'd rather be with Heather.

I'll be damned if I'm going to feel sorry for myself, so I put on a pair of fitted black jeans, heeled sandals I hope I won't regret later, and a flowy pink tank top. I do my hair and my makeup, and by the time I'm ready to leave, I feel . . . *good*. I'll never have a Playboy Bunny body—and the thirty pounds I've gained since starting college aren't getting me any closer—but when I make an effort instead of throwing my hair in a sloppy bun and pulling on the nearest T-shirt, I don't think I look half bad.

On my way out of the dorms, I pass Steve and Heather. Steve's eyes go wide when he spots me. I didn't do this to make him regret breaking up with me, but seeing him look at me like that isn't a *bad* feeling.

I'm nervous to take the Metro alone, but we've done this as a group a few times now and I researched it online. It's just one line I have to take to get from our host-college dorm to the Eiffel Tower exit.

Once I'm on the train, I actually smile.

I'm in *Paris*. I've wanted to come here since I watched *Forget Paris* with my mom when I was ten years old. Maybe it's better that I can wander the city without Steve. I don't want to be worried about pleasing him or giving him the constant reassurance he requires.

When I exit the train and climb the stairs at the Champ de Mars station, the crowds are intense. I clutch my cross-body purse out of habit. I've heard too many stories about women having their purses sliced right off them.

But there's the Eiffel Tower. Right in front of me, and it's bigger than I could imagine. It's *massive.*

"A flower, pretty lady?" a man asks, pressing a rose at me like a gift.

I shake my head and keep walking, making my way to the long line of people waiting to take the elevator up.

Easton: Where are you?

Me: Oh, so now you're going to respond to my texts?

Not even his delayed response can sour my mood. I'm on my own personal cloud nine.

Easton: I was away from my phone. Where are you?

Shay: At the Eiffel Tower, bawling my eyes out because it's so damn beautiful.

Easton: Be more specific.

Shay: More specific than the Eiffel Tower?

Easton: Which level? Give me details with those words you use so well, Shayleigh.

Shay: The middle one. I haven't taken the final

elevator to the top yet, but right now I'm looking out over Paris. The sky is so clear I can see Sacré-Coeur in the distance.

I bite my lip, hesitating. Is it dumb to take a selfie? *Screw it.*

I lift my phone and snap a picture of myself, my hair blowing in the breeze and the city behind me. I send it off before I can overthink it.

Me: There. Happy?

And because he wouldn't be Easton if he didn't make me completely question my actions, he doesn't reply. I shake my head and tuck my phone back in my purse.

Focus on the moment, Shay. You can text Easton later.

I take one deep breath after another as I look out over this city I've dreamed about visiting for so long, trying to breathe it in. I want to remember everything, and not just the view but the *feeling*. My love for Paris isn't all that different than the feelings I once had for Easton—an acute longing I could never quite explain, years of expecting it to change, and then this feeling of *rightness* while I'm here.

I wipe tears from my cheeks and sigh. I'm an emotional mess right now, but I love it. I might not be able to have Easton, but I'm claiming this city. She's mine, and I'm coming back someday—without Steve and without the college group.

"I'll come back when I can see all of you," I whisper. "And we'll really get to know each other."

"Are you talking to the tower or the city?"

My heart stops before slowly thudding back to life. *Easton?* I spin around at the sound of that deep voice I haven't heard in so long.

Easton gives a wide, goofy smile and steps closer. "I didn't mean to interrupt your private conversation."

I shake my head, try to rehinge my jaw. There's no way this is real. Just no way.

He takes another step closer. He rakes his gaze over me, and I can't tell if he's trying to make sure I'm okay—as if the breakup could have left a physical mark on me—or if he's *looking* at me. God, I want it to be both, but the nagging, insecure part of me reminds me of the weight I've gained and of the flawlessly beautiful pop star he's been seeing.

"Paris suits you."

"What are you doing here?"

He cups my face in his big hands and wipes away my tears with his thumbs. "You've waited your whole life for this trip, and that ass ruined it. I couldn't have that."

I open my mouth to explain that I'm not crying because of Steve. He sucks, and the timing of the breakup was rotten as hell, but we've been going through the motions in our relationship for a while. These are happy tears. But I don't get the chance to explain, because Easton dips his head and sweeps his mouth over mine.

I *must* be dreaming.

No kiss can feel this good. The flick of a guy's tongue across my lips shouldn't make the same buzz go through me as the climb to the top of a roller-coaster's first peak. The way his hand slides into my hair shouldn't feel as comforting as my own bed at the end of a long, exhausting day.

But he pulls away, and no matter how many times I blink at him, he's still there. Easton Connor just kissed me on the Eiffel Tower, and I can't even process it.

His eyes roam over my face a thousand times. "Sorry."

"Sorry?"

He nods. "I was afraid you'd accuse me of offering a pity kiss and refuse me." His lips quirk into that bad-boy smile I love so much. "So I didn't want to ask."

I touch my fingers to my lips. That *happened.* "Was it a pity kiss?"

"Hell no."

I'm pretty sure that's not true, but I smile anyway. "You're really *here.*"

He laughs. "Do I need to kiss you again to convince you?"

I open my mouth and then close it again. It's too much and not enough, and I'm happy and baffled all at once. I want to ask a thousand questions, but there's something so magical about this moment that I'm afraid it might fall apart under the weight of my disbelief.

"Shay? Are you going to say anything?"

"No. I'm not."

His smile falls away. "Is that bad? Shit, I was trying to do a good thing, and—"

I put a finger to his lips and shake my head. "Shh." I reach for his hand and lace my fingers through his, turning to face the view.

He stands beside me, studying our hands, our intertwined fingers. "You're not mad that I came?"

"I'm not mad." I smile. I might smile forever. "I can't believe you came to Paris for no reason other than my broken heart."

He shrugs. "Maybe I was just in the neighborhood."

"Right! Of course. You're a big-shot NFL player. You probably fly to Paris for dinner all the time."

His lips twitch. "Totally."

"It's no big deal."

"Nope. Not at all."

I swallow hard. "Big deal or not, thank you. It means a lot to me."

He presses a kiss to the top of my head. The gesture is almost brotherly, and that only confuses me. I release a breath and make a promise to myself—tonight, I'll enjoy Paris. I will not analyze Easton's kiss. I will not try to make it into more than it is or obsess about tomorrow. In return for this gift from the universe, I'll enjoy the moments as they come and expect nothing.

We hardly talk for the next hour as we take in the view, but it's not an awkward silence. Not for me, at least. For me, it's just an awed reverence for the moment as I try to memorize every detail—the sun sinking into the Parisian horizon, the feel of his fingers threaded through mine, and the thrill of everything below looking so small. It's crowded up here, but I barely notice anyone else, and when he pulls my back to his front, we might as well be the only two people in the world.

"Shay? Shayleigh, are you okay?"

I turn and blink at Steve.

His eyes go wide when he sees Easton. "Are you . . . You aren't really . . . I mean, you can't be . . ."

Easton smiles easily as he faces Steve. He extends a hand while keeping one arm around my waist. "Easton Connor. Nice to meet you."

Steve blinks at me and then at Easton. "Holy shit. I knew you two texted sometimes, but I didn't know . . ." His eyes dart back and forth between us like he's trying to solve some complicated mathematical equation. And I get it. Of all the girls Easton could choose to have in his arms in Paris, I don't fit. I'm just a chubby, awkward nerd girl who followed him around when I was a kid. I'm not anything like what he deserves—not like the popstar who's been hanging on his arm at L.A. bars. I'm just . . . me. Which is why I know tonight is special. It's why I know this moment is a singular gift and not the beginning of something new.

Easton pulls me closer to his side. "And your name?"

"I'm . . . uh, I'm Steve."

At first, I wonder if Easton will remember. Steve's been a huge part of my life during the last two and a half years, but Easton's never even met him. I see the moment the name clicks into place for him, see the recognition in his eyes as they go wide. "Ah. I see."

"I'm such a big fan. Huge. I can't even believe I'm meeting you right now."

Part of me finds a moderate amount of satisfaction in his stammering, but the rest of me just wants him to leave so I can return to my happy bubble—my dreamy evening with Easton.

"It's always good to meet a fan," Easton says with a nod.

"Have a nice night." He leads me away, dropping his arm from around my waist only to take my hand again.

"Thank you," I whisper.

"For what?"

I shrug. "For making it look like we're together. For making him wonder if maybe he gave up a good thing."

He stops and turns to me, cupping my face in both of his hands. "If and *maybe*?" He shakes his head. "Shay, he's an absolute fool for letting you go. And a bigger fool if he had to see me with you to figure that out."

I swallow hard. "Thank you."

He narrows his eyes. "But you don't believe it, do you? You don't realize that you deserve better than some prick who couldn't even be bothered to wait until you were ready and tried to pressure you into having sex with him."

I blink at him. "You remember that?"

"Of course I do. I had to use all my restraint not to fly home and give him a piece of my mind." He turns in the direction Steve left, glaring. "I'm afraid to ask what happened."

I laugh. "I was with him for two and a half years. What do you think happened?"

He releases a low growl and rolls his shoulders back, but I squeeze his wrist. I don't want him to pummel poor Steve.

"It didn't happen that week. He waited until I was ready." I tug on Easton's arm until he meets my eyes again. "Please get that look off your face."

"What look?"

"That big-brother protective look. Stop. We're in *Paris*. Watching you get arrested for homicide would really put a damper on an otherwise lovely evening."

His lips twitch. "You think that's my big-brother look?"

"Isn't it? You're as bad as Carter, trying to scare off any guy who looks at me." I blow out a breath. "It's no wonder you two get along so well. You both wanted me to be a virgin forever."

His eyebrows shoot up. "I . . . never said I wanted that."

My cheeks heat, and I really want to change the subject. I turn away, shivering a little. The sun has set, and the air's cooled.

Then Easton's behind me, holding me, his warmth seeping into my back. "Trust me, Shay. I've never thought of you as a little sister." He blows out a breath, and I feel it against my ear. "I want to kiss you again."

My stomach twists. He's only here because he hated the idea of Steve ruining my trip. He's swooping in to play the hero, but that doesn't make this *real*. I crane my neck to see his face. "Don't ruin this with your pity kisses, East."

He spins me in his arms and tilts my face up with one big hand. His eyes are darker than before, his lips parted. I want to feel those lips again. "Is that what you think this is? Even when I said it wasn't? Is that what you thought it was about when I touched you on New Year's Eve?"

My face burns. We've never talked about that night.

"I have wanted to kiss you for so long." His gaze dips to my mouth then down to my cleavage, and I feel hot all over. "Carter gave me hell about it because he could see it on my face, but you were too young and I had to resist. Until I had you in my arms and I couldn't say no."

My heart is beating so fast that I feel like I ran the stairs up here. "I'm not too young now."

His nostrils flare. "I know."

Kiss me. Do it now. I might beg. Instead, I ask, "What's next?"

Some of the darkness lifts from his eyes. "Next, you let me take you to dinner."

Easton

Shay's lipstick marks her wineglass, making it impossible to
focus on my food. I can't think of anything but those lips and
the way she moaned into my mouth when I kissed her.

I forgot how it feels to be close to Shay—how she calms my
anxiety and simultaneously ties me up into knots of desire.

She's just heartbroken and on the rebound.

She's been raving about Paris since we sat down, chattering
about everything she's seen in the last few days and what she'll
see in the upcoming weeks. If I had to guess, I'd say it's equal
parts nerves and sincere enthusiasm that has her cheeks pink
and her words running into each other like a traffic jam.

"But what about *you*?" I ask. "How's college? What's your life
like?"

She reaches for her wine and swirls it in her glass. She's old enough to drink in France, but she's only had a few sips. "I'm not like you, East. I'm just an average girl with an average life."

"That couldn't be further from the truth. You're so damn smart and talented. Everything you do is interesting, and I hate that he made you question it even for a minute."

"I'm not questioning it right now," she says, peeking up at me through her lashes. "What about you? I thought you were dating that pop star."

I put down my fork and take a long sip of my wine. "Scarlett," I say. There's not enough wine in this bottle to truly prepare me to talk about Scarlett Lashenta. "I was. For a while."

"And . . .?"

Where do I start? With Scarlett's constant drinking? With her battle with addiction that I'm pretty sure she doesn't want to win? With the way *everything* about her life is dramatic and she prefers it that way? "We split up, but you probably already know that."

"I try not to read the gossip sites," she says, but her blush turns her cheeks a vibrant pink and gives her away. "Though sometimes it's hard to resist."

I laugh. "I meant that I thought you'd have figured that out, because I wouldn't have kissed you otherwise."

Her cheeks blaze a darker shade of pink. "Oh. Right."

I huff out a breath. "This is totally unfair, you know. You can log on to Perez Hilton every time you want an update on my life, but how am I supposed to know what's going on with you? You don't even post on Facebook."

"I mean, phones still work, last I checked? And it's not like we haven't talked at all since you moved away."

"Sometimes I wonder about you and want to know what you're up to without interfering with your life." My smile falls away. "I was serious when I told you I didn't want you changing your plans for me. I couldn't let you switch to UCLA when you'd never mentioned the school before. You're living your dreams."

"I wouldn't have actually . . ." She blows out a breath and studies me. The silence seems to pulse between us. "Maybe I would have, and maybe it's good that you didn't let me."

But how tempting was it? I could picture her at UCLA, taking classes and visiting me at the Demons' training facility, coming home to me at night. But how many opportunities was she going to miss? And what about all the days I traveled with the team? I didn't have any right to fuck with her life like that. Her brothers would've hated me for it. I would've hated myself. "How's your family?"

She nudges her food around on her plate again. "Dad's sick."

"Shit." I sit back. It's hard to imagine Frank Jackson sick. He's nothing but a pillar of strength and stability in my mind. "Like, the flu or what?"

She shakes her head. "Like, *sick* sick. He . . ." She draws in a ragged breath, as if she needs to fortify herself, and I know what's coming. "Cancer."

That news is a punch in the gut. Frank Jackson was such an important part of my childhood. He was like a father to me. He was the example of a father that my own dad never bothered to stick around and be. "Is it bad?" I know it's a ridiculous question. If it weren't bad, she wouldn't look like the weight of the news was crushing her. I'm just not sure how else to ask it.

"He's fighting it." The words sound sticky, as if she has to shove them out around tears she's too stubborn to shed. "But some days, I'm not sure he's going to win."

"I'm so sorry, Shay. I know how close your family is. This must be really hard."

"I'm surprised Carter didn't tell you."

"Well . . ." I shrug. The truth is that I haven't done a very good job keeping up with Carter. He'd probably be hurt if he knew I texted Shay more than him. That or he'd kick my ass. "It's hard to stay in touch when we don't see each other anymore."

She cocks her head to the side. "But you kept in contact with me."

Because I can't seem to let you go. "Maybe I should try harder."

The statement sounds as weighed down by guilt as I feel, but she waves it away. "Nah, he's busy too. He joined the Jackson Harbor Fire Department last fall and is loving life."

I laugh. "I can see Carter playing the hero."

"He loves it. Mom, however, hates it. She's proud of him, of course, but she . . . frets."

"I'm sure." I grin, thinking of Mrs. Jackson. "She still sends me care packages at Christmas with homemade cookies." My smile falls away as I remember last Christmas, when Scarlett threw the whole box away and accused me of trying to make her fat to keep her. I was so pissed and told her I'd had no intention of sharing the damn things.

"What's going on in that mind of yours?" Shay asks. "You look . . . disturbed."

I take a deep breath, in and out, visualizing the stress and pushing it away. "I never told you . . . I had to see a shrink my first year in the NFL," I say, evading her question. "I didn't have you around to help anymore, so I had to learn how to deal with it on my own."

She winces. "I'm sorry."

"No, it was good. I mean, I'm glad I finally learned some coping strategies."

"I thought football was one thing you never felt anxious about."

"Not the games, but everything else." I look at the ceiling, remembering how overwhelmed I was by all the decisions that first year in the league. My agent helped, but it was still too much. "It was a lot, but I figured it out."

"I'm glad. I guess you don't need your own personal comfort creature after all."

"Is that all you thought you were? My *comfort creature*?"

"I didn't mind." She dodges eye contact, studying her food instead, but she's smiling. "It let me be something more than the tagalong little sister."

"Shay?" I wait until she meets my gaze. It takes a while, but I'm patient and she's curious. "There's no one else I would've dropped everything for at the last minute. No one else I would have flown to Paris to see. You haven't been a *tagalong* to me in a really long time."

She bites her lip, and when she releases it, I have to tamp down the urge to reach across the table and touch the marks her teeth left behind. When she smiles at me, everything feels right with the world. "You've always known the right thing to say."

Shay

*P*aris doesn't sleep at night. Or if she does, it's not until long after I've fallen asleep. It's eleven, and customers loiter at tables in front of brasseries, drinking wine, smoking, and talking. Cars roll by, and the moon creeps higher in the sky, bringing me closer to the moment when I'll have to say good night. I dread that moment with everything inside me. I'd keep walking forever with aching feet and my exhaustion-fuzzy brain if it meant I didn't have to let go of Easton's hand.

Dinner was amazing. Not the meal—I have no recollections of what the food tasted like—but the experience. I've been with him for four hours and I'm right back to the lovesick girl I was the last time I saw him. Maybe worse. My chest already aches when I think of saying goodbye tomorrow night. I still can't believe Easton came to Paris when he can only stay one night. He has to get back for a PR obligation—some black-tie event where he's promised to appear—so he'll leave only twenty-four hours after he landed. *Insane.*

"When do you have to be back to your room?" he asks, stopping to look at his phone.

"I'm a big girl now." I bite back a grimace at my word choice. *Big girl, indeed.* "No curfew."

"When do you *want* to go back to your room?"

I shake my head. I'm in no rush to return to Heather and the sounds of her sneaking Steve into our room after lights out, them making out in her bed. And yet that's all secondary to how much I don't want my time with Easton to end. "I wouldn't go back at all tonight if it was up to me."

He smiles, and it's a smile I haven't seen on Easton many times. It's big and wide and makes his eyes shine. "Do you . . . Would you want to stay with me? I have a room."

"So we wouldn't be sleeping in the streets?"

He pinches my side. "You're such a pest."

I squirm, trying to avoid his tickling hands, but he's stronger and bigger and spins me around. Then I'm in his arms, his body pressed to mine, his gaze on my mouth.

I lift a hand and tentatively touch his cheek. "Where's your room?"

"No idea." I feel his laugh more than hear it, and he nods up the block. "But my driver is right up there."

His driver. "You're so fancy these days."

He grins. "Nah. Just trying to impress a girl. You're sure about this?"

"Are *you* sure?" I ask, my voice a little shaky.

He huffs out a laugh. "It's not even a question. Tonight, I want as much of you as you'll give me."

"So it's a plan."

He leads me to the car, and the driver jumps out and opens the door for us. I slide in first, and Easton follows.

Outside my window, the lights of Paris glow, making this fantasy seem even more like a dream. Last night's bus tour doesn't hold a candle to riding in a private car around Paris with Easton—and Steve and Heather have nothing to do with that. "It's beautiful, isn't it?" I ask.

"It is. I see why you've been so excited to visit."

I look over my shoulder and find his eyes on me, not the lights outside. "You look worried."

"I'm not sure if I can trust myself with you tonight. You might have to tie me to the bed so I keep my hands to myself."

"If that's what you want." I stick out my tongue.

"No, Shayleigh. That's not what I want."

"But you only kissed me the once when you got here."

He frowns. "You're broken-hearted. I want to be a better guy than the one who takes advantage of the pretty girl on the rebound."

"My heart's not broken, Easton." I shake my head. "I'm pissed off, and my pride is bruised, but Steve and I grew apart months ago. We'd planned for this trip for so long, I think both of us were just trying to hold on until we made it through. The suckiest thing about it was his timing, but now I'm riding around Paris with Easton Connor and I'm liking the way things turned out."

He skims his fingers down my arm. "Then come here."

I scoot over in the seat and angle my body toward his.

"Closer," he says.

I scoot more, until my thigh presses against his.

He smiles. "Still not close enough."

I laugh. "To get any closer, I'd have to sit in your lap."

His hands go to my waist. "That's a plan I can get on board with."

I stiffen. I'm all too aware of the thirty pounds I've gained in the last two years and of the fact that I wasn't small to begin with. But rather than ruin this, I pull my legs under myself on the seat. I grip his shoulders as I straddle him, trying to keep my weight on my knees so I don't crush him.

His hands cup my jaw. His eyes dip to my cleavage. And if I didn't know better, I'd think I'd become someone else—that I had a different face, a different body. The way he looks at me makes me feel beautiful. When he kisses me, I liquify and forget all my insecurities.

He slides his hands down my back to my ass, tugging me tighter against him until I can feel the long ridge of his erection through my jeans. "Do you remember that night in your room?" he whispers, his breath warm in my ear.

Do I remember? Hell, it's moved from memory to my favorite fantasy. I wonder how many times I've relived that night in my brain. "Of course I do."

"I almost left as soon as you fell back asleep."

"Why?"

"Because I wanted more. And I thought you might give it to me. And then I'd hate myself."

I run my fingers down the line of his jaw. He hasn't shaved since before he flew here, and rough stubble abrades my fingertips. "I would've given you anything." The idea is terrifying. He touched me and made me come, and I was ready to throw away my plans and move across the country to chase him. If we'd made love that night, I would've been a mess.

"I never expected you to wait for me, but I hate that he got that piece of you."

I turn, watching the lights flash by outside my window. "Is this about my virginity? Was that first time a guy was inside me somehow more important than what I can offer now?"

"No. I'm just jealous, Shay. Jealous as fuck that the timing was right for you and him and not for you and me." He cups my face. "Jealous that no matter what happens tonight, when you go home it'll still be easier for you to be with him than me."

Easton is jealous of Steve. This baffles me. Half of my brain is convinced this is a dream. The other half is pretty sure I've somehow slipped into an alternate reality. "I wanted more that night too," I whisper. Because in this timeline, I get to say exactly what I'm thinking. "You touched me, and then I wanted to . . ." I swallow. "I wanted more."

His lips brush mine, then open, and he sucks at my bottom lip. When he tilts his head and nibbles up my neck, shivers of pleasure race along my skin. He flicks my earlobe with his tongue before sucking it between his teeth. I lean into him, half mortified by the moan that slips from my mouth. He wraps me up tighter.

I close my eyes, afraid the moment might disappear if I focus too intently on anything. If this is a dream, I don't want to wake up.

The car stops too soon, and I reluctantly drag myself off Easton's lap just as the driver opens the door.

"Le Pavillon de la Reine," he says. "Sir, your bags have already been taken to your room."

I climb out, and Easton follows me, taking my hand and leading me into the beautiful old building and up the stairs. He uses his key to unlock the room and holds the door open for me.

Easton's hotel room is nothing short of spectacular. It's a suite, of course. The room is so beautiful that when he flips on the lights, my nerves fall away and all I can do is wander around and take in the opulence. Parquet floors, high ceilings, big windows, and chandeliers. It's not fancy the way upscale U.S. hotels are. This is old-Europe fancy. I grew up wanting for nothing, but I've never in my life stayed in a place this nice. I didn't even know Europe had hotel rooms this big. They're known for their tiny spaces.

It's not until I make it to the back of the suite and am studying the piles of plush bedding that I remember why I'm here and what's about to happen. My nerves tie my stomach into knots.

"It's a really nice room," I say lamely, turning to him.

He looks around, and I'm suddenly aware that he's been so busy watching *me* that he's just now taking in the space for the first time. "I made my assistant track down the nicest available suite in the city. I got lucky that this one had a last-minute cancelation."

His *assistant.* For a beat, I wonder if I even know this Easton— the one who doesn't have to worry about money, the one who reserves the nicest available suite in Paris, the one who has an assistant and a driver. But that worry's gone in a blip. He's still Easton. He's still the boy who bought me a signed copy of *Harry Potter and the Philosopher's Stone* for my fifteenth birthday. The one who always looked back for me when I was swimming to the dock with the boys, just to make sure I was okay. The one who makes me feel beautiful when he touches me.

"Do you want some wine?" he asks.

Toeing off my shoes by the door, I shake my head. I don't want anything that might make me forget part of this night.

He drags a hand through his hair. "We should've gone by your dorm and gotten you clothes. I'm not thinking clearly tonight. I'd like to blame jet lag, but"—he drags his gaze over me—"I'm totally distracted by your presence."

I snort. He's been saying stuff like that all night, so maybe I should be used to it by now, but it's so outrageous. Him distracted by *me*. "I can just sleep in one of your T-shirts or something."

He prowls forward, his eyes skimming slowly down my body. "I wouldn't mind if you slept in nothing." When he's a breath away, he slides his hands up under my tank, and I'm way too conscious of his big hands on my soft stomach.

"I've gained weight," I blurt.

He cocks his head to the side, studying me. "Are you worried about it?"

"It's just college, you know? Stress and convenience food and . . . beer." I laugh, nodding. "There's definitely a beer factor in this tummy as well. Anyway, I wasn't exactly little before, and now . . ." I shrug, hoping the gesture says, *What you see is what you get.*

He squeezes my side with one hand and brings the other hand to my lips, pressing a finger against them. "Do you think the freshman fifteen is going to make me suddenly not attracted to you anymore? I think you're beautiful." He slides his hand from my side to my breast, and his thumb grazes my nipple. "These curves have driven me crazy for years. The summer before I left, I couldn't look at you without my brain serving me really dirty thoughts. Every day we were both at the cabin, I was fighting embarrassing erections and trying to hide my infatuation from Carter. Unsuccessfully, I might add. You can ask him about it."

The thrill of his admission sends my stomach into a series of somersaults. "I had no idea."

He shrugs. "I promised myself I wouldn't touch you until you were eighteen." He gives a bashful smile. "I'm honestly surprised that I made it."

I study his face, looking for any sign of a lie or exaggeration, but I see none. I want to believe Easton really has been attracted to me all this time, but it's so incongruous to the way I see myself that it's hard. "I think you're crazy," I say with a nervous laugh.

"I might be a little. When it comes to you." He dips his head, skimming his lips up and down my neck. No sucking, no open mouth, tongue, or teeth, just the slightest pressure of his soft lips. I shiver. "You know what you do to me. You felt it on the way here."

The reminder sends a thrill through me. I felt it, all right. Felt *him*.

"You turn me on so much. That hasn't changed in the last twenty minutes, but if you're not ready for us to—"

"No." I shake my head. "It's not that. Easton, I want this." *I don't know what tomorrow brings. I don't know how long I get you. I don't know if I'll ever get a night like this again.* They're words I can't let myself speak, so I just repeat, "I want this."

I muster all of my courage and pull off my shirt.

He steps back and has such wonder in his eyes as he looks me over that I have to check if maybe my body isn't how I remember it. All I see are my breasts practically spilling out of my black satin bra—I *really* need to buy new lingerie—my soft tummy, and the waistband of my jeans digging into my hips.

Easton reaches out with shaking hands, unbuttons my jeans, and drops to his knees as he pulls them down. I step out of the denim and watch him toss it to the side, but he doesn't stand. He stays on his knees, curving his hands around from the front of my thighs to my hips. He slides rough palms down and up again, and when he sweeps around to cup my ass, my whole body clenches. There's *heat* in his eyes as he looks at me, and there's reverence in his pose.

"You deserve to be worshipped," he murmurs as if he can read my thoughts. Then his mouth is on me—starting just above my knee and kissing his way up. Mouth and teeth and tongue trail a wet path toward the apex of my thighs and send a blaze of need rushing through me with every centimeter he inches closer to my cotton panties.

I say a silent prayer of thanks that I'm in cute underwear. It's not a matching set or something super sexy, like I'd have chosen if I knew where this night was going, but I could've chosen worse than a black satin bra and purple panties with a black lace trim.

I'm entranced by the sight of his mouth on my skin. He trails his tongue across the crease of my hip, right along the lace trim, following it down inside my thigh. I tremble so hard that I'd probably fall over if he weren't holding me up with those big hands, like he's afraid I might run away. He nuzzles me right between my legs, breathing in deep, like he's trying to smell me, and the sight is so erotic. I don't know if I'm breathing.

"You're so wet." His eyes flick up to mine. "Were you like this in the car? I wanted to touch you right there. I've never forgotten how it felt to make you come on my hand."

Me neither.

Slowly—so slowly I could cry—he hooks his thumbs into the sides of my panties and pulls them down my legs. When his eyes land on me—on my sex, bare and exposed—he curses. "Look at you, so bare. You're full of surprises."

"Steve liked it if—"

He pinches my ass, and I let out a breath at the sweet sting. "I don't want to hear his name on your lips right now." He guides one foot and then the other from the purple cotton then blows a cool stream of air right between my legs. "If you're thinking about him, I'm not doing a very good job."

He stands and nudges me backward until the backs of my thighs hit the bed. I lie back then prop myself on my elbows and look up at him, a potent mix of awe and lust making my breath come short. He guides his fingertips over my shoulders, my collarbones, down between then over my breasts and down my stomach. He lowers himself to his knees beside the bed and sweeps his hands out to my hipbones then back in, nudging my thighs apart as he continues his teasing path down my legs.

His eyes are so dark, so hungry, that by the time he comes back up to my thighs, I can hardly remember why I was nervous. I don't care about anything but his hands on me and the way his fingers are inching closer to the ache at the apex of my thighs.

I'm not innocent. There's not much I haven't tried, but the majority of my experience was with Steve. And this is *Easton.*

Everything seems new. Everything feels like a first.

As he hooks my legs over each of his shoulders, his grin is the perfect combination of smugness and delight. He lowers his mouth between my legs, and I can't remember how to breathe.

His tongue is as patient as his fingertips, and the pace of his strokes is nearly torturous. I have to fight to keep my hips on the bed, but then he slides his hands beneath my ass and tugs me closer to the edge of the bed. He holds me there, devouring me, his short beard scraping at my inner thighs. When I rise off the bed again, he tightens his grip and groans in approval as he strokes my clit faster with his tongue.

Receiving oral sex has always made me uncomfortable—it's too vulnerable, too intimate—but his tongue sends my thoughts scattering. He slides two fingers inside me and touches some spot I'd chalked up to mythical before this moment. I lose all control and come against his face with a violent jerk of my hips.

He stays right there, licking me through the aftershocks, stroking me as I slowly find my way back to earth.

When he stands, he watches me as he strips out of his clothes and slides on a condom. His eyes are on mine, and he's . . . smiling.

"What is that look on your face about?" I ask. My cheeks blaze hot.

"I'm just realizing I'm not going to want to let you leave this room tomorrow." His gaze dips to my sex. "Christ, Shay. I want to make you come over and over again." He trails his fingers over me and I shudder. "I almost came just listening to your sounds."

I reach for him. I want to feel the weight of him on me and kiss that smile.

"In a minute." He guides my legs around his waist, and I wait for him to climb on top of me, but he stands there at the edge of the bed, his big hands curled around my hips as he lifts them off the bed and slowly enters me.

My breath hitches and my body stretches around him. I'm so tender from my orgasm that the pleasure is almost too much, but it's so damn sexy to watch him look down, his eyes fixed on the place where our bodies are joined.

He moves slowly at first. His thrusts are gentle, tentative, like he plans to do this all night. But I need more, and when I arch my back and reach for him, he finds my clit with his thumb, stroking that spot I thought was too sensitive for more contact. My body clenches and he squeezes his eyes shut. "Damn, Shay. You feel unreal. I can't even . . ." His hips jerk and his pace increases. I can feel him trying to hold back and love that he's losing the battle.

It's my turn to watch him fall apart, and it's glorious. He tries to keep his gaze locked on mine but surrenders to it, throwing his head back and growling, gripping my hips like he's afraid I might disappear.

Easton

"Can I tell you a secret?" Shay asks.

We're tangled together in the dark, and I don't even know if she realizes it, but she hasn't stopped running her fingers up and down my torso since I came back to bed. It's like she can't stop touching me, and I fucking love it. "What's your secret?"

"I'm writing a novel."

I grin even though I know she can't see it. "Of course you are. You're Shay." For as long as I remember, she's always been reading or talking about a book. She was always coming back from the bookstore or camped out at the library. Books and Shay don't just go together—I can't think of one without the other.

"Are you laughing at me?"

"No. I think it's awesome. I guess I always assumed you'd end up writing something."

"You don't think it's stupid?"

"Why would I think that?" I smooth her hair back, wishing I could see her face.

"I don't know. Lots of people write books and nothing ever happens. I'm not sure I'll ever be good enough to get it published, but I had this story in my head and I wanted to try to get it down."

"Will you tell me about it?"

I can feel her hesitation in the stiffness of her body, but she releases a breath and it falls away. "Don't laugh."

"I wouldn't."

"It's about a nerdy high school girl who falls for her brother's best friend. He's a football player."

I smile so wide that she'd probably laugh if she could see me. "I like it already. A little autobiographical story there, Shay?"

She smacks my stomach. "No."

I wrap my arms around her and roll her under me. I kiss her neck as I find her hands, clasping them in mine and guiding them over her head. "You told me once that you had a crush on one of your brothers' friends," I murmur, settling a knee between her legs. "I wanted to think it was me."

She arches into me, and I wonder if she knows what a turn-on it is that she responds to me so quickly. So completely. "Of course it was you. It was always you, Easton."

My throat goes thick with all I want to say. I wish I could just show her the inside of my heart—touch her hand and telegraph what it is she makes me feel. She's the one who's good with words. I don't know how to do that, but I do know how to support her. "Write your book, Shay. And when you're done, you'd better tell me so I can remind you how awesome you are and how much the world needs to read the stories only you can tell."

She shudders under me as if I've just whispered an erotic secret in her ear. "Everyone deserves someone who makes them feel the way you make me feel."

"I only speak the truth."

"In that case, I need you to answer a question for me."

"Anything."

She's quiet for several long moments, and I use the time to kiss a path from her ear down to her collarbone, and her measured breaths go jagged. "Easton, is this a 'just because we're in Paris' thing?"

I lift my head reluctantly before I reach her breast. "What? What does that mean?"

She pulls out of my arms, and I feel her looking at me in the darkness, but I can't make out her features. We're supposed to be sleeping, but I should've known I couldn't sleep with her naked next to me and insisted we keep the lights on. I want to see her. All of her. "It's okay," she says. "If this is, like, something we only do once. I can understand that."

I take her face in my hand, skimming my fingers over her soft cheek. "You know what I've been asking myself since we got here?"

"What?"

"If there's a way I can have you without being the reason you give up your dreams."

"I don't understand. Why do you even *want* me, Easton?"

"Because you're Shay."

She laughs. "That's not actually an answer."

"Well, why do you want *me*?"

She scoffs. "Because my heart beats faster every time you're close. Because any time I know I get to see you or talk to you . . . any time I'm even expecting a text message from you makes me feel like a kid on Christmas Eve. Because when I have your attention I feel like the luckiest girl in the world."

"Yeah." My voice shakes, as unsteady as this feeling in my chest. This is all so tenuous, and I'm fucking terrified I'm going to screw it up somehow. "It's pretty much the same for me."

"You feel like the luckiest girl in the world?"

I release her hands and grab her sides. I trap her with a knee on either side of her waist and tickle her. She squirms with laughter under me. Then her back arches and our bodies are flush again and we're not laughing anymore.

I lower my mouth to hers as I slide my hand up to cup her breast. "Come see me this summer," I say against her lips. "Come visit me in L.A. before training camp. I know you can't stay—you need to finish your degree—but visit, sleep with me, and be there when I get home every night." I swallow hard. I don't know what I'll do if she says no. I've never wanted anything more. "Everything after that we can just take a week at a time."

"Okay," she says. "I'll be there."

I grin. "Does that mean Shayleigh Jackson's going to be my girlfriend?"

"I don't know. I'm so convinced I'm going to wake up from this crazy dream any minute now."

I nuzzle my face in the crook of her neck and pinch her nipple. "Then let me prove you're not dreaming."

*p*aris with Easton is nothing short of a dream. I can't imagine a life in which this day doesn't remain one of my favorite memories.

I told my professor that a family friend was in Paris and got permission to spend the day with him while my classmates continued with previously scheduled activities.

Easton and I used every second we had. We took a boat ride down the Seine, walked up the steep hill to Sacré-Coeur, and shared gelato from a street cart outside an art gallery in Montmartre. When we walked the streets of Le Marais by his hotel, he insisted on buying me this lavender-and-lemon-scented soap, and a pretty pink-and-purple scarf. I tell myself it's a good thing he has to leave tonight. If he didn't, I'd probably get myself in trouble trying to get out of more time with my classmates so I could be with him. But I don't want him to go. In Paris, we're in this bubble—a microcosm where *Shayleigh Jackson and Easton Connor* isn't an absurd joke but an actual possibility.

His driver takes me back to the dorms to drop me off before he heads to the airport, and he kisses me so long in the back of the limo that I find myself straddling his waist again.

He groans and grips my waist with the possessive strength I love so much. "You're going to make me late for my flight."

"Sorry." I blush, but there's no real embarrassment. Not after all we shared last night. "I know you need to go. I just don't want you to."

He tucks a lock of hair behind my ear and studies my face. "I don't want to either. But I see you next month, right? You're not going to chicken out on me? You'll fly to L.A.? Stay with me in Laguna?"

In truth, I'm terrified to visit Easton. That feels more like the "real world" than Paris ever will. Will he realize then, when we're in the middle of all the flash and glitz of his life, that I don't fit?

"I can already tell you're overthinking it." He runs a thumb across my bottom lip. "I can see it on your face."

"I can't believe we're going to try to make this real."

"Believe it, Shay."

"I'm scared."

"I want this, and you do too. It might be hard, but it's just a couple of years, and then we'll figure out what's next." He kisses me hard one more time before whispering, "Next month. You and me."

I want it to be true, but it almost feels like I want it too much. My stomach flips. How can this work when I don't fit in his world?

Part VI.

Now

Easton

A week after my tour with Shay, I'm back on the Starling campus for another meeting. We all know I'm going to take the job, but we need to do this dance just to make sure they appreciate what they're getting.

Even though it's cold as fuck outside and my body is no longer accustomed to this ice-and-snow shit, I parked on the liberal arts side of campus on the off chance I might run into Shay—because I'm just that pathetic. I swing into the library for a coffee and am relieved to see the grumpy barista is busy with another customer.

I hand the girl at the register my travel thermos. "A large black coffee, please."

"You got it." She winks at me and turns to fill my cup.

My gaze snags on the man talking on his cell at the end of the bar. George motherfucking Alby. Shayleigh's secret boyfriend. Jesus. What a pompous ass. I hate him, and even though I know my feelings are completely biased and entangled with irrational jealousy, they're there. I'm not interested in investing the energy to change them.

"I miss you too," he says softly. Hell. Is he talking to Shay? His grin turns lascivious. "Save that for tonight. It'll be worth the wait. I promise, Buttercup."

God, he *is* talking to Shay. The barista puts down my mug to help her coworker find something beneath the counter, and I will her to hurry. I don't think I can handle listening to Professor Douche sweet-talk Shay.

"Nah, don't be like that," he croons. "We're *both* so busy through midterms." He hums and closes his eyes. I half expect him to reach down and adjust himself in front of the whole library. "Anything for you." He chuckles. "I won't even make you beg this time."

Bile surges up my throat. Fuck it. Coffee isn't worth this. They can keep the mug.

I turn on my heel, leave the kiosk, and push out of the library. And practically run into Shayleigh Jackson.

She steps back at the last second, saving us both from a head-on collision. "Easton, what are you doing on this side of campus?" She frowns. "Hey, are you okay?"

Jealousy is a giant drill twisting in my gut. "Fine. I was just getting some coffee."

Her gaze drops to my empty hands just as the bubbly barista rushes out of the library with a steaming cup. "Mr. Connor, you forgot your coffee."

I grimace as I accept it. "Right. Thanks so much."

Shay snorts. "Rough night?"

"Not exactly." I watch the girl head back in and see George pull the phone from his ear. I look back and forth between him and Shay. Is he already ending another call, or was he sweet-talking someone other than Shay?

I throw another glance over my shoulder. Professor Douche is still in the coffee shop, now chatting with another man who looks like he's probably faculty. "Did you just get off the phone with . . . your man?" Since I know she's afraid the word will get out about their relationship before she's defended her dissertation, I don't use his name.

"No." Her brows pull down together and her lips pucker in the cutest fucking pout. Fierce possession claws at me. *He doesn't deserve her.* "Why do you ask?"

I wave toward the windows to the view of the man in question. "I just saw him in there. He was having an interesting phone conversation with someone he called *Buttercup.*"

"Okay . . ."

"Is that what he calls you? *Buttercup?*"

"No." She shakes her head. "You're being weird, Easton."

"If *you're* not Buttercup, I wonder who is." I fold my arms. "I wonder who he was just talking to on the phone."

She sighs and grabs me by the arm to pull me away from the library entrance and around the side of the building. She tilts her head to the side. "Listen. I know you don't like him, but I'm not asking you to. I don't need your approval or your friendship. If you recall, I've lived just fine without it for over a decade."

"Not quite a decade," I whisper, thinking of that night in

Chicago. She hadn't talked to me in years, but when she needed someone, she came to *me*. That meant something.

Her eyes narrow to slits. "Are you planning to rub my nose in my mistakes?"

"Shay—"

"I don't care if you like George or if you think my relationship is doomed to fail, but I'm not going to let you stir up trouble where there is none."

"I'm not stirring anything. I'm just stating facts. I heard him on the phone, and he—"

She holds up a hand. "Stop. Just . . ." She shakes her head, her jaw tight. "Please just stop."

"I don't want him to break your heart."

"Right. Because I guess that's your job."

The blow lands just as she intended it to, and I flinch. "I never wanted to break your heart either." The last word sounds as broken as I feel.

She tilts her face up toward the sky, and I can't help but notice how pink her cheeks are in the cold, how red her lips are. "You think that just because you're back here, just because you're not married, we should go to dinner, catch up. I should dump my boyfriend and let you be part of my life. Hey, maybe when it's convenient for you, I could take you back to my place and we could find out if I've picked up any new skills in bed in the last seven years?"

I suck in a breath. "You really hate me, don't you?"

"You *broke* me." She might as well have just plunged a knife in my gut. It would hurt less, but I can only swallow and take it. I deserve every word. "Forgive me if I'm not rushing to sign up for another round."

She walks away, and all I can do is lean against the side of the building and press a hand to the ache in my chest.

Shay

*I*t's snowing again, and I stare at the flakes falling outside the window when I should be giving my attention to this stubborn dissertation chapter.

George is always hot and keeps his apartment cool, so I'm bundled on the couch in my hoodie and a pair of leggings, a fuzzy blanket tucked around me. George sits at the kitchen table, grading papers. A month ago, I considered this my happy place. But since Easton came home, my time with George feels forced, like I'm faking my way through a relationship that was never meant to go this far. My phone buzzes beside me on the end table. When I see Easton's name, my stomach flips.

> *Easton: I'm heading to Chicago for a few days. I'll be back to close on the new house, then Abi and I will be*

official Jackson Harbor residents.

I blame my visceral reaction on old habits. I've spent so much of my life loving him and having to wait for his attention that my brain is programmed to pump out adrenaline when I finally get it—but then I see it's a group text sent out not just to me but also to my brothers.

That definitely makes more sense. After the way we parted on campus yesterday, he probably isn't interested in having any one-on-one conversations with me. I'm a little surprised I'm included at all.

A pang of nostalgia sweeps through me as I remember his first couple of seasons in the NFL and all the group texts that blew up my phone after every game. Why'd we stop those?

Ethan: Lilly is so excited to meet Abi.

Easton: You have no idea how grateful I am for that. Abi is nervous about the move.

Carter: Hurry back. Need someone who can push me at the gym!

Levi: Fuck you too, Carter. I creamed your ass on that triplet this morning.

Jake: Let the old man be delusional, Levi. Today he believes he can keep up with a pro athlete, but the day we decide to run a 5K, all the excuses come out.

Brayden: Accurate.

Ethan: Y'all know you can stay relatively fit without killing yourselves competing with each other, right? Been doing it for years.

Carter: Really, Ethan? Do you even lift, bro?

Ethan: Oh, fuck off. I could out-bench you all every day of the week.

Levi: Every day except the ones ending in Y.

Easton: You have no idea how much I missed this nonsense.

I'm staring at the screen and grinning like an idiot when George brushes his knuckles over my shoulder. "You're awfully attached to that phone this afternoon."

Shame washes over me. George isn't anti-technology, but he doesn't like when people are glued to their screens, and he's been known to pull out his old typewriter from time to time to pound out a draft of an article. I'd blame his aversion to technology on his age, but he's only ten years older than me. The guy's been forced to use computers since high school.

I roll my shoulders, shrugging off the guilty feelings. "Easton was just updating everyone on his plans and my brothers were going back and forth, giving each other shit."

He arches a brow, waiting for more.

I wave a hand. "They're just being idiots."

"Hmm." He dips his head and grazes his lips across the crook of my neck. I pull away without thinking, and his expression cools. "What's going on with you?"

Good question. "Nothing. I'm just . . . There's a lot on my plate right now. I'm still feeling a little lost about the future." We haven't talked about it since last week in his office. I haven't wanted to bring it up again.

He straightens and folds his arms. Gone is seductive George. He's pulling out his Dr. Alby face. "You're a defense away from completing your dissertation, and you have half a dozen interviews lined up for jobs."

"So?"

"So why aren't you excited? You've worked for this for years."

"Why are *you* so excited? Doesn't it bother you at all that I might not even live here next year? That I might be on the other side of the country?" *What the hell was that ring in your coat pocket? And who the hell is Buttercup?*

His eyes flicker. I don't think he actually moves, but I can feel him retreat. "Shay, this is the nature of academia. We have to take what we can get. New PhDs in this field are lucky to find a tenure-track position at all. We don't get to be picky about where we live."

"I know that."

"Then please explain what's going on in your head."

"If you're not Buttercup, I wonder who is." I mentally shake myself. I've never worried about George's faithfulness before, and then I let Easton go and make me question it. I'm not sure what upset me more—the fact that Easton assumed a decent guy who

wanted to date me must also be a cheater, or that the possibility didn't wreck anything in me. George and I might not be forever, but I'd be hurt if he wasn't faithful. I might not be ready for that ring, but I'd be upset if he planned to give it to someone else. *Wouldn't I?*

Fuck. I can't avoid this anymore. "When you forgot your coat at the restaurant that night, a ring box fell out."

He squeezes his eyes shut and shakes his head. "That's what all this craziness has been about? You saw my ring and thought I was going to *propose*? Shay, we . . ." He grimaces then reaches for my hand. "I care about you, and I can't deny how appealing I find the idea of *not* letting you go. But that's a far cry from marriage, isn't it?"

"I didn't . . ." I sigh, and he arches a brow. "I couldn't think of another explanation for what I saw."

"It's a family heirloom. It was my grandmother's, and I'd tucked it into my pocket to take it to the bank. Why didn't you just ask me?"

"I panicked."

Sighing, he moves my laptop to the coffee table and pulls me off the couch to stand in front of him. The blanket falls to the floor, pooling around my feet. "What exactly do you want from me, Shay? Promises of all my tomorrows? Do you want me to beg you to stay here when you've worked so hard to go?"

"No. Of course not." But it does seem strange that watching me go seems so easy for him. *I just don't understand why I'm never enough.* But it's not fair to put that on George when he's not the one I'm so desperate to have choose me.

He steps closer and slides his hands to the small of my back, pulling my hips flush against him. "I know how hard you've worked for this. I'm not going to be the guy who expects you to arrange your life around him."

"I'm not asking you to be that guy." I swallow. "It's just odd that you don't seem to care that this thing between us has an expiration date."

"I thought we were just having fun. *Enjoying* each other." He lowers his mouth to mine, and I stiffen but don't let myself pull away.

I pour myself into the kiss, willing myself to feel whatever it was that made this feel so good before Easton came back to town. But every movement of our lips and tongues seems clinical. I want to melt, but kissing George feels *wrong*.

George backs toward the bedroom, his mouth still on mine. "Come on, Buttercup."

I pull back. "What did you just call me?"

He blinks, but color rises into his cheeks before he hides his face in my neck again. "I don't know."

"You called me *Buttercup*."

He shrugs. "You're cute."

"You've never called me that before. Do you call someone else that?"

He licks my collarbone. I hate that I can't see his face. "Who would I call that?"

"I really don't know." I just stand there as he trails kisses up the side of my neck and strokes up and down my arms. *Buttercup.* I can't deny the coincidence.

"Come to bed with me. We haven't been together in two weeks."

I wriggle out of his embrace. *Buttercup.* What is this I'm feeling? It's not jealousy. It's not even hurt. It's *disgust.* "Stop."

He steps back, letting me retreat. "Seeing that ring gave you a convenient excuse to pull away, but what's your excuse now?"

"I don't need an *excuse.* I'm not in the mood."

"Seems like you're never in the mood anymore. Not since that football player came to town." *And there it is.* His dark eyes are colder than the snow piling on the windowsills. "That's what this is about, isn't it? You're chickening out about the jobs, about moving away, not because you're serious about this genre-fiction whim but because you don't want to move away from *him.*"

There is so much in that statement to unpack. I start with the part that pisses me off the most. "Genre-fiction *whim*?"

He rolls his eyes. "What do you want me to call it?"

"I don't know—my novels, maybe? My potential career as an author? My dream that this fucking institution beat out of me for no good reason? I've been writing novels since I was eighteen. Twelve years isn't a *whim.*"

"Okay." He holds up his hands. "Hell, Shay, you can't be pissed at me about me not taking this seriously when you've never breathed a word about it to me before."

Because I didn't tell anyone. No one but Easton. "That's fair, but I have told you—and many times—how important my family is to me. I hate the idea of leaving them, and I won't uproot my life for a job I don't want. Considering my options at this stage of the game isn't cowardly; it's prudent."

"Prudent? Is that what you call throwing away opportunities because you're feeling like a little girl with a crush?" He sneers, shaking his head. "I thought you were better than that archaic nonsense."

"What if I told you my family is more important to me than my career? What if I told you I'd walk away from academia forever if it meant I could live down the street from my brothers and watch my nieces and nephews grow up?"

"I'd tell you that you're being immature and you'll regret shaping your life around everyone else instead of building it around yourself."

"I don't need you to understand my decisions to know they're right for me. I don't need your approval."

"Of course you don't. That's my point. Live your life. Don't make your choices based on anyone else." He reaches for my hand. "Come on. I'm sick of arguing. Let's go to bed."

I pull away. "I'm going home."

He drags a hand through his hair. "You're going home angry." He says it like it's the dumbest possible choice.

"Yes. I am." I roll my shoulders back. "I think we should stop seeing each other."

"What?"

I wave a hand between us. God, I don't even know how this started. Teagan's right. Sleeping with George wasn't just unwise, it was completely out of character for me. "Whatever this is? We need to step away for a while."

"You wouldn't be saying that if that ring was for you, would you?" His frustrated expression transforms to a sneer. "I see now. You *want* a proposal. You're looking for a declaration of love, a promise that I'll provide for you forever as if you're a child and not an independent woman?"

I grab my purse from the table. "You don't see me at all."

"I see a scared little girl."

"Fuck off, George."

Shay

Apparently, I'm capable of flipping from adoring girlfriend to vindictive ex in no time, because the day after my breakup with George, I'm determined to find out if there is a Buttercup.

One thing I know for sure is that I owe it to the woman George is seeing to tell her we've been sleeping together. If he didn't tell me about her, chances are he didn't tell her about me. But the problem is I don't even have a name, let alone a way to get ahold of her. I can't exactly ask George for her contact info. I doubt he'd be interested in supporting my mission.

So I find myself doing what any slightly unhinged ex-girlfriend would do: I wait for George to leave campus on Thursday evening, and I get in my car and follow him to Chicago.

There are a thousand things wrong with this plan, the least of which is the possibility that following him tonight will be fruitless. Even if he does have some side piece in Chicago, what are the chances he goes straight to her on a Thursday night? But I don't have any better ideas, so I follow him the two and a half hours on the interstate, staying a couple of cars back, and hope for the best.

In truth, the downtime of the drive is kind of nice after months of a packed schedule. I'm behind on my pleasure reading, so I listen to a new release on audio from one of my favorite romance authors. By the time we're pulling off the interstate, I'm in a pretty good mood.

If he just goes home and not to his girlfriend's, I'll call up some of my old college friends who still live in the area and enjoy a nice dinner. But when I follow him into a residential area and he pulls into the garage, I realize I'm a little disappointed. This is his house. He's told me all about it, and I recognize the big front porch and the swing in the front yard from his descriptions.

I park along the road a couple of houses down to regroup. I tried to prepare myself for this possibility, but I really don't want to drag this out any longer. I don't relish the idea of delivering bad news, and I want to get it over with. What the hell am I supposed to do now?

I'm barely even paying attention when George comes out the front door with his daughter. *That* strikes me as strange. I thought she lived with her mom during the week, and I would've thought he'd need to make a stop to get her. Did her mom meet him here?

There's a tire swing hanging from the big maple tree in the front yard, and he lifts her onto it and starts swinging her. A wave of guilt flashes over me. I'm being a vindictive ex trying to find his other girlfriend, and here he is, playing with his daughter. I turn on the car with a resigned sigh. Dinner and friend reunions aren't appealing anymore. I'd rather just drive home.

I'm pulling away when I spot a woman coming out of the house. She has the same blond hair as the little girl—maybe her mother. She goes up to George and loops her arms behind his neck, kissing him full on the mouth. Wait. Who is she? Did the girlfriend bring his daughter over? It never occurred to me that he might have a serious relationship with *Buttercup*. Or maybe . . .

Maybe that *is* the mother of his child.

I rack my brain for the name of the woman. *Merritt.* He's mentioned her before. She's a professor at Loyola.

I park my car again, a few houses down in the opposite direction this time, so I have to turn in my seat if I want to watch them. I pull out my phone, search *Loyola professor Merritt*, and click on the top result. Merritt Reddy, associate professor of anthropology. The picture is definitely the same woman who just stuck her tongue down his throat.

Are they reuniting? I never got the impression it was a contentious separation, so I guess a reunion is possible, but this is the first time he's been home since we broke up *yesterday.*

When I look toward George's yard again, the three of them are headed back inside.

Someone knocks on my window, and I jump. A woman's standing at my door, disapproval all over her face.

Shit. I roll down my window. "Hi."

"Can I help you with something?"

"Oh, no. I'm fine." I smile and reach for the window button

again, but she shakes her head.

"I'm on the neighborhood watch, you see. So I need you to tell me why you're here, or I'm going to call the police."

Fabulous. My face heats, and I decide to use my embarrassment to my advantage. "I'm a student at Loyola and I was coming by to talk to Dr. Reddy about getting a reference letter for graduate school, but . . ." I duck my head. "Well, then I saw her with her child and realized I need to wait until her office hours." I turn my phone to her so she can see that I have Merritt's contact page pulled up on my phone. Her office hours are right beneath her photo.

"Well, she deserves time with her family like anyone. You were right to rethink your plan."

I nod. "This works out, though, in a way. I was getting her a couple of theater tickets as a thank-you, but I think I should make sure it's enough so she can take out her whole family. Do you think she'd want to bring her boyfriend and his child?"

The woman purses her lips. "You mean her *husband* and *their* child? Yes, I imagine she would. They're both so busy. Don't get enough time together as a family."

Husband? My stomach is in a perpetual freefall. "I didn't realize she was married. I thought she was . . . divorced for some reason." *I thought they just had a child together. I thought they were never very serious.*

"Dear no. They're an odd couple, but they moved in right after their wedding five years ago and have been living there together since."

"They weren't . . . separated or something? Recently, I mean." I force a laugh. "I'm so silly. I thought she was single and would've felt so bad not getting enough tickets!"

She waves a hand. "You're just confused because her husband works out of town a few days a week." She straightens as if realizing this was a poor choice of information to share with a suspicious stranger. "You should probably get going before someone thinks you're up to no good. Just find her during her office hours, and don't bother her at home."

"Right. You're absolutely right, of course. Thank you so much."

I've been sleeping with a married man. And they're not just married. They're married and have a child together. It's unreal. My brain refuses to process it. I feel like I'm watching a TV show or having a nightmare. Every time I try to process what I've done, my mind pushes it away. That's not me. I wouldn't do that.

But I have. And I can't take it back.

I leave the neighborhood and pull into the fueling station just before the interstate. I throw the car in park, put my head on the steering wheel, and cry.

Easton

"What kind of man goes house-hunting with his ex?" Maven asks, horror all over that pretty face women love. I met him in downtown Chicago this morning for brunch, a much-needed reprieve from Scarlett and her eccentric housing tastes.

I shrug. "A man who wants his kid to be within a few hours of her mom?"

"Better man than me," he mutters. "She planning to live in Chicago full-time?"

"Nah, she's planning to split her time between Chicago and L.A. But who knows what will end up happening? You know Scarlett."

"That I do," he says, grabbing his menu.

I follow my buddy's lead and try to figure out what I want for breakfast. The place is nice, but one look at all the fancy "waffle sundaes" on the menu is a blow to the gut. Shit like that makes me miss my daughter even more intensely. I talked to her last night, and she's doing great. It's not like she's unaccustomed to me being away, but I'm ready for us to settle into our life in Jackson Harbor and for time apart to become the exception.

"You can bring Abi down here next month," Maven says, reading my damn mind. He and I played together on the Demons for three years before he was traded to Chicago two years ago. He was my favorite receiver, and when they replaced him, I felt like I was being asked to win games without one of my arms.

I tap my menu, pointing to a picture of a chocolate, maple, bacon, and whipped cream waffle monstrosity. "I'm telling you now, this is the one she'd get. And then her mom would freak that I let her have sugar."

He laughs. "Well, take a damn pic of it and text it to her. Tell her Uncle Maven is going to treat her when she comes to visit."

"Done."

"Two coffees," our waitress says. She slides our steaming mugs on the table and pulls out a small notebook. "Have you had a chance to look at the menu?"

"We'll need a minute," Maven says. He gives her a lascivious once-over. "Everything looks *so good.*"

The waitress blushes. "I'll be right back, then."

I narrow my eyes at him. "Really? You can't make it through breakfast without hitting on our damn waitress?"

Maven grins. "I mean, I *could*, but why would I want to?"

I grunt and look back down to my menu, only to see a familiar form in my periphery. "You've got to be kidding me."

Maven follows my gaze—obvious as hell, but I don't actually

care. "What?"

Professor Douche slides into the booth across from us. *Fucking awesome.* This is exactly how I want to spend my morning.

"Who's that?"

"Professor Douche," I mutter. "What the hell is he doing here?"

Maven's eyes go wide, and he gives Shay's guy a dismissive once-over before turning back to me. "Speaking of, how *is* the love life?"

I tear my attention off George and focus on Mav. "What love life?"

"Oh, now you're going to pretend you *weren't* hoping to get back together with the best friend's little sister? What's wrong? Did it turn out she's serious about Mr. Manbun?"

"Serious enough about him that she won't talk to me." I squeeze the back of my neck. Hell, Shay's refusal to talk to me probably has nothing to do with George Alby and everything to do with how I fucked up.

A flash of blond hair in my periphery sends my attention back to Professor Douche's table. He stands to greet her and . . . holy fucking shit, he's kissing her. Like, open-mouth, face-eating, should-probably-get-a-room kissing.

Mav's attention slides to the table across from us before coming back to me. "But that's not your girl."

"No," I say. "That is *not* Shay." *Fuck.* I can't believe what I'm seeing. Can I take a picture? Would that be going too far?

"Well, score one for Team Easton. Does she know?"

"I don't think so."

"Holy shit, man. You're gonna tell her, though, right?"

My jaw ticks. "I think I have to, but I doubt she'll believe me." She certainly didn't appreciate it when I told her about *Buttercup*.

He hisses. "What a fucking mess."

"No argument from me there." They're sliding into the same side of the booth now, but they're all over each other. I drag a hand through my hair and blow out a breath. "Listen, you mind if we jet? I suddenly lost my appetite."

"Sure. I understand." Maven pulls a twenty from his wallet and throws it on the table to cover our coffees.

I stand and head toward the door, but after three steps, I turn around and go to George's table.

He's so absorbed with his company that he doesn't even notice me scowling down at him. I clear my throat. "What do you—" He blinks at me. "Easton."

"Let me guess," I say. "This is Buttercup?"

The blonde frowns. "What are you talking about?" She looks to George. "Who is this?"

George shakes his head. "Someone I know from work."

"Who's Buttercup?"

I grunt. Jesus, how many women is he stringing along?

"Did you need something, Easton?"

I think through my options. I'm just a hair too civilized to punch him, though he definitely deserves it. "Nah. I'm good. Just wanted to let you know I'm here." I pause a beat. "And I'm paying attention."

His date arches a brow. "Who do you think you are to interrupt our meal like this?"

George smiles at me, unfazed when he should be horrified.

"He thinks he's a big shot just because he's an athlete."

Oh, fuck that. He realizes I'm going to tell Shay, right? "Shay deserves better than you," I say.

Maven grabs my arm and tugs me toward the exit. "Come on, East. Let's get out of here."

Shay

*M*olly is the last person I expected to insist on a small wedding. I knew Brayden would be on board for anything she wanted, and I expected something elaborate.

Molly runs the new Jackson Brews Banquet Center and specializes in over-the-top, beautiful weddings. She's so good at them, in fact, that I always assumed she'd have one of her own. But when Brayden proposed last fall and they started talking wedding plans, Molly made one thing very clear: she didn't want all the fuss. All that mattered to her was having her mom and all of the Jacksons there. She wanted Noah to walk her down the aisle and my siblings standing beside them as they said their vows.

Upon hearing this, my mom burst into tears. It's a good thing we aren't a competitive bunch, because in that moment, Molly may have become Mom's favorite.

Molly and Brayden decided to have the big day at our family's cabin about thirty minutes outside of Jackson Harbor. At the time, I didn't think anything of it. They were planning it for the spring on the tiny beach in front of the lake, and I was thinking of Molly in a white dress, of Brayden with that dumbstruck, loving look he's had on his face since Molly moved back from New York. I was *not* thinking of Easton Connor being back in town. I wasn't thinking of the house where we played Never Have I Ever and he snuck into my room after midnight to sleep next to me. I wasn't thinking of New Year's Eve.

Now I'm thinking of those things. Since he's practically family, everyone assumes he's coming. As twisted up as the idea makes me, I'd be disappointed in him if he didn't.

"I like *that* one, Shayleigh," Mom says.

We're trying on bridesmaid dresses. Molly decided she didn't want us all to match. She wants us to wear different spring colors in knee-length dresses of any style. I've realized since the minimal plans have been in motion that if I told Molly I wanted to show up in PJs, she probably wouldn't bat an eye. All that matters to her is Brayden.

I look down at the dress my mom likes so much. It's a warm peach strapless dress with a high waist and a poufy skirt that makes me think of 1950s swing dresses. It shows off my legs, toned from running and twice-weekly weights. I love my legs and I feel pretty in this, which is a plus. I have much more confidence than I did when I was a teenage girl in love with Easton, but feeling pretty still doesn't come easily.

I look to Molly. "Do you like it?"

"You look *amazing*," she says with a big smile.

"When are we finally going to meet the boy you've been seeing?" Mom says.

I force a smile. *Boy* is not the best word to describe George Alby. "I don't think that's going to happen, Mom." And I don't want to analyze why this is a relief to me—why the idea of introducing George to my family makes me a little queasy. And that feeling isn't a product of the breakup. It's always been there.

But why *didn't* I want my family to meet him? Was I worried they'd judge me for sleeping with the chair of my dissertation committee? Hell, *I'm* judging me. Or is it because I knew they'd recognize what I already knew on a gut level? George and I aren't a good fit.

"Why the secrecy?" Ava asks, coming out of a stall. She's wearing a blush rose one-shoulder gown.

"I love that on you, Av," I say, and my sister-in-law beams.

"It covers my mommy pooch," she says, patting her stomach.

I snort. "You *don't* have a mommy pooch."

"I do, and I like it, so hush!"

"Don't change the subject," Molly says. "Why the secrecy with the guy?"

"It's not actually . . . a *thing*," I say. I look down, studying the hemline of my dress. Again, I'm struck by how little I feel about ending this thing with George. It should be a blow. But maybe I'm just made wrong, because it's not. It wasn't even much of a blow when Steve broke up with me, and that was the longest relationship I've had. No, it seems Easton is the only man capable of leaving me in pieces when he walks away. "I don't think we're going to see each other anymore."

"I'm so sorry," Mom says.

Teagan is watching me. She's been uncharacteristically silent on the topic of George and Easton. I have a feeling I know why. She's met George a few times, and I don't think she likes him. "Did he . . . want more commitment or something?" she asks.

Right, because last time I talked to Teagan about George, I thought he was going to propose. Because I'm an idiot. "No. Neither of us were ready for that." I'll explain the rest to her later when we don't have an audience. "It's not a big deal. We were never serious." I sigh. "Honestly, it was never a good idea to sleep with someone I work with." Mom's eyes go wide, and I realize what I've said. "Sorry, Mom. Your baby girl isn't a virgin anymore."

She laughs. "I didn't figure you were, Shayleigh."

"To bigger and better things," Teagan says with a nod. Then under her breath, so only I can hear, she says, "Emphasis on *bigger*."

Swallowing a laugh, I elbow my friend then change the subject in case Mom can see all my secrets in the blush of my cheeks. "And *anyway*, it's not a good idea to get attached to anyone here when I'm about to uproot my whole life."

Mom frowns. "How's the job hunt going?"

"Better than expected." Maybe that's the problem. Did part of me believe I wouldn't be able to find a job? That I wouldn't have to worry about moving away from my family because I didn't think anyone would want me? "I have an interview in Oklahoma on Monday and then one at Emmitson in L.A. next month."

"Oklahoma? L.A.? Those are both so far." Mom looks like I just told her I'm planning to marry Satan. "You wouldn't move there, would you?"

"Mom . . ."

"I hear that it's really hard to find jobs in your field," Ava says in her typical peacemaking way.

I nod. "It can be. There's not exactly a shortage of English PhDs, so general wisdom says you go where the job is."

Mom wrings her hands. "But who wouldn't want you? I thought Chicago or Indianapolis—Ann Arbor, maybe? But L.A.?"

She thought I'd stay within a weekend's drive. Oh, God. Wouldn't that be nice? I wouldn't have to miss Sunday brunch. I wouldn't have to miss watching my nieces growing up. "I don't know how I feel about it." Maybe honesty's my best bet here. "I've worked really hard to get this degree, and it only makes sense to follow the job. That was always the plan. But I can't pretend I'm excited about living on the other side of the country and only coming home a couple of times a year."

Mom pales. "A *couple* of times?"

My heart squeezes. I always assumed she'd thought this through. "I haven't made any decisions yet, but . . ." I stare at my bare feet, too aware of all the eyes in the room focused on me. "I'm beginning to realize the first decision I need to make is whether I even want to keep working in academia."

"You don't have to take a job right away, do you?" Teagan asks. "Maybe you need a break so you can decide. A buffer year."

"I need a catering manager at the banquet center," Molly says. "I mean, obviously you're ridiculously overqualified, but if you just wanted to step away for a while, the job is yours."

"I love that idea," Mom says, clasping her hands together.

And it's official. Now Molly is *definitely* her favorite. She spins to me. "You could work for Molly until you find something closer, Shayleigh."

The idea pulls me in two directions. On one hand, I don't *want* to leave home. On the other hand, finishing my PhD and abandoning it feels like a degree of failure. "Maybe I'll put my application in," I tell Molly. "I'm just not sure yet."

"No pressure." She grins. "Just options."

I nod. "Options are good." My phone buzzes, and I stoop to grab it from my purse in the corner.

> Easton: I'm coming back from Chicago early. We need to talk. And before you say no, it's not about you and me. It's about something else.

"Is everything okay?" Mom asks. She's got this sixth sense when it comes to her kids. She always knows when there's something wrong. I swear, even though I've never breathed a word about my relationship with Easton to anyone in my family, I wouldn't be totally shocked if my mom suspected something had happened between us. That's just the way she is.

"Everything's fine." I force a smile and shove my phone back into my purse without replying. I *really* want to stop talking about myself. "Is everyone happy with their dresses?"

Molly scans the group, and everyone nods happily. "I think so."

"Then let me take my girls to lunch," Mom says. She looks at me. "I know you're very busy with everything right now, Shay, but come to lunch with us. You need to eat."

"I will. Lunch sounds good." That's a lie. Nothing sounds good. This morning, I tried to make myself eat oatmeal and ended up dry-heaving over the toilet for fifteen minutes. I'm glad I didn't know in high school what stress does to my appetite, because I probably would've sought it out just to lose weight.

I head back to the changing room, hoping that a locked door between my mom and me will dim her spider-sense.

"Shay," she calls right as I start to unzip. *Damn it.* She's going to realize I've been feeling sick, and when she does, she'll hound me about going to the doctor. I would, seriously, but there's no point. After Dad's funeral, I was sick for weeks. This isn't my first rodeo.

"Yeah, Mom." I hang the dress back up and try to infuse a smile into my voice.

"I think you separating from your boyfriend might be quite timely."

Yeah, because there's never a bad time to realize you're sleeping with a married asshole. God, if Mom ever finds out, I'll *have to* move. I can barely look her in the eye as it is. "Why's that?"

"Because Easton was asking Carter about you. Carter said he made it quite clear he was interested and planning to pursue something. Remember how much you used to like him? You followed him around like a puppy dog when you were little. It was the cutest thing."

I yank on my sweater dress with more force than necessary. "Not happening, Mom."

"Why not? He's an amazing man. You know this."

"Just not interested."

"Don't tell me you're not attracted to him anymore."

Why is this my life? I step out of the changing room. Instead of giving me her Cheshire Cat grin, Mom is studying me with her worried mother eyes. I take her hand and squeeze it. "Let me figure out where I'm going to be living next year before I start dating anyone, okay?"

She smiles, but there's something about the narrowing of her eyes that makes me think she can see through me. "You know, Steve's mom told me what Easton did when Steve broke up with you in Paris." She cocks her head to the side. "It was such a kind thing to do, and yet . . . you never mentioned it to me?"

There's a question in her words that I can't answer. I love my mom, and her approval means the world to me. George would say that's immature, but that's just the way I'm built. "It was a long time ago," I say, and I try to ignore the hurt that flashes in her eyes when she realizes I have no intention of saying anything more.

Easton

I wasn't planning to come back to Jackson Harbor until Sunday, but after seeing Professor Douche with his . . . *whatever* she was to him this morning, I couldn't wait to talk to Shay. Not that she replied to my text messages.

I thought about going to her apartment, but if there's anything I've learned during the last couple of weeks, it's that Shay doesn't spend much time there. It seems like she's always at work, the bar, or on her laptop in the apartment upstairs.

I'm not surprised to see her when I step out of the cold and into Jackson Brews. I *am* surprised to see that she's working—not tapping away at her laptop, but pouring beers behind the bar, taking orders, and mixing drinks like a pro.

I'm already high on her list of Least Favorite People, and I secured my place on that list years ago by sharing information she probably would've been happier never knowing. It was a mistake and I regret it to this day, but this is different, isn't it?

No matter how many times I think it over and plan my words, I know she's going to hate the messenger for what I have to tell her, but what if I didn't tell her and she found out I withheld that her boyfriend was screwing around with at least one other woman? There's no doubt in my mind that she'd consider that a much worse crime.

I slide onto a stool and am all too aware of the way she stiffens when she registers my presence. "Hello, Shayleigh."

She flicks her gaze over me quickly. And hell, if their coolers break, Jake can just have Shay keep the beer cold with her attitude toward me. "What can I get you?" *Ice cold.*

She already hates me. Might as well make myself public enemy number one by being the bearer of bad news. *Fuck.* Not just bad news. The shittiest news. "Can we talk?" I'm starting to sound like a broken record with this question.

She sighs, but she sounds more tired than annoyed. "Not right now, Easton."

I spot her brother pushing out of the kitchen. "Hey, Jake."

He lifts his chin at me and serves a basket of fried something to the couple at the end of the bar before heading down to our end. "What's up?"

"Can I steal Shay for a few minutes? I need to talk to her about something important. It has to do with . . . her dissertation committee."

He nods eagerly. "Please do. She's not even supposed to be here." I didn't notice, but now that he mentions it, Shay's not even dressed for work. Everyone who serves here wears jeans or a skirt and a Jackson Brews T-shirt, but Shay is dressed in a sweater dress that hugs her curves like whoever designed it was on a mission to torture me. "Cindy's pissed that she's going to make fewer tips because she has to work back here with Shay."

"I told her she can have the tips."

"And I told you that you aren't needed," Jake says. He turns back to me. "The only reason she's here is because she's procrastinating."

"Luckily, I can help with that," I say, smiling at Shay. "Why don't you grab a drink and meet me back there?" I point a thumb toward the back of the bar and head that way without another word. I'm better off not giving her the opportunity to deny me.

I slide into a booth, knowing there's a good chance she won't follow.

When she does, she doesn't take the seat across from me. She stands at the foot of the table like she's my fucking waitress or something. "What?"

Fine. We'll do it her way. I take a breath. "I just got back from Chicago."

"Obviously."

"I saw Professor D—George while I was there."

She lifts one shoulder in a shrug. "His daughter lives in Chicago. He spends half his week there."

George has a daughter. Didn't think Professor Douche had it in him. I wonder if the blonde knows. Or maybe the daughter is a convenient lie that allows him to lead a double life. "Shay, he was with somebody else."

She folds her arms and frowns. "Were you *spying* on him?"

It's official. She thinks I'm a psycho. Can I blame her? "It was a total coincidence that we were at the same restaurant, but it was a lucky one, if you think about it. I know it's not my business. I know you want me to stay out of your relationship—"

"And yet here we are."

"He was *all over* this woman."

She just stares at me.

Jesus. Was I wrong about this? Does she have some sort of open relationship with this guy? It seems so out of character. "That doesn't bother you *at all*?"

I swear hurt flashes in her eyes before she cuts her eyes away from me. "It doesn't matter."

How the fuck does that not matter? "Because you broke up?"

"Because we're . . . seeing other people."

"Clearly *he* is seeing other people. What other people are you seeing?"

She drops her arms. "Have a nice night, Easton. I have shit to do. And for the record, I don't need you barging into my life and trying to fix everything."

"When are you going to stop pretending we don't have anything to talk about?"

"When I'm feeling up for the conversation."

"How can I make you feel up for it, Shay? Tell me." I lower my voice. "If you'll listen to nothing else I have to say, at least let me apologize for your dad's funeral. I never should've told you. It was wrong, and it was selfish. I wish I could take it back."

She stares through me, and the ache in my chest amplifies with each second. "You're right. It was selfish, and I wish you could take it back too. But you can't. You can't change any of it, so please stop trying to bring it all back to the surface." She turns on her heel and walks away. I don't take my eyes off her as she strides purposefully all the way to the bar and disappears into the kitchen.

Fuck that. I push out of the booth to follow her.

"Hey, East. How's it going?" Carter asks. Unless I missed him when I got here—which, to be fair, is completely plausible—he must've arrived while I was talking to Shay.

"Just trying to get your sister to give me the time of day."

He lifts his chin, his jaw hardening. I wonder if Carter has ever noticed that his sister is all grown up now. But then he says, "Good luck with that."

I push into the kitchen after Shay and find her standing with her arms braced against the stainless-steel counter, her head bowed. "If you're here to give me more of your opinions on George, save your breath."

"You deserve better than him. Is that really what you want? A relationship with a guy who doesn't even realize how amazing you are? If you were mine . . ." My stomach cramps. She was mine. For the briefest moment, Shay was *all mine.* And I lost her. I knew I screwed up, but at the time, I was doing what I had to do. And I can't regret any choice that gave me my daughter. "I wish I'd handled everything better."

She releases a puff of air and shakes her head.

"What is it?"

"Nothing."

"Shay?"

When she turns and meets my eyes again, only bitterness glitters in hers. "You didn't have to sleep with me. You didn't even have to kiss me. You could've been the hero just by showing up in

Paris when I needed a friend. Then none of this . . ."

"You want me to regret that night or just apologize for what happened after?" I prowl forward, caging her against the counter. Her brothers are on the other side of the kitchen door and could walk in here any minute. I lower my mouth to her ear before I continue. "I don't regret taking you to bed. I'm not sorry that I made you moan my name even if the sound has haunted me, even if knowing how good we were together made me miss you that much more."

She uncurls her hands from my shoulders but doesn't push me away. I brush my hand along the side of her jaw, and her breath shudders out of her.

"Do you truly not feel this? Did it end for you?" I close my eyes. I need to back away, but I don't want to. She's letting me touch her. Letting me close. "Because it didn't end for me. I don't think it ever will."

She stares at me for a long beat before sliding out from between me and the counter and turning into the office just off the kitchen. Am I supposed to follow her or let her go?

Jesus, if I had any clue how to let Shay go, I would've done it ten years ago. I follow and close the door behind me. "We need to figure this out."

She spins back to me, her eyes blazing. "Do it yourself."

I huff out a laugh and prowl toward her. "What did you say?"

Those defiant eyes brim with tears and her bottom lip trembles. "I said *do it yourself.* I have nothing to say, but you're the one so determined that we have this conversation."

I come closer. She backs against the wall, and I keep coming until there are only inches between us. "That's real mature, Shay."

I cup her jaw and stroke her bottom lip with my thumb as I study her face. "This is what you want?" I dip my head and bring my mouth a breath from hers. "You want me to corner you and make you talk? Maybe I need to remind you how good we are together." I cock my head to the side, touching the bridge of my nose to hers. "You try to keep hating me, but you lose your grip on it when I get close, so I wonder what would happen if I got closer."

Her breath is sweet against my lips, and she grabs my arms and curls her fingers into my biceps.

"Is that how it has to be, then? You want me to press you against this wall and kiss you until you can't remember your name and can't blame yourself for letting your guard down?"

Her pulse quickens beneath my fingers and her back bows as she arches into me. "We have nothing to talk about."

"Bullshit. But maybe first you want me to track down that fucker you're sleeping with—the one who you're fine to let 'see other people'? I could throw my weight around a little. He'd probably leave you alone just so he doesn't have to deal with me." I drag my nose along her cheek until my mouth is at her ear. "Then you wouldn't have to tell him that you don't want him. You wouldn't ever have to admit that even after all these years, even after all the shit fate threw at us and all the mistakes I made, you still want *me* more than you'll ever want him."

She swallows, and when she draws in a breath, I think she's going to deny it. But she doesn't say a word. Her only response is sliding a hand up to cup the back of my neck. *Fuck yes.*

"I'm not going to do that for you." It takes every drop of my will to force myself to step back. "I want you to talk to me. I want you to scream at me for every shitty decision I ever made. Then I want you to kiss me and tell me I get another chance. I want you to break it off with that douchebag completely and be with me, but I'm not going to do it for you." I take another step toward the door. "You're going to have to make the choice yourself."

My hand's on the knob when she says, "East. Stop."

I turn back to her, just like she knew I would, and she's right there. She pushes me against the door with flat palms to my chest. Then she has a hand in my hair and is tugging my mouth down to hers. And the taste of her . . . *Fuck.* She's better than I remembered, and as soon as those lips part under mine, I'm all in—kissing her with more intensity than I've ever kissed anyone.

Our mouths are eager, desperate, nipping and stroking. This isn't making love with our mouths. If there's a kissing equivalent to fucking, this is it. Her hands tangle and tug in my hair and she presses herself against me like she's trying to mold us together permanently.

But I'm too damn tall and I need her closer. I grip her behind her thighs and hoist her up. I spin to press her against the door, and she hooks her feet behind my back, locking us into place, right where we match. She rocks into me, and *Christ.* So good. Her body. Her hands. Her mouth. Everything. All over.

I know what she's saying. It didn't end for her either. She feels something when I'm close. Despite my mistakes, she's never stopped wanting me.

Clinging to my self-control, I try to slow the pace, stroking a hand up her side, caressing the curve of her breast with my thumb. She tugs harder at my hair and bites my bottom lip until it stings. I'll give her whatever she wants. This girl could ask me to bleed out, and I'd be helpless to deny her. In seconds, my rhythm matches hers. I'm wild, frantic. I'm terrified she'll walk away again.

I pinch her nipple through her bra and greedily swallow the sound of her moan. She rubs against me, as desperate as I am for connection. When her hand comes down between our bodies and she unbuttons my pants, I groan. "Shay. Fuck. Slow down." Her hand's in my pants, stroking me, squeezing me.

"Condom," she says.

I pull away and shake my head. I don't have one. "Sorry. I wasn't prepared for this." But it's better, right? We need to slow down. To put on the brakes for a second and fucking talk about what's happening right now.

"Top drawer." She nods to the desk.

I don't want to let her go, but I know what she's saying— condoms, in there. "Good to know." I trail an open mouth down her neck. I'm so proud of myself. It's taking superhuman strength of will to ignore the fact that there are condoms a couple of yards away. I could be suited up and inside her in less than a minute. Instead, I stroke the nipple I just pinched and slowly lick the column of her neck. "You're as sweet as I remember," I say, but I want to sample every inch, just to be sure.

A frustrated growl tears out of her. "Condom," she repeats. "Shay . . ."

She untangles herself from me, dropping her feet to the floor and pushing me away.

I drag a hand through my hair and try to catch my breath— try to think one clear thought that doesn't involve *taste, suck, fuck*—but she's opened a desk drawer and pulled out a condom, and I'm a goner.

She holds my gaze as she inches a hand under her dress and pulls down her panties. They're black, lacy, and hot as hell, but they have nothing on *her*. She saunters back to me, a spark of challenge in her dark eyes. I'm a desperate fool, because when she frees my cock from my underwear, I can only watch, dumbstruck and entranced, as she rolls the latex over me.

She tangles her hands in my hair again, tugging me down to her. I try to kiss her gently, but she turns it savage fast, and I can't help but respond in kind—nipping, sucking, biting. I could eat her up right here. And *fuck*, I want to.

She hitches a leg over my waist, and I feel her notched against me—feel her heat and her wet pussy. I'm helpless to resist. I lift her and spin us around until she's pressed against the wall. I hold her gaze as I slowly lower her onto my shaft. My breath rushes out of me as she clenches around my cock.

"You feel so good," I whisper, and she covers my mouth with hers and moves her hips in a silent demand for action.

This isn't the reunion I've fantasized about. It's primitive need—her nails scraping down my back, her teeth sinking into my neck, her breathy plea of *harder* until I'm fucking her against the goddamn wall of her brother's office. Not what I imagined, but it's good. *So good.* I lose myself a little and forget where we are and why this is a bad idea, why this is too soon and too fast. My thoughts have narrowed to the most primitive instincts to thrust and retreat, thrust and retreat, my attention focused on the way her body perfectly fits mine and the sound of her moans as she buries her face in my neck.

She's close. I feel it in the sudden tension in her body, the way she's clenched around my cock. I slip a hand between our bodies and find her clit. She may have set the pace, but I'll be damned if she walks out of this office without coming. I stroke tiny circles around that sensitive spot, and her breathing hitches and her hips shift, seeking the friction where she needs it. When I give her what she wants, she bucks wildly against me. Her body squeezes so tightly as she comes that I forget to breathe. Then I'm coming right behind her with my own pounding thrust of my hips—barely breathing, barely thinking, barely anything but an animal seeking release.

I hold her, clutching her close as I bury my face in her neck. The smell of her is a drug. I want it on my pillow. I want it in my house. I want to wake up to this scent every day.

She grips my shoulders, squeezing before she pushes me back. I gently lower her to the ground. She searches my face, and I wait, wondering what she can really see in my eyes. Can she see how I feel about her or does she just see the man who hurt her?

"Thanks," she whispers, biting back a smile.

I choke on a laugh. "Um, you're welcome?"

Pans clang outside the office, and I wince. *Right.* We just had sex in the middle of her family's bar. In Jake's office.

"Have you seen Easton?"

Shay and I share a moment of wide-eyed horror at the sound of Carter's voice.

Someone clears his throat. "Don't see him, nope." *Jake.*

If I had to guess, "don't see him" means he knows damn well where I am and is trying to save me a beating. I definitely owe him.

"Well, if you do, tell him Scarlett Lashenta is out front asking for him."

I feel like I've been punched. Not because of Scarlett. I can deal with her. But because Shay's pink cheeks just turned ashen. Because this is really shitty timing. *Again.*

I catch her gaze and shake my head. "Don't freak out," I whisper.

Jake coughs. "Scarlett is *here?*"

"Yep," Carter says. "And not even a little incognito. She's holding court at the bar."

"I have to see this," Jake says.

The sound of their voices fades until I can only assume they've left the kitchen.

"She's right on time," Shay says, a cruel smile twisting her lips.

"She likes to be unpredictable," I tell her. "It's just the way she is."

She huffs out a wry laugh and bends over to grab her panties off the floor. "You'd better get out there before she comes in here looking for you. I'm sure she has some life-changing news."

"Don't do this. Don't shut me down." I swallow. "Shay, what just happened between us . . . That was too fast. I'm sorry."

She pulls her underwear up her legs then smooths down her dress. She won't even look at me. "Stop being a prude. We scratched that itch, and now we can move on."

Is she kidding me? "You're going to drag me in here, beg me to fuck you senseless against the wall, and then go back to being *cold*? Back to hating my guts?"

She shrugs. "That's all we're good for, Easton. *Fucking.* Getting each other off." She rakes her gaze down my body and back up. "And you're good, I'll give you credit for that. But I do remember you having a little more stamina."

I don't take the bait. If she wants to judge me for lasting less than ten minutes when I've wanted her for years, she can fucking judge me. That's not the part of her little speech that bothers me. "We still need to talk." It sounds so ridiculous now with a used condom hanging off my dick and my ex-wife in the next room. Grabbing a tissue from the desk, I clean up the condom and zip up my pants.

When I turn back to her, she's frozen by the door, like she's torn between running away and chewing me out.

"Tell me what you're thinking."

"I'm thinking I was the most obvious person to warm your bed since you're back in this tiny town, but now she's here, so I can go."

I press a palm flat to the wall to steady myself. "That's fucking unfair, and you know it. I never assumed you'd climb back into bed with me. I want what we *had*."

"We talked. Then we fucked." She cocks her head to the side, ice-cold Shay returning so quickly I have whiplash. "Don't you remember how it goes? Next, you walk away."

"Shay—" I reach for her, but she shakes out of my grasp and pushes past me and out the door. I see her run for the back exit and watch the door shut behind her.

Part VII.

Before

Shay

June 3rd, ten years ago

I'm exhausted. I got home yesterday from my month in Paris. Mom drove to Chicago because she wanted to be the one to pick me up from the airport and the first to hear all about my trip. We spent the evening hanging out at one of her favorite lakeside restaurants as she regaled me with questions and demanded to know *every detail*.

I couldn't bring myself to tell her about Easton. My memories of our night and day together are so precious, and I want to keep them locked away like rare, ancient tomes whose pages can disintegrate with human touch.

Then last night I fell into bed, convinced I'd fall comatose for twelve hours, but I could barely sleep. After tossing and turning for six hours, I gave up, made a pot of coffee, and wished I didn't have this horrible, aching worry in my chest regarding Easton's silence.

When I can't handle it anymore, I text him.

Me: Are you free? I need to talk.

Easton: Give me two minutes and I'll call.

I set my phone down on the coffee table and squeeze my eyes shut. Just two minutes.

Another wave of exhaustion washes over me, and I lean back on the couch and put my hand flat against my chest. I just want to go home—my Jackson Harbor home, not this Chicago rental I share with three other girls. I want to curl up in my own bed and hide under my own blankets. I want Easton to find me there, crawl in bed beside me, and tell me it's going to be okay. Tell me he hasn't been avoiding me.

Easton texted me when he got home, but then his messages became . . . sparse. He said we'd talk when I got home from Paris, that he didn't want to bother me during my trip, but something felt off.

My phone buzzes, and I jerk upright, reaching for it. Easton's face grins back at me from the screen. It's a picture I took of him when we were eating gelato in Montmartre. He's grinning and has a smudge of chocolate on the corner of his mouth. The picture fills me with conflicting emotions so intense that I feel like I might be torn in two. Joy, because that was the best day of my life. And longing, because whatever we had in Paris is already slipping away.

It vibrates again, and I swipe the screen to accept the call. "Hello?"

"Hey, Shay. What's up?" His voice is all gravelly from sleep.

"I'm sorry. Are you awake?" *Idiotic questions for five hundred, Alex.* I flinch when I look at the clock. It's before eight here, which means it's not even five in the morning in L.A. "I mean, obviously you are now, but I . . ."

"No, it's fine. I normally get up at five anyway. Are you okay?"

No. You've barely talked to me since you left Paris. "I just wanted to hear your voice." I hate the sound of the sob in my throat.

"Yeah. Listen, I'm sorry I haven't called. I came back to a mess here and I just had to deal with everything. I'm glad you texted. I was planning to make this call today."

This call. Like it's one very specific conversation he needed to check off a list and not one of hundreds he plans to have with me. "Wha—why? What's going on?" But I already know. I hear it in his voice. *We can't be together in the real world.*

"It's Scarlett. She's . . ." He blows out a breath. "I can't get into details. She's a very private person, but she needs me right now. I think . . ."

"You think what?" My voice breaks. I already know. I'm going to make him say it anyway.

"I think I need to be here for her. I need to help her."

"Okay . . . but that doesn't mean you can't call."

"Shit," he mutters, and I imagine him scrubbing his hand over his face. "Shayleigh, I've always known you were too good for me."

"No." Tears roll hot down my cheeks. "Don't give me that."

"Why not? Isn't it true?"

"No. It's not true, and it's a lame excuse. If you're freaking out about what happened between us when we were in Paris, then that's on you. Don't try to pretend that you're pushing me away because I'm just *so great*. Don't try to pretend you're doing me a favor."

"East?" I can barely make out the small voice in the background. Feminine, worried. "Who is that? Are you coming back to bed?"

"I'll be there in a minute," he says.

Nausea roils. I feel like my insides have just been pulverized. "By help her, you mean fuck her? Is that code or something?"

"Jesus, Shay, it's not like that. She's . . ." He blows out a breath. "Scarlett is pregnant."

For a minute, I'm sure I've misheard him. I'm positive this cannot be happening.

"Shay? Are you still there?"

"She's pregnant." Saying the words doesn't make them any easier to swallow. *How? Fucking* how *could this work out like this?*

"Yeah." I press my hand to my stomach, and I'm almost surprised not to feel blood seeping out on my fingers. *She's pregnant with Easton's baby.* All I can hear is the soft whoosh of his breath through the phone. He's breathing as hard as I am.

"I grew up without my dad around. I always promised myself that if I was ever a father, that would be my first priority. Do you understand?"

I nod, even knowing he can't see me. Yes, I understand. I know that Easton wants to be the kind of dad who's there for everything—who always puts his kid first. He'd never walk away from a child he knew about, and being put in any sort of situation where he felt like he had to would destroy him. Yes, I understand too well.

"Shay?"

"Congratulations, Easton." The sob rises up my throat, and I choke it back. "I know you'll be an amazing father."

Part VIII.

Now

Easton

I followed Shay to the parking lot, but she was already in her car and driving away.

Fuck. Fuck. Fuck.

I'm going to have to track her down. We can't leave it like this after what just happened. But first, I need to deal with the woman waiting for me at the bar.

"Easton! Surprise!" Scarlett slides off her barstool and pushes through the crowd that's gathered around her. I've developed a good relationship with my ex-wife over the years, but I'll never understand her need for surprises. And tonight's visit to Jackson Brews is *definitely* a surprise.

She wraps her arms around my stomach and hugs me tightly. Jake and Carter watch every move. Jake looks a little pissed. Carter looks confused.

"What are you doing here?" I ask Scarlett, pulling out of her hug. She's an affectionate person, and while I know she hugs everyone, I don't need Shay's brothers thinking this means we're patching things up. When I decided to come back early from our Chicago house hunt, I was under the impression that she was going to keep looking without me. Kinda hard to look at Chicago homes when you're not in Chicago.

"I was thinking—why buy a place in Chicago when I can buy a home *here* and be closer to you and Abi?"

I squeeze the knot of tension at the back of my neck. "Why don't you stay in Jackson Harbor for a few days before you make that decision?" Chicago is too "small-town feel" for Scarlett. Jackson Harbor isn't going to be her thing.

She beams and flips her long red hair. "Is that an invitation?"

"It's not my town, Scar. Do what you want."

"I mean, are you inviting me to stay with you and Abi until I make my decision?"

Oh, *hell no*. Not only do Scarlett and I get along a thousand times better when we don't live together, but I wouldn't do that to Shay. "Nope. You could stay in a hotel or get a temporary lease, but you and I don't work under one roof, remember?"

She sticks out her bottom lip in a pout. "So says *you*."

I look at my watch. Every minute that passes is a minute Shay has to decide we made a mistake. I reach into my pocket for my keys. "I need to get out of here. Talk to Jake or Carter about the best hotels nearby."

*S*hay lives in a third-floor walk-up a couple of blocks from the bar. I know this thanks to Mrs. Jackson, who was pleased to hear that I wanted to swing by and bring Shay some dinner, since she's been working so hard lately. To make good on my promise, I grabbed pizza and a six-pack of beer on my way over.

But when I get there, no one answers.

A gray-haired lady opens the door across the hall. "She's not home yet."

I swallow. "Do you know where she is?"

She shakes her head. "Hardly ever sleeps here, far as I can tell."

Because she's with George? Is that where she is now? Jesus. I can't believe this night. "Here." I hold out the pizza. "You like pepperoni and jalapenos?"

She takes the box and pulls a piece from inside before backing into her apartment. "Thanks. I'll tell Shayleigh you came by."

I stand outside her apartment like an idiot for at least ten more minutes. When she doesn't come home, I text.

> *I never chose Scarlett over you. She would lose that matchup every time. I chose my daughter over myself.*

Shay

"I slept with Easton," I blurt when Teagan opens the door.

"I'm sorry—what?" She makes a few fish faces like she's trying to talk and is failing. "You . . . *slept* with him."

I cringe. "Maybe 'sleeping' isn't the right euphemism. There was no sleeping. And no bed." I thread my fingers through my hair and tug. "Just a wall and some very athletic fucking."

Her eyes are wide. I've been shocking her right and left, it seems. "Okay. Well, that's not exactly what I had in mind when I told you not to make any decisions."

"I know." I rub my head. "I really do. It's just . . . Oh my God, Tea, my life is a mess. I broke up with George, then Easton threatened to kiss me until I talked about *us*, and I pulled him into Jake's office and practically demanded he do me against the wall."

"I'm sure that was very difficult for him. Should we go down to Hallmark and get him a card?"

I didn't even mention the worst part. *I just realized I've been sleeping with a married man.* Nausea turns my belly, and I push past her, down the hall, and into the powder room by the garage. I throw my purse on the floor and barely turn in time before I vomit up the little lunch I was able to choke down. I hear Teagan behind me, running water in the sink.

She sweeps my hair to the side and puts a cool, wet cloth on my neck. "Is this always your reaction when you have athletic wall sex?"

I spit and flush before leaning against the wall and closing my eyes. "Don't know. That was a first for me."

"Well, you've been missing out." She clears her throat. "I mean, I'm assuming you agree? Was it good?"

I can't look at her. I'm too afraid I might see what a mess I am reflected in the panic of her expression. "It was great until his ex-wife showed up."

"Wait. Scarlett Lashenta was at *Jackson Brews*?"

She's silent so long that I realize it's not a rhetorical question and open my eyes. "Teagan, focus. She's the bad guy in this story."

"A bad guy with some really catchy tunes," she says, then ducks her head at my glare. "Okay, okay. So what happened after the evil pop star showed up? Did she catch you in the act? Oh my God, was she pissed? Did you fight?"

I scowl. "You might be enjoying this too much."

She snorts. "Says the girl who just had great athletic wall sex."

"Teagan!"

"*Your* words, not mine."

"We were in the office and heard Carter and Jake looking for Easton and saying she was in the bar." My cheeks heat when I remember. I'd just had him inside me, begged for *harder* into his ear. And then I heard her name. "I did not handle it with grace."

"Do I want to know what you did?" She grabs another washcloth from the vanity drawer, wets it, and hands it to me.

"Thanks," I whisper. I leave the first cloth on my neck and dab the second on my sweaty forehead. "I told him we're only good for getting each other off and stomped away."

She nods as if this was a perfectly reasonable response.

"You're the best, Teagan. And I'm not just saying that because you didn't hide while I puked."

She sighs. "About that . . . I'm not sure if you're aware, what with how quickly everything's been happening, but as your best friend, I'm woefully under-informed here. Would you like to back up to the part where you broke up with George, or go even further than that and explain your history with Easton?"

"George. I guess."

"Okay. So you told your mom you weren't going to see each other anymore, but what happened exactly? What was with the ring?"

"He *said* the ring was a family heirloom he was taking to the bank." I press the back of my hand to my mouth as another wave of nausea hits. "But it turns out he's a liar, so who really knows?"

She nods slowly. I'm so grateful that she's not freaking out on me about all this. "So George is a liar. This is a good reason for a breakup."

"That's just it. I didn't even know the truth when I broke it off with him. Everything's too complicated right now, and there are so many variables. I wasn't sure I wanted George to be one of them." I groan. I'm annoying myself. "And he was kind of pissing me off by implying any future that didn't involve an academic position would be an immature choice."

Teagan sinks to the floor and leans against the cabinet. "What a dick."

"That's not even all. There's also the part where Easton heard George talking to someone on the phone and calling her *Buttercup*, and then George was kissing me and called *me* that, which he's never done before."

"You think he was cheating?"

"It's worse than that," I whisper. "He was cheating, but not on me. *With* me."

She grunts. "Well, who gets to decide that if neither of you knew about the other?"

"No, Tea. *I'm the other woman.* George is married."

"Wow." She wraps her arms around her knees. "I think you're more mature than I am. I'd probably be in jail by now."

"I need to tell her he was sleeping with me." I draw in a breath. "It's the only way I can forgive myself for being involved with a married man."

"Don't be so hard on yourself. You had no way of knowing."

Intellectually, I know she's right. This isn't my fault. But when it comes to marriage and families, I've always believed everyone is culpable. "I hate him. We weren't even using condoms. If he's really sleeping around, God knows what he could've given me."

Her eyes go wide. "You weren't using condoms?"

"I'm on the pill, and he said he'd been tested. I thought the whole not-planning-to-fuck-anyone-else part was implied."

"Shay, you've noticed your symptoms lately, haven't you? The queasiness? Aversion to alcohol? The constant exhaustion?" She points to the toilet. "The *puking*."

I wipe my forehead one last time then my mouth. "It's the stress. It jacks with my stomach."

"But you weren't using condoms."

I wave a hand. "No worries, *Mom*, I'm on the pill."

"But—"

"And I haven't missed a period."

Her lips buzz with her dramatic exhale. "Thank God. Sorry, that's the first place my mind goes." Her smile falls away. "But you do know you should get tested for STIs, right? Just in case?"

I wipe my face again. "I know. I'll call my doctor." My purse vibrates from the middle of the bathroom floor, and I frown at it.

Teagan arches a brow. "Is that your phone or a malfunctioning sex toy?"

I roll my eyes but then lose my smile. "I'm afraid it's Easton. I said some pretty shitty things to him, and I'm not ready to be a mature adult and apologize."

"Given that he threatened you with kisses and was coerced into wall sex, maybe it might be a decent idea to cool off before you talk."

I nod. This is reasonable. But I'm staring at my purse, willing it to do that *buzz, buzz, buzz* thing that happens when someone sends one text after another. But it was just the one.

"Do you want me to look?" she asks. I nod again and watch with way too much anticipation as she pulls my phone from my purse, unlocks it, and opens my texts. Her forehead wrinkles as she reads.

"Is it from him?"

"Yeah." She turns the phone to me so I can read.

> *Easton: I never chose Scarlett over you. She would lose that matchup every time. I chose my daughter over myself.*

My breath whooshes out of me, and the nausea comes roaring back.

"Okay. So there's still a lot I don't know about you and Easton, it seems," Teagan says. She takes my hand and squeezes it. "You know you can tell me the truth, right? I won't judge you if . . ."

"If I was Easton's mistress? If he cheated on Scarlett with me?"

She grimaces, probably because of my word choice. "I understand better than most people that many situations are more complicated than they appear on the surface."

"Like with you and your ex?" I don't know everything about Teagan's past—I guess we both have secrets—but I do know she and Carter got together when he was pretending to be her boyfriend to protect her from an old flame.

"Something like that," she says.

I reread Easton's text. Then I read it again. I already knew he was choosing his child. How can I explain that the true motive behind his decision made it so much harder? I couldn't hate him. I couldn't be angry about his choice when it was the only choice to make. "Ten years ago, he and Scarlett broke up after dating for probably six months," I say. "And not long after that, my long-term boyfriend broke up with me while we were in Paris."

"Seriously?"

"Yeah, and I didn't want my family to worry, so I only told Easton. He surprised me by showing up, and we were together for the first time. We were going to give being a real couple a shot—despite the distance and how different our lives were. We both wanted to try. But then he found out Scarlett was pregnant, and all our plans just . . . They weren't relevant anymore." I swipe my thumb across the words of his text. "I knew he wasn't choosing Scarlett over me. I knew he was choosing Abi, which pretty much means I'm a terrible person."

"No," Teagan says. "Not at all."

"Tea, I wanted him to choose me over his child and then resented him for years when he didn't." The shame of it makes me feel ugly, and I bow my head to hide my face. "Who does that?"

She makes a face. "*Is* that what you wanted, though? For him to choose you over his child? You didn't ask him to walk away and shirk his responsibility."

"To Easton, asking him not to be with his daughter's mother would've been the same as asking him to walk away from his daughter. He didn't have a family growing up. His dad was shit. He called when it suited him but ignored East the rest of the time. He wanted better than that for his daughter."

"But Abi isn't even his kid, right? And didn't I read that he *knew* she wasn't his?"

I shake my head. "He didn't at first. I don't know exactly when he found out, but when he married Scarlett, he believed she was having his baby. I think by the time he found out the truth . . ." I shrug. "Easton's a good guy, and I'm sure he's a good dad. DNA wouldn't change his love and sense of responsibility toward his little girl."

"Don't beat yourself up. Easton made choices, and those choices affected you. You had every right to be upset."

I shrug. "Maybe. Maybe not. But I can't change how I felt then, only how I act now."

"Interesting."

I know that face. Teagan has *opinions* and she's not sharing. "Tell me what you're thinking."

She bites her bottom lip and shakes her head. "I don't know if you want to hear my thoughts."

"I do. Seriously. I'm stuck with mine all day." I tap my head. "I'm kind of making myself nuts and desperate to hear someone else's take on the situation."

She blows out a breath. "Okay. I'm thinking that you swore you want nothing to do with Easton, but as soon as he's back in town, you break up with your secret boyfriend. Meanwhile, Easton is everywhere—at brunch, at the bar, even taking a job at your college. And your reaction to a fight with him is to have some against-the-wall sex. Doesn't that tell you anything?"

"It tells me I'm a mess and that the sixteen-year-old pathetic crush part of my brain hasn't been completely overridden yet."

"Or . . . maybe you still have feelings for him."

I might always love him. "I didn't break up with George so I could date Easton."

"But do you *want* to?"

"*Date* him?" My laugh sounds a little crazed. "Nothing I want from Easton could ever be that simple, but I think for a minute tonight maybe I believed we could make it work. But then Scarlett showed up, and I flipped out."

Teagan stands and offers me her hand. "Another sleepover?"

"Is Carter working?"

"No, he's just meeting some friends at the bar. He'll be back soon."

I shake my head. I don't want my brother guessing at how messed up I am right now, not with his relationship with Easton and history of protectiveness. "I think I'll go home. It's been a long day, and I fly out to Oklahoma tomorrow for my Monday interview."

"Shit, I forgot about that. You're not going to cancel?"

"I don't know what I want to do yet, so it would be silly to shut down my options." I guess this means I won't see Easton until after he comes back with his daughter and moves in. I force a smile. "And anyway, time away is probably good. I need to figure out how to apologize to Easton for Hulking out on him tonight."

And I need to figure out how I feel. Because when I got that condom from the desk, I thought maybe I could try with him, and that confidence fizzled away when I heard Scarlett's name. I need to figure out what exactly I want from him, and right now I'm so scared to feel these old desires that I'm not sure I can trust my judgment.

Easton

I'm back at Jackson Brews, Scarlett is settled into a room at the Tiffany B&B, and Shay is God knows where. I'm loitering in the hopes that I'll see her. She never replied to my text, and my stomach sours every time I consider that she might be with Professor Douche.

Jake clears his throat and nods to the kitchen. "Can you help me in the back with something, East?"

"Sure." I put down my beer and follow him into the kitchen.

Grimacing, he leans against the counter and runs a hand through his sloppy mop of hair.

"What do you need?" I look around the kitchen for something heavy that needs lifting or boxes that need to be unpacked—anything to explain why he brought me back here. What I *don't* do is look at his office or even walk near it. I won't return to the scene of the crime with Jake watching.

Not that it felt like a crime. It never feels wrong when I'm with Shay.

Jake takes a deep breath, opens his mouth, then snaps it shut again. What the hell?

"What's up, Jake?"

"Listen." He winces, like just having to come up with words is causing him physical pain. "I've never had to do the protective-big-brother thing. I respect Shay and know she can make her own decisions."

I arch a brow. "Why do I get the feeling there's a big *but* waiting at the end of that sentence?"

"I heard you and Shay fighting in the office tonight." He rolls his neck. "Then I heard you . . . not fighting."

"Oh." While under a different set of circumstances, I'd be happy to own up to what I was doing with his little sister in there, I have a feeling Jake doesn't want to hear that Shay seduced me into a veritable hate-fuck against his office door.

"Oh? That's all you have? Seriously?" He mutters an impressive string of curses. "This is when you're supposed to tell me it wasn't what I think. *Dammit.*"

I scrub a hand over my face. "Jake . . ." But what do I say? *Yeah, I screwed your sister in your office, but only when she insisted? Don't worry, we used a condom from your desk?*

"First of all, regardless of how the rest of this conversation goes, let's just establish that's my *office*. I'm going to have to have my cleaning lady in to disinfect the place. The only sex that's permitted inside this kitchen is between me and my wife. Got it?"

I laugh, but it's forced. This conversation is painful. I've had testicular exams less awkward. "Sure."

He folds his arms. "Are you serious about her, or is she just some convenient lay to you?"

My brows shoot up. "You're kidding, right?"

"Of course I'm not kidding. You think I'm enjoying this conversation? This is *Shay*, Easton. She's . . ." He shakes his head. "Do you remember the guy she was with in high school and college?"

Steve. How could I forget the ass who had her so nervous he might call it quits if she didn't give him her virginity? The guy who stayed with her only to dump her *in Paris*? I bet I know more about Steve than the Jackson brothers do. "Yeah, I remember him."

"They dated for, like . . . three years?"

"Two and a half." I wonder if she ever told her family that I met her in Paris. Obviously she didn't tell them what we did there, but she could have admitted we spent time together. Fuck, after the bomb I dropped when she got back to the States, I bet she didn't talk about it at all. That would be like Shay. She'd rather pretend she wasn't hurt than risk my relationship with her family.

"And then there's this mystery guy she's been seeing from her work. The guy I assumed she was still seeing until she . . ." He pulls a face. He doesn't have to finish that sentence for me to understand what he means. He has the face of a brother who now has more knowledge of his baby sister's sex sounds than he ever wanted to have.

"They're seeing other people." The words taste bad. Shay isn't the kind to sleep around. While I wouldn't judge her if she were, that's not what she's about. She's a long-term kind of girl. I know she is. We've both carried this thing for each other for more than a decade. But as the guy who just had a quickie with her in the bar office, I'm not sure I'm the one to judge her choice to have casual sex with some asshole professor.

Jake shakes his head then turns to the counter and starts unloading plates into stacks at the end of the service line. "Did you know she always had a thing for you?"

I meet his eyes. "Always as in when?"

Jake shrugs. "*Always* always."

I'm pretty sure any *thing* she had went both ways. "Did she say something to you?"

"She never talks about that stuff. Not to me, at least. But she didn't have to tell me. I could see it. She followed you around every time you were over. After you moved away, every time Carter brought you up, she'd hang on every word."

I swallow the lump in my throat, faced again with how much I lost when I fucked up with her. But even with the horrible ache of that knowledge, I can't regret going down the path that gave me Abi. "I've had a thing for Shay for a long time too." It's ridiculous that I've never admitted that to anyone other than Shay herself. Carter only knew I couldn't keep my eyes off his sister. He didn't understand that there was more to it than a gut-level physical attraction.

"Is that what this is?" Jake asks. "This is all about you having *feelings* for my sister?"

I rock back on my heels. "*Strong* feelings." Those words are too weak, so I try again. "I like Shay. A lot."

He looks me up and down. "Good. Because you're a pretty big dude, and I don't know if I'd survive if I tried to kick your ass, but I'd have to try if you were using my baby sister for sex."

Me using *her* for sex? *I think you might have that backward, Jake.* "I want something real with her. A relationship. I've wanted that for years, and now the time is finally right, but it might be too late. I'm doing everything I can to convince her to give me a chance."

Jake nods. "Okay. But from here on out, please exclude fucking in *my office* from your list of *everything you can.*" He shudders. "I can't unhear that."

"Got it."

"I trust you not to hurt her," he says, which is a bigger kick in the nuts than he realizes. "Now, excuse me. I need to find a neurologist to cut the memories of tonight from my brain."

I baked. I don't remember the last time I let myself make anything with sugar and flour—high school? Maybe middle school?

I used to bake with Mom all the time. I loved it, loved the feel of sweet, buttery treats melting on my tongue, fresh out of the oven. And my love for it showed around my stomach and hips.

But last night when I couldn't sleep, I got out of bed and made chocolate chip cookies for Easton and his daughter. Because nothing says "sorry about the hate-fuck" like a plate of baked goods.

The trip to Oklahoma was a bust. I knew from the moment they picked me up from the airport that the job wasn't a good fit for me. I don't have a good explanation—just that it didn't feel right. They said they'd contact me with their decision in May, but I already know I won't leave my family for that position. If George wants to judge me for that, so be it.

I park my car by Easton's Lakeview Drive home and grab the tray of cookies from the passenger seat with shaking hands. I feel a little bit like some sweet suburban housewife welcoming the new family to the neighborhood. I've rehearsed my speech in my head a dozen times. *"I know I wasn't very welcoming when you were in town, and I'm sorry. If you're living in Jackson Harbor, you'll be part of my life, and I want us to be friends."*

"Friends" might be a stretch. I don't think I can be *friends* with Easton Connor. It might physically hurt too much. But my behavior during his last visit left a bad feeling in my stomach. I'm not proud of myself.

Taking a deep breath, I walk up his front steps and knock on the door.

I braced myself for Easton's anger or his disarming charm. I braced myself to maybe see him shirtless or in a business suit.

I did not brace myself for the bright-eyed twenty-something beauty who answers the door.

"Can I help you?" she asks. She's in a T-shirt that's cut off just above her navel and a pair of fitted shorts that cover less than the panties I'm currently wearing beneath my jeans. Her hair is in a high ponytail, her eyes are bright, and her smile is . . . perfect.

I am such an idiot.

I stumble back a step. "I think . . . Sorry, I . . . Wrong house." I'm such a liar. This is definitely the right house. Not only did I confirm the address with Ellie before I came, but everyone in this town knows what house belongs to future NFL Hall of Famer Easton Connor.

I turn on my heel and rush down the steps, still carrying the goddamn tray of cookies. I'm enough of a mess that I might eat these things if I weren't in some sort of chronic state of vague illness lately. This stress is gonna be the death of me if even cookies don't sound good.

I run smack into a bare-chested Easton, and the cookies fly everywhere. Good thing I wasn't counting on a binge. "Shit. Sorry. Fuck." *Busted.*

"Shayleigh." He says my name so softly. Not like a curse—which I'd deserve after the way I treated him the last time I saw him—but like a song.

I drop to my hands and knees, picking up the cookies to save myself from having to look him in the eye.

"What are you doing here?"

"I was just . . . I just . . ."

He sinks down with me. When I plop a pile of pieces onto the plate, he grabs my hand. "Were you bringing those to me?"

"Yeah." I take a breath. "They were for you and Abi."

He arches a brow, waiting, and I will myself to say the words. *"I'm sorry I treated you like my own personal sex toy. I'm sorry I pretended there's never been anything between us but sex. I'm sorry I freaked out when your wife showed up."*

They don't come. Instead, my gaze is fixed on his bare chest and the sweat rolling between his pecs and over his washboard stomach. Professional sports do amazing things to a man's body, and as I'm acquainted with every inch of this one, I can attest that the benefits go far beyond the aesthetic.

"Shay, my eyes are up here." Scowling, I lift my gaze to meet his. He laughs. "Want to see the house?"

"Um, your . . . girlfriend is there." I doubt she's a *girlfriend* per se, but referring to her as his latest screw seems rude.

"My who now?"

God, I'm such an idiot. After the way I treated him, he certainly shouldn't be waiting around for me, but she doesn't even look familiar. Is she from around here? Or did he bring her from L.A.? "Blonde, perky boobs." I hold up a pinkie. "About this big."

"Are you talking about *Tori*?"

I return to my cookie retrieval. "Don't know. Didn't get her name. She just answered your door."

"The blonde who answered my door would be Tori, my *nanny*," he says with a freight-ton of emphasis on the last word. He's not just saying she's his nanny; he's saying I'm freaking mental for assuming something else. I know it to be true, so I'm not going to argue.

"Oh." I shrug. "Your nanny, then. My mistake, but I'm sure people make it all the time."

"Since she's barely twenty years old. I would hope not."

My eyes flick up to meet his. "I was twenty when we were in Paris."

He rocks back on his heels with a deep breath, then pushes himself to standing. Because I'm a bitch. Obviously. *Shit.*

Guilt washes over me. I abandon the cookies and stand. "I ruin everything. I was coming to apologize."

He arches a brow. "Really. And what were you going to apologize for?"

He's going to make me say it. Sonofabitch. "The *sex*." I grind out the word.

His lips twitch again, and then he stops fighting it and full-on smiles. "I didn't need an apology for the sex." He rakes his gaze over me and back up. "I *liked* the sex, Shay. You're right. We are good together. I didn't take issue with the sex. I took issue with the part where you made assumptions and refused to talk to me."

I swallow. And here I am, making more assumptions. "Fair enough."

He nods toward the house. "Want to come inside? I could make you some coffee and . . ." He rubs the back of his neck, and the movement does such good things for his pecs and biceps. Is he intentionally trying to use his body against me? He immediately knocks down that theory. "Abi's home. You could meet her. If . . . if you wanted."

There's something about seeing him like this that gets to me. He's not exactly insecure but more guarded and hopeful, and I realize I'm nodding.

He beams and takes the tray of broken cookies before striding past me and up the steps to his house. I follow, half convinced I'm making a terrible mistake.

I'm a few steps inside the door when the *nanny*—I am an *idiot*—greets me a second time. "Hi again!" She looks from me to Easton and back to me again. "You had the right house after all."

I hear Easton's quiet chuckle. "She's not been here before, Tori." He takes the tray of broken cookies from me and hands it to Tori. "We had a cookie accident outside, but no one was hurt. Can you take care of that for me? I'm just gonna show Shay around."

"Okay! Abi's had breakfast and now she's upstairs organizing her makeup in her bathroom."

Easton grins. "Awesome."

He grabs my hand, and the contact sends such a shock of warmth through me that I simultaneously want to yank my hand away and curl into him. My body hasn't gotten the memo that last Saturday was a blip and Easton and I aren't happening again.

It's so scary to have such a strong reaction to him. If I'd been asked six months ago, I'd have said I was over him, or as over him as I'd ever be. I think you call that "willfully ignorant." It's just too hard to get over Easton. Maybe I'm incapable on a cellular level.

"I promise I'll get you that coffee in a minute," he says, tugging me toward the stairs. "I want you to meet Abi first."

The pride on his face makes my ovaries explode, and I know in that moment that any bitterness or resentment I thought I felt toward his life in L.A. doesn't apply to his daughter. I know it doesn't matter that Scarlett lied. It doesn't matter that Abi shares none of his DNA, because she is his. In every way that counts, she's his daughter.

I follow him up the polished wood stairs. I love how warm this house feels. It's not a marble showplace where everything is intended to dazzle and flaunt his wealth. It's his *home*—where his daughter will run and play and hang out with her friends. This is where she'll grow up and know that no matter what drama happens in the world beyond, she's always safe and loved when she's inside these walls. This will be his safe place too. The start of his new life.

At the top of the stairs, he turns to the right and knocks twice on the wooden door before pushing it open. "Abi?"

"I'm in my bathroom," she calls.

He gestures into the room, and I follow him inside. His

daughter's space is decked out with white furniture and a mermaid bedspread topped off with sequin pillows. There's still a pile of boxes stacked against the wall and a few others sitting open in random spots on the floor, but the room already hints at the personality of its new occupant. Mermaids, sequins, teal and turquoise everything. The two tall, coordinating bookshelves are empty, but I smile at them. Looks like Easton has a reader on his hands.

I follow him into the attached bathroom and spot Abi's long red ponytail. She's sitting at the small white vanity with an oval mirror and a high-end spa's worth of cosmetics and polishes in front of her.

"I'm organizing my nail polish by color," she says. "That way I won't buy more of a shade before the last one is gone."

Easton shakes his head, a crooked smile on his face as he watches his daughter. "Only you would have so many nail polishes that you need to organize them like that. Are you going to do the same with your lip glosses?"

"Obviously." She grins as she positions a bottle of polish carefully into a drawer. "It's not my fault that Mommy likes to buy me pretty stuff."

"As long as it's only for play, it's fine with me. But no makeup at school."

She rolls her eyes. "Mom lets me wear it whenever I want."

He shrugs, unfazed by this tiny bit of defiance. "Mom has her rules, and I have mine."

"Yeah, yeah." She finally lifts her head, and her smile falls away when she spots me.

"I wanted you to meet my friend Shay," her dad says, pointing the same warm smile at me he gave her.

"Hi," I say.

"I've heard about you," she says.

That is unexpected. "You have?"

"Yeah. You're daddy's friend. The girl who is prettiest and smartest and who writes books."

My breath catches, and I look at Easton, who just shrugs and gives me a lopsided grin.

She sighs. "I tried to write one when I was seven, but I didn't finish. Maybe I'll finish a book when I'm ten."

"You did more than most people do just by starting," I say. To be fair, I feel a little hypocritical giving advice on this subject. I'm good at writing books, then tucking them away to never be seen again. If I wanted to get serious about being a novelist, I'd need to get good at revisiting those drafts, facing their weaknesses and reworking them until they were better. And then I'd have to be willing to let someone else judge them and find them lacking or not. Instead, I'm sitting on an opportunity to query a dream agent and writing something new instead of fixing the old stuff. "I bet you could if you decided you wanted to. You just have to put in the work."

"That's what Daddy says too. But I'm not in a rush."

"You don't need to be. You can just enjoy being a kid right now."

"Daddy says that too." She stands, and I realize just how little she is. I wonder if that's genetic or from being sick. A pang spears through my chest imagining how it must have been for Easton when she was in the hospital.

Maybe it's just because she reminds me of Lilly, but I love her already.

"Shay hasn't seen the house," Easton says. "I thought maybe you'd like to give the tour."

Her eyes go wide. "I would love to!"

After the best tour I can imagine—complete with "this is where I can do my tumbling" and "this is the dining room, but all we ever used our old dining room table for was puzzles, so I don't think this will be any different"—Abi retreated to her room to finish organizing, and Easton led me back to the kitchen and poured me a cup of the coffee he promised.

"Thank you," I say as he pulls a carton of half and half from the fridge. I doctor my coffee and watch him take a big sip of his. "Abi is really sweet."

His expression softens. "She's pretty great, and all things considered, I think she's taking the move well. We were both ready for a change."

I glance toward the stairs. "I know you're still settling in, but why isn't she in school?"

"When the news broke about her . . . biological father . . ." He takes a breath, as if the words hurt, but then he shakes it away. "The kids at school were brutal, and we ended up pulling her and homeschooling. She'll continue homeschooling through the end of this academic year, but in the meantime, I'm visiting Jackson Harbor schools to figure out my options. I'm happy homeschooling is an option, but I don't think it's the best long-term choice for Abi."

"You'll find something." I give him what I hope is an encouraging smile. "Who knows? Maybe you'll send her to the same public schools we went to."

He smiles at this and stares into his coffee. I wonder if he's remembering those days. Before college. Before the NFL. When everything was simpler in his life and mine. "I owe you a huge apology, Shay," he says, lifting his eyes to meet mine.

I put my coffee down. Right, the whole reason I came over. "I'm pretty sure you have that backward."

"I had no right to interfere in your relationship with George. I know it doesn't excuse anything, but I couldn't stand the idea of you being with someone who doesn't treat you right. For what it's worth, I believed I was doing the right thing."

"I shouldn't have lost my temper that day outside the library. You had every right to be concerned."

"I deserved everything you said to me. I never meant to make you feel like I don't think you're capable of making decisions for yourself." He draws in a deep breath and hesitates for so long I get the impression that the next part is hard for him. "I have to accept that there's nothing about you being with someone else that will ever sit right with me, but that doesn't mean I have the right to judge your relationship. You know yourself. You know what's right for you."

I don't know why I told him George and I were seeing other people. I didn't want him knowing the truth, but I could've just said we'd broken up. I think, at least in part, I was trying to keep some distance between us, but I'm pretty sure that ship sailed the minute I unbuttoned his pants in Jake's office. "George and I aren't together."

He straightens. "You're not? Since when?"

"Since before you and I . . ." I make a circular motion with my hand. "And you were right. About George. Sort of, at least."

"What does that mean?"

I blow out a breath. "He wasn't cheating on me with someone else. He was cheating on someone else with me." My eyes burn, and anger pulses through me at the reminder. *That lying sonofabitch.* "He's married."

Easton blinks. "You're kidding."

"I wish I were." My eyes prick with tears. I'm not heartbroken, but my pride is so battered it has a limp. "After we broke up, I decided I wanted to find out who Buttercup was, and . . ." I shrug helplessly. "I guess I know now."

"What a fucking asshole. Jesus, Shay, I'm so sorry." His eyes are full of anger, but he shakes his head like he's trying to keep his emotions in check. "If it helps, I take no joy in being right about this."

The sincerity in his voice makes the tears spill over. "I feel like a fool."

He puts down his coffee, cups my face in both of his hands, and wipes away my tears. "It kills me to see you cry. To know he had your heart to break. He didn't deserve you."

"I wasn't in love with him. I'm embarrassed and my life is a little confusing right now, but my heart isn't broken." *Not like it was when you walked away from me.* "You know what hurts the most?"

He shakes his head. "What?"

"He made me the other woman. I never got the choice, but that's what I was, and now I need to tell his wife the truth. She

262

deserves to know."

Something flashes across his face. *Pain. Regret.* I know he's thinking of the night of Dad's funeral. I haven't stopped thinking about that night since I followed George home. I felt like Easton cracked my entire foundation with what he said that night.

"I know what you're thinking," he says. "But it's not the same. Your situation is different."

"His wife still deserves to know."

"Of course," he says. "You do what you think is best."

I step away from his touch and pull in a long breath. "I'm sorry I lied to you about George and I seeing other people. I was too much of a coward to admit the truth."

He flashes me that crooked smile and takes a step closer. "Does that mean you'll give me a chance?"

If only it were that simple. I bite my bottom lip and study his beautiful face—the blue-green eyes, the hard lines of his jaw, the faint stubble he hasn't shaved away today. I have no business pursuing a relationship with anyone until I figure out what's next for me, whether that's in Jackson Harbor or somewhere else entirely. "I think we should only be allowed to touch when we're in Paris. I tend to lose my mind when we do it stateside."

Hurt flashes in his eyes. "Shayleigh, what happened in Chicago—"

I put my fingers to his mouth before he can say more. "Don't say it was a mistake."

Gently, he takes my hand from his mouth and squeezes my fingers in his. "The only mistake I've ever made with you was not trying harder to choose you and my daughter both."

I melt. "You're not making this no-touching thing easy, East."

"I have no intentions of making it easy for you."

"I just broke up with a married man, I'm about to defend my dissertation, and I have to decide where I want to live next year—assuming I even *get* a job. You and me? We can't happen right now. I'll be your friend, though."

He searches my face, and the tenderness in his eyes makes me want to yank him to my side of the line I just drew in the sand. "I'll take it."

Part IX.

Before

September 22nd, seven years ago

"**H**ow's Dad today?" I ask in a whisper, quietly shutting the door behind me.

Mom bows her head. It's brief, but the quick movement speaks volumes. She's steeling herself to share bad news. "He wants to talk to you."

I put my purse on the foyer table. "He's awake?"

"Yes. Go on in."

But I don't want to. I already know. I can hear it in her voice.

The grief isn't new. We've all been grieving on and off for four years as we rode this roller-coaster cancer buckled us into without our permission. But what I hear today is different. A resignation. A . . . lack of hope.

My throat clogs with a sob and my eyes burn, but I lift my chin, swallow back my tears, and pull back my shoulders. I can't fix this, but I can be strong for them both. It's the only thing I have to offer.

Death has a smell, the scent of decay and rot, and it's shoved up my nose when I step into my parents' bedroom. Dad's hospital bed is raised so he's sitting up, and his frail hands are wrapped around a cup of water.

"Hi, Daddy."

His hands shake as he sets the water on the bedside table. "Shayleigh." Even his voice is weak. This disease has stolen everything from him—his career, his strength, his pride. But not his family. Fuck cancer. Never us. "Come here."

I'm not sure how my legs get me from the doorway to the chair beside the bed. With every step, I think they might collapse. But I make it, each step steadier than I feel, and lower myself into the chair, taking his hand. "Hard night?" I ask. It's a space-filler question. There's no point to it when every night for months has been terrible. And every day.

I ask it for myself. Because I need a few more breaths in a world where no one has confirmed what I've suspected for weeks now—that there's no fighting this, that treatments will only make him sicker, and that it's time to let go.

"Not terrible," he says.

I laugh for his benefit. "You liar."

He wraps his fingers around my hand. My dad used to be so strong. These hands picked me up hundreds of times. They gripped my knees when he carried me around on his shoulders, showed me how to hold a baseball bat, checked my forehead for fever, and turned the pages of my favorite bedtime stories. "We've talked to the doctors."

I nod. Because I know. Because I'm hoping he won't make me hear the words if I can just show him that I get it. I know what comes next, and my chest aches until it's an effort to breathe through it.

"I want you to know that I would suffer for years if it meant I'd win this fight. I'd do it for you kids. If I had any chance of winning, I'd do it just so I could come to your wedding and walk you down the aisle. I'd do it just so I could watch you become a mom."

Tears rolls down my cheeks. I try to be unshakable, to be strong for him, but I can't. "I don't want you to hurt," I whisper. "Don't worry about me."

He strokes the back of my hand with his thumb. "I do worry about you. My only girl. My sunshine. You've always carried so much for your brothers—always been there to help them navigate the emotionally muddy waters when they struggled. You're like your mom like that. A light in the darkness."

My chest shakes, and I draw in one ragged breath, then another. A tear plops onto the back of my hand, and Dad rubs it away with a trembling thumb.

"I hope you know how proud I am of you."

"I do. I know."

"I know you have more to worry about than boys and falling in love, but since I'm not going to be here, I want you to promise me you'll protect your heart. Don't give it to anyone who will be careless with it. Don't settle for anyone who doesn't make your soul sing."

"Dad . . ." I shake my head. This isn't fair, but we've had years we didn't think we'd get, and I know it's time. "I love you."

He pats the back of my hand. "I love you too, sweet girl. To the moon and back."

Another sob rips from my chest, and I sink to my knees beside his bed, letting my daddy stroke my hair with those frail hands that used to be so strong. Letting him comfort me through my tears one last time.

Easton

"Can't you call him or something? Tell him who I am and that I want to see him?"

"Ma'am, no one is allowed back to the players' rooms without prior authorization."

I thought I recognized that voice when I got off the elevator, but I can hardly believe my eyes when I see Shayleigh Jackson arguing with security in my hotel.

"Please? We're friends. He'll want to see me."

"If you're friends, you should call him."

"She's with me, Troy." I rush forward before Shay can do something reckless like try to push by him. I can't see her face, but I can hear the desperation in her voice, and I wouldn't put it past her.

Shay spins around and barrels into me, throwing her arms

around my waist. I wrap her up against me and close my eyes as I memorize the feeling. It's been so long and . . . God, when did she get so small? She feels tiny in my arms.

Troy arches a brow in question, and I nod, reassuring him that she's welcome here.

I smooth back her hair and tilt her face up to meet mine. The tears rolling down her cheeks slice into me and hurt nearly as much as the news Carter delivered yesterday. "Let's go somewhere we can talk in private."

"I'm sorry," she says. "I couldn't fall apart on my family. I couldn't do that to them."

I kiss the top of her head. "You can fall apart on me. Come on." I thread my fingers through hers and lead her to my room.

"You know? About Dad starting hospice?"

The door shuts behind me with an ominous *thunk*. Shay turns, folding her arms and searching my face as I nod. I haven't been home in years, but tomorrow, when the Demons head back to L.A. on the team plane, I'm going to rent a car and drive up to Jackson Harbor. I have to see Frank one last time. "Carter called. He's pretty torn up."

"Me too."

"Come here." She doesn't move, doesn't drop her arms or rush toward me and bury her face in my chest like she did in the hall.

It's as if now that we're here, now that we're alone, she's second-guessing her choice to come to me, and I can't have that. I close the distance between us and pull her into my arms. Her arms are still folded against her chest, but I stroke her hair, her back. "I'm so sorry," I say. "It's not fair."

And I am. So sorry. Frank Jackson's the closest thing I ever had to a father—which is a sad state of affairs, considering the man who provided half my DNA is still alive.

I feel the moment Shay surrenders to the need to be close to me. She drops her arms and wraps them around me. She stops reinforcing that dam inside her and lets it break. Her tears rack her small frame and she trembles in my arms, shakes and clings to me like I'm the only thing keeping this grief from pulling her under.

I don't know how long we stand there—just inside my hotel room, my arms wrapped around her, her tears soaking my shirt—but when she pulls away, it's with a deep breath and a lift of her chin that tells me she's determined to be strong.

I search her face—those deep chocolate eyes I've dreamed of so many nights and the sweet pink lips that are pouty without trying. She searches mine in return, and I wonder if she's missed me as much as I've missed her.

"I should probably go. Your wife . . ."

I cock my head to the side, waiting for her to finish that sentence. When she doesn't, I say, "Scarlett might not like you being here, but since she's currently living with Grant Holland, she doesn't have much room to talk."

Shay grimaces and looks away.

"You already knew."

She shrugs. "I try not to pay attention to celebrity gossip. I don't believe most of what they say."

And rightly so. I've had some un-fucking-believable shit written about me since entering the league. But the recent round of media attention regarding Scarlett is at least partially true.

Partially because there's all sorts of speculation about our recent separation, and most of it involves me being cold, unfaithful, an ass, or all of the above. Nobody's come close to the truth—that I married her because she was pregnant with my daughter and we were never really in love. Or that it gets lonely being married to someone who doesn't love you—a feeling I'm as familiar with as Scarlett is.

"We're separated." I shrug as if it's nothing. As if I didn't spend years sacrificing everything to try to give my daughter the family I wanted for her, only to see it fall apart anyway.

"I'm sorry, Easton." She swallows. "How's your daughter? Abigail, right?"

I nod. "She's amazing. Talks up a storm, sings all the time. But she's going through this fussy phase where she never wants to eat, and I think she's losing weight." I shake my head. Abi has a doctor's appointment on Tuesday. "I'm sure everything's okay. She's stubborn, and when she doesn't want to eat, she doesn't want to eat, but the protective father in me needs a doctor to tell me that."

"That makes sense." She shifts from one foot to the other. "I bet you're an amazing dad."

"I try. Most of it I've just had to figure out as I go."

"As a girl who was raised by an amazing dad, I have to say it's *everything*." More tears spill down her cheeks, and I'm being torn apart.

I don't know when I cupped her face in my hand, but I watch my thumb clear away a streak of tears. *She came to me.* "I'm glad you're here." My chest feels too tight. Fuck, I've missed her so much. "I'm so sorry about how I handled the pregnancy. I was trying to help Scarlett stay sober and generally freaking out about becoming a father. And—"

She presses a thumb to my lips. "Not tonight, okay? I don't want to talk about that tonight."

Right. She has enough to process.

I nod, but she doesn't move her thumb. Instead, she presses down until the tip is in my mouth, almost between my teeth. I touch it with my tongue, and her eyes darken. I want more than this tiny taste, more than I can have. I don't know how long we stand like that—her thumb between my teeth, her face in my hands, our bodies so close that I can smell her lemon-and-lavender soap.

I'm not sure I take a single breath until she steps back and my hands drop helplessly to my sides. She drags her bottom lip between her teeth and holds my gaze as she unbuttons her shirt and lets it drop from her shoulders, and my situation with the oxygen shortage doesn't improve a bit.

My mouth goes dry at the sight of her smooth ivory skin, her breasts cupped in the simple white cotton of her bra. I follow her hands, watching as they unbutton her jeans and push them down her hips.

I've fucked up so many times where Shay is concerned, and tonight she came to me upset, grieving. Maybe the right thing to do is to tell her to keep her clothes on. Maybe letting her strip makes my sins cross over into unforgiveable. But I'm willing to accept every label, every hit to my character and blow to my ego if it means I get to touch her.

She steps out of her jeans, and I can't take my eyes off her. I love that her bra is simple, nearly virginal, love that her panties aren't a match but a bright pink. They're cut to sit high on her hips and barely cover her ass. I love how easy it is—how uncalculated. She didn't put on her sexiest panty set and come here to seduce me. She's just wearing whatever she's wearing. But who am I kidding? She could be wearing fucking pantaloons and a chastity belt under her clothes, and I'm sure I'd still be hard as a rock watching her strip for me.

I can't help but notice the changes, though. I memorized her with eyes, hands, and mouth in Paris, and I know every inch of her. She's lost weight. Too much. I want to ask if she's okay, if she's been sick—Carter hasn't said anything, but damn, she's so frail—but I don't. She's always been so self-conscious about her appearance, and I don't want her thinking she's not beautiful when she takes my breath at any size.

"Say something," she whispers, and I realize I've just been staring, trying to catalogue every change while her hands shake at her sides.

"You're beautiful." Is there really anything else to say? But the more honest part of my brain whispers that there's so much more. *I want you. I need you. I've fucking missed you.*

She looks down and swallows. "Better, huh?"

My stomach knots. I hate that she never saw herself the way I saw her. "You've always been beautiful. I've told you that before."

Her lips part as she blows out a breath. "I'll never look like your Scarlett Lashenta."

The words are a kick in the nuts. They're a reminder that my decisions shackled this girl—this *woman*—with insecurities. "I'm glad for that." My wife's name floats in the room, a reminder that I'm entangled in a different world than Shay, a more vicious one, a reminder that we can't be seen together without that world taking a swing at her. "Shay . . ."

She gives a small, sad smile and turns her back to me, striding toward the bed.

I close my eyes and count my breaths. *In. Out. In. Out.* I know why she's here now—I understand exactly what she wants from me. And I want it too—holy shit, do I want it. I want to give her what she came here for tonight, provide the comfort I know she needs. More than that, I want *her*. But my life is a fucking mess, and I can't drag her into that. Scarlett may have moved out, but our lives are still entwined. I have to work out my shit so I can give Shay more than another night of pleasure.

When I finally lock on to my resolve, I follow her into the room and find her crouched in front of the minibar, digging through it. The sight of Shay in her underwear, frowning at a bottle of tequila, makes me grin.

She holds it up. "Not much here, but do you mind?"

"Help yourself."

She unscrews the lid and takes a sip, grimacing. "Shit."

When she offers it to me, I shake my head. I don't drink much during the season, but even if I did, I don't trust myself to drink tonight. I already only have a tenuous hold on my self-control, and even a drop of alcohol might obliterate that.

She shrugs. "Suit yourself." She takes another sip as she scans the room. "I really expected you to be in a fancy suite or something. This is . . . almost a normal-person hotel room."

I chuckle and sink into a chair on the opposite side of the minibar, crossing my feet at the ankles as I sit back. "When I was a rookie, I had to have a roommate. I definitely prefer this."

She lifts the mini bottle. "Here's to being a big shot and having your own room." She drains the rest of the tequila and wanders to the window, pulling the curtain aside to peer out at the view. I can't stop looking at her—at her perfect nipples peaked against the thin white cotton of her bra, her bare legs, her toenails painted a dark purple. I wouldn't have imagined she could be more beautiful. If she'd asked, I would've told her not to lose the weight, that she was perfect as she was. But now? She stands taller, her chin higher. She wanders around my room nearly nude with a self-confidence that was perhaps the only thing she was missing before. It's the confidence that makes her shine, gives her thinner, stronger self an edge on the old Shay. I wonder if she knows that. Or if she thinks that when she walks through a room and men stare at her from every direction, it's because her stomach's flatter and her hips are narrower.

Slowly, she saunters toward me, her eyes locked with mine. Every step closer steals oxygen from my lungs. I can hardly catch my breath, and I know the only relief will be in touching her. She stops in front of me and swings a foot over my extended legs until she's straddling my thighs. It would be so easy to bend and press my mouth against her stomach, cup my hand over those pink panties. I could grip her hips and hold her in place while I slide off the chair to the floor between her legs and bury my face in her pussy. I'm dying to taste her again. I want to fill my head with the sounds she makes and the smell of her. Fuck, I want to make her come and claim her as mine in the most primitive way.

"I keep waiting for you to kick me out," she whispers. Swallowing, she props a knee on either side of my hips and lowers herself onto my lap. The little bottle of tequila is still in one hand, and she wraps the other behind my neck.

"You can stay as long as you want." When she shifts her hips forward, she presses against the hard length of my cock through my jeans, and my breath rushes out of me.

"You're killing my newfound ego. You know that, right?"

I arch a brow, curling my fingers into the arms of the chair. "How so?"

"I'm here thinking I'm all cute now, thinking that if I strip, you'll want to touch me again. You don't seem to mind that I'm almost naked, and yet . . ." She tosses the empty bottle onto the bed before cocking her head to the side and studying me. "I'm on your lap like this, and you're not putting even a finger on me." Something like regret flashes in her eyes. "Do you want me to leave?" The question is asked in a whisper so quiet it's almost like she wants to hide from the possibility that I might.

I release the arms of the chair and place my hands gently on her waist. "Not unless you want to." She presses into my erection, and my eyes float closed. *Fuck*. "But Shay, we shouldn't have sex tonight."

She stills. "Shouldn't? Or you don't want to?"

I try to laugh, but it catches in my throat and comes out like a grunt. "Trust me, there's not much I want more right now." I tighten my grip on her waist. "But I've fucked up with you before, and I don't want to do it again. Jesus, you haven't even talked to me in *years*, and now you're on my lap."

She bites her lip. "I've always been an all-or-nothing girl. You know that."

"I do." I trace the soft lace waistband of her panties with my thumb, my brain warring with my baser instincts. "Let me get through this mess with Scarlett. Let me . . . fix my life. *Then* I can give you what you deserve."

She threads her fingers through my hair and tugs lightly. "I'm sorry I couldn't talk to you after Paris." She looks away. "I am sorry about that."

"Hey." I take her chin in my hand and turn her face back to mine. "I'm the one who's sorry. You don't owe me an apology."

She reaches for the hem of my shirt and tugs until it's off. She traces invisible paths down my chest with her fingertips, circling the cluster of bruises over my ribs. "What's this from?"

"Nasty hit."

"Don't you wear pads?"

I laugh. "Yeah, but even pads can't save you when a two-hundred-sixty-pound lineman pummels you."

She scoots off my lap and bends, placing the smallest, gentlest kiss to the nasty purple-and-red skin. Pleasure bolts down my spine like her mouth's on my cock and not my ribcage.

When she looks up at me, her eyes are full of lust and desperation. And maybe grief. "I'm so scared and lonely," she whispers. "All I want is to lie with you and lose myself for a few hours. The rest can come later."

I slide a hand into her hair and lead her mouth to mine. My muscles tense then relax at the contact. She tastes like tequila and smells like lemon and lavender, and I've missed her so much. "You're an all-or-nothing girl, and you deserve the *all*."

She draws in a breath right against my mouth. "I don't want another night of nothing."

I wrap my arms around her, stand, and carry her to the bed. I don't know when I'll be able to give her everything she deserves, but tonight, I can give her this.

Part X.

Now

Easton

I spent the beginning of the week unpacking and trying to make the house feel a little more like home, but on Wednesday, I had to drive to Grand Rapids to go to a few meetings. I'm not officially starting until this summer, but I'm being kept in the loop regarding recruitment, and I like to be at all the coaching and athlete meetings.

I head into the house from the garage and drop my keys in the mudroom. I follow the smell of homemade spaghetti sauce and find Tori in the kitchen, stirring a pot on the stove. Abi's nowhere to be seen.

"How was my girl's day?"

"It was okay. She's upstairs now," Tori says. "I think she might be a little homesick tonight."

"Hence the sauce?" I motion to the makings of my daughter's

favorite meal.

She shrugs. "Maybe it will help."

This was bound to happen sooner or later, but my chest aches nevertheless. Even though I know it'll be for the best in the long run, I hate that this transition is going to be tough for Abi on any level. "Thanks, Tori."

I head to the twisting stairwell at the front of the house. When I was a kid, I used to drive by the big houses that line Jackson Harbor's Lakeshore Drive and dream of what it must be like to own a place like this, to have a big enough family to fill it. One out of two isn't bad, and even if it's only me and Abi forever, I can be okay with that.

I find my daughter in her room, sprawled on her bed looking at pictures of her friends on her iPad. "Hey, squirt. How's it going?"

Frowning at me, she sits up and curls against the headboard. "I don't have any friends here."

"Not yet." I try to keep my voice upbeat, but the tears in her eyes slay me. "But you will with time."

"How do you know? What if I never make any friends? What if no one here likes me?"

"You met Lilly a couple of days ago, and she likes you."

She shrugs. "I guess."

I look at my watch. It's a school night, but it's only five. "Maybe Lilly could come over for dinner, then you two could play a little after. Would you like me to ask?"

She nods eagerly, so I give her my best reassuring smile and pull out my phone to text Ethan. He replies quickly.

Ethan: Shay is taking Lilly to gymnastics at 6. You should take Abi. All the kids get a trial class before you have to sign a contract.

I turn the phone so my daughter can read it, and she smiles for the first time since I walked into her room. "Can we *please*?"

Spend our night with Shay? *Twist my arm.*

The girls giggle excitedly as they put their flip-flops back on after practice.

"What did you think, Abi?" I ask my daughter. "Did you like it?"

"I *loved* it!" She's practically vibrating with excitement as she grabs Lilly's hand. "I want to be in Lilly's class, though."

"I'll talk to the girls at the desk and see what I can do."

"It's the intro-level class," Shay says. "Since she's just getting started, this would be a good spot for her, and we could carpool."

"Carpool?"

"Well, I don't take Lilly every week, but she likes me to watch her, so I do a lot of the time. When I'm the one driving, I wouldn't mind swinging by to get Abi."

I arch a brow. "You think I'm going to miss out on spending an hour every week with my new friend?" I shake my head. "No, we're friends now, and I'm going to enjoy this hour."

Shay's cheeks turn pink.

"Is Abi's dad your boyfriend, Aunt Shay?" Lilly asks.

LEXI RYAN

Abi spins around and stares at me. "Is she?" She doesn't sound upset about the possibility, which is a relief, to be honest.

"Not yet," I say, winking at Shay. Her cheeks bloom to a darker shade of pink. "Right now we're just friends, but you never know what surprises life has in store."

Shay licks her lips. "We're good friends. We don't need to be more." I think it's even obvious to the eight- and nine-year-old girls watching us that Shay is trying to convince herself.

"Would you be okay with me inviting Lilly out for ice cream?" I ask.

Shay nods. "I think that would be fine."

"What do you think, girls? Ice cream?"

The girls' cheers fill the corridor, and half a dozen parents turn disapproving frowns toward us. I pull my keys from my pocket. "Come on. We'll all ride together, and I'll bring Lilly and Shay back to get their car after. It's my treat."

The girls both want banana splits, which Shay and I agree is way too much ice cream and sugar. The girls argue that's unfair, since it's "practically half fruit." We compromise when they agree that they can share one.

I get a hot fudge sundae, and Shay has a small cone of vanilla ice cream. I know she didn't choose it to sexually frustrate me, so I try not to stare, but I can't deny that seeing her tongue and mouth at work puts serious ideas in my head. I'm hopeless.

The ice cream place has a tiny playground in the back, and after the girls finish maybe half their banana split, they're begging to play. It's warm enough today that they don't want to wear their jackets and cool enough that Shay and I insist they do. We watch them play and talk.

Lilly asks Abi about school, and Abi tells her she's going to go to a Jackson Harbor school next fall. Lilly tells her all about her teacher and the kids in her class and begs her to go to *her* school. I watch them, hoping that Abi has a friend in Lilly who she can count on, the way I always did in Carter.

"When will she see her mom?" Shay asks quietly beside me. "Or does Scarlett not . . .?"

"Oh, no, Scarlett's involved. She'll see her." I scrape a bit of ice cream off the side of the dish. "That's actually why I was in Chicago before. I was trying to help her find a place so she can split her time between L.A. and there. That way, when Abi wants to visit her mom for a weekend, she doesn't have to take a four-hour flight. And anyway, it'll be good for Scarlett to get away from that scene."

"I'm glad to hear it. I know you're an awesome dad and you'd give Abi everything she needs, but it's good that her mom still wants a relationship with her."

"They have a great relationship, actually. Scarlett spoils her a little, but she loves her madly." I study Shay's dark eyes and feel a pang of regret that I didn't try to keep up with her while I was in L.A. Once I had to let her go the second time, I just didn't trust myself, but regardless of what else happens between us, I *do* want us to be friends, and she doesn't know anything about my daughter's mother. "Scarlett's not a bad person, Shay. She's just . . . She was brought up in L.A., in the middle of all the money and fame. Her parents weren't like ours. They had totally screwed-up priorities and don't understand what life is like for normal people. Scarlett really has matured since becoming a mother."

"I thought she was nice when I met her."

I frown. "You met her? This last time she was in Jackson Harbor?"

"No, I met her after Dad's funeral. She . . ." Shay cocks her head to the side. "You didn't know she came to talk to me?"

Well, fuck. "No. I didn't." The words come out with a bite Shay doesn't deserve.

Shay shakes her head. "It wasn't a big deal. She just wanted me to understand why you were staying married."

My stomach sours. "She shouldn't have done that. I wanted to tell you myself."

"But I wasn't taking your calls."

I look away. It hurts to remember those days. The grief of losing Frank to cancer and losing Shay to circumstance. The panic and fear of watching my daughter fight for her life.

"Hello, Shayleigh."

I blink away my memories as Professor Douche steps up to the bench where Shay and I are sitting.

"George," she says tightly. "What are you doing here?"

"I was just at your apartment. I wanted to check on you." His gaze is all over her, and I want to punch him. This asshole is *married,* and he just went to her apartment. I'd bet my Laguna house he was going to try to talk her into bed while he was "checking" on her. "How are your revisions coming?"

She flinches, and I wonder if it's worry about her dissertation or anger that she's trying hard to keep off her face. "They're fine. I'm almost done."

"They need to be in by Monday."

"Not a problem."

His gaze shifts to me, and he chuckles, shaking his head

before turning his eyes back to Shay. "Looks like you were right about him."

She stiffens. "George—"

"What does that mean?" I ask.

George shrugs. "She said you only fuck her when it's convenient for you. And here you are. I figured that was why she ended things, but she wouldn't admit it." He laughs again as he walks away. "You two enjoy yourselves."

When I pull my eyes off the asshole hipster to look at Shay, she's staring at the ground. "You told him that I only fuck you when it's convenient for me?"

She closes her eyes. "He put words in my mouth. They might have felt true, but I didn't say it."

I flinch. *They felt true.* "You haven't told him that you know about his wife, have you?"

"No," she whispers. "I haven't seen him and haven't wanted to." Standing, she tosses the remnants of her cone in the trash can then wraps her arms around herself and shivers. "Can you take me and Lilly back to my car? I want to go home."

"What will you do if he shows up?" I'm not entitled to this jealousy—this anger. But I wield it anyway. "You said your heart's not broken, but Shayleigh, if you could see what I see when you look at him—"

"I'm not heartbroken over him, Easton." She swallows and her eyes brim with tears. "I'm heartbroken over what he made me by hiding his marriage. I haven't even told his wife yet." She presses the back of her hand to her mouth. "I'm trying to cope with the fact that I pushed away the man I . . ." She swallows. "I didn't talk to you for *years* because I didn't want to be the reason your daughter lost her father, but now I may very well be the reason this other little girl loses hers, and I didn't even love him."

She's killing me. "Shay—"

"I can't talk about it anymore tonight."

I want to hold her, but every time I process her words, I hear the truth. I'm the root cause of this pain. *"I pushed away the man I loved."* She loved me. She didn't say the word, but I heard it anyway. Part of me has always known it, even if she never said it. Now it's just a matter of finding out if I can earn that love again.

Easton

Scarlett picked up Abi and took her to Chicago for Easter weekend. They got a suite at the Four Seasons and are shopping and going to the aquarium. That leaves me to spend the weekend alone in Jackson Harbor until Abi comes home Sunday morning—though I'm not interested in spending it alone at all.

As I climb the stairs to Shay's apartment, I feel like a teenage boy about to go on his first date. I grabbed pizza again, but I'm hoping this time I won't have to give it to the neighbor. When I texted earlier, Shay said she'd be home and didn't argue when I said I was going to swing by. Since I'm focusing on the little victories with her, that felt like a prize.

I shift the pizza box and knock with my free hand. Shay opens the door to her apartment wearing flannel sleep pants and a tank top with a picture of Shakespeare that says, "OMG. I *literary* can't even." Her hair's piled in a messy bun on top of her head, and her makeup's been washed away. She looks younger like this. More vulnerable. And I hate myself for every time I've hurt her.

"Nice shirt," I say.

She looks down as if she's forgotten what she's wearing. "Thanks. Lilly gave it to me for Christmas." She leans on the doorjamb and arches a brow. "What did you need?"

You. "I thought we could hang. Talk. Whatever. Abi's with her mom for the weekend."

She folds her arms. "I'm not sure it's a good idea for me to let you in here."

"It's a great idea. This is the kind of stuff *friends* do. But if you prefer, we can hang out in the corridor." I grin, but inside, I'm a mess. If friends is all she can give me, then I'll take it. From Shay, I'd live on the scraps if it meant I didn't have to let her go. After what she said on Wednesday night about pushing me away for Abi's sake, I feel lucky that she'll talk to me at all.

"What if I just close the door?" I can tell she's trying to keep a straight face, but her lips twitch.

"You know that eighties movie with John Cusack? Where he holds up the stereo outside her window? It'd be like that. But for friendship."

She rolls her eyes. "I'm so sure you're going to pull a *Say Anything* to get me to talk to you."

I give her my best cocky grin. "Test me."

She stares at me for a long time as if she's trying to decide if I'm bluffing. Hell, now that she's doubting me, I kind of hope she makes me do it. I'll have to go buy a stereo from Target, though. I hope they still sell those. Holding up an iPhone and Bluetooth speaker just doesn't have the same appeal.

Stepping back, she opens the door wide and waves me in. "Come on, then."

I step inside and right past her, as if I've been here a hundred times before. I keep walking until I'm on the other side of the small living room and reach the kitchen. I plop the pizza box on the counter and open it up. "I got your favorite. Pepperoni and jalapeno, and those cheese-stuffed breadsticks."

When I turn, she's on the opposite side of the kitchen island. "No, thanks."

Well, shit. I probably should've asked about her food preferences too. I abandon the pizza and walk toward her. "Can I order you something else, then? Chinese? Thai? Wings?"

"I had oatmeal."

"For *dinner*?"

She shrugs and tugs open her fridge. There's not much in there—some sliced melon, cottage cheese, milk, lettuce, and a variety pack of Jackson Brews beer. "Want a beer?"

"Sure." I pull a slice of pizza from the box and take a bite. I hate to eat in front of her, but I'm starved.

She grabs an IPA for me, but I notice she doesn't get one for herself. She pops the lid off for me and hands it over. "That smells so good." She closes her eyes and groans.

And now my dick's hard. "It is. You should have a piece."

She stares longingly at the box. "I don't eat that stuff anymore."

"Why not?"

She waves a hand over her body, as if this explains anything. "Because this is better. And I might be fully recovered, but greasy foods still remind me of my binge-then-starve days."

I frown as I look her over. She was always self-conscious about her weight. And then sometime between Paris and when she came to my hotel room in Chicago, she'd thinned out. I remember being worried about how frail she looked. "You had an eating disorder."

She laughs, but the sound is dark and cold. "Yeah. Between grasping for control when Dad was dying to trying to deal with lifelong insecurities about my body . . ." She shrugs.

"I never understood why you were so self-conscious."

"I know." She holds up a hand and shakes her head. "Intellectually, I know that you thought I was beautiful and whatever."

"And *whatever*? I was head over heels for you just the way you were." I hate the idea of her making herself sick.

"Does your family know?"

"Mom does. She's the one who took me to the counselor after Dad died. She said her heart wouldn't ever recover from losing Dad if she had to watch me waste away too. I asked her not to tell the boys, and she agreed. I'm all better now, though, so stop giving me that look."

"But you still don't eat pizza?" I take another bite and watch her consider how to answer this.

"Part of my recovery was identifying triggers for me—emotional triggers, food triggers. It's not like I had a healthy relationship with food before I lost the weight. The anorexia was just a new manifestation of existing issues." She shrugs. "So as I recovered, I had to deal with those issues and try to form new, healthy habits. I choose not to eat foods that make me feel angry with myself after. For whatever reason, I can drink a beer or have the occasional ice cream sundae without feeling like my life is spinning out of control, without feeling like food is some evil sin I've succumbed to again. But I associate pizza with . . ." She bites her lip, like she's trying to keep the words in.

"With what?"

"Self-loathing?" She laughs, and I can tell it's because she's uncomfortable sharing that and not because she thinks anything's funny.

"Does it bother you for me to eat in front of you?"

"Not at all. Seriously, I've come a long way. And I've learned to love my body through exercise. I love what it can do—how I feel after a long run or after squatting heavy weights."

Bigger or frighteningly thin, she's always been beautiful to me, but I have to admit the healthy curve of her glutes and the muscle in her shoulders look good on her. And the confident sway of her hips looks even better.

She shrugs. "I still have my moments, but I'm in a pretty healthy place."

"I'm glad to hear it. Maybe we could run together someday. I enjoy it too."

"I'm not like my brothers. I like to enjoy my workouts—not kill myself to compete."

I've worked out with her brothers a few times now. They like to do CrossFit-style workouts and bust their asses to beat each other. As a lifelong competitor, I love that, but that's not always what I'm looking for when I go to the gym. "I promise I won't race you." I glance around the kitchen as I finish my second slice of pizza. The space is small but tidy. There's a stack of books beside her laptop on the table. "Were you working?"

She nods. "I just finished up the last of my revisions and sent my final dissertation off to my committee."

"That's incredible. Why aren't you out celebrating?"

She snorts. "A night at home with no work is my idea of a celebration. And anyway, nothing's official until after my defense."

"But your committee's read it at this point, right?"

"Yeah, they've read pieces of it along the way and given me feedback. George has read everything except my most recent revisions."

"Then you should be fine. Right?"

She wraps her arms around herself and seems to shrink. "Assuming George doesn't hold it against me when I tell his wife he slept with me."

Well, shit. "You think he will? Do you think you should wait?"

"If I wait, I'm only doing it to protect myself, and that feels wrong. I should never have slept with him to begin with. I might not have known he was married, but I went to bed with him when he was the chair of my committee. This is part of that fallout, like it or not, and I can't wait to tell a woman her husband is unfaithful just because it's inconvenient to me." She straightens a stack of papers on the counter. "Knowing and not telling her makes me complicit."

"What happens if George holds it against you? What if he doesn't . . . pass your dissertation or whatever?"

"Then I don't get my PhD, and I'm suddenly under-qualified for all the jobs I've been interviewing for."

Jobs that will take her away from Jackson Harbor. I close up the pizza box while I consider this. Fuck. I'm so selfish. I don't want her to leave, but if that's what she wants . . . "Did you ever email that agent?"

She ducks her head, and I already know the answer before she says, "Not yet."

I grab a napkin and wipe off my hands. "Why not?"

She studies the stack of papers and straightens it again. "Because reading and writing fiction has always been my safe place. The stories I read as a kid got me through high school when I thought the size of my body made me less important than skinnier girls. And writing got me through college—when I was so stressed, it was there to help me unwind." She looks up at me through her lashes. "It was there to help me work through losing you. Both times."

"It'll still be that, won't it? Even if you try to make a go of it?"

She swallows and cuts her eyes away. "There's a really good chance I'm not good enough. Most people aren't."

I cross the small kitchen and take her chin in my hand, guiding her to meet my eyes. "I believe in you."

"You haven't even read my stuff."

I shrug. "I'd love to, if you wanted me to. But even without reading, I have faith that you can tell an amazing story. You grew up with a book in one hand and a pencil in the other. At this point, it's probably written into your DNA."

She studies my face and then her gaze shifts from my eyes to my mouth, and the energy in the room changes. The tension between us becomes a palpable thing.

"If we weren't just friends," I say softly, "this is when I'd kiss you."

Her breath catches. "Is it?"

"Yeah, but that would only be the beginning. Once I tasted

you, I'd want more, and I'd end up lifting you onto the counter so you could wrap your legs around me." I tuck a lock of hair behind her ear and skim my fingertips down the side of her neck. "Then I'd kiss you here because I know how much you like it."

Her lips part and her pupils dilate. "You were always good at figuring out what I like."

"Because figuring out what turns you on turns *me* on. But once I started tasting you, I'd be greedy for more, and I'd end up with my face between your legs, licking you until you were begging me to fuck you."

Her chest expands on a ragged inhale. "But we are just friends."

For now. Nodding, I skim a finger over her bottom lip. "I'm gonna be the best fucking friend you've ever had, Shayleigh Jackson."

"Hmm. I guess that remains to be seen."

I allow myself one last touch before dropping my hand and stepping back to give her the space she needs. "Well, it's Friday night and your best friend is here to celebrate your completed dissertation. What do we do next?" I smile to cover the truth that I'm terrified she's going to ask me to leave.

She looks to the living room and then back to me. "Before you got here, I was about to watch a movie. Do you want to watch it with me?"

I grin. *Little victories.* "Sounds good. What are you watching?"

"*The Princess Bride.* It's one of my comfort movies. Is that okay? If not, we can—"

"It's great." She could tell me she planned to watch a documentary on drying paint, and I'd be game. I doubt I'll be able to keep my attention on the screen anyway. I'm just glad to be spending time with Shay.

We both sit on the couch, keeping a friend-appropriate distance between us, and she pulls her feet up under her as she starts the movie.

I watch her posture go looser and looser and her eyes get heavy. We're not even thirty minutes in when she falls asleep. She shifts in her sleep and leans against me, using my arm as a pillow. Her neck's at an awkward angle, and her body's torqued. I hate to imagine how knotted her neck will be if she stays like this long, so I grab a pillow, put it in my lap, and guide her to rest her head on it.

Then, like any friend would, I spend the rest of the movie watching her sleep. *Totally reasonable friend behavior.*

After the credits roll, the TV cycles into a screensaver, and the sudden quiet startles her awake. She blinks up at me. "East?"

"Hey."

"Have I been sleeping long?"

"Movie's over."

She rubs her eyes but doesn't jerk away from me, so I'll consider that a win too. Slowly enough so she can stop me if she wants to, I cup her face in one hand and trace the line of her jaw and the shell of her ear.

"Was it as good as the first dozen times you saw it?" she asks sleepily.

"I enjoyed every minute," I say, though I didn't waste a minute looking at the screen once she was sleeping in my lap. She stretches her arms overhead, arching her back, and my gaze snags on her hard nipples pressed against the image on her thin

T-shirt. There's a real possibility I'll get a semi from the sight of Shakespeare's face from here on out, and that's just screwed up.

"I should go to bed," she says.

"If you want."

Silence pulses around us, thick with sexual tension. "And you should probably leave."

"If you want me to."

"I don't," she whispers.

I take that as my green light and hold her gaze as I skim my hand down her neck, across the swell of her breasts and the peak of each nipple. She leans into my hand and moans softly at the light friction.

"I can't give you anything but friendship right now," she says, even as she leans into my touch.

"I'll take it."

"We really could be great friends."

I roll her nipple under my thumb. "The best."

"We should do that, then." She gasps when I pinch her opposite nipple. "Is this breaking the rules?"

"Only if you say it is." I trail my fingers between her breasts and over her stomach, slipping them beneath the waistband of her flannel pants. "What do you say? Is this allowed?"

She lifts her hips off the couch. An invitation.

I stroke back and forth beneath the elastic and circle her navel with my thumb. "This is your call, Shayleigh. You make the rules."

"I can't be . . ." She squirms under my hand, no doubt fighting the instinct to guide my hand where she needs it. "It's not fair to you. I might not even live here much longer."

The idea of her leaving is a kick in the chest, but I push that pain aside. "As your best friend, I'm sure I won't want you to leave whether I touch you tonight or not."

Her eyes are closed and her tongue darts out to graze her bottom lip. I can barely breathe I want her so badly.

"Can your best friend touch you?" I ask, hearing the desperation in my voice. "Can I make you come?"

She opens her eyes and searches my face. "Please?"

That's all I need. I cup her between her legs. She's so wet, and I've barely started. She parts her legs for me, giving me easier access to her slick folds. I circle her entrance. Once. Twice. She whimpers, and I plunge a finger inside her. She's so hot and wet and tight. Her eyes shut again, and those soft pink lips part. I want to kiss her, but the way our bodies are positioned, I can't, so I watch, my gaze switching between the way she's moving against my hand and the pleasure on her face.

I stroke her cheek with my free hand. I wasn't lying that night at the bar when I told her I wanted her to choose me, but I lied when I implied I wouldn't play dirty to get her there. We've spent too many years apart, and if the insane chemistry we've always had is what's going to make her give this a chance, then I'll use it to my full advantage.

I add a second finger to the first and find her clit with my thumb. Her body clenches tightly, and blood pulses to my cock.

"As your friend," I say, eyes fixed on her hips now and how she's fucking my hand, "I think you should know you have the perfect pussy."

She grasps the hand that was stroking her cheek and turns her head to pull my index finger into her mouth. She licks then closes her mouth around it and sucks. Pleasure barrels down my spine, and I imagine her on my cock, the suction, how hot she'd look with her lips stretched over me.

Without meaning to, I've increased the pace of my hand, fucking her deeper and harder with my fingers. Her teeth scrape my knuckle and she gasps, her whole body tensing before she finally lets go and her orgasm pulses around my fingers.

I turn my touch gentle. Slow. I'm guiding her down, reluctant to pull away until I have to.

When she opens her eyes, they're foggy with lust and there's a small, satisfied smile on her lips. "You're one hell of a friend."

I smirk. "Told you so."

She removes my hand from her pants, and I groan. I could touch her all night, but if playtime must be over . . .

I lift my fingers to my mouth and suck off the taste of her. She watches me with wide eyes and releases a little whimper that speaks volumes. I'm not the only one who wants more tonight.

Sitting up, she turns to face me on the couch and slides a hand down my chest to my stomach. "Your turn?"

I push off the couch and adjust myself in my jeans. I'm so fucking hard right now. "I should go."

"Are you sure? I can . . ." She shakes her head, and I can see her scrambling to decide what she's okay with. How far we can go within her rules. "I can return the favor."

I brace a hand on either side of her on the back of the couch, then lean forward until my lips are almost touching hers. "Next time you touch me, Shay, it won't be because you're returning a favor. It will be because you want to. Full stop. No hesitation."

"I . . ."

I pull away. Last time I got her off, we switched gears so fast that I couldn't even enjoy how beautiful she looked all flushed and satisfied. Today, I want to take a picture and frame it above my bed. "I'll see you Sunday."

She blinks at me. "Sunday?"

"Jackson family Easter dinner. At the cabin." I smile and look her over, thinking of tequila and drinking games, first kisses and crossing lines. I can see in her eyes that she's thinking about those things too. "I'm *really* looking forward to it."

Shay

The Jacksons have brunch every Sunday morning at ten. If someone's schedule doesn't allow for it on any given week, so be it, but the time is always the same. The only exceptions are when Christmas falls on a Sunday, and every Easter, when we skip brunch and meet at the family cabin for a big dinner.

This Easter will be our biggest yet. Everyone will be here, including Easton and Abi. Even if I'm nervous about spending time around Easton with our tentative "just friends" arrangement, I'm glad he and Abi have somewhere to spend the holiday.

Jake is in the kitchen, working on the ham and a potato-and-sour-cream casserole. Nic is making half a dozen pies because that's her way of showing us all how much she loves us. I'm hoping my stomach can handle some of this stuff. Not only is it delicious, but I suspect I've lost a few pounds, and I don't want to sink back into the cycle of feeling victorious every time the scale shows a lower number.

"Do we drink red or white with ham?" Teagan asks, holding up both bottles. She's in a pink spring dress today and looking as bright as the sunny day outside.

I position the last fork in place at the table and shrug. "I don't think it matters."

Still holding the wine, she presses the back of one hand to my forehead. "What is wrong with you? You're supposed to say *both*."

I laugh. Because she's right. Typically, that would be my answer, but I'm not drinking tonight. Partly because Easton's going to be here, and I'm afraid even the tiniest loosening of my inhibitions might land me in his bed, but mostly because my stomach is still screwed up and I don't want wine ruining any chance I have of eating a halfway decent meal. I'm sick of not having an appetite and living on dry toast. Even coffee upsets my stomach these days. Sad times indeed. "I'm ready for my stress levels to go down so I can eat and drink like a normal person again."

Teagan plops both bottles down on the table and props her hands on her hips. "Have you gone to the doctor yet?"

I look over her shoulder to my brother Jake in the kitchen and down the hall toward the girls in the living room to make sure no one heard her. "Would you lower your voice, please?"

She arches a brow.

"Not yet. I've been kind of busy, but I'll call on Monday."

"I've heard that before."

"I know, I know." Maybe I'm stalling deliberately. Every time I fall asleep at my computer or sleep twelve hours when I'm normally good with seven, I think about how tired Mom was before she found out she had cancer. I think of Dad losing his battle. Maybe part of me knows that I need to take this seriously and I'm too scared of what I might find out.

I hear the front door open and the sounds of Easton and Abi's voices as Carter lets them in.

Teagan flashes me a grin. "Carter said that Easton said you two watched a movie together Friday night," she says in a conspiratorial whisper.

My cheeks burn at the memory of Easton on my couch. His hand. His wickedly dirty mouth. "What else did he tell him?"

She smirks. "Nothing that should make you blush like *that*. What happened? He told Carter you wanted to just be friends for now, but he's putting all his cards on the table with your brothers. He wants more, and he wants them to know his intentions so he doesn't have to deal with any 'protective brother' bullshit when he finally gets his shot with you."

I know how Easton feels. He hasn't exactly hidden his intentions. Yet hearing Teagan tell it like that gives me massive butterflies.

"Abigail!" Lilly's scream is followed by the sound of little feet running on hardwood.

"No running in the house!" Nic calls.

"Lilly! I went shopping with my mom in Chicago this weekend. She took me to the American Girl Store and bought me a new doll. Do you like her?"

"She's beautiful! I have one upstairs. Come on, I'll show you. Did you like Chicago? I've been there before and it was just so big. There are so many people."

"It's nothing like L.A.," Abi says. "There are even more people there."

"No way."

The sound of the girls' chatter quiets as they head upstairs, and Teagan and I exchange smiles.

"They're adorable together, aren't they?" Easton says.

I spin and see him at the threshold to the dining room, his hands tucked into his pockets. He takes me in slowly, and those blue-green eyes darken. "Happy Easter, Easton," I say. He looks . . . *edible.* Tailored black pants, a sky-blue oxford with the top button undone and the sleeves rolled to his elbows. His forearms are a work of art, and my mouth goes dry as I ogle them and remember the muscles there bunching as he worked between my legs.

"Happy Easter." His husky timbre is the stuff of wet dreams. Or maybe that's the memory of what we did on my couch. *Both.* "Thanks for having us."

"I'm not the one who invited you."

His lips twitch. "This is true."

"Easton," Carter calls. "Do you still suck at pool? Come downstairs so I can kick your ass."

"Language!" Lilly shouts from upstairs, and Easton laughs, delighted by her bossy reprimand.

"Do you need any help?" he asks me, looking the table over. It's set beautifully, if I say so myself.

"Go play with Carter," I say. "He's missed his buddy all these years."

Easton drags his bottom lip through his teeth and gives me one final head-to-toe once-over that leaves my skin tingling. "As you wish." He winks then heads to the basement.

Teagan grabs a plate off the table and fans herself. "Holy sexual tension, Shayleigh. You two are gonna fog up the windows in here if you keep looking at each other like that."

I pull out a chair and sit because I'm suddenly lightheaded.

Teagan chuckles. "You okay?"

"I'm . . ." I put my fingers to my lips. I'm so many things.

"Lemme guess, starts with an *H* and rhymes with *corny*."

I grab a napkin from the place setting in front of me and toss it at her. It floats ineffectually to the floor at her feet.

Laughing, she picks it up, refolds it, and returns it to the plate in front of me, but her face is serious when she says, "It's okay to give him another chance. He lives here. He has custody of his daughter. Everything's different now."

Yeah, it really is. This time I might be the one who ends up in L.A. while he's here.

*D*inner was the usual chaotic and boisterous affair of a dozen conversations happening at any given time and enough food to feed a small army.

I take kitchen duty after the meal ends, partly because I'm one of the few people here who isn't responsible for a child of some sort, and partly because I could use the time to get my thoughts in order. The day turned out nice, and everyone's outside enjoying the mild temp and sunshine by the water. I find myself lingering—towel-drying and putting away dishes rather than leaving them in the rack, wiping down the counters a second time, even going as far as to organize the little we keep in the pantry.

I don't understand why until I look out the window and see the girls chasing Noah barefoot in the sand and all my brothers standing around a fire talking. *This might be my last Easter living in Jackson Harbor.*

The thought strikes me and cuts through the little energy I have like a sharp knife. I pull out a kitchen chair and sink into it.

"Why so sad, Short Stack?"

I turn away from the window to find Easton sitting down opposite me. "I'm not sad."

"Could've fooled me."

I shake my head. Not sad. I'm a little disappointed that the truth didn't hit me sooner, and maybe even a little embarrassed, but not sad. "I'm just thinking."

"Tell me."

I nod toward the window, toward my family. "This is how I want to fill my life." I swallow, overwhelmed with the rightness of the choice. "Not with scholarly articles and stacks of papers. Not with tenure and postdoc work. I've enjoyed getting my doctorate, but when I choose what comes next, I want it to include this."

He follows my gaze out the window. "I can't blame you."

"You don't think it makes me a quitter? Or a coward?"

"I guess that depends." He takes a deep breath, and I wonder if it's fair to either of us to ask him this question. I already know he'd like me to stay. "Are you giving up a dream? Are you turning down a job you want because you're scared of starting new somewhere?"

"Being a college professor wasn't ever a dream. It was just . . . a job." I laugh. "And pursing a PhD was the best way to drag out my school years when I wasn't ready to enter the real world."

He's watching me. "Close your eyes."

"Why?"

"It's a little visualization exercise. Just do it."

"Okay." I obey and wait. What is he doing?

"I know it's hard, but try to forget what's stressing you out right now. Imagine everything works out easily, and five years have passed. The stress is gone. The decisions have been made and you're happy."

I smile. It's a relief to imagine being beyond this moment in my life. It's not a hardship to imagine when I've moved past these worries, past my defense and my career choices, past George and the decision of how I'm going to tell his wife the truth.

"It's five years from now," Easton says, and his deep voice helps me relax. "You have the day off and you wake up on your own. You roll out of bed and walk out of your bedroom. Where are you? Who's there? How do you feel? What are you doing with your day?"

"I . . ." The image is so clear, and my heart aches with how badly I want it. *This* future.

"Keep your eyes closed," he says softly. "Look around. Step outside if you want. Grab your planner and open your calendar—what do you have coming up this month? This is the life you built, and you love it. Study the details. What makes you smile? Like any life, there's good and bad, but what are the parts that make the tough moments worth it? What excites you? Here, in this moment, five years from now, you can find all the answers you need."

It's easier than I would have imagined. Everything is so clear—the sunny room I wake up in, the smell of coffee in the kitchen, the warm feel of someone wrapping me in a hug from behind before I turn to smile. I open my eyes and find him watching me. "That was incredible."

"Did it help?"

I nod. "I'd already decided, but yeah. The visualization helped nail it down. Thank you."

His throat bobs as he swallows. "Where were you?"

"In Jackson Harbor, and I have a family." I study him and wonder if I'm a fool for having the same dreams for my future now that I had when I was a twenty-year-old college student studying in Paris. The idea of moving to L.A. doesn't thrill me, but the idea of staying home, of letting my choices be guided by my family? Does it really matter if that makes me a small-town girl? Or old-fashioned? Maybe those things aren't bad. Maybe they're just *me.*

"That sounds like a good start," Easton says.

"I think for me it is. There are people who thrive by revolving their life around their career, but there's no career I want enough for that."

"What about writing?"

I smile. Leave it to Easton to refuse to forget my whispered dreams. "I'm not sure even a career as a novelist would be enough to substitute for living near the people I love the most. But that's moot, isn't it? I can do that anywhere . . . if I'm ever lucky enough to do it at all. And until then, I just need a job that pays the bills and allows me to live my life. There are so many opportunities with my family's business that I'd enjoy. A job that gives me a sense of satisfaction and lets me spend my free time with my favorite people in the world." I shrug. "For better or worse, that's enough for me."

He takes my hand and strokes his thumb across my knuckles. He's quiet for a long time, and when he does talk, he draws in a deep breath first. "Take a walk with me?"

"I'd like that. Do you need to tell Abi?"

He shakes his head. "Nah. I told Carter I was coming in here to ask you on a walk, so he's going to keep an eye on her."

I'm wearing flats with my dress, so I trade them for a pair of canvas tennis shoes on the way out the door. The fresh air feels good, the sun amazing after the long winter, and I find myself smiling as we stroll the property. There's so much left to do and decide, but I already feel better having made my decision. I'll have to call Emmitson University next week and cancel my interview. I don't need to waste their time or mine.

We wander past the house and away from the beach toward the pole barn where we keep the snowmobiles and store the boat and lake equipment during the winter. Easton knows this property as well as I do, having spent a good chunk of his teenage summers and weekends hanging out here.

"Thank you for taking me through that," I say after we've walked for a while. "It was helpful."

"I can't take the credit. When I was trying to decide whether or not to retire, my therapist did that exercise with me. I found it . . . insightful."

"And your vision brought you back here?"

"Yeah." He looks down at me. "I guess we have that in

common. I think it was the right decision, too. It's such a relief to see Abi happy, but I owe that to your family. You all welcomed us and made us feel . . ."

I smile. "Welcome?"

He smacks my ass lightly. "Pest. I was going to say *not alone.*"

"Well, I think that's what friends do." I take his hand and intertwine our fingers. "I like being your friend, Easton." And maybe, if I stay, we could work on being something more.

Something flashes in his eyes, but he looks away before I can place the emotion. "About that . . ."

We keep walking, but I squeeze his hand. "What?"

He lifts our hands and studies them. Mine is so small in his, but to me, it's the perfect fit. He shakes his head. "Nothing."

I glance at the pole barn over my shoulder and smile. "Come on." I tug him toward the barn, and he follows.

I enter the security code on the door and push inside. It's darker in here, the only light from the high windows on the garage doors, but there's enough to see and it's still nice and cool, unlike in the summer, when the metal walls turn it into an oven.

I shut the door and smile up at him. "When I was a teenager, you and I were alone in here once. You were in a pair of swim trunks, shirtless, and I was looking for the big float for the lake."

"I remember. You were wearing a black swimsuit and . . ." He bites a knuckle dramatically, and I laugh. "Carter was pissed at me that day."

I hoist myself up on the counter in the workshop at the back of the barn. "I got sick of looking and sat here," I say. "I was so self-conscious about my body, but I thought . . ." I bite my bottom lip. Even more than a dozen years later and with a world more self-confidence, it's hard to make myself say the words. "I thought you were looking at me."

He prowls forward. Slowly. *Too* slowly. "I was."

"I think I believe that now, but I didn't then. I couldn't have. So I did what I always did when I needed to cheer myself up. I told myself a story."

Easton stops two feet away and tilts his head to the side. "What kind of story?"

"I imagined I was the kind of girl you'd look at—"

"Not a stretch, since you were."

"And that you desperately wanted to kiss me."

"I did."

"I told myself you were going to stop tinkering with Jake's old bike and notice me sitting here."

His nostrils flare. "I noticed."

"Maybe if we'd been friends then—like we are now—I would've had the courage to tell you I wanted you to kiss me."

"Maybe if we were friends, I would have had the balls to ask." He steps closer, and even sitting on the counter, I have to look up to see his face. He nudges my thighs apart and takes another step to stand between them. He strokes a whisper-soft path up my thigh, pushing my dress aside on the way. "Do you want me to kiss you, Shay?"

"We are friends, right?" I whisper. "I like being your friend. Do you like it?"

He buries his face in my neck, and I gasp at the feel of his tongue flicking the sensitive skin behind my ear. "I like this." He sucks my earlobe between his teeth. "And this."

I whimper. "Yes, me too." I turn my head, searching for his

mouth, and he kisses me hard. His hands are in my hair, and our tongues collide. Desperate. Searching.

"As your friend," he says, his voice all low and gravelly when he breaks the kiss, "I couldn't help but notice the way you were looking at me tonight."

"How did I look?"

"Like being friends might not be enough for you. Like you were thinking about me getting you off on your couch. Like you were thinking that maybe next time, you want more from me."

My breath catches as his knuckles graze the damp cotton between my thighs. "I can't stop thinking about it," I confess, fighting the urge to rock into him.

"Me neither." He dips his head to the swell of my breast above the neckline of my dress, opens his mouth, and bites down gently.

My breath shudders out of me. "I want to touch you."

He groans against my breast, and I wiggle away from him and hop off the counter. He turns, watching me, and I drop to my knees, working at his buckle. "Christ," he whispers. But he doesn't stop me, and the desperation in his eyes is enough to send a shock of pleasure right through my core.

I free him from his jeans and nearly gasp at the feel of him in my hand—hard and silken against my palm. Hard *for me*.

He rocks into my fist, groaning. "Shay. Fuck, that's good."

I lean forward and press my mouth to the tip of his cock. The way he jerks under my lips sends a rush of power through me so potent I feel like I could do anything. I run my tongue along the underside then grip him at the base of his shaft before I take him into my mouth.

Maybe this is reckless, but we've already crossed lines, and right now, there's nothing I want more than to make him come.

He threads his fingers through my hair, not so much to guide me but as if he's trying to hold me, to keep more contact between us. I work my mouth over him, pulling him deep for a few strokes before releasing him completely and licking his tip with my tongue.

When I pull him deep again, he tugs lightly on my hair. "Shay."

I look up at him, increasing my suction. He releases a loud groan and the metal walls around us vibrate.

He closes his eyes. "Shit, I want to come inside you."

I release him and stroke his wet shaft in my fist. "Condom?" The word breaks on my tongue because I want that too.

He grimaces. "Fuck. I'm sorry. Are you . . . on anything?"

I bite my lip. It's so damn tempting. "Yes, but I haven't been tested since I found out about George's . . . indiscretions. Until I know I'm healthy, we shouldn't risk it."

Swallowing hard, he nods. "I get it."

I grin. He thinks this is over, but I'm not done yet. "Just enjoy letting me live out a teenage fantasy," I say, and I'm treated to another groan as I take him back in my mouth and suck every bit of pleasure from him I can.

"What were you going to say earlier?"

We're walking back to the main house and the sun is setting. It's a beautiful evening, but I was reluctant to leave our bubble in the barn.

He smirks at me. "If you think I can remember anything resembling the English language after what you just did with your tongue..."

I smack his arm, blushing. "Would you hush?" I look around, but we're out here alone. "Before we went into the barn, I said I liked being your friend, and you acted like you wanted to say something about it. Is this... You'd tell me if this was getting too weird for you, right?"

He reaches for my hand as if he needs the support. I don't hate it. "Remember how I said my therapist walked me through that exercise?"

"Yeah."

He squeezes my fingers gently. "When I imagined my future, I didn't just see Jackson Harbor. I saw you."

My stomach flips. I saw him too. I was just too scared to say it. I'm still too scared.

His steps slow, then he stops altogether as he turns to face me. "If you truly want to be my friend and nothing more, I'll take it and consider myself lucky. But I'm done pretending I'm not in love with you."

Can a stomach drop and dance all at once? Because mine is. We've never said those words. And now... "East."

He scrunches up his face and shakes his head. "I screwed this up twice, and while I regret that the way I handled things hurt you, I can't regret my choices, because now I have Abi. She might not be my blood, but she's my..." He shifts his gaze skyward, and my heart twists as I watch his eyes fill with tears. "She's my proudest accomplishment."

"She's amazing," I say. "And so are you, Easton. She's lucky to have you as a dad." It's really just that simple. I love the way he is with her. I love how unequivocally he puts her first. I love . . . *him.* And now, looking into his eyes while the cool spring breeze whips my hair around my shoulders, I know I've loved him forever. Even when my heart was broken and I tried to lock it away to protect it, I never stopped loving him.

He tilts my chin up and studies my face. "I've never felt like I was in a position where I could choose you both, so I made myself stay away. I kept my distance until I could have another chance with you that might actually last. Something solid enough to weather the worst storm. I want that chance, Shayleigh."

I want all of that, but I can't deny this piece of me that hesitates. This cautious bit of my soul that's sending up a warning signal that we've been here before. I've believed in the improbable and was crushed. *Twice.* "Why do you want me, Easton?" It's only once the question passes my lips that I realize it's not the first time I've asked. I asked him when we were in Paris.

"Because of who you are. Because we're good together."

"But why?"

He grimaces then shakes his head. "I'm not good with the romantic words."

I try not to crumble. I don't want it to matter, but he was doing so well, and I asked and ruined it. "I think you're better than you believe you are."

"You're the writer." He lifts my hand to his mouth and kisses my knuckles. "Do you think I could make the past up to you? Do you think you could love me too?"

Reaching up, I stroke my fingers across the stubble on his jaw.

"Easton, I never stopped loving you." He dips his head, lowering his mouth toward mine, but I stop him with a fingertip to his lips. "Loving you is part of who I am."

He must see the hesitation on my face because the worry doesn't leave his. "But . . .?"

"But I'm scared."

"Even having decided that you're not moving? You're still . . . You don't trust me."

"I don't trust *life*. I don't trust all the things out of our control. Things happen and choices have to be made and . . ."

"I'll prove it to you, then." He nods, and I see his determination in the set of his jaw. "I'll have to prove you can trust me. That I won't hurt you again."

I press my palms against his chest and rise onto my tiptoes as I slide them up to his shoulders.

He dips his head, stopping with his lips a breath from mine. "When you pictured your future today . . . could you make any room in there for me?"

"No, Easton." I shake my head, and his face drops. "I don't need to make room because you were already there."

He wraps his arms behind my back and lifts me off the ground, crushing my body to his as he kisses me. I kiss him back and try to ignore the nagging feeling that tells me I've invited heartache back into my life.

Shay

*D*o doctors' offices intentionally turn down the heat in rooms where women are wearing these flimsy exam robes? Because as I sit on the edge of the table and wait for my doctor to join me, I'm practically shivering. I think my toes might be turning blue.

I wrap my arms around myself and sigh. The fact that I'm even here instead of just getting a quick STI panel drawn up at the lab speaks to the magnitude of my hypochondria. Symptoms? Exhaustion. Queasiness. And a side of I-could-fall-asleep-any-fucking-where.

I'm a doctoral candidate slated to defend her dissertation in less than a month. I don't need to talk to my doctor. I need a nap. Or at least that's what I've been telling myself for the past few weeks. But even when I made sleep a bigger priority, it didn't make any difference. And according to the scale on the way in,

I've lost weight.

Please don't be cancer.

Fear is an icy hand on my lungs.

There's a soft knock on the door.

"Come in," I call.

Dr. Hassell steps into the room and closes the door behind her. "How are you, Shayleigh?"

I smile. I like my doctor. I started working with her in graduate school when the weight loss started destroying my body. It's so weird. Everyone praised me for getting thin, but it was killing me. My hair was falling out, my periods stopped, and I could see my ribs when I stood naked in front of the mirror. Funny that vanity was the thing that made me finally accept that I had an eating disorder and needed help to overcome it. "I'm . . . tired." I laugh, since that's why I'm here. "But I guess you already know that."

I expect her to stand behind the room's laptop and start noting my symptoms, but she doesn't. Instead, she takes the seat next to the table, sitting sideways so she's facing me.

"I know it's ridiculous to come in for being tired, but I lost my dad to cancer, and my mom's primary symptom before her diagnosis was fatigue, and—"

"Shay, it's understandable."

My cheeks heat. "I feel like a hypochondriac."

"When was your last period?"

"A few weeks ago?"

"And was it a full period or just a little bleeding?"

I shrug. I've been heavy, and I've been anorexic. My period was never regular until I got a handle on both and went on the pill. "It was light, I guess. That's not uncommon for me." *Shit.* My eyes instantly fill with unexpected tears. Am I going to have to get a hysterectomy before I've even had a chance to start a family? I wipe at my cheeks. "If it's uterine cancer, do you think . . . will I still be able to have children?"

Dr. Hassell grabs a tissue from the box on the counter and hands it to me. "Shayleigh, I don't believe your symptoms are from cancer—uterine or otherwise."

I dab my cheeks gently then blow my nose with the grace of a trumpeting elephant. "Sorry. I'm just under a lot of stress right now, and it's making me emotional." I force a laugh. "And making me jump to conclusions, apparently. It's just stress, right? All this . . .?" I wave a hand in front of my face to indicate the hot mess express that I've become.

"Stress could be a contributing factor to your symptoms, but according to the urine sample you gave my nurse, you're pregnant."

I blink at her. "I'm . . . Excuse me? What?"

Her smile is gentle. "Pregnant."

My brain takes so long to make sense of the word that it might as well be from a foreign language. "How could I be . . . I'm not even . . . I'm on the pill. I haven't missed a period."

"Some women continue to have light periods at the beginning of their pregnancies." She stands to look at her computer. She taps the screen and scrolls through something I assume is my chart. "As for your birth control, of course nothing's one hundred percent, but the pill can fail if you're on antibiotics. Have you been prescribed anything for a sinus infection or—"

I shake my head. "No. No antibiotics. Are you sure? Maybe

they mixed up the cups or something?" But even as I say it, I remember the conference in Florida a couple of months ago. I got food poisoning and was sick for days. I rarely forget to take my pill and am sure I didn't miss it on that trip, but how much good can it do if you can't keep anything down? "I was sick," I whisper.

She gives me a sympathetic nod. "That can happen too."

I used condoms for two weeks after that food poisoning. Just in case. But that doesn't account for the sex I had leading up to my sickness. In fact, before I ate the bad shellfish that made my weekend a total pukefest, it would have been better described as a sexfest. *With a married man.*

"I don't do OB anymore," she says, "but I can get you a referral if you'd like to continue with the pregnancy or even if you're not sure yet."

"I'm sure," I say quickly. I understand why she might question it—a single woman with no boyfriend in sight—but of all the things I've been questioning about my life as I wrap up my doctorate, my desire to have a family is not one of them. When I visualized my future, I pictured children.

I just imagined they'd be Easton's.

Fresh tears pour from my eyes as I imagine his face when I tell him the news. "Shit," I whisper. "You must think I'm such an idiot."

"Not at all. You had every reason to take the sudden change in your energy levels seriously. And I'm glad you did. We'll make sure all the lab work looks good too, of course, and send those results over to your OB when you chose one. My staff can get your appointment set up for you." She taps on her keyboard a few times then hesitates. "Do you . . . have a preference for your obstetrician?"

"Not my brother," I blurt. Even if I *was* ready to drop this bomb on my family—and, hello, I'm not—I wouldn't want him to be my doctor. I know he's good at his job, but that's just weird. My family is close, but not check-your-dilation close.

"I wouldn't advise anyone to choose a family member. I'm sure your brother would feel the same."

I nod along as she goes through some basic pregnancy advice, and I accept the pamphlets she offers. But I'm trapped in my own mind, nausea tearing me apart as I realize I have to tell George I'm pregnant. I have to tell his *wife.*

I've become the kind of woman I swore I'd never be.

Part XI.

Before

Shay

October 15th, seven years ago

I've had months—hell, years—to prepare for this, and there's still something so surreal about seeing my father in that casket.

The last days were a slow trudge to a finish line none of us was sure we wanted to see. When he finally crossed and we saw the end to his pain, we were all . . . *relieved*. We've grieved, we will continue to grieve, but death itself was welcome.

After a four-hour visitation, my feet are screaming and my fingers ache from all the consoling handshakes. I just want to go home to Mom's place and curl up on the couch with a cup of hot chocolate, like I'm a kid wrapping up a particularly hard day of school and not a grown woman who's about to bury her father.

"Almost done," Mom says next to me, flashing me a shaky smile.

I nod. *Almost done.* Then tomorrow, we'll return for the service and put my father in the ground. My throat thickens at the thought.

It's been a day of whispers and respectful silence, but I straighten when the whispers change, when they seem to roll through the room and heads turn toward the door . . . where Easton Connor has appeared and is hugging Carter with the fierceness of an old friend who understands your heartache better than anyone.

I didn't know Easton was coming. I didn't ask. Didn't even think about him until now.

A shiver races up my arms at the sight of him. He looks so impossibly broad in his black suit, but my mind instantly strips it off him, remembering the sight of him under me in his hotel room, the feel of his rough hands on my thighs as I rode him.

Mom squeezes my hand. "You're flushed. Do you need to sit down?"

I shake my head. "I'm fine. It's almost over."

Slowly, Easton works his way through my family members, inching closer to us with each condolence.

When he reaches me, it's not the memory of three weeks ago that makes my knees weak but the emotion in those sea-green eyes. I've been so focused on Dad and being there for my family the past few weeks that I haven't had time to talk to Easton, let alone consider how this loss would affect him. How could I be so selfish and forget what my dad meant to Easton? Dad was always there when Easton's own should have been.

Easton doesn't say anything. He pulls me into his arms and buries his face into my neck. His body trembles slightly. "I'm so sorry," he whispers, his voice thick.

I stroke down his back over and over, and when he finally pulls away, the tears I heard in his voice are streaming down his cheeks.

"Easton," Mom says, grabbing his forearm. "Thank you so much for coming."

Easton's gaze stays glued to me for a long beat before he finally turns to her. "Your husband was an incredible man. I'm so grateful he was part of my life."

"Come on," Jake says, taking my hand. "Let's go back to the house and get something to eat."

I swallow and give one last look to Easton, like I'm drowning and he's my life raft. Mom's taken him over to the casket and is telling him the story about when she bought Dad the suit he's wearing. He thought it was too expensive and a waste of money, but Mom insisted that with his build, he needed something custom-fitted to him. Dad declared that at the price they paid, the damn thing better fit him till the day he died and make him look as handsome as George Clooney when he was laid to rest.

Jake tugs my hand. "Mom will be okay," he says. "Unless you needed to talk to Easton again?"

What is there to talk about, really? Do I want to use my father's funeral as the opportunity to confess that part of me has always waited for him? That I'd probably wait for him forever? "No. Let's go."

*E*aston came to the house, and it was like old times. There was so much laughter and food and reminiscing that it felt more like another holiday than a wake. That's just how Dad would want it, but I kept catching myself waiting for my father to walk into the kitchen.

It's strange how our brains work, because the dad I had for the past few years was sick more often than not. Thin and weak. Bald. But when I imagine him walking into the kitchen, I imagine the tall and strong father from my childhood. The pre-cancer dad. Even at the end, the reality of his condition only hit me in blips. Most of the time my brain didn't process the changes. *Couldn't.*

If he were here, he'd follow the sound of our voices into the kitchen. Dad always chased the crowd—loved the house to be full and was happier in the middle of chaos than alone with a good book, like me. He'd go straight to Mom, like always, as if he needed to touch her and convince himself she was real, because a lifetime together would never be enough. Then he'd sit down at the table and listen. That was what he liked best about big groups. He didn't want to be the center of attention or talk constantly, but he loved hearing everyone's stories. And when he did speak, you listened, because you knew whatever he gave you would be good.

"Are you okay?"

I didn't even realize I was staring into space, but I blink away from the alternate reality and turn toward Easton. His eyes are so gentle, his hand warm as it cups my shoulder. I nod. "I think it might take me ten years to accept that he's gone." I say it softly, knowing the words might send any number of people into another crying jag if they overheard them.

"I get that." He points to the back doors. "Some fresh air?"

"I'd like that." I grab a couple of beers from the fridge and follow Easton outside. It's dark, well past sunset, but we don't bother with the lights. He stops on the patio, but I shake my head and lead the way to the treehouse, climbing the old ladder one-handed until I reach the privacy of the fort my father built for us.

I'm sinking to the floor and pulling the bottle opener from my pocket when I hear Easton's feet scraping against the rungs and spot his head poking into the tiny wooden house.

"I don't think I've been up here since I was ten," he says, pulling himself inside. He's too tall to stand, so he stays on his knees and crawls to the wall opposite me, extending his long legs so they're next to mine.

"You probably haven't fit since then," I say, squinting at him through the dark and smiling. I grab the battery-operated lantern from the wall and click it on. It's not much, but it's enough to cast a warm glow around us—enough so I can see his face. "You hardly fit now."

He glances up at the ceiling, way too close to his head, even seated. "Eh, there's plenty of room." He nods to the two beers beside me. "Is one of those for me?"

"If you want." I open them both and hand one to him.

His sigh fills the space a beat before his sadness. "This is the first time since I was drafted that I've had more than a single drink during the season."

"Your body is a multimillion-dollar temple."

"This temple is all I have. Without this, I don't have shit." His words are slightly slurred, and I wonder how many he's had. I know he was drinking while talking to my brothers. I had a few too. I'm tempted to get sloppy drunk, but Mom's here and she wouldn't like that.

"You always thought you were nothing without football," I say. "I never believed that."

He gives a small smile and sighs. "Thanks." He traces the lip of his beer with his index finger, and I can tell he's trying to work up to say something important. Something I probably don't really want to talk about right now. "Mom's sorry she couldn't come. She wanted to be here."

I smile. I can handle talking about Ms. Connor. Easton may have grown up without a dad around, but his mom did everything in her power to make up for it. "How is she?"

"Busy. Happy. Finally pursuing her passions instead of just trying to get by."

"Art, right?"

He nods. "She's obsessed with watercolors. She's really talented and doesn't give herself enough credit." He lifts those sad eyes to me. "A lot like you, I guess."

He's so close to me up here, but with our legs stretched out between us, he feels so far away, so I roll to my knees and scoot across the plywood floor to sit beside him, shoulder to shoulder. "I love the way you take care of her—the way you didn't question it when you joined the league. You just did it." When I tilt my face up to look at him, I catch him studying me, his gaze glued to my mouth. "You're a good son. I bet you're a good dad too."

He blinks away. "We need to talk about what happened in Chicago."

"I'd rather not right now," I whisper, focusing on the frogs in the distance, the cicadas singing in the trees.

"I need to." He wraps an arm around my shoulders and kisses the top of my head. "I want to be a good dad more than I want anything. I'll never be like your dad—I travel too fucking much, for one—but I want to try to be as close to that as I can manage. Everything I know about being a good father came from him."

I take a deep breath before rising to my knees and turning to straddle him. His eyes go wide and his jaw slackens, and for a moment, the look of wonder in his eyes is worth all the years of longing—of wanting and feeling like he was so far beyond my reach.

He grips my hips and slides his rough thumbs under my shirt, rubbing absent circles there. His eyes are glassy and his cheeks are flushed. "Shay, I'm serious. I need to explain."

I shake my head and bring my mouth to his. I know this is complicated. I'm in grad school; he's in the NFL. I'm just an average girl, and he has models knocking down his door. And never mind how my family will react . . . I brush my lips over his. "Not tonight," I say. His mouth is soft against mine, but his hands tighten at my waist. "I know we have things to figure out, but we can do that another time." I tug his bottom lip between my teeth.

He groans, then shoves me away—and not gently. "Shit. I'm sorry. We can't."

I scramble to the opposite wall, my pride stinging.

"Fuck. So sorry, Shay." He rubs at his mouth with the back of his hand, and he might as well have slapped me. Is he rubbing away my kiss? "Shit, shit, shit."

My own apology sits on my tongue, but I trap it there. When

he said we needed to talk, he didn't mean figuring out the details of *us*—he meant he needed to explain that there isn't going to be an *us*. I'm such an idiot. Why did I expect anything else?

I draw my knees into my chest and close my eyes.

"Shay," he whispers. "God, I screwed this all up."

"Don't."

"You're fucking amazing. And if things were different . . ."

"Please stop."

"Do you know what I admire most about your father?"

I press my forehead to my knees. I can't handle this right now—this conversation, this *rejection*. And if he tries to bring Dad into it, I'm going to fall apart.

"He was there. For all of his kids. For his wife."

I squeeze my knees tighter, trying to tune him out because his words are bringing the tears back, coaxing them from the pit of my stomach and into my chest where there's nothing but chaos. I feel myself shaking and pray he can't see it. Why did I kiss him? Why did I think he'd choose me?

"And when things were falling apart between them, he *stayed*."

I whip my head up. My eyes burn and my stomach aches, but *those words*. "What? What do you mean?"

"You think he and your mom were always happy? You think they didn't have tough times? They're human, Shay, and they both made mistakes. And when he thought he was in love with someone else, he didn't let that keep him from doing the right thing."

"Dad was never in love with anyone else."

"Ann, his administrative assistant at the construction

company. She was my mom's best friend and told Mom everything. They were in love, but your dad didn't want to tear apart your family. He sold the whole company to prove to your mom he wanted to start over."

"No. You misunderstood." I shake my head and scoot toward the ladder. "You don't know what you're talking about."

"He wanted you all to stay together. Frank knew his kids needed to have both of their parents all the time. That's what I want for Abi."

"Shut up." I don't bother to wipe away my tears. I have to get away from here—away from his poisonous words—as fast as I can. I race down and slip on the last rung. Pain is a hot spike driving up my leg and radiating out around my ankle.

I fall to the ground, clutching my ankle, and roll to the side.

Easton is next to me in a flash. "Shay, look at me. Tell me what hurts."

I must have screamed when I landed, because I hear the soft thud of feet coming across grass from the house. "Is she okay?" It's Carter. "Shay, what's wrong? Is it your ankle?"

It's my heart. "I landed wrong," I say, avoiding Easton's gaze, even though I feel it on me so intensely it burns.

"Here, let me help you up." Carter slides a hand under my shoulder and hauls me to my feet. I gasp the second I try to put weight on the bad ankle. "Do we need to go to the hospital?"

"No. I just need ice. I'm fine."

Easton goes to the side opposite Carter. I don't want Carter to ask questions, so I don't deny his help.

Carter asks anyway. "What were you two doing up there?" *Ever the protective big brother.*

"Just talking," Easton says. He reaches forward to open the door, and I hobble inside, letting them half carry me to the couch. "I'll grab some ice," he says when I sit, then he disappears in a rush to the kitchen.

Carter reaches around me to pull the lever on the reclining sofa to elevate my feet.

"What happened?" Jake asks.

"She fell out of the treehouse," Carter says.

I smack my brother's arm. "I didn't fall out. I missed a couple of rungs on the ladder and landed wrong." The sharp pain has subsided to a dull, throbbing ache. "It's just twisted. I'll be fine."

Easton returns with a bag of ice and apology all over his face. His eyes are hazy. He's drunk. He probably didn't have any idea what he was talking about before. My dad has never loved anyone but my mom. He wouldn't—

My stomach lurches. "I think I'm going to be sick."

Jake grabs an empty popcorn bowl off the end table and shoves it in front of me before the three beers I've had tonight rise from my throat and splash into the bowl in a nasty cocktail of alcohol and stomach acid.

"I'm so sorry, Shay," Easton says. I can't look at him.

Carter tenses beside me and throws an angry glare in his direction. "What did you do? You made a pass at her up there, didn't you? You fucker. Didn't you *just* tell me that you're trying to work things out with Scarlett?"

"Stop it," I say, but the words are wrapped in a sob I can't hold back. *He's working things out with his wife.* And dear God, that hurts, but nothing feels right in a world where what he said about Dad is true. "*When he fell in love with someone else . . .*"

"Are you sure you're okay? You don't need to go to the ER?" Carter asks.

I'm not okay. But there's nothing in the emergency room that can fix me.

♡

Scarlett Lashenta is sitting on my front porch.

No. Pretty sure that can't be right.

I drag my hand over my eyes, trying to rub the sleep out of them. But when I open them, she's still there—sitting on the front porch of the off-campus two-bedroom I'm renting with friends for the summer. "Can I help you?"

Scarlett tucks a lock of silky red hair behind her ear and gives me a weak smile. "You're Shayleigh Jackson?"

"I am."

"I've seen Easton's pictures of you two in Paris together. You're even prettier in person, though." She bites her bottom lip. Her *perfect* bottom lip. If I tried to wear red lipstick like that, I'd look like a clown. This woman looks Photoshop-perfect in real life. "I was hoping we could talk? About Easton."

My stomach cramps. I haven't seen him since he left Mom's house the night of Dad's funeral. He's texted, saying he wants to talk. I've ignored him. "Is he okay?"

"Oh, yes. He's fine. Well, as fine as he gets. You know Easton. Every time there's a major change in his life, he struggles a bit, so the new QB coach is getting to him."

I didn't know he had a new coach. I guess we didn't talk that much about his life, now that I think about it.

"You seem like a really nice girl, Shayleigh. At least, that's what I've come to believe from Easton's stories."

"Thanks." This is so surreal. Scarlett Lashenta is sitting on my front porch telling me I'm *a nice girl.* Two nights ago, I was climbing onto her husband's lap and trying to seduce him.

"You don't strike me as the kind of person who'd set out to tear apart a family." Her blue eyes fill with tears. "I don't believe you'd want a little girl to be without her daddy. That's why I'm here."

Maybe this *is* a dream. Or a nightmare. It was bad enough to have Easton push me away. I don't need to hear it from Scarlett too. "I don't know what you mean."

"I know what happened between you and Easton in Chicago." She waves her phone as if this explains everything. "But when he slept with you, he didn't know what he knows now."

"Okay?" Why is she here? Easton made his plans clear. He wants to stay with Scarlett because he seems to think I'm just like whatever woman he claims my dad fell in love with. *He was drunk and talking crazy. Dad never loved anyone else.*

With a sigh, she cocks her head to the side. "He hasn't told you, has he?"

"My father just died."

"About Abigail." She toys with her pearl necklace. "She has leukemia."

My stomach drops to my feet. "What?"

She turns away, staring into the overgrown rosebushes lining the front of the porch. The blooms are brown and dried, and the whole flowerbed looks atrocious. When she turns back to me, tears glisten in her eyes. "She needs us to be a family right now, and I'm here to ask you to stay out of his life."

The words are a knife to the gut. "That won't be a problem."

"Are you sure about that?"

"Why are you here? Easton already told me he's not going through with the divorce."

She wipes away a stream of fat tears. "Between you and me, I don't think our marriage stands a chance if you're in the picture, and I need it to work. Abi needs it to work." She drops her gaze to her shoes and shakes her head. "I'm not trying to hurt you. I'm hoping for your mercy. I'm hoping you'll understand why I'm asking you not to make it harder than it is for him, why I'm asking you to let him focus on his child."

Part XII.

Now

Shay

The first person a woman should want to see after she finds out she's pregnant is the father of her baby. And yet I find myself on the steps of Easton's beautiful home, the lulling sounds of the lake behind me.

When I ring the doorbell, I'm not sure what I plan to say, but my body is locked up with worry. Whenever I get him, something pulls him away from me again, and it looks like this time isn't going to be any different.

The second Easton opens the door and he smiles, though? A strange sense of calm washes over me. He drags his eyes down my body and slowly back up before taking my hand and pulling me into the house.

"Abi and Tori are spending the afternoon at the library," he says with a grin. And just like that, his mouth is on mine. His hands are sliding up my shirt and mine up his. We don't even make it past the foyer before we're naked and on the floor—greedy hands and mouths and desperation the backdrop to the breathy sounds that fill the air.

I'm not sure I could ever get used to the fact that Easton wants me like this—that I can have him anytime I want him. Or I could, *before.*

I push the thought away and focus on the rough grip of his hands on my hips and the wet sweep of his tongue across my nipples.

"I've been thinking about you all day," he murmurs as he kisses his way down my stomach. "I don't know if I actually slept last night. I wanted you in my bed."

I slide my fingers into his hair and tug him up. "Easton."

He lowers his smile to my mouth and kisses me until everything else falls away. He only stops his touching and kissing—his *worshipping*—long enough to put on a condom and position himself between my legs. He pauses there, so close to where I need him, and frames my face with his hands. "We're really doing this," he says softly, reverently.

I lift my hips, seeking him, needing him. *One last time.*

He slides into me and moves so tenderly that tears sting the backs of my eyes. "I love you."

"I love you." All I can do is bury my face in his neck and hold on, because it's only love, and that's never been enough.

And when we're spent and breathless, once my tailbone feels tender from the hardwood floor, he rolls us over so I'm on top of him and wraps his arms around me.

"Sorry about that," he says.

I close my eyes and focus on the rise and fall of his chest with his heavy breaths. "Why sorry?"

"I was thinking about you, and then there you were." He chuckles. "I don't know, Shay. After years of thinking about you, of missing you and wanting you, it's going to be hard to pace myself now that you're mine."

Emotion clogs my throat at that, and I can't reply. I can hardly even breathe. *Now that you're mine.* But for how much longer?

He rolls us to our sides before standing and helping me up. He scoops our clothes into a big pile in his arms. "Coffee?" he asks with an arched brow.

I bite my lip and shake my head. "I'm good."

He smacks my bare ass. "Then go get in bed. We have three hours until Abi gets home, and I want to spend it all naked with you between my sheets."

I try to smile, but this morning's news weighs heavily on me and I can't quite make my lips obey. This is all a preview of what could have been, and I'm being sliced apart from the inside.

"Hey." He cups my jaw. "Did I hurt you? Are you okay?"

"You didn't hurt me." *But I'm not okay.* "Come on." I don't want to share my news while we're standing naked by the front door. "I'm going to go upstairs and clean up. I'll meet you in bed."

His eyes flare hungrily again and his gaze dips down and back up, but I turn away before he can meet my gaze. This feeling in my chest when he looks at me like that and I know what I have to tell him? It's a little bit like heartbreak.

Easton

Something is wrong with Shay, and I think I know what it is.

I open the curtains in my bedroom to expose the picture windows and the floor-to-ceiling view of Lake Michigan. I wasn't kidding when I said I wanted to spend the afternoon in bed with her. While she cleans up in the bathroom, I run downstairs to grab a plate of fruit—grapes, fresh strawberries, a few mandarin oranges—and a pot of coffee in case she changes her mind about it.

When I return to the bedroom, Shay's in my bed. She curled on her side with her head on my pillow as she reads the back cover of the military suspense novel from my nightstand.

"I liked this one," she says.

I smile. I'm going to love trying to keep up with her. "I wouldn't have thought you'd have time for pleasure reading while you were working on your dissertation."

She huffs out a laugh, but there's no humor in it. "Maybe if I hadn't made time for pleasure reading, I would've finished a couple of years ago."

I set the plate of fruit and carafe of coffee on the dresser before climbing into bed with her. "You're really here." I pull her back to my front and press my hand flat against her breastbone.

"I am," she says. "It's unreal. I didn't think we'd ever . . ."

I press a kiss to her bare shoulder. She didn't believe we'd make it work. One night in Paris then a night in my hotel room in Chicago before her dad died. I want us to have a chance, and it's always been yanked away from us before we could settle in.

"We're going to make it," I say. She stiffens in my arms, and I instinctively hold her tighter. "I know you're scared. I know you don't trust this to work, but . . ." I force myself to relax my hold. "I'm struggling to not be selfish. I want you in my arms all the time, but I know you have other things to do this week."

"You're the least selfish person I know," she says softly.

"Maybe I just hide it well." I mean it as a joke, but it doesn't sound like that. "I've been pretty selfish with you."

"Not with Abi. Not with Scarlett."

I shrug. I don't particularly want to talk about my ex-wife while Shay is in my arms, but there's still so much of our pasts we haven't hashed out. If she wants to talk about this now, we will. "I've had my moments, but don't paint me as a martyr just because our situation is unconventional."

Turning in my arms, she presses her palm to my chest, as if trying to measure the beats of my heart. "When did you find out Abi wasn't yours?"

"When Abi was sick, I wanted to see if I was a match to donate bone marrow. Most of the time, parents aren't a match, but I wanted to try anyway. Scarlett panicked that it was like a DNA test or something and they'd tell me I wasn't Abi's father." I close my eyes as I remember her stopping me on my way out the door. Her panic. Her tearful confession. The way she begged me not to leave her. "She told me she'd lied because she'd wanted to give her child the best, and she believed I was meant to be Abi's father."

"What did you do?"

"I grieved a little, I guess. Now it *truly* doesn't matter to me. She's my daughter, but when I first discovered she wasn't biologically mine, I had to rearrange my perception of everything. Including my marriage and how hard I was willing to bend to make it work and how long I was willing to continue what felt like a ruse at that point. Scarlett and I were married in name only. When she moved back in after Abi's diagnosis, I insisted she sleep in a different room until we figured out what we really wanted. The day of her confession, I went from wanting to stay married for my three-year-old daughter's sake to wanting to stay married because I was afraid she'd take Abi away from me if we divorced. What claim did I have if she wasn't even my blood?"

"That's awful."

I stroke Shay's hair and twist to press a kiss to her forehead. "I don't think she would have. Hell, she barely fought me for primary custody when we finally did divorce." I sigh. "Scarlett knew—knew before she even held Abi for the first time—that I was the best choice she could make for her daughter. While I resent the lies and manipulation, I understand that Abi was always her priority. Just like she was mine."

"Can I ask you a question?"

When she doesn't immediately ask, I say, "Of course."

She worries her bottom lip between her teeth and watches me for a long time before speaking again. "Do you ever think about the decision you made when you found out Scarlett was pregnant?"

My breath catches in my chest. *Painful.* I think about my decision to stay with Scarlett a lot, but in the context of Shay, I think about it almost compulsively. If I could rewrite the past, I would've found a way to be Abi's father without marrying Scarlett. But even from this vantage point, I can't see how that would've happened. Scarlett didn't want to be alone, and if I'd known Abi wasn't mine before she was born, I wouldn't have felt so determined to make us a family.

Shay studies my face. "I'm not judging your decision either way," she says, misinterpreting my silence as defensiveness. "I just wonder if you've ever considered how you could've handled it differently if you'd known the truth. What would you have done if you'd known Abi wasn't yours?"

My chest tightens.

"I don't mean about us," she says in a rush. "I mean, do you think you would've married Scarlett?"

I pull back so I can see her face. "But there *was* an us."

"Barely." She looks away when she says the word, and I wonder if it feels like as much of a betrayal to her heart as it does to mine.

I take her chin in my hand, guiding her to meet my eyes. "Not barely."

"It was one night in Paris, Easton."

"Does that make it any less real?" I take her hand and press it to my chest. "Does what I felt here not count because I only got one weekend to touch you? To hold you? What we had was real. Maybe it didn't last long, but it was the most honest thing I've ever felt for any woman. Even when I thought Abi was my daughter, you were part of the equation. It wasn't an easy choice."

"But what if I hadn't been in the picture and you'd known she wasn't yours? Would you have stayed? Would you have wanted to be Abi's father?" Her face falls. "That's not a fair question, is it?"

"She's my daughter in every way that matters, Shay. I cannot imagine what my life would be like if I didn't have her, and I don't want to." I swallow the lump in my throat. She's asking me a serious question and she deserves an honest answer. "No. If I'd known she wasn't mine, I wouldn't have stuck around. Raising another man's child is a heartache I wouldn't have signed on for if I'd known."

She nods slowly.

I wrap my arms around her because I can feel her pulling away. "Does it bother you? The idea of getting involved with a man who's already a father? Does it bother you that Abi remains my priority despite our DNA?"

"No. That doesn't bother me." I see the truth in her eyes, but it doesn't explain the stiffness in her body.

"What about Scarlett? Will it bother you that she's around sometimes?" I blow out a breath, realizing I should address the possibility of Scarlett moving to Jackson Harbor now and not later. "Will it bother you if she decides she wants her second home to be here and not Chicago?"

She blinks at me. "She's thinking of moving *here*?"

I nod slowly. "I was trying to talk her out of it, but I'm not sure what's going to happen now."

"Oh. I guess that could be good for Abi."

But not for her? Is that what she's thinking? "Scarlett can live right next door if she wants to, and it won't change the fact that I want you."

She curls into my chest and closes her eyes.

I stroke her back. "Hey, Short Stack. Talk to me. Are you okay?" *Please don't panic. Please don't give up on this before we even have a chance to begin.*

"Will you . . . just hold me for a while?"

"Of course. You're talking to the guy who wants to hold you forever, remember?"

Dr. Merritt Reddy
Associate Professor of Anthropology
Office Hours, MWF 2 to 5

I hold my breath as I stand in front of Dr. Merritt Reddy's office. I've questioned my decision to come here dozens of times and nearly turned my car around on the interstate. I should've gone to George first, told him and let him decide what to tell his wife. But can I trust him to tell her the truth? If I leave it to him and he doesn't tell her, I'll walk around feeling guilty forever. She deserves to know about me as much as *I* deserved to know about her.

I hate him for putting me in the position he did, but I refuse to hate myself. I need to do this.

I lift my fist to knock on the wooden door, but it opens before I can, and I'm suddenly standing in front of the woman I saw George kissing in his front yard. Her long blond hair is tied back today, and the glasses on the tip of her nose rise higher when she scrunches up her face in a frown.

"Can I help you?"

"Um, yes. I'm . . . Yes. Dr. Reddy, my name's Shayleigh Jackson. I was wondering if we could speak privately?"

Sighing, she rolls her shoulders back and presses her office door open, gesturing me inside. "I was going to get some coffee, but I suppose that can wait."

"Thank you." My voice shakes and I fear I might throw up on the lovely blue and gray rug covering her office floor. *So, this is what it feels like to destroy a family.* I'm a walking, talking time bomb, and she's just invited me into her office.

She waves to the gray armchairs just inside the door and waits for me to sit before she takes the one opposite me. "You're George's PhD candidate, is that right? I understand you've really blown away the whole committee with the work on your dissertation. George is very proud of you."

Bile rises in my stomach. She's not making this any easier. "I'm surprised he talks about me at all," I admit.

"Oh, of course he does. George lives and breathes for his graduate students. You've been a bit of a passion project for him the last couple of years."

You have no idea. "Have you and he . . . been together long?"

She smiles. "It's all relative, I suppose. We've lived together for ten years or so, been married for five. Our daughter is four."

I feel lightheaded, and the room feels like it tilts sideways. I gulp in air.

"You look a little pale, darling. Can I get you some water?"

"No, I'm fine." I just want to get this over with. "I'm really sorry to come here like this, Dr. Reddy. I want you to know that I thought a long time before I decided to come."

She arches a brow. "Okay."

"Before I say anything else, I want you to know that regardless of what you decide to do, I don't like being in this position. Family is everything to me. But I had to come."

She folds her hands in her lap and studies me with a tilt of her head. "Maybe you should start at the beginning. You're not making much sense."

Another wave of nausea slams into me, and sweat breaks out on my forehead. I close my eyes and focus on my breathing. *In and out. In and out.* "George and I have been . . ." God. I cannot say it. I can't be the reason this family falls apart. Can't be the reason this woman loses her husband or their child loses her father.

Too late for that, Shay.

She holds up a hand. "Before you do this, I want you to ask yourself if you really want to be the kind of woman who lies and manipulates to steal a married man who doesn't even want her." The kindness from her voice earlier is gone now.

"What?" Heat blazes in my cheeks. She thinks I'm here to tell her lies? In an attempt to . . . *steal George from her*? Does she know we slept together?

"He told me you were being rather immature about everything."

What exactly did he tell her? I feel like they've been laughing at me behind my back, and it feels . . . ugly.

Her lips quirk. "Darling, I'm not sure what kind of man you thought George was, but he's happily married with a daughter he adores. He doesn't want you."

"I'm so sorry. You have no idea how awful I feel, and I regret what I'm here to say, but it's nothing but the truth."

She holds up a hand. That's when I notice the ring on her finger. The ring I thought he'd gotten for me. The one he told me he was taking to his safe deposit box. *Such a liar.* "Stop. Please. My husband already told me that you threw yourself at him and he turned you down. And now you're trying to rewrite history so I'll—what? Step aside and you can keep him for yourself? Stop while you're ahead. I'm embarrassed for you, and this whole scene is insulting to me and to my husband."

"I'm sorry. I . . . What?"

"What do you want from me? Pity? Poor little grad student fell in love with her professor and doesn't want to let him go." She shakes her head. "He told me about you. How you're so scared of what's next that you're looking for a man to take you under his wing. I think he made it clear that he will not be that man when you tried to take him to bed."

I feel like I've been slapped, but at the same time, anger makes my nails bite into my palms. That fucking *liar* told his wife I tried to sleep with him. Is this some crazy dream? Am I still in bed with Easton? Maybe I fell asleep and only dreamed about making excuses to leave. Maybe I haven't actually left for Chicago yet. But I swallow, lift my chin, and say what I have to say as clearly as I can. "I don't know what your husband told you, but I'm only here because I thought you deserved to know the truth. George and I have been sleeping together. Until last week, we were in a relationship."

"Sure you were." She sighs. "You're a lovely girl, and I know why you'd be interested in my husband. I wasn't surprised when he told me you came on to him. You're not the first student to get romantic delusions."

My face is so hot, and I can't decide if I'm embarrassed or angry or some other emotion that strikes in the middle of this Bizarro World alternate universe I've found myself in. She truly believes that George turned me down and I'm here because I'm jealous.

"I know it can be intense to finish a dissertation, and I'm sure you're dealing with a lot of emotions right now. But I'm not sure what you hoped to accomplish by barging in here and trying to ruin a good marriage. Do you think this will make him want you?"

I grab my purse off the floor and slip it onto my shoulder. "I'll leave now." I stomp toward the door but stop when my hand is on the handle. Slowly, I turn around. "If you knew the truth, if you'd listen, you'd be as angry with him about this as I am."

"Child—"

"No. You don't get to treat me like a little girl. I'm thirty years old. This isn't about me having some crush on your husband. The problem here is that he never told me he was married. Not when he started sleeping with me. Not after. I didn't know about you until last week." Her jaw drops, and I think I've finally shocked her, but I push past my mild satisfaction at that and keep going. "If you were wise, you'd hear me out. We *both* deserved to know the truth, especially considering he and I were having sex without condoms. By keeping the full truth from me, he denied me the choice that should've been mine to make, and now I'm pregnant with a married man's baby."

"You're . . . pregnant?" She's pale. She actually looks like she might be sick.

I shake my head slowly. I'm not done. "And by assuming I came here to lie, by assuming I'd go to such disgusting lengths because I *want him*, you're only enabling a lying womanizer. Shame on you. If you want to believe him, go for it. Personally, I want nothing to do with him."

Something flickers across her face, but I'm too angry to analyze it. I've said what I needed to say. I'm done.

Easton

Me: Come over for dinner? I'm grilling steaks.

Shay: Not tonight. I'm tired.

Me: You could come over and nap? My bed is pretty damn comfortable if you recall.

Shay: I just need a night at home.

I want to ask if she's sure everything's okay, but I already asked that when she left my house this afternoon. I want to ask if the idea of Scarlett moving here is freaking her out, but I already asked that too. I want to tell her I love her, but I'm a little afraid that this time she might not say it back.

Shay

I got back from Chicago around nine and went straight to Teagan and Carter's. Carter is helping Easton with the equipment setup in his new theater room, and Isaiah is visiting his grandmother. I knocked twice before strolling right into their house and sitting my pregnant, emotionally exhausted ass down on their couch.

"Here. You look like you could use this." Teagan emerges from the kitchen and hands me a bottle of beer.

"No alcohol for me."

"Still the stomach thing, huh?" Shrugging, she returns the beer to the fridge. "Coffee?"

"I'm actually trying to cut back on my caffeine intake too."

This shocks her. "You really must be feeling ill. But honestly, the coffee is probably harder on your stomach than the alcohol, so good call."

There are a dozen excuses I could easily use to not drink alcohol or caffeine, but now is really as good a time as any to share my big news with my best friend. I clear my throat. "About that . . . I went to the doctor this morning. It turns out there's an explanation for my exhaustion. A . . . pretty obvious one that also explains the nausea and food aversions."

Her jaw goes slack and she lowers herself into the chair. "You're pregnant."

Tears burn at the back of my eyes. I know if I speak I'm gonna open up the floodgates. I really don't want to cry again today, so I just nod.

"Holy shit." She puts her beer down and rushes back into the kitchen. She yanks open the freezer. "Ice cream?"

I nod again and watch as she fills two large bowls with chocolate peanut butter chunk swirl. My favorite.

She doesn't say another word until we've each eaten several bites. "Are you okay?"

I'm sure she must have a thousand questions, but I'm so grateful she chose to start there. "Yeah. I mean, I'm getting there, at least."

She watches her bowl as she pushes a spoonful of ice cream around. "It's definitely George's?"

I laugh. God, for a blessed moment in the doctor's office, the possibility that it was Easton's crossed my mind. No, not possibility—dumb hope. "It's George's." I put my ice cream down on the coffee table. "Easton and I talked Sunday, and I decided I wanted to stay in Jackson Harbor and give him and me a chance. And now instead of going out on dates with him and finding a job in the place I really want to be, I need to figure out how I can blow them away at my L.A. interview so I can start over somewhere else."

"Wait. Is that what you *want* to do? Start over?" She shakes her head. "Why? I don't understand."

Because I'm too ashamed to raise a married man's child in front of my mother. Because I'll do anything to avoid disappointing her like that. Because I can't ask Easton to raise another child that isn't his. "It wouldn't be unexpected, would it? It's what I'm supposed to do next."

"The only thing you're *supposed* to do next is figure out what makes you happy." Teagan puts both of our bowls in the sink before returning to the living room. "You didn't answer my question. Is that what you want?"

"I've spent the last eight years of my life working on this PhD. I'm a good teacher. I'm a grown woman. I can do this."

"Of course you can. I have every faith in you, but why move to L.A. if you don't want to live there? Why leave your family?"

"Because I can't look my mom in the eye and tell her I'm having a married man's baby." I close my eyes and hot tears stream down my cheeks.

"You didn't know, Shay. Just explain. Your mom will understand."

Shaking my head, I open my mouth to explain, but I can't. I can't speak the truth Easton broke me with. Saying the words feels like a betrayal to my father's memory. "The whole thing makes me feel like an idiot, Tea. It's like I'm looking at a map with a million different roads, and the only rule is I can't stay where I am. I see all these options, and everything's confusing, but there's one thing I know for sure."

"What's that?"

I meet my friend's eyes. "The timing and logistics might be awful, but when I sat in the doctor's office and she started asking me about my periods, my biggest fear wasn't that I might be pregnant; it was that I might have something terrible wrong with me that would keep me from having kids. I want this baby."

She takes my hand and squeezes it. "Then start there, but don't assume you have to leave. Your mother will love you and this child no matter what."

"And what about Easton?" My voice cracks.

"I don't know, baby. I think he's the only one who can answer that."

"Will you come with me to my ultrasound tomorrow?"

She pulls me into a hug. "I wouldn't miss it."

Shay

When I got to campus this morning, there was a note from the department secretary in my mailbox saying Dr. Alby needed to see me in his office. I planned on talking to him this morning, but judging by this note, his wife already had a conversation about it with him last night.

I hope she chewed his ass out—and not in the sexy way.

When I knock on his office door, I'm numb.

"Come in!" His tone is decidedly grumpy. Good. That makes two of us.

I push into his office and shut the door behind me.

When he tears his gaze away from the computer, his eyes lock on that closed door. "Shay. I think it would be better if you kept that door open."

What a fucking *asshole.* "Really? You didn't mind me closing it when you were cheating on your *wife* with me." Oh. Wow. That felt great. Why was I putting this off?

He blows out a breath. "Merritt told me you came to her office last night. And before you get all high and mighty with me, you should understand that I made the decisions I did based on my gauge of your maturity level. After the way you handled speaking with her, it's clear that I made the right call."

In this moment, I see George clearly for the first time. Honestly, I'm disgusted with *myself* for getting personally involved with him. I've always known on some level that George needed taking down a notch, but why on earth didn't I ever find his ego annoying? Like, vagina-shriveling unacceptable. I shake my head. "My *maturity* level? What a convenient excuse that must've been for you—to lie to your wife and keep me in the dark about your marriage so you could fuck me. You *knew* I would've turned you down if you'd told me the truth."

He rocks back in his chair, chest puffed up, nostrils flaring with anger. "I suppose now you're going to act like you didn't want to? Play the victim card and say I coerced you through the mentor-mentee power dynamic?"

I shake my head. "I never thought that. Your evaluation of my work and guidance of my research always felt completely separate from our personal relationship."

He swallows and his chest caves in. *Good.* At least he's been a little worried about it.

"I didn't sleep with you for academic favors," I say, realizing we need to get this cleared up first. "And I never felt like you used your position on my committee to get me in bed."

He scrubs a hand over his face, nodding. "Okay. Good, good,

good. This is good to hear."

"That's a lot of *good* in reference to a situation that's pretty fucked up, George. You're not off the hook for not telling me about your wife. Not with me, at least. If she wants to ignore what you've done, that's on her. Even if I wanted a relationship with you, I wouldn't forgive you for keeping me in the dark. I don't have the energy to hash out how I feel about your lies right now."

He smirks. "Is that a good thing or a bad thing?"

I cock my head to the side. "What exactly did your wife tell you?" *Did she tell you I'm pregnant?*

"She told me to get out." He shifts uncomfortably. *Ass sore, George?* "And then she told me I needed to talk to you."

"She's right. We do need to talk."

He stares at me and when I don't immediately explain, he says, "Spit it out."

"I'm pregnant."

He goes pale then seems to shake away the instinctive panic. "The football player works fast."

"The baby isn't Easton's." I stare at him, but when he only stares back with that constipated confusion face, I say, "I'm eleven weeks and four days pregnant." I pull the ultrasound picture from my purse and place it in front of him on the desk.

He stares at the black-and-white photo with wide eyes. "Can you be sure it's mine?"

What a *dick*. "Before Easton came to town, you're the only one I'd slept with in years."

When he lifts his eyes to mine, they're angry. "You told me you were on the pill."

"I was. It looks like I got pregnant during that Florida

conference. The doctor said if I was that sick, the birth control wouldn't have worked right."

"The chances, though . . ."

I point at the picture. "Right there. *There's* the chance."

He stares at me for a long beat, and I watch as the possibility clicks into place in his mind. "I can't marry you, Shay. You've been acting weird since you saw that ring, but I've never given you reason to believe I wanted that from you. I don't want to lose my wife."

"If you think I want to marry you after all I know now, you've lost your goddamned mind."

"I mean, I'd want a paternity test."

"Would you? And what then? What would the proof of a paternity test change for you?" I shake my head. "I might not like how this happened, but I'm not upset to know I'm going to be a mother."

"Well, at least that's one of us." He blows out a breath. "You got just what you wanted, didn't you? An excuse to stay home. An excuse to ignore everything you've worked so hard for so you can . . . what? How will you support this kid? Are you going to be a fucking *bartender*?"

I know that shot is supposed to hurt, but it doesn't. I don't care what he thinks of me, of my family or my choices. "I'm only telling you because it's the right thing to do. Not because I expect anything from you."

He looks dumbstruck. I wonder how many other women he's been sleeping with while not using condoms and pretending to be single. Maybe even other women at this college who thought they were protecting their own reputation by keeping the secret.

"I think it would be easier all around if you make this decision regarding the baby in the same way I told you to make the decisions regarding your career," he says. "Don't factor me into the equation."

"Would you sign away your rights to the child?"

He shrugs, as if I'm asking for something meaningless. "If that's what you want, that's fine with me."

I take a breath. "And when I defend my dissertation, I expect you to do the same. Evaluate me as if we were never together, as if we were never involved."

"You think I'm going to evaluate you unfairly because of all of this? I have the highest regard for academic integrity."

I laugh. "Because *academic* integrity is everything, right? Apparently, for you, it's even more important than personal integrity." I take the ultrasound photo from his desk, tuck it into my purse, and leave his office.

Maybe it's not wise to walk away with bitterness between us when the future of my degree hangs in the balance. If I'm going to move away and start over, I'm going to want this degree I've busted my ass for. But it was worth it.

Easton

Me: Everything okay? I missed you yesterday.

Shay: I'm dealing with some stuff at school. I've had some unexpected changes that complicate things.

Me: Can I help?

Shay: I need to do this myself.

Me: Will I see you at gymnastics tonight? Abi is excited.

Shay: No, Nic's taking Lilly.

Me: You're avoiding me.

*Shay: I am. Kind of. Give me some space, Easton.
We'll talk, but I need to take care of me right now.*

"What do you think about this one?" Carter asks, twisting the solitary diamond band between two fingers. "Is it too simple?"

I shove my phone into my back pocket and swallow my heartache. Because when your childhood best friend wants you to come along to pick out an engagement ring for the love of his life, you do it. "Simple isn't a bad thing." I study the diamond. "And that one doesn't strike me as simple at all. Just . . . solid. Like you two."

He grins. "I think so too." His gaze flicks to the pocket where I just put away my phone. "Was that my sister?"

"Yeah."

"She still avoiding you?"

I drag a hand through my hair. "Yeah."

"Are you gonna do something about it?"

Do I look like an idiot? "She wants space."

He frowns. "What'd you do?"

I shake my head. Carter doesn't know about our history. I never told him about Paris or that she came to me when she found out their father was entering hospice care. Maybe it's time to own up to all of it. "I didn't do anything this time," I say carefully. "But she has every reason to be cautious."

"Meaning?"

"Listen, I'd like to tell you the whole thing, but if you beat in my face, *you're* the one who has to explain your actions to my sweet, innocent daughter."

His eyes go wide. "Oh, hell. We're gonna need beer, aren't we?"

I nod. "We should probably do this at the bar."

I'm officially avoiding my apartment. I started packing it up yesterday in an emotional rush of energy. Even if I planned to stay in Jackson Harbor, and I don't, I'd have to leave my tiny third-floor walk-up. It won't be practical with a baby, never mind that it only has one bedroom.

I go to Teagan's and smile when she opens the door. "Can I hang for a while?"

"Always."

"Want to order in? I think I'm officially past the no-appetite part of this pregnancy and into the clichéd cravings part."

"I . . ." Her gaze shifts to the living room just beyond the foyer.

And that's the moment when I realize Teagan isn't home alone. In the living room, Carter stops with a beer halfway to his lips. And halfway between me and the couch, Easton stands paralyzed, staring at me in wide-eyed shock.

"Easton's here," she says quietly. "Nic took both girls to gymnastics."

Shit. I wasn't ready for this yet. I might not ever be.

I turn around and open the door she just closed, pushing outside onto the porch.

"You sonofabitch!" I hear Carter say behind me. "I listened to your whole damn sob story, and now you're telling me you got my sister pregnant?"

I close the door before I can hear Easton's response. The porch swing is either too high or I'm too short, because my feet dangle a good foot off the ground as I let the swing rock me back and forth.

When the door opens again, I look up expecting to see Teagan, but it's Easton stepping out onto the porch with me. Easton, who doesn't want to raise another man's baby again. Easton, who just wants a simple life where he can focus on his daughter and avoid all the drama.

He studies the spot next to me, and whether because of my mood or because he can't stomach the thought of being that close to me right now, he seems to think better of sitting there and leans against the porch rail instead. His jaw ticks as he stares at me. "You're pregnant."

I nod jerkily.

"And it's not . . ."

I shake my head. I wish it were Easton's. The thought takes me back to when I was twenty years old and so immature, trying to wish myself pregnant so maybe he'd choose me over Scarlett.

But of course, I wasn't. Easton was always too careful for that.

He pivots and faces the street. Good. Maybe this'll be easier if I can't see his face. Even if . . . even if watching him turn his back on me shakes me at my fault lines.

"I didn't know until this week," I say. I cannot stand the idea of him thinking even for a minute that I'm like his ex-wife—that I would have deceived him the way she did.

"That's why you asked, though," he says. "Monday . . . when you asked if I'd make the same choice."

I swallow. "I know you probably don't want to talk to me right now, and I don't blame you. I'm leaving for the airport in the morning."

He spins to face me. "What?"

"For the interview in L.A."

"Your brother's getting married on Saturday."

That's what he's worried about? That I'll miss the wedding? "I'll be home in time for the family dinner Friday night, no worries."

"I mean . . . You've put family first. You decided to stay, and now you're gonna run away and leave them all behind?"

I don't want to talk about moving away from my family. I just . . . can't. I shrug uselessly.

"Does he know?"

"He knows."

"And is he going to L.A. with you?"

"No." Does he think that's how this works? That if I can't have him, I'll take *George*, despite the lies? Despite the fact that my heart belongs to Easton? My thoughts muddle and blur, and the world around me seems hazy. "All I know is I have to have a way to take care of this baby. I have to make that my priority."

He closes his eyes. "By moving to L.A."

"There are some things that aren't clear to me, but I want to be a mom. This baby was unexpected and unplanned but not unwanted."

"How can you say that when *he* is the father? He was married and slept with you."

"So were you!" I push myself off the swing. I shouldn't have come here. But one thing is clear. I have to move. Because I don't think I can survive seeing Easton all the time and knowing he'll never be mine.

"Were you going to tell me?"

"I should've told you the second you opened your door on Monday. I know that. I just . . ." What excuse do I have? *I wanted one more time with you*? *I didn't think my heart would survive losing you a third time*?

His eyes are watery, and he tilts his face up to the ceiling of the covered porch. "Trying to raise this baby alone in L.A. is a big mistake."

"I don't need your approval." I walk to where I parked my car on the street, only looking back when I open the door. He's not running after me. He's just standing there, staring at the ground. I didn't realize that part of me was hoping that when circumstances turned against us a third time, he might choose me anyway. And watching him stand there, watching him let me go, I feel my heart break once more.

Easton

*S*hay walked away, and I feel like I've been hit by a truck.

It's been an hour since she stormed off the porch at her brother's house and left me behind to deal with my shock and confusion.

She's having his baby.

There's part of me that keeps waiting for her to track me down and say it was all a bad joke. A mistake. *Anything.*

We've never been able to get the timing right. Before I left for L.A., she was too young. Then Scarlett was pregnant; then Abi was sick. And now . . .

She's having his baby.

"You look like hell," Carter says, sliding into the booth across from me.

Shay walked away, and I came to Jackson Brews. I let the

nanny know I'd be home late, and I fully intended on getting completely shitfaced. But so far I haven't had more than a couple of sips of my beer, and the double Bulleit I ordered sits untouched in front of me.

"You okay?" he asks.

"She's having his baby." The words are no easier to say after an hour of hearing them on repeat in my head.

Carter grabs my bourbon and takes a big swig, grimacing a little as he puts it back down. "The situation's so fucked up. First of all, I can't even wrap my brain around Shay getting involved with this guy to begin with, but then, get this—according to Teagan, she had a talk with him and they agreed he wouldn't be part of the baby's life. Who does that?"

I snap my head up. "She said that?"

"Apparently. Teagan said she didn't want George involved, and he was uninterested." He shakes his head. "Seriously, he's just gonna have a kid out there and not even care?" Carter releases a humorless laugh at my arched brow. "Right. I guess you'd know something about that with your dad."

"I never understood it either. My first thought when I found out Scarlett was pregnant was just to figure out the best way I could be a dad to the kid."

"And then it turned out you weren't Abi's dad at all."

"Don't say that." The words come out harsher than I intended, but I don't care when his felt like a blow.

"Shit, I'm sorry. I didn't mean it like that."

"I know, but Abi and I talk about it. We talk about how words matter and we choose the words we use for our relationship. While I might not be her biological father, I am her dad. *That* has nothing to do with DNA. Fuck, look at my father. He's the best evidence to prove that doesn't mean shit."

"I'd say *you're* the best evidence of that, East. You are a great dad to Abi."

The pride on his face makes my throat go thick, and I have to swallow a lump of emotion I'm not equipped to deal with right now. "Thanks."

He leans back in the booth. "I'm supposed to let my little sister raise a baby on her own in another state?"

"She'll land on her feet. This is Shay." *But it burns like hell.*

"It's not that I don't think she can do it. She's going to be an amazing mom. But hell, Easton. I watched your mom. It was so much harder for her than it was for my parents, and there were *six* of us. It's just harder without a partner, and I don't want that for her." He sighs. "Also something you're familiar with."

I roll my pint glass back and forth between my palms. "Not exactly. Scarlett might not be the most consistent parent, but she is involved. She loves Abi and makes sure she knows it. That alone is worth so much."

"Where's your head with all this?" Carter asks. "Is this . . . The baby, the move to L.A.—is it really a deal breaker for you?"

"She didn't give me a chance to make a decision. She didn't even tell me, just changed her plans to exclude me." I realize that's the part that hurts the most. She was ready to leave for her interview without telling me at all. Was she going to wait until the news made its way back to me through the grapevine? Or maybe she planned to call me from California and tell me from there. Was she too scared, or did she—

I cut the thought off before it can fully form. I know she

wasn't planning to pretend the kid was mine. That's not how Shayleigh functions.

"Teagan said Shay's a mess about it," Carter says, and I know he's poking around for more.

"That makes two of us."

He takes another sip from my bourbon. "Sorry. I didn't realize I needed this."

I shake my head. "That's okay. You can have it. I don't have the stomach for the hard stuff tonight, after all."

"Can I ask you a question?"

"Yeah," I say wearily. The last person to preface a question with that was Shay. She wanted to know what I would have done if I'd known Abi wasn't mine. In retrospect, it's pretty obvious that she didn't tell me about her pregnancy on Monday because I gave the wrong answer. Every second since she walked away from me this afternoon, I've been mentally poking at my answer—testing it for inaccuracies. But I gave her my honest response.

"Are you in love with my sister?"

"Fuck, I thought you were going to ask me something difficult. Yes. Of course I'm in love with her. Madly."

Carter's eyes widen and his jaw goes slack. I've shocked him. I don't know if he wasn't expecting that answer or if he wasn't expecting it to come out so easily. "Wow. I thought you two might be on your way there, but . . . already?"

"Always." I squeeze my eyes shut. "And I'm pretty sure it goes both ways."

"Me too," he says softly. "But if you love her, why are you letting her do this?"

I scrub a hand over my face. "Fuck, Carter. I think she might be a better person than me, because she stepped back twice. Two times she stepped back so I could do what I needed to do for my daughter. And if she wants to move to L.A. and raise this kid on her own, then I . . ."

"You don't want her to stay?"

"Yes, I want her to stay. I want her to be here with you guys. She'll be all alone out there. I want her to have help." I shake my head. "I know her well enough to know she thinks this makes her like Ann. I bet she doesn't want your mom to find out that the father is married." Other than that foolish slip with Shay, Carter's the only one I ever told about Frank's infidelity.

"Since when does Shay know about Ann?"

I drop my gaze to the table, and Carter curses. "I shouldn't have said anything. In the moment, I was trying to explain that I want to be as good a father as Frank was."

"By bringing up that you thought he was a cheater? Jesus, Easton, it's not even true."

I lift my head. "What?"

"It's not even true. When my mom was sick, when we thought we might lose her too, I finally talked to her about it, and she said it's not true."

"But your father sold the whole business. Ann said he was in love with her but felt awful about it and sold the business as a way to recommit to his family."

"Ann was his assistant at the construction company. If she was the problem, he could have just replaced her. He sold the company and started the brewing business because that's what he wanted to do." Carter swirls the bourbon in its glass. "She *was* in love with Dad. Mom knew, but Dad didn't reciprocate. It was awkward, but Ann had a kid at home, so Mom and Dad didn't want her to lose the job, and since plans to sell were already in the works, Dad just rode it out."

I think back to the woman Mom called a friend for so many years. Why did I believe her when Frank never gave me a reason to believe he was capable of being unfaithful? "I can't believe I spent all this time taking Ann's word for it."

"I can't believe you told my sister. Jesus, how long has she been walking around thinking our father was a cheater?"

Shame heats the back of my neck. "Since the night of his funeral."

He releases a colorful string of curses then drains his glass. "Well, you're gonna have to fix that shit. Dad loved Mom. Beginning to end. Even if that story had been true, using him as an excuse to stay in a bad marriage was bullshit."

I lift my beer with a shaking hand and take a sip. Then another. "I've always been afraid I'd turn out like my father. All I knew to do to prevent it was follow Frank's lead."

"But you weren't following his lead. Your lives were nothing alike. You were just doing what you thought was right, and anyone who sees you with Abi knows you're nothing like your dad. You did the best you could for her, and she's turned out great." He pauses a beat. "But this isn't about Abi. This is about Shay. Be honest, do you only want her to stay because you think she'd be better off close to family, or do you want her to stay close to you?"

"It's complicated." I shake my head. "I love her, I want her, but I can't pretend this pregnancy doesn't change anything. I don't know if I can raise another man's kid."

"Seems like you're doing a pretty good job of it with Abi."

"It would be different this time. Knowing out the gate . . . Would I treat the child differently? Would I always favor Abi and scar the other kid for life?"

"Is that really what you're worried about?"

"I don't know. I'm fucked up about this right now, and that's the most honest answer I can give you. I know I'm the worst kind of hypocrite. I hate the idea of her having his baby, but I have no idea how to let her go."

Carter gives me a sad smile. "But you're a fucking adult, so you either have to learn to be okay with the first or figure out the second."

"She's not going to give me a chance to be okay with anything. I found out by accident, and I'd barely processed it before she walked away."

"Maybe after the last two times, she's having trouble believing that this time you would choose her." He pushes an envelope across the table. "She asked Teagan to give this to you. I offered to deliver it."

Carter leaves, and I don't even say goodbye. I stare at the envelope, at my name written in Shayleigh's loopy script on the front. I don't know how long I sit there like a coward before I find the courage to open it.

Shay's a writer, a fucking genius with words, so I expected a long letter. Instead, I get two sentences.

I never blamed you for choosing Abi. Even when it hurt, I always loved that about you.

Shay

*M*olly and Brayden's wedding isn't a big or formal enough affair to warrant a rehearsal, but the couple decided they still wanted to do the traditional "rehearsal dinner"—just to spread out the festivities a little.

We hired Nic's sister to watch all the kids and met up at Jackson Brews for dinner, and I found myself the only Jackson sibling without a date. Everyone is settling down and settling in. Hell, none of my brothers have ever been as happy as they all are right now. And me? My life is a deck of cards and I've just stepped into an endless game of fifty-two pickup, but knowing my brothers are so happy makes me feel a little steadier, though my own future is foggy at the moment.

Despite the meal being over, no one seems in a rush to go. I totally understand why my family is lingering, but I just got off a plane an hour before the meal, so between jet lag and first-trimester exhaustion, my bed is calling my name.

I tap Mom's arm. "I'm going to head out."

She squeezes my hand. "We didn't get a chance to talk about your interview. Do you like the school?"

I'm flooded with adoration for this woman. She didn't just birth me. She raised me and loved me and showed me what it means to be a mom. Because of her, I know I'm going to do all right by this baby. "The campus was beautiful, and I think the interview went well. They're going to make a decision by the end of the month."

"I don't want you to go, Shay, but I'll be fine if this job is what you want. We'll all miss you, but we're your family no matter where you live." Her gaze flicks to my untouched wine—Brayden poured—and back to me before curling her lips into a knowing smile. "You have news you've been keeping from me, and I can't figure out why."

My laughter takes even me by surprise and comes out as a bit of a giggle-snort. "Of course you know. You probably knew before me."

"I knew the day Easton came back to town and you didn't drink your champagne. You're a fan of liquid courage, and something had to be off for you to push it aside that day."

She knew before I did. Of course. "I found out Monday," I whisper. "And I'm scared and surprised, but I'm not sad—not about the baby part, at least."

"The man from school is the father?" she asks.

I nod.

"Will he be involved?"

I shake my head.

"Maybe that's for the best, huh?"

"How would you even know that?"

She wipes my cheek, like she's washing away a messy child's dinner. "He didn't make you happy. I could see that."

"After we broke up, I found out . . ." I squeeze her hand tightly. "He's married, Mama. I didn't know, and now his wife has asked him to move out and a little girl might grow up without her dad." I drop my gaze to our hands. "And I think it would be easier to move away than to see you every day knowing I've disappointed you. I'm so ashamed."

"Why is that your shame to carry if you didn't know?" She leans forward in her seat and pulls me into her arms, rocking me back and forth gently. "I could never be disappointed in you. You make me proud every day."

I give myself three deep breaths before I say, "I didn't want to be like Ann. Tearing apart families."

"Ann Friedman?" Mom releases me and gives me her patented *I thought I told you to say no to drugs* look. "What about this situation makes you like her?"

"Easton said Dad was in love with her."

Mom snorts. "In her dreams. Don't you remember Ann?"

"A little."

"Do you remember the time she told everyone—including the police—that she was held up by Santa Claus at the bank? And then security footage showed her giving the money to that homeless guy right outside?"

I nod. "I'd forgotten that."

"Or the time she told you that you wouldn't get your period

if you never wore red?"

Oh, wow. I'd forgotten that too. "She was a little nuts, wasn't she?"

"She just marched to her own drummer. She had a thing for your dad and"—She points to her head—"trust me, the comments she made that implied her feelings were reciprocated were the reason for all this gray hair. But she never threatened our family, because your father wasn't interested."

"What's happening over there?" Levi asks from across the table. "Are you two okay?"

"We're fine," I say quickly. I'm so glad I didn't share that story with anyone else in the last seven years, but I wish I'd asked Mom.

Mom lifts a brow then nods meaningfully toward my brothers. I nod too, giving her the permission I know she's looking for. "Shay's expecting a baby. We're just happy about a new blessing for this family."

"You're *pregnant*?" Levi says, and Brayden says, "What the fuck? I didn't even know you were seeing anyone." And at right about the same time, Jake says, "Is it Easton's?"

"I'm not the baby's father." The soft, achingly familiar voice has me tearing my gaze off my brothers and whipping around to look at Easton. I don't know when he walked into the bar, but he looks about as tired as I feel. He's wearing a loose white button-up with sleeves rolled up to his elbows and khaki slacks. "But I'll be the dad if Shayleigh will let me."

I didn't think it was possible, but those words seem to stun my entire family to silence. Especially me. Even Mom's quiet, though she is *smirking* beside me.

"What did you just say?" I ask softly.

Easton smiles. "I said it'll depend on you, but I've made my choice." His intense gaze slides from my eyes down to my shoes, and something inside me shimmies in response. His nearness sends an electric current of energy through me every time. "You look . . ." He swallows hard and attempts a smile. "Just beautiful."

I glance down at the simple blue dress I borrowed from Teagan. It's fitted through the body and stops at the knees. I won't be able to wear dresses like this much longer . . . at least not if I don't want to advertise my pregnancy. "Thank you."

"Can we talk?" he asks. He casts a glance over his shoulder and toward the exit. "I have some things I'd like to say. In private, if that's okay."

I nod, grab my purse, and lead the way out to the back. I don't look to make sure he's following me as I head through the kitchen, but I don't have to. I feel him there.

I hesitate outside Jake's office. The last time we were in there . . .

"I thought maybe we could talk down on the beach," Easton says. "It's a nice night."

"I'd like that." I'm in heels, but we're only a couple of blocks away, and I can kick them off as soon as we get to the sand.

We're quiet as we walk toward Lakeshore Drive, neither in a hurry to start this conversation. I don't know why he's waiting to say what he has to say, but I know why I am. I *want* what he offered in the restaurant, but I'm afraid he's not offering it for the right reasons. I want Easton to be my family, my partner, and my baby's dad—even if he'll never be its genetic father. But I also know how honorable Easton is. I know why he offered what he did.

"I won't ask if you meant what you just said to my family," I say, mustering my courage. "Because I know you did." His face is guarded as he waits for me to say more. "Easton, I would never ask that of you. I couldn't. It's too much."

The light turns at Lakeshore Drive, and he takes my hand as we cross. His touch is everything I've spent the last forty-eight hours telling myself it isn't. It's comfort and peace and *home.*

We cross to the beach, and he waits while I kick off my heels, never letting go of my hand. The air is cool and the sand is cold against the bare soles of my feet, but it's welcome after the heat of the crowd inside the bar.

"It doesn't mean I don't appreciate it," I say, when we've walked for a couple of minutes and he still hasn't replied. "I do. And it's tempting but . . . I know how you feel."

He swallows. "But do you really know? Because I don't think you do, and that's on me."

"I know you want to protect me. I know you care about me."

"Do you know that I want to be with you?"

"Of course I know, but things are complicated, and I get that."

He shakes his head. "You've asked me before. You've asked me why I want to be with you, and you asked because you needed me to explain it. You asked because you *didn't* believe it. Ask me now."

"What?" I blow out a breath and search for the courage not to take anything from him he doesn't truly want to give. "Easton, you and I have never gotten the timing right. No one will judge you for how you feel about this pregnancy."

"Ask me why I want *you.*"

My heart squeezes as I remember having this conversation

before. When I asked him in Paris, he needed me to find the words. And he stumbled when I asked him at the cabin on Sunday. It shouldn't have mattered and it did. I shake my head. "I can't do this right now."

"Ask me."

Does he know how fragile I am? Does he understand that I don't have the energy or the emotional fortitude to write my own love poem? "I already know. Same reasons *I* want to be with *you*, right?"

"Ask. Me." He squeezes my hands, then whispers, "Please."

"Why do you want to be with me?"

He grins, like the question itself is a gift. "I want to be with you because I think about you all the time. Sometimes when you're away from me, I convince myself I've made up how good it feels to have you close, because there's no way one person could make me feel so damn *good*. But then I'm near you again—like right now—and I know I was right."

My heart somersaults. I did need to hear this, whether I knew it or not.

"I want to be with you because I was born with this anxious kernel in me that whispers that I'm going to fall short. But when you're there, when you're looking at me with those big brown eyes, when you're in my arms, when I hear you laugh—those whispers are silenced.

"I want to be with you because you knew who you were before anyone else, because some days I feel like I'm floating in space and still don't know who I am, but being next to you is like always having steady earth beneath my feet.

"I want to be with you because the sight of the Eiffel Tower at dusk makes you weak in the knees, and because you see the world with a reverence that makes me realize how much I've missed by walking through life blindly. I want to be with you because when I think of happiness, I picture that day we took a boat ride down the Seine, and I watched the wind whip your hair in your face. I think of how beautiful your smile was that day—how you rivaled the sun—and how *whole* I felt just because you were by my side."

I open my mouth, and he presses an index finger to my lips. "I'm not done."

I laugh, but I think it might sound like a cry. Maybe it's both. "Okay."

"I want to be with you because you stepped back to let me be the kind of father I thought I needed to be, because you believed I could make the right choices for me and my daughter. I want to be with you because life is short, and I want to spend the rest of mine with you by my side. And because you're my family. No matter what you decide or where you go or where you live, you're a part of me the way Abi's a part of me. You never stole my heart. You tucked a piece of yourself into it and made me better."

"You know you can't say stuff like this to pregnant women." I sniffle and look around desperately. "I don't even have a tissue."

He pulls a handkerchief from his pocket. "I brought it for you. I figured I'd either need it for your tears or my bloody nose—which I'd probably deserve." He shrugs. "Can I go on?"

I wipe my face and nod.

He exhales slowly, then starts again. "I want to watch you grow with this child and hold your hand while you learn what it means to be a mother. Because I know you're going to be incredible, whether you do it alone or with someone by your side. But damn it, Shay, I don't want you to do it alone, and I don't want you to do it with anyone else. I want all of your babies to call *me* Dad. I want to be the person who wakes up with you during the sleepless nights and who reminds you that you're kicking ass when the kid turns three and becomes a miniature demon. And hey—lucky for you, I've been there and can assure you that they *do* grow out of it."

I laugh and feel hot tears spill down my cheeks.

"I want to take you to Paris and hold you during thunderstorms. I want to read your books and wake up to the smell of you on my sheets. And maybe it's not fair of me to say so, but I want to do all that with you here. In Jackson Harbor, *home*. Because your family is awesome and I know your mom doesn't want to miss watching her grandchild grow. But if what you need is in L.A., I'll move back there. I'll find a way to protect Abi from the press. I'll figure it out. But when I say I love you, I need you to understand that I mean everything I just said, because I can't live thinking you don't really know how I feel and I'm shit with the romantic words."

"I think you're pretty good," I say, then I hiccup. Because tears.

"I had a lot of notes and time to prepare. I was really nervous."

"I liked it," I whisper.

"Once I sat down and got going it was easy, but not at first. To me, it's so obvious and it never occurred to me that you needed to hear it. I should've realized a long time ago that it isn't so clear from where you stand. You're the woman I love. The one I want. The future I want. If you want me."

"Of course I want you." I loop my arms behind his neck.

"Why?" he whispers, and there's a smile in his eyes.

"Because of who you are. Because you're the man I love and the one I want."

He wraps his arms behind my back and pulls me close. "That's more than enough."

Shay

Brayden has never smiled as much as he has since he started dating Molly, and never smiled as big as he did standing on the sand behind our family cabin and saying his vows.

The service was beautiful. The pastor gave a speech about how a marriage ceremony isn't about two people making vows and committing to each other—as that's already happened one way or another before the ceremony—but about the community accepting them as a couple. When the pastor spoke about love withstanding even the toughest trials, I found myself turning to Easton, only to find he was already watching me. Our eyes locked as the pastor spoke about the patience of the heart and reward of love, and Easton smiled. A private smile just for me that made my heart race and my knees go weak.

The reception is a small gathering—or as small as anything

with my family can be—but everyone is seated at tables on the back patio that overlooks the lake. Molly hired her chef from the banquet center to do the cooking and brought some of her waitstaff out to serve us. There's no microphone when I stand to give my speech, and I'm grateful for that. The worst thing about having an English degree is that when people ask you to give a speech or write a letter, they have really high expectations. At least if I screw this up, my voice won't be amplified.

I smile at my new sister-in-law. She's flushed and glowing, holding Brayden's hand and her son Noah on her lap. She truly looks like this is the happiest day of her life.

I lift my glass. "Molly, I always wanted a sister. You probably don't know this, but it wasn't until the little hellion that is my brother Levi turned three that Mom announced she wasn't going to have any more children. Before him, she'd intended to continue popping out babies until her body wouldn't cooperate anymore. While I understood why Levi would make even my most-patient mother tap out of the child-raising business, I was crushed."

Everyone laughs, and I wink at my mom, who shrugs like *Can you blame me?* Levi doesn't look too offended. He knows the story.

"All of my brothers were relieved at the news because, let's face it, things were getting kind of crowded. But not me. I'd been wishing for a sister, and it looked like my chance was gone. What I didn't realize when I was a kid was that I'd be lucky enough to get five sisters. Molly, you're perfect for my big brother. You make him smile and laugh and somehow even get him to stop working from time to time." Everyone laughs softly, and I take a breath before continuing. "And you're good for me too," I say, the words breaking a little. I glance around the patio. Teagan's wearing a shiny new engagement band, and I choke up a little at the reminder. Ava's holding her one-year-old daughter, Lauren, while Jake keeps an arm around her shoulders. Ellie's leaning on Levi, and Nic has her fingers intertwined with Ethan's. By the time I look back to Molly, I think everyone understands why I feel so damn grateful. "You're all better than sisters. I'm a pretty private person and I never wanted to burden anyone else with my troubles, but in you, Molly, and in Ava, Ellie, Nic, and Teagan, I don't just have sisters. I have friends I can go to any time life is rough. Thank you for being brave enough to come back to Jackson Harbor. You're a piece of this family as essential as one of my brothers." I throw Levi a look and grunt. "Except maybe him. We'd be all right without him."

"Heeey!" Levi says over everyone's laughter. "This is family time, brat!"

I blow him a kiss and shake my head. "But seriously, Molly. Today you're not just marrying Brayden. You're stuck with all of us—even Levi—and we're lucky enough to have duped you into thinking this is a good thing. I'm grateful for you and Noah, and so thrilled to call you both Jacksons. Here's to you and Brayden." I lift my glass of sparkling apple juice in the air. "May you always be lucky enough to know what a gift you have in each other."

Everyone cheers, and I lower back into my seat.

Easton leans over, his mouth brushing my ear. "Do you know how wild I am about you?"

I smile. "I might have an idea."

He nips my earlobe. "Good. Just checking."

Easton

When dinner's over and everyone's dancing on the beach, I stand and offer Shay my hand. "Dance with me?" I nod to the beach where all of her brothers are entranced by their dance partners. "Brayden and Molly want everyone out there."

She bites her bottom lip. I want to bite that lip myself, but biting leads to sucking, and sucking leads to roaming hands, and . . . Well, we're expected to be out here for the next couple of hours, so I'm trying to pace myself. "I suppose. If I have to."

I lead her down to the beach.

Shay loops her hands behind my neck, and I settle mine at her hips as we slowly sway to the music.

I scan the family surrounding us and shake my head. "Carter was right."

She cocks her head. "About what?"

"I told him he shouldn't propose today. That it's a little . . . I don't know, faux pas to propose at someone else's wedding."

"I don't think Teagan cared when he did it. She just wants to marry him."

"Oh, I think she cared." I pull her closer and rub a hand up and down her back. "I think she likes celebrating with your family. He proposed here because she's part of this now. Officially."

She smiles. "She's stuck with us."

"Lucky girl," I whisper.

"You've been stuck with us since you were a kid," she says. "Don't deny it."

"I wouldn't dare. I consider myself lucky too, but I wasn't as lucky then as I am now."

"For a guy who says he's not good with words, you are *such* a charmer." She closes her eyes and rests her head on my chest.

Warmth floods through me. That sense of *rightness* clicks into place. Everything is working out. Scarlett even found a place in Chicago yesterday. She said it's a better fit for her than Jackson Harbor and that she didn't want to get in the way of my fresh start with Shay.

"Can I dance?"

Shay and I still our feet at Abi's request. With a small smile, Shay steps back and nods at me, getting out of the way so I can dance with my daughter. I grab her hand before she can get far.

"How about we all three dance together?"

Abi grins. "Okay!"

We all hold hands and sway to the music. And I don't think I've ever been happier.

Epilogue

EASTON

Twenty-nine weeks later

"Easton! Oh my God, Easton! Get in here!"

There's a special speed I can run through my house. I call it the I-think-my-girlfriend's-in-labor speed. That's the speed I use as I fly down the hall and into the den. I grab the doorframe as I turn the corner and narrowly miss falling on my ass on the hardwood floor. I'm still bruised on my right side from when I thought she was in labor last weekend.

I'm not sure what's more embarrassing about that—that she was doing it to show the girls how fast I'd come, or that, as she pointed out, this isn't my first rodeo and I'm well aware that babies don't just fall out seconds after contractions start.

Shay's sitting at her desk, staring wide-eyed at the computer screen.

I try to play it cool and hide that I ran here. "What can I do for you, Dr. Jackson?"

She rolls her eyes at the name, but hell, she earned it. "I have a reply from that agent."

"The one you queried last week?"

"No, the one whose contact info you gave me. Remember, I sent her my manuscript last month."

I was starting to think my buddy had given me a false lead when she wasn't hearing anything back. "What'd she say?"

"She loves it." She presses both hands against her mouth and shakes her head. "Actually, what she says is she *loves, loves, loves* it. Three *loves*, Easton."

"I told you it was good."

"And baby, I appreciate that, but how much YA romance do you really read?"

"I don't have to read the genre to know a good book when I read one."

She makes a face. "Am I going to be this emotional *forever*?" Then . . . *three, two, one,* tears.

I guide her out of her chair and pull her into my arms. Admittedly, hugs aren't the same these days, with this big watermelon she's carrying around on the front of her, but I'm not complaining. Shay is beautiful pregnant. It never did anything for me with Scarlett, but the sight of Shay's rounded belly makes me want to pull out a camera and catalogue every inch and curve of her. I did that one night, but inevitably ended up pulling out *other things* before I finished.

"I'm so proud of you," I murmur into her hair. "I knew you could do it."

"It doesn't mean anything yet. I told her I'll sign with her, but now she has to find an editor who wants to buy it."

"One step at a time." I run my hands down her back then back up her sides. Slowly, I lower my mouth to hers and kiss her. She squeaks against me, and I pull back. "Are you okay?"

"Easton, I think I need to go to the hospital." She grimaces.

"What? Are you in pain?" I look around on the floor. "Did your water break? Does something feel wrong?"

"I've been having contractions all morning. I just didn't want to tell you, because you've been a little high-strung about this, but they're about three minutes apart now, and—"

I'm already running to the nursery to get the hospital bag. I've nearly perfected my I-think-my-girlfriend's-in-labor speed and I'm back in a flash. "You ready?"

"You're ridiculous," she says, but she's smiling.

"I'm . . ." I sink to my knees and press a kiss to her rounded belly. "I'm desperately in love."

"I love you too," she says.

I nod. "Yes, that, but I was talking to the kid." I cup her stomach in both hands. "What do you say, kiddo? Are you ready to meet your daddy?"

Shay cries out and crumples to the floor at the same time. I catch her on her way down. "I think we need to go."

SHAY

I was seven years old when I fell in love with Easton Connor and thirty-one when I made him a daddy for the second time. He wasn't my baby's biological father, but I was a romantic at heart who didn't believe family lines were drawn at blood.

When they put my baby in Easton's arms for the first time, I saw the love in his eyes and just knew he was the best choice I'd ever made for myself or my child. Because I'd been through enough heartache and loss to know when something's worth fighting for. Because he made me feel beautiful and believe in fairytales again. Because I loved this man with the light brown hair and blue-green eyes who looked at *our* child like I'd just given him the best gift in the world. And, later, when our hospital room was full of happy, celebrating Jacksons, when Franklin Jackson Connor was sleeping in my arms, I smiled with the knowledge that someday I would marry Easton Connor.

It was my secret. One I vowed to keep to myself until the time was right. Easton didn't know my plans.

And I had no idea he had a ring in his pocket and was about to propose in front of my entire family.

The End

Thank you for reading *If It's Only Love*, book six in The Boys of Jackson Harbor series. If you'd like to receive an email when I release a new book, please sign up for my newsletter on my website.
I hope you enjoyed this book and will consider leaving a review. Thank you for reading. It's an honor!

Contact
I love hearing from readers. Find me on my Facebook page at www.facebook.com/lexiryanauthor, follow me on Twitter and Instagram @writerlexiryan, shoot me an email at writerlexiryan@gmail.com, or find me on my website: www.lexiryan.com.

Acknowledgments

I'm filled with gratitude for everyone who helped me with this book. As always, to my family first. Brian, my husband and reluctant "deadline widower." Thank you for believing in me, for listening to me, and for being the calm to my constant storm. If I know how lucky I am, does that mean I can keep you? To my kids, Jack and Mary, you are so freaking cool, and I'm so proud of you both. I'm the luckiest mama ever! Thank you for inspiring me to be my very best. To my six siblings—thank you so much for making me love big families so much that the Jackson family made sense to me. Thanks to my mom for checking on me when I work too much.

I'm lucky enough to have a life full of amazing friends. Thanks to my writing friends who sprint with me and talk me off the ledge when the book looks like a disaster. To my hand-holding, hair-stroking, and pep-talking BFF, Mira Lyn Kelly, my eternal gratitude.

To everyone who provided me feedback on this story along the way—especially Heather Carver, Samantha Leighton, Tina Allen, Lisa Kuhne, Dina Littner, Nancy Miller, and Janice Owen—you're all awesome. I appreciate you all so much!

I have the *best* editorial team. It truly takes a village. Lauren Clarke and Rhonda Merwarth, thank you for the insightful line and content edits. You push me to be a better writer and make my stories the best they can be. Thanks to Arran McNicol at Editing720 for proofreading. I've worked hard to put together this team, and I'm proud of it!

Thank you to the people who helped me package this book and promote it. Sarah Eirew took the gorgeous cover photo and did the design and branding for the whole series. A shout-out to Lisa Kuhne for helping with admin when I'm drowning. Nina and Social Butterfly PR, thank you so much for all your work! I love working with you and your awesome assistants! To all of the bloggers, bookstagrammers, readers, and reviewers who help spread the word about my books, I am humbled by the time you take out of your busy lives for my stories. My gratitude will never be enough, but it is sincere. You're the best.

To my agent, Dan Mandel, for believing in me and always believing the best is yet to come. Thanks to you and Stefanie Diaz for getting my books into the hands of readers all over the world. Thank you for being part of my team.

Finally, the biggest, loudest, most necessary thank-you to my fans. Because of you, I'm living my dream. I couldn't do it without you. You're the coolest, smartest, best readers in the world. I appreciate each and every one of you!

XOXO,
Lexi